D1589213

THE
BABY
SITTER

Emma Curtis was born in Brighton and now lives in London with her husband. After raising two children and working various jobs, her fascination with the darker side of domestic life inspired her to start writing psychological suspense thrillers. She has published five previous novels: *One Little Mistake, When I Find You, The Night You Left, Keep Her Quiet* and *Invite Me In*.

Also by Emma Curtis

One Little Mistake
When I Find You
The Night You Left
Keep Her Quiet
Invite Me In

THE
BABY
SITTER

EMMA CURTIS

CORVUS

To Ollie and Emma

Published in Great Britain in 2023 by Corvus,
an imprint of Atlantic Books Ltd.

Copyright © Emma Curtis, 2023

The moral right of Emma Curtis to be identified as the
author of this work has been asserted by her in accordance
with the Copyright, Designs and Patents Act of 1988.

All rights reserved. No part of this publication may be
reproduced, stored in a retrieval system, or transmitted in any
form or by any means, electronic, mechanical, photocopying,
recording, or otherwise, without the prior permission of both
the copyright owner and the above publisher of this book.

This novel is entirely a work of fiction. The names, characters
and incidents portrayed in it are the work of the author's
imagination. Any resemblance to actual persons, living
or dead, events or localities, is entirely coincidental.

1   3   5   7   9   10   8   6   4   2

A CIP catalogue record for this book is
available from the British Library.

Paperback ISBN: 978 1 83895 972 2
E-book ISBN: 978 1 83895 974 6

Printed and bound by CPI (UK) Ltd, Croydon CR0 4YY

Corvus
An imprint of Atlantic Books Ltd
Ormond House
26–27 Boswell Street
London
WC1N 3JZ

www.atlantic-books.co.uk

MIX
Paper | Supporting
responsible forestry
FSC
www.fsc.org
FSC® C171272

Prologue

November 2013

Her parking place has gone, which is not a huge surprise in Culloden Road, and Claudia is forced to park at least six houses away. There's no let-up in the weather; if anything, it's worse, with thunder rolling and gutters overflowing. There are few people out. Just a man running in the opposite direction holding his briefcase over his head, and, walking towards Claudia, a woman in a quilted black coat with a huge fur-fringed hood. Claudia wraps her coat around Tilly and carries her, clamped against her waist, to the house, fumbling for her keys with wet fingers. She drops them and they fall between the olive tree in its waterlogged terracotta pot and the wall of the house. Resting Tilly's weight on her knee, she crouches in the wet and delves amongst the spiderwebs. To her surprise, the pot shifts and a stranger scoops the keys up and hands them to her. It's the woman in the black coat. She's pulling the tip of the hood forward to keep the rain off her face, her wide sleeve obscuring her features.

'Thanks.' When the woman doesn't continue on her way, Claudia adds, 'It's Nadine, isn't it?' and unlocks the door. 'You're a little early, but don't worry. It's fine.' She's embarrassed by the nasty egg on Tilly's forehead and the

1

plaster covering the cut, and is about to explain that it looks worse than it is when her mobile rings. 'Sorry, would you mind holding Tilly while I get this?'

They go inside and Nadine takes Tilly, who is thankfully still fast asleep. Claudia fishes her mobile out of her bag and answers it.

'Hang on, Joe.' She cups a hand over the mouthpiece and turns to the agency babysitter. 'Give me two minutes. Take your coat and boots off and make yourself comfortable in the front room. Tilly won't wake up.'

And then she leaves her daughter with a stranger and walks into the kitchen, phone clamped to her ear, listening to Joe telling her he's going to be late and will meet them at the theatre. She gives him a hard time because tonight was meant to be perfect; a new beginning. She asks what's keeping him and he says something about an incident and having to speak to the parents. She tells him about Tilly's tumble and they have a short conversation, no longer than a minute and a half, then she goes to find Nadine.

The front room is empty. Claudia's first thought is that the babysitter must have needed the loo and has taken Tilly with her because she didn't want to leave her alone, so she waits at the bottom of the stairs, listening for the flush and becoming increasingly uneasy.

'You okay?' Her voice sounds strangled.

When she goes to investigate, her anxiety is off the scale. She checks every room, then hurtles downstairs and into the street, yelling their names. Across the road, Kate is letting herself into her house, her wet hair hanging in rats' tails around her face.

'Claudia?' she shouts, peering through the downpour. 'What on earth's happened?'

Claudia is barely able to form the words. 'Tilly. She's taken Tilly.'

Kate checks the road and sprints over. 'What do you mean? Who's taken her?'

'The babysitter.'

Just then, a woman in a camouflage coat and a brown woolly hat with an enormous bobble hurries over from the other side of the road, lifting her hand to wave a greeting.

'Wow! This weather,' she exclaims cheerfully. She has a South African accent. 'Are you Mrs Hartman? I'm Nadine, from Mulberry Nannies.'

SHE LIED: MONSTER MUM JAILED

by Greg Davies

A 'quick-tempered' mother who killed her baby has been jailed for 15 years. Claudia Hartman, 25, was today convicted of killing Tilly Hartman, aged 8 months, and concealing the body.

In her statement, Mrs Hartman said that her baby was stolen by an unknown woman who she took to be an agency babysitter. However, her testimony fell apart when police investigating the crime found traces of Tilly's blood in the Hartmans' sitting room.

Colleagues of Mrs Hartman, a primary school teacher, painted a picture of a woman who was fantastic with the children she taught but found it hard to form relationships with the staff and avoided social events. A friend described her as 'overly possessive' of husband Joe, 34, head of Overhill School in Surrey. Another described her as jealous of her husband's slavish devotion to their child.

After the discovery of the blood, Mrs Hartman changed her story, confessing that Tilly had fallen off the sofa and cut her head on the corner of the coffee table.

When asked why she hadn't sought medical attention for her daughter instead of going shopping, Mrs Hartman said the injury wasn't serious, and that Tilly had cried immediately and afterwards had been her normal giggly self. She later confessed that she had in fact been on her way to A&E but had become anxious, worrying that her baby would be taken from her, given that she had suffered from postnatal depression and psychosis and had secretly stopped taking her medication. Mrs Hartman insisted she had told the truth in the rest of her statement.

The prosecutor alleged that Tilly had in fact died in the accident, and accused Mrs Hartman of concealing the body and fabricating the story of the abduction to cover her negligence. He described her account of her psychosis as an exaggeration.

Mrs Hartman's GP said that although aware of her condition, he had considered it under control and had no reason to believe she had ceased to take the pills. Mr Hartman had also thought his wife was taking her medication as prescribed.

PART ONE

Chapter 1

CLAUDIA

The buzzer sounds, the door opens, and Claudia Hartman steps blinking into the outside world, the strobing effect of several cameras flashing at once a sudden and brutish welcome. Clutching a clear plastic bag containing her mobile phone, her keys and the black leather shoulder bag she came in with, she covers her face with the crook of her arm. It's 6.30 a.m. and still dark. A chill wind whips across the prison car park. She stands with her back to the door and tries to adjust quickly to a change as seismic as birth. For a split second she's so frightened of what awaits her that she wishes the guard would drag her back in, tell her it's all been a terrible mistake, she should never have been freed.

The minicab driver doesn't get out to open the passenger door; instead he waits, windscreen wipers shunting from side to side, headlights picking up the rain. Between Claudia and the car there are at least a dozen journalists, burly in their winter coats, steam puffing from their mouths. They barrel towards her, microphones held aloft, blocking the wind.

9

'Claudia! Do you have anything to say to your ex-husband?'

'Why did you change your plea?'

'How are you going to survive on the outside when no one wants you?'

That last question comes from someone at the back, and the tone is different; it's more personal. It's also a question she has asked herself, a question that cuts right to the heart of her. She has a feeling of being hollowed out as she squints to see who asked it, but the flash bulbs blind her. It was a woman, though. She sees a figure holding a large black umbrella that obscures most of her face. Her chin is swathed in a scarf and she's standing apart. She doesn't look as though she belongs with the rest.

Claudia sways, grey with exhaustion. Her last night in the cell was peppered with yells and taunts. No one was happy that she was getting out. The women felt cheated, even though they'd spent years tormenting her. The guards offered little protection, believing middle-class Claudia Hartman considered herself better than them. They would miss the fun of taking her down a peg or two. If only she'd said what her lawyer had advised her to say sooner, it might have taken the heat out of the situation, they might eventually have got used to her and been kinder, but it took a long time to admit defeat and say the words. *I am guilty.* It still sticks in her craw.

She gasps, feels the cold air in her throat and marches forward, pushing against arms and coats, gagging on breath stinking of coffee and cigarettes, bacon butties and fried eggs. She reaches the car, pulls open the door and dives in.

The driver picks up an envelope from the front seat and reaches back to hand it to her. Then he pulls away, moving deliberately slowly, allowing the few who are fit enough to run alongside the car. Someone raps hard, a pale face coming out of the darkness, and Claudia shies away. Only then does he put his foot down.

He doesn't speak. Occasionally, he raises his eyes to the rear-view mirror, gives her a hard stare before returning his gaze to the road. Her mother booked him through a local firm, so she assumes he's used to picking up freed inmates, taking them and their smell and their miserable bags of belongings back to whatever halfway house has been organised. She wonders how many he drops off outside detached houses in neat suburban cul-de-sacs. The man is in his forties and there's a photograph stuck to his dashboard of two little boys in school uniform.

Claudia turns her head and watches the urban landscape roll by, and her eyes widen, taking it all in, aching from the stimulation. The envelope is on her lap, under her hand. She picks it up. The name on it has been typed. *Claudia Hartman*. She wrinkles her brow. Could it be an invoice for the cab? That would be odd, unless it was her stepfather, Robert, who organised it and this is him being unpleasant. It would be typical of him to take a dig at her without telling Louisa, her mother. Robert had never warmed to her. Coming into her life three years after the death of Claudia's father in the car accident that had injured Louisa, he had made her feel like the cuckoo in the nest. Even more so when Jason was born.

She hasn't heard from her half-brother since before her conviction. In the meantime, he has married and produced two children. She's seen the pictures: the family together in Shires Close for Christmas, playing in the garden with Grandpa Robert, building sandcastles on a beach in Cornwall. She supposes she and Jason are estranged; at any rate, she's not going to bother him. She adored him as a child, and it hurts that he can walk away. Louisa maintains it's his wife, Amelie, who is behind it, but Claudia doesn't believe that. Her mother is trying to lessen the pain, but prison has a way of letting you know who your real friends are.

She opens the envelope, pulls out an A4 sheet and unfolds it. The note is typed as well. Just the one line.

You were safer inside. Outside you are dead.

She clutches the back of the driver's seat. 'Who gave you this?'

'I don't know, missus.'

'Was it a man or a woman?'

'Woman.'

'What did she look like?'

'Dunno. Ordinary. She banged on my window. I opened it and she slipped it through, then she walked away.'

Claudia sits back. Could it have been the woman who seemed out of place amongst the journalists? She folds the note, slips it back into its envelope and puts it in the plastic bag. It's only to be expected, given that the world has been encouraged to hate her, but even so, this isn't a good start. Who was it, though? Someone who knows her, or a stranger?

Spits of rain splay across the windscreen and chase each other to the corners. The minicab drives past Hampton

Court Palace and through Bushy Park. Workers standing at bus stops look frozen. Cyclists in top-to-toe Lycra zip by. Claudia's eyes follow the rhythmic flash of their fluorescent detailing, their revolutions matching the beat of the windscreen wipers, round and round, thwack, thwack, thwack. It's hypnotic, and before she can blink her way back to reality, she's back in her own car on that day, Tilly strapped in behind her. The rain has gone from steady to torrential in the five minutes since she left home, surprising her and everyone else attempting to pass through Kingston. People are hooting, frustrated. Ahead of her she sees cars climb the pavements. Behind her the traffic is at a standstill. There must be a flood where the road dips beneath the railway line. She considers her options, then swings the steering wheel hard round, grimacing as she takes the last possible left turn, even though it's no entry, and drives home, into hell.

She mustn't go back there. She must move forward, make the devastating lie she told worthwhile, make it up to her daughter. The thought of Tilly growing up not knowing she was stolen has always been bittersweet. People say she's dead, because it's impossible these days to keep a baby off the radar, but without a body, there's no proof of that. Claudia has to keep the faith: Tilly is alive; she has been loved and well treated. If she doesn't believe that, she will collapse under the weight of her own guilt.

She wonders what Joe is doing now. He would have been warned that she was about to be released as a matter of course. She imagines him waking next to his second wife, spooning his body against hers like he used to against Claudia's. He'll press his face into the crook of Sara's neck and shoulder, blocking thoughts of Claudia, but he won't be able to block Tilly. No matter how much he wants to put the past behind him, their daughter will make her presence felt. He gave up on Tilly, choosing to prioritise his mental well-being, and Claudia will never forgive him for that.

They turn into Shires Close. Behind them, several cars and a motorbike pull into the kerb, not caring if they're blocking driveways. Doors fly open, men and women swarm with those who are already waiting patiently. Even more than her emergence from prison, this is the money shot: Claudia Hartman arriving at her parents' home with her tail between her legs. She presses herself rigidly against the back of the seat, her stomach squirming.

The driver twists round. 'You need to get out.'

She detects a note of sympathy, even though he immediately turns away and starts keying his next ride into the sat nav.

All she has to do is barge past them. They can't prevent her from going inside. She has the key; her mother dropped it in at reception last week, when they came to visit the day before they left for an extended visit to Robert's relatives in South Africa.

That had been an unpleasant surprise, but she got it. Robert didn't want to be in the country when it all kicked off. Anxious to spare her mother anxiety, Claudia had insisted she would prefer to navigate the transition period alone. It was at least partly true.

'Go on, lady. You'll make me late.'

'Yes, okay. I'm going.'

She pulls the handle and pushes the door open. The

noise drops off and the silence bulges until it pops like an overblown balloon and they're all shouting at once.

'Claudia! How does it feel to be out?'

'Hey, Claudia, over here! What have you got to say to your neighbours?'

'Will you be seeing your ex-husband?'

'Do you regret what you did?'

And then louder, more forcefully, a male voice bellows. 'Where did you bury your baby, Claudia?'

Chapter 2

SARA

'It's either a scammer or your mother,' Joe said when the phone rang.

Joe was a great one for the zinging one-liner, his mind as rangy and elastic as his body, but with the earliness of the hour, and given that they'd been expecting a call for the last few days, Sara only raised a smile with difficulty.

Joe reached for the phone because he was closest, and Sara had Maeve, their eighteen-month-old daughter, on her knee. He read the caller display. 'It's Michael.'

'Oh God.' Michael Chancellor was Joe's lawyer.

Joe's fingers rose to rub at the vertical frown lines between his eyebrows. 'Morning, Michael. This is early even by your standards.' He left the room, the phone clamped to his ear.

Above her, Sara's husband paced the spare bedroom, which he used as an office. She lifted Maeve into her high chair, put a bowl of Weetabix in front of her and waited, hoping it wasn't what she thought it was. There was a sliver of logic to that hope, hinging on Claudia Hartman having caught COVID in the late spring of 2020, when it surged through the prison population. She'd had pneumonia the year before, which had damaged her lungs, so when Michael phoned Joe to inform him that his ex-wife was dangerously ill, Sara had prayed that Claudia would die. Maybe she was dead now, either from her compromised health, or because the other prisoners had been so incensed she was being freed that they'd taken matters into their own hands.

After a while, she heard his guitar. The melody made her think of a time at the beginning of their relationship when she had begun to wonder if she'd ever break down the barriers. He'd told her that if his mood took a downturn and he couldn't stop thoughts of his daughter crowding in, music was the one thing that helped. It was the shift of focus, both mental and physical.

Five minutes later, the stairs creaked and Sara set down her mug of tea, folded her arms and waited. When he came in, Joe fixed her with his eyes, his expression rueful.

'She's out.'

Sara sprang up and went into his arms. His dressing gown smelled slightly stale. 'What did Michael say? Is she going to be a problem?'

'I doubt it. Staying away from us is one of the conditions of her parole. She can't come here, and if she does, she'll be recalled. Michael is all over this.'

'Are you all right?' she asked. The tension in his face scared her.

'I'm fine. It's not as if it's a surprise.' He arranged his mouth into a smile. 'It's a bit like when you know someone is dying, but it's still a terrible shock when they go. I've known for months that she's coming out, but I'm still finding it hard to take in now it's actually happened.'

Maeve started to whinge; she was a jealous little thing.

Sara pulled herself out of Joe's arms reluctantly and went to her. She picked her plastic spoon up off the floor, washed it and handed it back. Her daughter hated being fed.

'It's good that she confessed,' Sara said. 'It draws a line.'

'There is no line, at least as far as Claudia is concerned. She admitted guilt because it was expedient.'

She looked at him sharply, alarmed by the dull monotone. His face was impassive. 'Joe?'

'I can't talk about this now. I need to get a shower and get on. I've got a day full of meetings.'

'Can't you cancel and stay here with us? It is half term after all.'

'Sorry, darling. They've been in the diary for weeks. And frankly, I am not going to allow Claudia to disrupt our lives.'

'Is that what she wants?'

'I don't know. I hope not. Sorry, I didn't mean to worry you.'

'I'm not worried about me, I'm worried about you. I don't want her bringing the nightmares back.'

Joe put down his coat and stroked her cheek, brushing back her hair. For the son of an Irish father and a half-Italian, half-British mother, he was a surprisingly even-tempered man, but that even temper somehow didn't diminish the crackling energy apparent in his long, nervy hands and mobile face. With his wiry black hair laced with grey, bright blue eyes and smile that combined mild amusement with warmth, he could still turn Sara's knees to jelly. Even now, when it felt like their lives were about to be upended.

'I admit the thought of her being free makes me sick,

and it isn't going to be easy, but as long as I have my two favourite girls, I'll weather it.'

Joe left. The house slipped into its routine. Tidying up, shadowed by Maeve, Sara wondered where Claudia was now, who had picked her up from prison, how it felt to walk out into a grey autumn day with a bag of belongings musty from being stored in a cardboard box for the best part of a decade.

Two years ago, Claudia, Joe's ex-wife, had confessed to the manslaughter of their baby, having previously refused to admit guilt. She'd had her fill of prison life, Sara assumed, and wanted out even if it meant admitting to what she had done. It wouldn't make much difference, since no one had believed in her innocence anyway. As a baby killer, Claudia's life had been over for a long time, even with mitigating circumstances taken into account. There would be no second chance.

Sara picked up the iPad and went to the news. Claudia's release was the top item, and the press had gone to town, knowing the public relished stories about the car-crash lives of the privileged. There was little mention of Sara; just a brief acknowledgement of the woman who had taken on Joe Hartman, the attractive, grounded, common-sense wife who had given him a new daughter. The perception was that she wasn't as worthy of copy as her predecessor, and that was the way Sara preferred it.

She pushed the iPad away. Claudia couldn't touch her. Whatever had once tied her to Joe was broken and could never be fixed. Even so, she spent the entire day on edge, waiting for the knock on the door that never came. She moved around the house touching her possessions, as if to ward Claudia off, resting her fingers on the table, the bed, on Maeve's cot; things belonging to her and Joe.

Deep in her heart, in a dark place she tried not to acknowledge, taking what Claudia Hartman had once valued gave her, not satisfaction exactly, because that would be mean-spirited, but a kind of piquancy that was hard to explain and even harder to justify.

Chapter 3

CLAUDIA

The studio flat smells of wet paint. Claudia is touched that her mother has redecorated. Louisa originally had the double garage converted after her husband died, to create a second income, and when Claudia was growing up, it had been let to a series of young people working at Sandown, where Louisa, before she retired last year, had been the events coordinator.

It's basic: a white box with a pale wood laminate floor that bounces when she walks on it. The front door opens onto the close, the back door onto a fenced-off decked area with a gate to the garden of her parents' house. A shower room and a kitchenette bookend the back door. In the living room there's a window to the front, a sofa bed, a wardrobe, and a table which serves as a desk. Claudia plugs in her phone, then sits down, pulls her chair in and slides across the sheet of typed instructions. This isn't about when to go next door and feed the cat, how to use the oven, when the bins go out, useful phone numbers – that one is stuck to the fridge under a magnet. This is from Robert, who has been concerned enough about how the neighbours will react to her presence to compile a list of dos and don'ts.

Don't try to talk to people, even if you know them.

Don't ask favours.

Do leave the studio as seldom as possible, and try to do it when there are less likely to be others around.

Don't use the front door of number 7 when going in to feed Frank.

As if she needs telling.

Robert had been against her moving into Shires Close, but Louisa stood up to him. Her daughter would always be welcome.

'You haven't thought about what Claudia living here will mean, love,' he had said, sitting next to Louisa at the cramped table in the visiting room when the proposition was first mooted. 'People will think what they think. We can't stop them. It doesn't matter what we believe. She admitted guilt. That puts us in a difficult position.'

'You know why I did,' Claudia whispered. 'The only way to find out what happened to Tilly is for me to be free.'

'But you're never going to be free. How can you be?'

'I'll clear my name. I don't know why you can't understand that. I didn't take her, so someone else did. I intend to find out who it was. I'm going to get her back.'

Robert clasped his hands on the table. 'We only want what's best for you, but there's a risk this situation will make our lives very uncomfortable indeed. The neighbours won't like it.'

'They'll just have to get used to it,' Louisa said. 'This is non-negotiable.'

Robert, a man who knew exactly which side his bread was buttered, had given in with a grumble. 'Just don't make a nuisance of yourself, and don't try and persuade them you're innocent. You'll only put their backs up.'

22

'Don't worry. I wouldn't risk being recalled. But that doesn't mean I can't investigate. There's always a way.'

'Claudia . . .' her mother said.

'Don't you want to know what happened to your granddaughter?'

'Of course I do, but not like this. It's more important to me that you're safe.'

'Safe?' She held her mother's gaze until it was painful and Louisa had to look away.

'We'll need ground rules,' Robert said, bringing the conversation back to the practical.

'It's all on the list,' Louisa said. 'You've covered everything.'

Claudia forced a weak smile. 'You don't have to worry. I'll keep myself to myself and I won't stay long. Just until Culloden Road is sold.'

'If you need any help . . .'

'I'll use my solicitor.'

'It shouldn't take long,' Robert said, brightening. 'And it'll have appreciated a lot since you went inside. Frankly, we need the money. Almost a decade of covering your share of the mortgage, well, that's at least seventy grand you owe us.'

'We don't need to go into all that now,' Louisa said.

'You'll get it back.' Claudia appreciated them hanging on to her interest in the house, but Robert never missed an opportunity to mention it.

There was a silence, then Robert looked around, checked no one was listening and spoke under his breath. 'You said you put her body in the river.'

'I had to tell them something.'

'So she's not there?'

'For God's sake, Robert,' Louisa said. 'Don't make her feel worse than she already does.'

'Sorry. You're right. She has enough guilt to contend with without me putting my oar in.' He looked straight at Claudia when he spoke. Louisa wouldn't have seen the sneer in his expression.

'I don't feel guilty, Robert. The person who should feel guilty is the person who stole Tilly.'

It was a lie. Claudia does feel guilt, a white-hot, searing guilt that she'll never shake off. She had looked away, and when she looked back, her daughter was gone. The idea of being able to forgive herself is laughable, but she doesn't want Louisa to know how futile and pointless everything feels to her. She understands that she has to allow her mother to have hope.

'I have no idea where Tilly is. I didn't kill her and I didn't get rid of her body. I just want her back.'

In that barren visitors' room time crushed like a tin can under a heavy foot, and she felt the hurricane of confusion and panic in the moment she realised her child was gone. She raised her head and saw her pain reflected in Louisa's eyes.

Her parents stood up, their visit over. Her mother embraced her and turned away to hide her emotion; her stepfather surprised her by opening his arms. After a hesitation, Claudia went into them, felt his breath close to her ear.

'I want you to know,' he murmured, in a voice she barely recognised, it was so cold, 'that I believe you killed our grandchild.'

'I didn't . . .' She tried to get away, but his embrace was like steel.

'I believe you did it, and I always have, but I pretend for your mother's sake that it isn't the case. The sooner you get your own place, the better. I wish you well in your future life, and I hope you find redemption, but please do not outstay your welcome. I have a certain standing in our community. And remember, the only reason you go into the house is to feed Frank and pick up the post. I don't want you making yourself at home there.'

She has a shower in the tiny bathroom, sloughing the prison from her skin. She can't scrub hard enough. Afterwards, the sight of her reflection in the full-length mirror screwed to the back of the bathroom door is a shock. Her posture is terrible. It deteriorated in prison as she strove to efface herself. Glimpsing her stretch marks, she is swept up in a wave of misery. When she gets dressed, she feels as though she's encasing the rawness.

Her mobile rings, making her jump. It's been such a long time since she last heard its ringtone. The caller display reads: *International*.

'Mum?'

'Oh, thank goodness,' Louisa says. 'You're home. I was so worried. How are you?'

'I'm okay.' She has already decided not to mention the threatening note. 'Thanks for leaving food.'

'I was glad to. I have an account with Tesco for online shopping. The password is Frank2015. You might find that easier. How's the studio?'

'It's lovely. Very cosy.'

'I'm sorry. I should have been there for you. I can't bear to think of you leaving that place on your own.'

'It's fine. I'm fine. And Robert was right: why should you have to deal with a media invasion? None of this is your fault.'

'Have you . . . Do you have any plans?'

'Not really.'

'Have you spoken to anyone?'

'Who would I speak to?'

'Joe, I suppose. Or Kate.'

'I can't speak to Joe, Mum. You know that.'

'I only thought . . . well, he might contact you, mightn't he? About the house.'

'That's what lawyers are for.'

She feels smothered by her mother's concern, and even though she wanted to speak to her, she now wants to be left alone.

'I've got to go. I'll call you tomorrow.'

As she runs her eye down Robert's list again, the stark reality of her situation sits like a boulder in her stomach. She mustn't care. Only Tilly matters. She whispers her mantra under her breath. 'I have been to hell. I am unbreakable.'

Chapter 4

CLAUDIA

Her mother has hung a variety of pictures on the walls of the studio in an effort to make it more homely. Tasteful neutrals, a misty landscape with a deer, some pebbles, sand dunes and silver birches, which probably came from IKEA along with the furnishing. On the desk is her old laptop, plugged in; above it Louisa has hung Claudia's final school photograph. Claudia can't understand how her mother could possibly have thought she would have wanted it displayed, but she nonetheless finds herself drawn to it. She leans on the desk and peers at the faces. She finds her seventeen-year-old self on the back row towards the centre, taller than the two girls either side of her. Her hair, which she normally wore in a ponytail, is down.

Sitting in the front row, with the rest of the staff, is Joe. He's wearing a blue shirt and cream linen jacket, and his smile is huge. She runs her finger over his face. He was, must still be, an incredible teacher. She envies him his career. It breaks her heart that she isn't allowed to teach any more. She can see him now, strutting in front of the whiteboard, pretending to be a character from a Shakespeare play, the girls in stitches.

The headmistress, Miss Colville, is in the middle of

that row, posture erect, expression bland. Claudia feels her hatred of the woman in her stomach and is surprised it's still so present, after everything else that has happened.

Joe and Claudia had kissed for the first time on Claudia's last day at Lady Eden's, and Miss Colville had walked in on them. Claudia had been seventeen, Joe twenty-six, but the headmistress had made him feel like a paedophile and called Claudia a disgrace. Now, looking back, Claudia concedes that she had been too young, and Joe, despite scrupulously keeping his distance, despite barely brushing her fingers with his, shouldn't have allowed her to fall in love. But she had, and so had he. Miss Colville had protected the school by sweeping the incident under the carpet, but she had been vile, and that had almost destroyed them.

Joe had resigned, and gone to work in the state sector, pushing Claudia away for both their sakes. He had told her she needed space to grow up, and that he would wait. The split had been painful, and the relief of coming back to him four years later so intense she'd thought she might die of it.

Miss Colville's unpleasantness and the way she'd taken what felt suspiciously like sadistic pleasure in making Joe and Claudia squirm was the reason why they didn't attend her memorial service. Claudia feels a pang of guilt. Perhaps they should have paid their respects. It was petty not to have done so. After all, Miss Colville's reference for Joe, if not exactly glowing, hadn't mentioned what she'd seen.

'I warn you, Claudia, nothing good will come of it,' she'd said when Claudia had passionately defended Joe's honour. Miss Colville had been proved right, although it had been too late by then for her to derive any satisfaction from it.

There are around four hundred children and staff in the photograph, so the scale is tiny, but Megan Holt's face jumps out at her. Megan, with her mournful brown eyes and her forehead scattered with spots, had grown up at number 12, on the opposite side of the turning circle. She'd been undersized and plain at fifteen, but Claudia thinks she would have turned into a good-looking woman. Her suicide had been a huge deal, the police swarming the school and Shires Close. They had talked to Claudia; she still remembers her reply. 'I didn't really know her.' They had been puzzled. 'But this seems like a close-knit community. And Megan's mother is your mother's best friend, isn't she?' Claudia had flushed. 'I mean, I knew her, but she was younger than me, and she wasn't really my type of person.'

The newspapers had printed articles describing Megan as *a promising young scientist*. Some girls, Claudia remembers, had claimed friendship out of a perverse desire for reflected glory. Claudia had kept quiet about her own behaviour. Her guilt over that *piss off*, casually thrown at Megan only hours before she died, wasn't going to go away. She wishes she knew who told the family years later.

If only she'd had the maturity to understand what was going on. She had felt mature at the time, but she certainly hadn't been. Joe had been absolutely right to put some years between them. Instead of rejecting her, she could have told Megan that she wouldn't always feel pulverised by things she had no control over. She swallows back a sudden ache in her throat; she would have been wrong about that. Pulverised exactly describes her permanent state.

She takes the photograph off the wall and slides it

29

behind the wardrobe. She doesn't need a reminder. Nowadays she can understand the impulse to end it all.

When it's time to leave for her appointment with her probation officer, Claudia pulls the hood of her coat over her head and darts out of the house. Cameras flash and voices clamour for attention. She has upset the quiet order of Shires Close.

A woman carrying a toddler on her hip – a little boy with tufty strawberry-blond hair – strides with purpose from one of the houses on the opposite side of the close. Claudia recognises Tilly's old babysitter. Megan's little sister. All grown up now.

'Claudia Hartman,' Anna says. 'You shouldn't be here. I think it's totally inappropriate, frankly.'

Claudia holds her head high, but her instinct is to shrink. Her shoulder blades, rammed back, carry as much tension as bridge cables.

A journalist thrusts a microphone at Anna, but Claudia doesn't hear his question as she hurries away.

'Don't get too comfortable,' Anna shouts after her.

She'd forgotten that her mother told her Anna and her husband had bought number 13 after Connie died. It had surprised her that Anna had chosen to live next door to her parents, but the husband was a property developer and knew he could make money. It was more of a surprise that they hadn't moved on once the house was finished. On-tap childcare was the most likely reason. Even so, she finds it strange. But then there is a lot about the Holts she doesn't understand.

In 2013, seven years after Megan killed herself, they

discovered what Claudia had said to her only hours before she died, and cut Claudia's family out of their lives. It was the day Tilly went missing and she had been catapulted into a terrifying nightmare from which she still hadn't awakened. But the upshot was, Frances and Patrick finally had someone to blame for what had happened to their own daughter. Despite having been a close friend of Louisa's for years, Frances Holt offered the minimum emotional support, and according to Louisa, these days she barely nods in passing.

But Claudia didn't know anything about this at the time. Tilly had been taken and her world had shrunk to a hard, hot little kernel. Nothing else mattered.

Anna, though, was a link to the past. The fact that she'd cancelled at the last minute had been the reason they'd booked the agency babysitter. If Claudia could only talk to her, get her to explain what had happened that day, maybe she'd have another piece of the puzzle. She'd have to pick her moment, but it was worth a try.

Chapter 5

ANNA

Mum is standing outside her front door as I march back across the close clutching Max. She frowns, but I shake my head. I do not want to talk to her, or to be told I shouldn't have confronted that woman, or that it would be healthier to reflect on my feelings around Claudia Hartman than project them onto her. It is actually a pain in the arse having a psychiatrist for a mother. She has an 'I'm listening' look that is intensely irritating. Why the fuck I agreed to buy Connie's house, I do not know. We were going to sell it in the new year, but that plan has been put on hold until Claudia's gone, because Owen thinks it'll attract rubberneckers and people will expect a price reduction.

Still, the free babysitting goes some way towards compensating for the irritation. And this house is gorgeous. I put Max in his high chair and pull the lid off a Petits Filous. Bad mother. But it's been one of those mornings.

'Hey, babe.' Owen strolls into the kitchen freshly shaven and gives me a kiss, then bends to kiss his son, who offers him a spoonful of yoghurt. 'Sorry, mate. I'll have to pass. What did you say to her?' he asks.

'I let her know she wasn't welcome here.'

'Harsh.'

I scowl. 'Do you think I'm being unreasonable? I'm not. This is the woman who told my sister to piss off when she was only wanting some help.'

'Claudia was insensitive, sure, but hardly culpable.'

'If she hadn't been so mean and dismissive, Megan might not have felt so alone. Claudia didn't have to be a bitch. She chose to be one. You should be on my side.'

'I am on your side. You're right. What she did was unforgivable.'

'Thank you,' I huff.

Owen throws back a coffee, munches a piece of toast, then grabs his phone and keys and he's off. He never used to dash out this early. I watch from the door as he reverses off the forecourt. Now that Claudia has left the house, all but one journalist has driven away. A stocky man in a bulky coat gets out of a grey hatchback. He wanders over, smiling.

'Greg Davies,' he says. 'Mind if I ask you a question or two? It seemed a bit personal just now. Do you know Claudia from before?'

'I used to babysit for her.'

'Ah. Right. The one who cancelled, yeah?'

I frown. 'I was ill.'

'What's your problem with her? She's done her time; this is her family home. What is it about her being here that upsets you so much?'

'I'm not upset. I'm just irritated. She's brought you lot here, hasn't she? We just want to live in peace.'

'I understand,' he says. 'It's tough when you have your own little one to be reminded of a tragedy, especially when you played an indirect part in what happened. It's hard not to feel guilty, even when you know you've done nothing wrong, isn't it?'

I turn on my heel and slam the front door in his face.

Chapter 6

CLAUDIA

She needs to see Joe. It's important to her to look him in the eye and tell him she did not hurt Tilly. He needs to know she's innocent, despite the later admission that led to her release.

It's going to be hard. Joe put up with a lot when they were together: her suspicion that he was seeing someone behind her back, her need for reassurance, her constant fear that she'd never be enough. It had become a self-fulfilling prophecy. But what was said in court, that vile accusation the prosecution had made, repeated after she'd been found guilty by the gutter press, that the appalling crime she was alleged to have committed had its roots in her irrational jealousy of the other female in the house, was simply not true. She had never, ever been jealous of Tilly. The dreadful unfairness of it, the knowledge that people think it, is devastating.

Greg Davies. That was the journalist's name. He had called her a monster and the media had run with it. She had refused to give him an interview, had slammed the door in his face, and that had been his revenge.

She is banned from approaching Joe's family, so she's going to have to be clever. Maybe Kate can help with that.

She isn't banned from the Shaws. She bites her lip. There might not be an injunction, but Kate hasn't contacted her since she went inside. Like Joe, she drew a line. Claudia has had plenty of time to wonder why the people closest to her slipped away when the going got tough, and she can only imagine that it's her own fault, a glitch in her personality. She makes people feel uncomfortable. She was a loner as a child, her relationships fragmenting too easily under pressure. Until Joe. She'll visit Kate anyway. She doesn't exactly have options.

After seeing her probation officer, Claudia walks into central Kingston, head down, hood up. If she looks shifty, the area is too crowded for it to be an issue. Everyone's busy; no one cares. In Old London Road, she passes the antiques emporium where she used to buy presents for Joe; quirky things that he kept on his study shelves. She peers through the window of Canbury Books and sees Kate behind the till. Taking a steadying breath, she pushes open the door.

'Kate . . .' she says, then stupidly starts to cry. She wipes the tears away and grimaces an apology.

Kate's assistant sidles out from behind the counter and makes himself scarce. Kate goes to the door, locks it and switches the Open sign to Closed.

'I'm sorry to just turn up like this.'

Kate gives her a wry look. She hasn't hugged her. In the past, they always hugged hello and goodbye. Claudia wonders if this is left over from the pandemic, or if it goes deeper.

'Don't be sorry.' Kate hesitates, discomfort written all over her face. 'It's good to see you, but—'

'Did Joe tell you I was out?' Claudia doesn't want to hear about the *but*.

'His wife called me.'

'What did she say? I mean, was it . . . like a warning? Or just passing on the news?'

'She was letting me know. There was no agenda.'

'I really need to talk to you.'

'I don't see what there is to be gained by talking.' Gentle but firm; that was always Kate's way. But for once, it chills Claudia.

'Maybe nothing for you, but a lot for me.' She's trying not to be challenging, but from Kate's expression, it's clear she's failing. 'You must know that I couldn't have done the things they said I did.'

Someone pushes at the door a couple of times, then walks away.

'I can't help you. I can't get involved.'

Claudia wipes her tears with the back of her hand. 'I need you to persuade Joe to see me.'

'Claudia—'

'I'm Polly's godmother,' she blurts out in desperation.

'Polly has a new godmother.'

Claudia's mouth opens and closes like a fish. She can't find the words.

'Sorry,' Kate says. 'That was uncalled for. Claudia, Paul and I have talked. We thought you might get in contact and we decided it was better to draw a line.'

'Do you have any more children?' Claudia tumbles over her words. 'Ignore that. You don't have to tell me anything personal.'

'Polly has three brothers: Henry, George and Kit.'

'Three boys. Wow.' She lifts her eyes to Kate's face, searching for anything that might hint at the warmth that had been between them. 'I would have loved another baby.'

Kate doesn't respond, and Claudia hurries to fill the silence. 'Why did you turn against me?'

'I didn't. I supported you when you had postnatal depression. I really wanted to help. I came over to be with you as much as I could, but later on you twisted that into some warped narrative of me trying to take over your household and steal your husband. I didn't know you were washing your pills down the drain. You didn't tell me. Your behaviour got completely out of hand. You were constantly harping on about my fixation with Joe, wanting to talk to me about it.' Her voice rises. 'You were the one with the fixation. I was a new mother, for God's sake, and in love with my husband. You used to set traps for us, organising suppers then watching me and Joe like a hawk, giving us opportunities to be alone. You were so transparent, it would have been funny if it hadn't been so pathetically sad.'

Claudia picks at her thumbnail, pulling at a tag of flesh. The pain is sharp. 'Was it you who spoke to that journalist; who said I was over-possessive of Joe and jealous of Tilly?'

'I didn't speak to any journalists, Claudia. I wouldn't do that.'

'Who then?'

'I have no idea. It could have been anyone.'

'It was kind of you not to stick the knife in when everyone else did.'

'That was because of Joe, not you. Paul and I kept quiet for Joe's sake.' She shakes her head, mouth folded. 'You'd done enough anyway. You didn't need us to make you look more culpable than you'd already made yourself.'

They stare at each other, then Kate relents. 'Please try to understand. Too much has happened. You should make new friends. Friends who didn't know you before. I can't be there for you. I have to protect myself and my family.'

Being dumped by a friend, Claudia thinks as she wanders away, is worse than being dumped by a lover. Two adults she cares deeply about, Joe and Kate, have distanced themselves. If they don't want anything to do with her, what hope does she have? Her mother loves her, but Robert will be glad to see the back of her. Even her half-brother hasn't reached out. She is alone in a way she has never thought possible, a small grey planet floating in a sparkling galaxy.

Chapter 7

SARA

'Sara Hartman?'

'Yes?' Sara swivelled away from the front door, startled. She was carrying Maeve on her hip and fumbling with her bunch of keys with her free hand. 'Can I help you?'

The stranger was attractive, in a shabby way. Something in his posture, combined with a pair of well-cared-for combat boots, suggested a previous career in the military.

'Greg Davies. *London News*. How do you feel about your predecessor's release this morning?'

'I have nothing to say.'

'It must be hard for you, knowing she's out. When do you expect her to get in touch with your husband?'

Sara bit back a swear word and fitted the key in the lock. 'I have no idea.'

'It's understandable that you'd feel threatened.'

'I feel nothing of the sort.'

'That's interesting. You must be very confident of Joe's affections.'

'He's my husband,' she said incredulously. 'Can you please leave? You can see I'm busy.'

'Take my card,' he said, proffering one.

She tore it in half and flung the pieces back at him. 'Get lost.'

Davies smiled. 'No problem. Call me if you change your mind. Beautiful baby, by the way.'

Sara slammed the front door and marched into the kitchen, putting Maeve down and struggling with the zip on her coat, almost tearing it off, she was so hot and bothered. She drank cold water straight from the tap, then sat down and pulled the iPad towards her, typed in Claudia's name and tapped Images. Years ago, she had obsessed over Claudia's face, hungrily examining the haunted eyes, the unwashed hair and the ugly rawness round her nostrils. Claudia had appeared confused, recoiling as cameras flashed and journalists thrust microphones into her face. Her gaze had darted around, desperate to find somewhere safe to land, while a police officer, his arm about her shoulder, warded off the crowd.

In another photograph, Joe looked like he wanted to punch someone. He was so obviously traumatised, stripped to the bone emotionally. Sara had never seen him so exposed. He kept something of himself hidden and he always would. She told herself it was natural, that it was about his ability to live in a world without his daughter, but the more she looked into those shell-shocked eyes, the more she wished he would show that vulnerability to her.

Joe ruffled Maeve's hair. 'I'm sorry for being such a bear.'

He kissed her on the lips. She smelled alcohol on his breath, but she didn't say anything, even though he rarely drank during the day. It was the timing that worried her. It fed into her fear that Claudia Hartman still had the power to throw him into an emotional crisis beyond anything she could alleviate.

'I've had an email from Claudia's solicitor,' Joe said. 'We're going to have to either buy her out or sell this house.'

'You're joking.'

When Sara had moved in five years ago, selling 26 Culloden Road had been an option, but her feeling had been that Joe wanted to stay, even though he said it was up to her; that somehow he had an idea that Tilly might come back one day. It seemed perverse, particularly to Sara's mother, who had tried to persuade her to do the opposite, but Sara had been so keen to get it right, she'd actively encouraged him, and in the end, she found she rather liked living where Claudia Hartman had once lived.

'Why on earth would I joke about that?'

'You mean sell and give half the proceeds to Claudia? What happened to not allowing her to disrupt our lives?'

'I spoke too soon.'

She waited to see if he had more to say, and when he didn't, she shook her head in disbelief. 'Where are we supposed to go?'

Joe made an effort to smile, to reassure her, but his expression made grim reading. 'It's crap, but we can get a bigger mortgage. You could go back to work. We could get rid of one of the cars.'

'Working wouldn't be practical while Maeve's so tiny,' Sara countered. 'And I am not going to be stuck at home with a baby and no car. I'll go mad.'

'We both have to make difficult choices.'

'Clearly,' she said, hearing the bitchiness in her voice but unable to do anything about it. 'So that the woman who ruined your life gets to spend the money. How can you even consider it? She doesn't deserve anything. She forfeited the right to leech off you when she killed Tilly.'

He turned on her with a look that chilled her blood. 'Will you stop it! She's not leeching off me. You know perfectly well that the Myhills have been paying half our mortgage.'

That was a mere detail and beside the point. 'Joe,' she hissed. 'You'll upset Maeve.'

'Sorry.' He took his glasses off and polished them on his shirt. 'I don't know why I stayed here. I don't know why I clung on to the past.'

She softened. 'But we've made it ours, haven't we? We've created new memories, created Maeve.'

'We can create memories somewhere else.'

'Perhaps you could help her out with rent or something? That would be better than us having to leave.'

'We can only act within the law. Claudia will get what she's legally entitled to, and then she'll move on. At least I won't be financially shackled to her. You don't want that, do you?'

She shrugged away from him. Joe had had time to think about it. She's suddenly suspicious. 'This hasn't come out of the blue for you, has it?'

He has the grace to look ashamed. 'No. I just didn't know how to tell you. I've spoken to an agent. I'm so sorry, but it's happening.'

'I was doorstepped by a journalist today. He wanted my reaction.'

Joe seemed relieved. 'Me too. Outside the school. What did you say?'

'I told him to get lost.'

'Good for you. Don't engage and they'll get bored soon enough. I'm sure they'll find plenty of people ready to give their considered opinion.'

'This isn't going to change things between us, is it?'

His eyes darkened. 'I hope not.'

Sara smiled uncertainly. That wasn't the response she'd been angling for.

Chapter 8

CLAUDIA

The thought of seeing Joe is all-consuming; a burning itch she can't scratch. If Kate won't help her, then she's going to have to make the first approach cold. She knows it's unwise, that she's exhausted and overwrought, but precisely because of that, she messages him, *We need to meet*, then she drops the phone like it's on fire and clamps her hands between her legs. Joe could go to the police with this. She has to believe he's still the decent man she remembers.

She misses him much more than she did while she was inside. Inside, she was able to blank him out most of the time. He never visited, not even when he decided to divorce her. He didn't call or show any humanity. Each official letter, each form she had to sign, had been a slice through her flesh.

Once, she had called her own home number, even though it was forbidden. Joe had picked up, listened to the recorded message telling him that the call was from the prison, and cut her off.

She paces the room. He owes her. They never said good-bye properly. Any communication regarding the divorce came through Michael Chancellor. Joe decided, without consulting her, that the best thing for all concerned was a clean break. He was hurting badly and she's forgiven the weakness that led him to make the decision, but she hasn't forgotten. What she understands is that he didn't want to hear what she had to say in case it made him feel bad.

When it's time to feed Frank, Claudia obediently lets herself in through the back door. Nothing has changed, not even the subtle smell of her mother's perfume. It's as though no time at all has passed since she was last in this kitchen, watching Louisa making coffee, getting down mugs and a pretty jug for the milk, hands visibly trembling. That was the day before Claudia was arrested; when she had been lost and frightened, her mother equally so.

Frank is being stand-offish, sitting between the small blue and white armchair in the corner and the curtains, tiger-stone eyes fixed on her, as if he's been warned. She picks up his empty bowl and takes it to the kitchen island. There's a pause. Frank pads over and sits beside her foot. He doesn't look up at her, still reserving judgement. She leans over and strokes his head, tracing her fingers over his knobbly skull, then rubs him just above his collar. She's pleased when he pushes back against her fingers and purrs. If only humans were so easy to win over. She takes a sachet out of the box and squeezes its contents into the bowl. Frank chases her to the corner, where she sets it down. She watches him eat, and then she leaves.

While she was out, Joe has replied. *Absolutely not. It would achieve nothing. If you need to contact me, call Michael.*

The tone is cold and hard. It's not him; not the Joe she remembers, not the Joe who was quick to laugh and happy to take the piss out of himself. Well, she can be cold and hard too.

You turned your back on me once before, she types. *I won't let you do it again. I swear to God I will keep up the pressure until I've seen you face to face.*

She waits a good fifteen minutes for a response.

Bushy Park car pk tomorrow 2 pm. It'll have to be quick.

Agitated by this exchange, it takes her a long time to fall asleep that night, even with one of the sleeping pills she's been prescribed. Every sound elevates her physical tension, jarring her nerves and causing an adrenaline rush that makes her sit bolt upright, ears pricked. The bark of a fox stiffens the joints of her spine. She lies back and crooks an arm over her ear, so that all she can hear is the rush of her blood, the noise it makes like wind gusting.

Chapter 9

Tuesday 24 October

SARA

Sara woke up at two in the morning, roused by Maeve calling out, 'Mama!' Yawning, she pulled her dressing gown around her and went down to the half-landing. She listened at the door to her daughter's bedroom, then went in. Maeve was standing in her cot, pudgy fingers wrapped round the bars. Sara picked her up, held her for a count of ten, then laid her down and drew the blankets up to her shoulders. Maeve stared at her in the darkness. She looked as though she was working up to a sleepy protest, but Sara placed a hand on her chest and murmured, 'Shush. Go to sleep now, darling.' She backed towards the door and stood there waiting. If she held her breath, she could hear the change in Maeve's when she fell asleep. Satisfied, she left the room and crept upstairs.

Joe's study door was ajar, a strip of blue light from his computer shining through the narrow crack. Sara hated the electronics being left on. Normally, if Joe forgot, it would go into sleep mode, but occasionally that didn't happen. She padded into the room and slid behind his desk, tapping the mouse. An image of her and Maeve filled the screen. She keyed in his passcode – his date of birth. She wasn't sure what instinct had brought her to the point where she was spying on her husband, but she clicked a file he'd minimised and found photographs of Claudia and Tilly.

She was angry at first, but the more she scrolled through, the sadder she felt. She rested an elbow on the desk, her chin in the palm of her hand. Tilly Hartman had been a gorgeous baby, old-fashioned-looking with her mop of dark hair and fat pink cheeks, so like Maeve at that age it made Sara wince. Claudia would have a shock if she ever saw Joe and Sara's daughter.

She had to accept, she did accept, that Joe was entitled to yearn for his child and that she and Maeve weren't enough to obliterate the memories, however much she might wish it. In Joe's shoes she would be exactly the same.

Joe's phone was charging on the bookshelves to her right. She reached for it, and after a hesitation entered his passcode – the same one; Joe was not particularly hot on security or even privacy – and went into his messages. The most recent exchange was with an unknown number. The first message had come in at seven minutes past three.

We need to meet.

She knew who it was from. Joe had deleted Claudia's number from his phone years ago, but Claudia knew his. Earlier, when his phone had pinged, he had said it was Lisa, his fifty-eight-year-old PA. Sara pinched her lips together. She imagined Joe's face, brow buckling, the minutes ticking by before he replied; felt the hurt rise up in her, and with it another emotion: fear.

She would do anything to protect this life, this family. And if that meant Claudia suffering, that was what would happen. No question. Sara put herself inside Claudia's head. Sitting at home with only her thoughts for company, of course she'd have Joe on her mind, of course she'd feel isolated and confused. It was what she would do to mitigate against this that worried Sara. Despite the shock of it actually coming to pass, it had always been a risk, and she'd always been ready for it.

The loo flushed. Skin prickling, she sent the phone back to sleep and replaced it on the shelf. It was too late to leave the room. Better to be found scrutinising photographs of Claudia and Tilly than Joe's messages.

She heard Joe's step behind her and turned, biting her lip, guilt spread across her face.

'Sorry. Did I wake you?'

'What are you doing?' Joe asked sleepily.

His hair was mussed, his eyes baggy. He was wearing pyjama bottoms but not the top. He draped his arms around her and kissed her neck, and she leant back into his bare chest and breathed him in.

'I was looking at pictures of your ex. I'm sorry. Maeve woke me up. I noticed you'd left your computer on, and when I came in to switch it off, I saw what you'd been looking at. Don't be cross.'

'I'm not cross. It's not surprising Claudia's on your mind.'

'And on yours.'

'But not in the way you're thinking.'

'Are you sure about that?' She pushed herself up off the chair, wound her arms around his neck and held his gaze.

'Of course I'm sure,' he said, his voice still thick with sleep. 'I love you. I promise you. I never thought I'd be happy again, but here I am. You can trust me.'

She didn't like it when people said that; it usually meant the opposite.

Chapter 10

CLAUDIA

Claudia has no idea how long she's been asleep when she wakes groggy and coughing, smoke filling her lungs. It takes her no more than a second to realise what's happening: the studio is on fire, flames consuming the curtains and lapping across the ceiling, eating up the oxygen. She cannot see a thing through the smoke and crawls towards the front door dragging the duvet with her. She tries to envelop the flames with it, but it catches light, and she drops it with a scream of pain. Terrified, she feels her way to the back door, but it's double-locked and her keys are on the windowsill at the front. She beats her hands against it, tries to kick in the panels, but it's too strong and won't give.

There's a small window above the basin in the shower room. She shuts herself in, rolls her damp towel against the base of the door and hauls herself up. She opens the window and gets her head and shoulders through, then her arms, but the lock catches on the waistband of her pyjama bottoms and she becomes stuck. Panicking, she fumbles to unhook it, then shifts her body from side to side until she's through, the frame scratching her thighs before she plummets onto the decking. She lies in a heap, panting, eyes streaming. Nothing seems to be broken, but her skin has been scraped raw in places and her burnt hand is agony.

And then there are sirens, loud and clear and spiralling. Barely seconds later, she hears her front door explode inwards.

She groans as she raises herself and makes her way round the side of the house. From the grass circle she watches the bulky silhouettes of firefighters, the spray from their hoses swallowed in steam and flame, as if it's happening to someone else. One of them shouts her name. They think she's in there. They probably think she's dead. She's freezing cold, but so shocked she can't speak or move. Then someone sees her and runs over, stripping off his coat. He wraps her in it, and she is safe.

Radios crackle. Pulsing blue lights are reflected in windows around the close. Claudia sits in the ambulance with a blanket draped across her shoulders while her burnt hand is dressed. The fire is out, black smoke rising from the ruin. Her hair is singed, her right hand has second-degree burns and she's thrown up twice, but she's otherwise unharmed. In the smoky haze she makes out the figures of her neighbours, pulled from their beds by the unfolding drama. She feels their hostility and wonders if it was one of them who wrote the note.

You were safer inside. Outside you are dead.

She wishes she had handed it in at the police station, because it's gone up in smoke along with everything else in the studio.

A police officer asks if any of her appliances might have been faulty. She gives him a blank stare.

'Like a hairdryer?' he clarifies. 'Or the fridge? Fridges

can combust. It's rare, but it does happen. There would have been an explosion if that were the case.'

'I don't know. I didn't hear anything like that.' She coughs to clear her throat and it hurts.

'We'll know more after the investigation. Do you have anywhere you can stay?'

She points to number 7. 'My parents' house.' She remembers and groans. 'The keys are in there. And my phone. Can I see if I can find them? They'll be near where the door was.'

The officer peers dubiously at the blackened, soggy mess. 'Sorry, love. Not until we know what started it. In the unlikely event it was arson, we don't want the evidence corrupted.'

Her mother's cleaner, Eva, has a key. Eva hasn't worked for her parents since the pandemic, because of underlying health issues, but her employment hasn't been officially terminated, so with any luck she hasn't returned it.

Claudia calls her mother. 'Sorry to wake you up,' she croaks.

'Claudia! Whose phone are you using?'

'A policeman's. Don't freak out, but the studio caught fire. I'm sorry, Mum, but it's gone. Everything's gone.' She's overcome by a fit of coughing, her eyes filling with tears.

'Oh my God. How on earth did it happen?'

'I don't know. They're going to investigate. It's just, I've nowhere to go. Is it all right if I use the house?'

'Of course it is. This is awful. Were you hurt?'

'I'm fine. Barely a scratch on me. Really, Mum, I escaped before it got bad.'

'Tell me exactly what happened.' Robert has come on the line. She repeats what she said to her mother.

'For Christ's sake,' he says. 'I don't believe this.'

There's nothing she can say to that.

'Get a case number from the police. I'll have to contact the insurers. You can stay in the house, but don't touch anything, and you're not to have your ex-con friends round, do you understand?'

'I understand. I don't have any ex-con friends, though. I don't have any friends at all, so you needn't worry.'

'And do not try and drag your mother back. She's here to rest.'

'I wouldn't dream of it.'

'I'll copy you in on any emails to the insurers, so make sure you cooperate. And tell the truth. Right. We'd like to get back to bed, so—'

'Wait. I need Eva's number. To get the keys.'

He sighs heavily. 'I'll hand you back to your mother.'

The neighbours are peeling away, muttering to each other, calling out goodnight. Someone even laughs.

Claudia gives the phone back to the officer. 'Do you think it might have been deliberate?'

'I doubt it. Who would do something like that to you?'

'You know who I am, don't you?'

He flushes slowly, from his throat up through his cheeks. 'I'm not here to judge, Mrs Hartman, I'm here in my role as a police officer.' He moves away. He hasn't been unkind, he hasn't sneered. She's surprised but grateful.

The paramedic offers her another bottle of water. 'Let's get you to hospital.'

'I don't need a hospital.' She starts to cough again, and presses her undamaged hand hard against her ribcage.

'You do. Smoke inhalation can cause all sorts of problems. We need to check you for carbon dioxide and cyanide poisoning among other things. The vomiting and shortness of breath is not a good sign.'

She shudders when she thinks how close she came to an agonising death. Who would want to inflict that on her? She hopes it was an accident, because if it wasn't, someone has been so thoroughly rattled by her release they want her gone for good.

You were safer inside.

Chapter 11

ANNA

Blue lights on the ceiling. Owen gets back into bed beside me.

'This is un-fucking-believable,' he says, for perhaps the fourth time.

I pull his arm over me, chilled to the bone after standing around outside in my pyjamas and dressing gown. I can't seem to get rid of the sight of Claudia being supported through the smoke-filled air to the ambulance, wrapped in a high-vis jacket. There was something childlike about her, as though she was glad to hand over control of her life to a man in a uniform.

Owen's breathing slows and I feel the moment he falls asleep, but for me oblivion is out of reach. I'm remembering that day, ten years ago now, when I joined the Hartmans' neighbours in Culloden Road, soon after news of Tilly's abduction had spread. Claudia came outside wearing a raincoat that must have belonged to Joe, because it was way too big for her even though she's tall. She looked childlike then too. I watched her face and wondered how anyone could survive that pain. But I wasn't a mother then. Now I understand that she had no choice but to survive.

Owen's long lashes sweep his cheeks. He has a perfect

face – like a film star – but when we met, it was his energy that attracted me rather than his looks. He reminded me of Joe Hartman, and I was in too deep before I realised that their energy came from very different sources. Joe's was in his enthusiasm, his urge to communicate, to make you feel the way he did about some long-dead writer like Thomas Hardy or the Brontës. It was never attention-seeking, always came from a place of generosity. Owen's energy, his bright light, is all about him.

The blue lights have gone, the close is silent. I spoon into Owen and try to sleep, but an image keeps sliding in, like a mouse under a door. Joe holding Claudia outside their house and staring at me over her head. I knew what that stare was asking, but he needn't have worried. I'd have kept his secrets for ever. Because I loved him.

Chapter 12

SARA

'Fire crew, police and paramedics were called last night to a blaze in Long Ditton. A property belonging to the parents of recently released convicted child killer Claudia Hartman was razed to the ground. Mrs Hartman has been treated in hospital for superficial burns. Police have not said whether the blaze was caused deliberately, but there is some speculation amongst neighbours that it may have been, given the publicity surrounding Mrs Hartman's release.

'Our reporter spoke to one of the residents of the quiet cul-de-sac where Mrs Hartman's family own a detached neo-Georgian house worth £1.2 million.

'"Obviously, it's a terrible thing to happen, but she really shouldn't have been allowed to move in here. We were all against it, but they insisted. And now look what's happened. If she'd gone somewhere else, maybe no one would have known where she was. We can't understand why it was allowed. There are young children living in the close. None of us feel safe."

'Louisa and Robert Myhill, Mrs Hartman's parents, were not available for comment. They are in South Africa, where they are taking an extended break.'

Joe switched off the radio. His back was to Sara. She was

still in her dressing gown, making coffee, and Maeve was asleep upstairs, the day not quite started.

'God.' She couldn't think of anything else to say.

Joe turned. His face was ashen. He sat down at the kitchen table, picked up the iPad and found the news item. There was a video, presumably taken by a neighbour. Sara set the cafetière down in front of him and watched over his shoulder. The ambulance was there, but she couldn't see Claudia. Some of the residents were outside, coats over night clothes, leaning into each other, staring.

'I can't believe it,' Joe said. 'Why would someone do something like that?'

'It might have been an accident.'

'Really? She's only just moved in.'

'All the more reason. Maybe it was a faulty electric fire. It was such a cold night.'

'She could have been killed.'

Sara put her hand on his shoulder and kissed the top of his head. She could feel the nervous tension in his body. This event had electrified him. He had exchanged messages with Claudia yesterday, arranged a secret meeting; and now this. It would add to the emotional impact of their reunion. She should say something, tell him she knew, but the words stuck in her gullet. She felt a powerful desire to teeter on the precipice, to test the strength of his love.

'I should do something,' he said.

'There's nothing you can do and nothing you should do. You are not involved in this.'

He raised his hooded eyes to her face. 'I can't just ignore it.'

'Yes you can, and you must. If you try to help her, she'll

only cling to you, because she has no one else. For God's sake, even her parents have made themselves scarce. Doesn't that tell you something?'

Joe didn't answer.

'Joe! You are not to see her. Promise me you won't.'

He hooked his clasped hands around the back of his head. 'This is incredibly hard for me. Whatever she did, Claudia has suffered.'

'But it's not on you. Think about me and how I feel. If she has such a strong hold on you, where does that leave us?'

'She doesn't.' There was a tinge of irritation in his voice.

'She's obviously on your conscience. Joe, listen. You must detach yourself from her. You absolutely have to, or she'll ruin our lives. Women like Claudia are like knotweed. They're impossible to get rid of unless you're brutal.'

Joe sighed. 'You're right.'

'You're not going to contact her?' She stared right at him, digging into his eyes. 'I need to know that I can trust my husband.'

'I'm not going to contact her.'

She couldn't speak, her throat closing as she absorbed the lie.

He pulled her down and kissed her. His lips felt cold. 'I'm all yours this morning. I've got to go in this afternoon, but only for an hour or so. I have a meeting at two.'

'Again? I thought you said you were ours for the rest of the week.'

She wanted to see him squirm. There was a short pause before he shrugged apologetically.

'A problem's cropped up with a couple of the Year 11

pupils. A bit of nastiness. It needs to be sorted out before term begins again. It won't take long, but you know what parents are like. Sometimes they just need a little soothing.'

Chapter 13

CLAUDIA

'Did you hear or see anything unusual before the fire?' the detective asks. He's standing at the foot of her hospital bed, a man of average height, rather lugubrious, late thirties, with brown hair and brown eyes. Earlier he introduced himself as Detective Sergeant Simon Ward.

Claudia hasn't slept; the only reason she knows the next day has dawned is because the levels of activity in the hospital have risen. 'I don't think so. The journalists left around nine. It was quiet.'

'What about smells? Did you smell gas, perhaps, or petrol?'

'No. Nothing.'

'You were released from prison to a media storm yesterday morning. You must have felt vulnerable.'

Claudia swallows. Her saliva still tastes of smoke. 'It wasn't easy.'

'Not the kind of attention you want, I'd imagine.'

She detects a note of judgement in the way both his eyebrows and his voice rise on the word *not*. 'I don't want any kind of attention.'

'It would make your life easier if people started to feel sorry for you, though, wouldn't it?'

What is he saying? She is so exhausted, her body feels like lead. The painkillers are dragging her into the mire along with her heavy limbs. 'Sorry,' she says. 'I feel a little muzzy.' She blinks her vision into focus.

'I wouldn't blame you for taking extreme measures, Mrs Hartman. You've had a tough time of it.'

'I did not . . .' She starts to cough. 'I did not set fire to my home. I wouldn't.' Her eyes are streaming. She presses the corner of the sheet into them.

'You're a liar, though, aren't you?' He smiles and pockets his notebook. 'The investigators will figure it out soon enough. Someone will be in touch once we have the results.'

Claudia washes herself carefully in the bathroom at number 7, the sterile dressings on her right hand protected by a freezer bag. Eva, a complete saint and the most uncurious person Claudia has ever met, brought the keys to the hospital and drove her back to Shires Close. Claudia stripped off her filthy socks and went straight upstairs to bed, where she slept until she was woken by Frank pummelling her through the duvet three hours later.

She should call Joe and cancel, but she can't bring herself to. He may not say yes again. She wonders if he's heard what's happened, and whether he'll even turn up. He might assume she won't come. She could end up waiting in the cold for him and making herself ill.

She'll go anyway, she decides. If he doesn't come, so be it. She has nothing better to do with her time.

The white spotlight above her head emphasises the puffy bags beneath her eyes. The smell of make-up when she opens the top drawer of the vanity unit takes her back to the bathroom in Culloden Road, with its claw-foot bath and duck-egg-blue walls.

Her mother has left behind stubby eyeliners and lip-sticks, old eyeshadows and powder blushers. Claudia picks her way through them, but her left hand is too shaky to do anything but smear lipstick clumsily onto her mouth. She feels like a clown from a horror movie and scrubs it off. This is the face she has to live with, marked by circumstances beyond her control, and stressing will not improve it.

A fit of coughing sears her throat. When she wipes her face on the towel, there's a smear of black. She remem-bers the detective and his insinuations. But she knows she didn't light that fire. Soon the police will too. It will be all right.

It's half past twelve. Her heart gives an odd little skip, as if to remind her it's there. She should ask Joe if they can meet at Ditton Hill Park instead, but what if he uses that as an excuse to cancel? Better not. Anyway, walking there and back will eat up an hour and a half of the day, which to Claudia feels like a bonus, until she remembers prison and the depressing concept of killing time.

Joe didn't ask why she wanted to see him, probably because it wouldn't take a detective to work it out. He'll think she needs money, or that she intends to ask for for-giveness. Perhaps he even thinks she wants him back. Their relationship was intense, but their passion wore off when she became ill. Joe did his best, but he was drowning too. There had been good days, though, and nights when they had lain tangled in the sheets, bodies glued together by their sweat.

Fifteen minutes to go. She checks on the journalists. They're still there, some of them taking photographs of the police officer standing guard in front of the ruin. She breaks out in a cold sweat and goes to the loo again.

It's time. In the silence, she can hear herself breathing hard. It isn't the journalists causing her anxiety, it's something unknown, something invisible but felt. She closes her eyes in desperation, pictures the walls of her cell, reaches out to touch them. She needs to be enclosed and protected. She makes herself go back to the prison in her mind; makes herself hear the clangs and hisses, the catcalls and groans, the spine-chilling bursts of laughter and even more spine-chilling screams. She has an olfactory memory of bodily odours, of aromas of overboiled greens and fatty chips drifting from the canteen; even the slightly fetid taste of the air. The windows were never opened, the air never fresh.

Her breathing slows, becomes more regular. She feels a failure for using the prison as a touchstone. In her heart of hearts, does she wish she'd never left? In prison, no one was waiting for anything from her, apart from an admission of guilt; no one expected anything of her, least of all herself. What choice did she have but to leave? Keep fruitlessly insisting on her innocence, keep trying to make people listen when they'd moved on, or change her plea and exist in limbo amongst people who feared and despised her? She had chosen the latter option because she owed it to Tilly.

She leaves the house by the front door, because whatever Robert says, she is not going to endure the ignominy of skulking out through the back and picking her way down the narrow and overgrown alleyway that runs behind the houses. From now on, in the close at least, she will hold her head up.

Frances Holt is standing outside her house; portly Charles Roache, chair of the residents' committee, cuts across the turning circle to speak to her. He keeps looking over at Claudia, his face stiff with disapproval, like some seventeenth-century pursed-mouthed Puritan.

The press move towards her, misted breath billowing as they shout questions. A woman who a moment ago had been talking to camera breaks through and positions herself right in Claudia's face.

'Woman to woman, Claudia. How did you feel when you realised you'd killed your daughter?'

Claudia flips from victim to aggressor, a Rottweiler baring its teeth. A survival skill picked up in prison. 'Get the fuck out of my way.'

There's a beat, then the woman smiles spitefully. 'You just wanted to not get caught, was that it?'

Claudia walks faster. The woman jogs along beside her, pushing her microphone into Claudia's face, her colleague walking backwards, camera on his shoulder, red light blinking.

'I'm not judging. I'm not here to do you harm. I'm offering you a chance to tell your story the way you want to. Don't you want your voice to be heard?'

'You know perfectly well that can't happen,' Claudia snaps.

'I understand the conditions of your probation, but there are ways of getting round that, if we're careful how we frame it. We could focus on your feelings as you negotiate life beyond prison. Come on, Claudia. Why not speak to me? Get it over with. Then I'll leave you alone.'

Claudia looks around for a means of escape. She cannot allow them to follow her, cannot let them see her meeting Joe. The policeman has moved away from his position and is pushing his way through the journalists.

'Put the camera down, please, sir.'

'We're not breaking the law, officer,' the woman says.

'You're causing a public nuisance.'

Claudia takes her chance, swings round and runs, heading into the neck of the close, a group of journalists in pursuit, microphones held out. It's almost farcical, until something hits her bandaged hand and she cries out in pain.

A car pulls up beside her, the passenger door is thrown open and a man barks, 'Get in.'

Claudia doesn't stop to think; she gets into the car, and has barely closed the door when the driver puts his foot down and they accelerate away. Only then does she realise how stupid she's been. She turns to see whose car she's jumped into. The man is wearing a beanie; he has stubble, and cracked lips from standing outside in the cold. The hands gripping the steering wheel are broad and weathered.

'Greg Davies,' he says, flicking her a glance.

The name rings a bell, and then she remembers. 'Oh my God. Stop the car right now. I'm not talking to you.'

'And I'm not asking you anything. I'm just doing a fellow human being a favour.'

'Is that right? You're no different from that bunch of piranhas. I suppose you've forgotten what you wrote about me, but I haven't.'

His fingers tighten on the steering wheel. 'I was doing my job.'

'And you're proud of that, are you?'

'What exactly do you want me to say?'

'Sorry might be a start. I know you have to write what the readers want to hear, but you went too far. It was too personal. It was misogyny.'

He drums the steering wheel with his thumbs. 'One. I'm not a misogynist. I like women.'

'Lucky us.'

'Two. I am, in point of fact, sorry.' He speaks gruffly. 'I reread that article last night and I admit I was out of order. So, well, this . . . this is a peace offering.'

It's an odd coincidence, so soon after the death threat; almost like he's involved.

'Writing anonymous letters is the act of a coward. I'm not going to be frightened into talking to you.'

'I haven't written any anonymous letters. What did it say?'

'Never mind.' She flushes. Of course he didn't write it. The cab driver told her it was a woman.

'But I do mind. I want to know what I'm being accused of.'

'It doesn't matter. I was wrong.'

He sighs. 'Listen, to prove I'm not after anything, I'll drop you off whenever you tell me to. I won't ask where you're off to or follow you.'

'Stop here.'

'What?'

'Here. Stop here.'

He pulls over. Turning to him, she catches the disappointment in his face.

'I expect you think you're building trust. I expect you think this is money in the bank for later. Well you're not, and it isn't. I will never talk to you. You're not sorry about what you wrote. I don't believe you had an epiphany, and I don't believe in your regrets. It was cynical and opportunistic.' She coughs into her hand.

'Congratulations,' he says drily. 'You've got my measure.'

She gets out, and leans back in. 'Thank you for the lift.'

'My pleasure.' He reaches over the passenger seat and pulls the door closed.

She waits until he's driven away before she starts walking.

Chapter 14

CLAUDIA

There's a moment, pausing in the entrance to the car park, scanning the vehicles, face stinging from the cold, when Claudia feels alive. Despite being weak with exhaustion, she stands tall, bandaged hand hidden in the capacious pocket of her mother's best quilted coat. A car door opens, and Joe emerges. He has come. The pure shock of relief tells her just how scared she'd been that he wouldn't. He narrows his eyes, checking it's really her. His mouth doesn't broaden into a smile, but hers does. She cannot help it. She walks towards him.

He gets back in the car. So they're not going to walk around the park like they used to.

She remembers the first time she ever saw him. She'd wandered into his classroom with no sense that her life was about to change, taken her seat, opened her English file on the desk, said something to a friend. Joe had entered the room a couple of minutes later. He put his scruffy brown leather bag on the floor, picked up a black marker pen and scrawled *Mr Hartman* on the whiteboard, then turned round. Everyone went quiet. He had something, an aura, an energy, that left the girls wide-eyed and smitten. She even remembers his first words. 'Right. Let's get started.' He was constantly moving, and it had seemed to Claudia that there was elastic holding his limbs together. Joe Hartman was both actor and teacher, the classroom his stage. They didn't know what had hit them.

Sliding into his car, she sees the baby seat, the toys beside it, the crumpled parking receipt, the discarded plum-coloured scarf. Joe grips the steering wheel, his gaze fixed in the distance. She absorbs his profile, his jawline, the shape of his mouth, the blue veins in his eyelids. She wants to touch him, and her fingertips tingle, remembering the rasp of his stubble against them.

'I'm surprised you came,' he says. 'I heard what happened. It was on the news.'

Claudia raises her bandaged hand. 'It wasn't much fun.'

'I'm sorry you had to go through that. It must have been terrifying. Your flat's unsalvageable, I suppose.'

She tucks a loose thread between the folds of the dressing. 'There's not much left of it. There wouldn't have been much left of me either if I hadn't woken up and managed to get out.'

'Do they know what started it?'

'They won't until the forensic investigators have been in. That's happening today. The police think it was an accident; the fridge was at least fifteen years old, and apparently they're notorious for combusting.'

'What do you think?'

'That it was deliberate.'

'If you started that fire yourself, if you're trying to make it look like the jury got it wrong, it won't work. The police aren't stupid. You'll be lucky if you're not done for arson.'

Surprised, Claudia stumbles on her words. 'I didn't do it.

You can't possibly think that. Someone left a note for me in the cab that picked me up from Bronzefield. It was a threat. It went up in flames like everything else, but I remember the words. "You were safer inside. Outside you are dead."'

Joe waits a second or two before responding. 'All right. I believe you.' He sighs heavily. 'Why am I even here, Claudia? What's the point of this?'

'I just needed to see you, once. To make you understand that I'm the woman you married, not the woman the press portray me as.'

He shifts round in his seat, one arm across the steering wheel. 'You've pleaded guilty to the manslaughter of our little girl. Do you know how hard it is for me to see you? Have you any idea?'

'Of course I do, but you're not listening. Tilly did not die in my care that day. I thought you understood that I had to lie to get out. I've lost everything because someone who hates me did a terrible thing and I was blamed. I have to find out the truth.'

'Don't do this.'

'Don't do what exactly? Speak out? Does having your carefully curated story contradicted upset you? Do you think I care about that? I put Tilly on the sofa. I turned my back, and she propelled herself off and cut her head. I thought I should take her to A&E just in case, but in the car she was chatting away, and conditions were awful so I decided to turn back. Then when I got home, there was a woman. She—'

'Stop, for Christ's sake.' Joe slaps his hand on the steering wheel. 'I understand that you believe what you're saying, that you've told yourself this version of the story so many times you think it's true, and I understand why. But the reality is that Tilly died in your care, and you panicked and dreamt up the story of the abduction. It was a huge mistake and it made things so much worse. When you realised that, you started exaggerating your mental health problems. You had me convinced for a while, but I sensed from the beginning that something wasn't right.'

'I did not imagine it, and I did not exaggerate my symptoms. I had stopped taking the pills. Life was so flat, so lacking in texture. There were days when I couldn't be bothered to move. Being depressed, well, that came and went, but there was always the hope of better days. It was a toss-up which was worse, but the pills took away my ability to think for myself. I found that hard to handle.'

'I get that, but you should have come off them under medical supervision.' He groans. 'I blame myself for not realising sooner. Believe me, you were a different person when you stopped taking the meds. You were insanely jealous. And because of that, we lost our daughter.'

Her head is ringing. 'That just isn't true.'

'How could you have coped with what happened when you weren't in your right mind? The shock must have been immense. Your instinct was to cover it up.'

She's prevented from defending herself by a coughing fit. Joe hands her a bottle of water from the cupholder under the dashboard and waits in silence until it's over.

'You okay?'

'Yes.'

'I can forgive you for leaving Tilly alone for a few minutes, but I cannot forgive you for turning my life into an utter nightmare. By telling lies, you prolonged the agony.'

74

'I did not tell lies.' She coughs again, tastes the grittiness of carbon on her tongue. 'I am not a liar.'

'This is getting us nowhere.' Joe sits back, his fingers tightening round the steering wheel. 'Until you accept what you've done, you are never going to find peace. If that's the way you want it, fine, but I have a new life now.'

'Well, I *don't* have a new life and I'm unlikely to get one. I'm going to find out who did this. I have nothing to lose.'

'You have a great deal to lose by drawing attention to yourself.' He sounds exasperated. 'The police won't reopen the case without evidence, and if there had been any, they would have found it the first time round. Don't you think it's time to make a new start? It doesn't have to be all negative. You could still make something of your life.'

'Like you have with your perfect wife and your perfect baby? Was it really that easy for you to move on? Were Tilly and I worth so little that you could just replace us with shiny new versions?'

Beside her, Joe crumples like an empty crisp packet. He grasps the top of the steering wheel and presses his forehead against the back of his hands, his shoulders rolling forward as he sobs.

'Joe,' Claudia says, aghast. 'I'm sorry. I didn't mean it. I know you're still grieving too.'

He wipes his eyes on his sleeve. 'Fuck.'

'When was the last time you cried?'

'The day you were sentenced.'

So he hasn't cried in front of his wife.

He blows his nose into a creased cotton handkerchief. 'There's a plaque for Tilly in Kingston Cemetery. Why don't you go and see it. It might help.'

Her mouth drops open. 'How could you? There's no hard proof Tilly is dead. As far as I'm concerned, she's missing.'

'I had to do it. I had to have some kind of focal point. So do you. What you did wasn't your fault, I understand that, but refusing to admit it now, telling yourself she's alive and well somewhere, that's not going to help you get better.'

'If she's dead,' Claudia says through her teeth, 'show me her body.'

'You need to accept reality.'

'Whose reality?' She scowls. 'Not mine.'

'So what happens if all your search turns up is proof of your own guilt?' Joe says as Claudia pulls her zipper up and winds her scarf round her neck. 'What will you do then? It'll break you.'

In the wing mirror, she sees a woman in a cream woolly hat and matching scarf standing like a statue about fifteen metres from where they're parked. It's hard to tell at this distance, but it seems as though she's interested in them. Claudia drags her eyes away. Joe doesn't appear to have noticed.

'Then that will be it for me.'

'You mean you'll give it up?'

'I'll never give up on Tilly.' She's hollowed out. It's time to go home. She didn't expect a miracle and she hasn't had one. 'What I mean is, I won't be able to live like this. Out here is worse than prison. I'd rather be dead.'

'I don't understand.'

'I'm not going to spell it out.'

Joe turns to face her, reddened eyes narrowed.

'When you were ill, you used to do that. You used to threaten me in that way.'

'I'm not . . .' She looks into the mirror again. The woman has vanished. 'I don't do that. It's not about that.'

'Emotional blackmail will not get you to any place you want to be. Do you understand? You're the one who'll get hurt by that kind of behaviour. I think you want me to worry about you, because it's a tie.'

'No. I—'

He cuts her off. 'Can I give you something to tide you over?'

'What?'

'If you're stuck for cash, I can help. I don't want you to suffer. It's in all our interests that you find some way to live your life.'

'No thank you,' she says stiffly. 'The only thing you can do for me is not hang around selling Culloden Road.'

'It's happening. I've signed a contract with an estate agent and they're taking the photographs tomorrow. Viewings will start next weekend.'

'Why did you stay there?'

'It's just the way things panned out.'

She studies his face. There are shadows beneath his eyes. Without thinking, she twists round in the seat and places her good hand on his neck, her thumb against his jaw. She feels the pulse of his artery beneath her fingers, feels his life flow through her.

'Stop it.'

She whips her hand away. The warmth has disappeared, leaving her feeling sad and stupidly vulnerable.

'I don't want to hurt you,' he says. 'But that's over and

done with. You need to move on. If there isn't anything else, I should get back to my wife.'

Tears spill down her cheeks. She wipes them away fiercely. 'Am I ugly enough now? You can go back to her safe in the knowledge that you don't want me any more.'

'Don't be ridiculous. You're still . . .' He shakes his head. 'You are still yourself. You think you're dead inside because you lost Tilly, but you're not; you're dormant, like I was. I genuinely want you to have a life that fulfils you.'

'I hate you, Joe.'

She opens the door and climbs out of the car, almost falling over herself to get away from him. She wipes her nose on her sleeve and hunches into her collar as she walks away. Stupid idiot. She said all the wrong things, alienating him even more when she needs him on her side. Why did she hint at killing herself? What had she expected?

She's even angrier with him. He made a conscious decision to believe the verdict, and in doing so, he chose to believe that Tilly was dead and his wife a killer. Claudia doesn't have the luxury of choosing a belief and sticking to it. She's had nine years in a cell to think about little else; no career, no new spouse and baby to distract her and apply balm to the sores.

Chapter 15

CLAUDIA

Claudia walks into Kingston to buy a new smartphone, but is told she needs proof of residence and three months' bank statements. Instead she buys a pre-paid phone that doesn't require any documents, then heads into John Lewis because it's warm and feels safe, though its familiarity is painful. Her mother used to bring her here when she was a child. She had loved the escalators, the way they took her up through the middle of the shop so that she could see everything around her; the mysteries of adulthood laid out like a magic carpet. Later, when she was married, she and Joe came here to choose baby paraphernalia before Tilly was born. They spent a small fortune, then had a cup of tea and a bun in the café with the view out onto the river. She remembers the feeling of her baby bump pressed up against the table.

She catches her reflection in a full-length mirror. Her face is grim, her singed hair weird, her mother's coat too big. Shame at touching Joe suffuses her. He was repelled. She's too hot. She needs to get out.

*

Bursting into the street, she drags cold air into her lungs and starts to walk. She passes a hairdresser's, hesitates, then pushes open the door and walks in.

'Is anyone free now?' she asks the girl at reception. 'I just need this sorting out.' She pulls at her hair. 'It probably needs cutting short.'

The girl can't hide her surprise. 'Give me a sec.'

She confers with a colleague, who glances over with a smile that immediately vanishes.

Dismayed, Claudia backs away, collides with a trolley carrying combs and curlers and sends it flying into a chair occupied by an elderly woman. Jabbering apologies, she hurries out of the salon and into the street. The day could not possibly get any worse.

She hugs the lapels of her coat tight across her chin. Despite the chill, Kingston is buzzing. Every time she sees a pram, she looks from baby to mother in a kind of panic before she remembers that Tilly will be ten years old and at school. She feels conspicuous, but no one notices her; mothers don't drag their children out of her path or bend defensively over their prams.

Outside the church, there's a gaggle of women with pushchairs, rolled-up yoga mats stored underneath. One of the babies seems familiar in his green and blue snowsuit. Her eyes lift to his mother, who notices her at the same time and wrinkles her nose as though she's seen a dog turd on the pavement. She whispers to her friends, who turn their heads and stare.

Anna.

'Can we talk?' Claudia asks, walking up. With no hungry press to record their exchange, this is an opportunity.

Anna's neatly tweezed eyebrows arch. One of the women laughs, and Claudia turns on her.

'If you have something to say, you can say it to my face.'

'Jesus,' the woman mutters.

'You're back in the close for five minutes,' Anna says, 'and you burn the place down.'

Claudia draws a breath, tells herself not to rise to it. 'I need to talk to you. I need to understand a few things about the day I lost my daughter.'

'How dare you? When I needed to understand what had happened to my sister, you didn't tell the police what you'd said to her. You have no feelings.'

'That isn't true.'

'Okay. Fine. Psychos have feelings too. Do I look like I care? You should leave Shires Close. No one likes you, no one's taking your side. I know for a fact your stepfather can't stand the sight of you, your mother is disappointed in you. If they loved you, they would've made damn sure they were in the country to support you. They couldn't get away fast enough. They're ashamed.'

'You can't possibly know that.' It comes out weaker than she'd meant it to, because of course she knows what Robert thinks. It's humiliating.

Anna gives her a snide smile. 'Actually, I do. Robert told Charles Roache and Charles told my mother. You'd be surprised how much our little community talks to each other.'

'I'm only surprised at how unforgiving and malicious you are. You know me. You babysat for my daughter. I was kind to you.'

'It was just money, so don't go thinking I liked you or

anything. I liked Joe. He was normal and funny and human. You, though, you were hard to get to know.'

'Where did you go that evening, after you cancelled me?'

'Oh fuck off.' Anna turns on her heel and, followed by her cohort, pushes through the door to the church hall.

Chapter 16

CLAUDIA

The light is going by the time Claudia gets back to Shires Close. She's done this walk alone hundreds of times before, and this certainly isn't the first time she's felt spooked. Back in the day, it was because Louisa was convinced there was a paedophile behind every tree, but this is different; this time the street lights feel sinister, the houses unfriendly.

Someone gets out of a car moments after she's passed it, closes the door and starts to walk behind her. Her heart is pounding, and she forces herself not to look over her shoulder. Ahead, the railway bridge looks like a mouth ready to swallow her. She is reluctant to walk under it and wonders whether she should start running. Then a metal gate clangs shut, and she almost gasps with relief.

Shires Close is quiet, the press pack dispersed. The burnt-out studio is a dark and jagged hump. It feels like a metaphor for her; a dirty reminder of her presence amongst the neat suburban houses. The police tape is still there, but the policeman guarding it has gone. When she lets herself into number 7, Frank slinks out of the kitchen and curves around her shins. She bends to stroke his head, and he pushes it against her. Whatever self-serving reason he has to be friendly, she's grateful.

The kitchen light is on. Claudia frowns and automatically eases the key between the clenched fingers of her left hand. She can't swear to it, but she's sure she switched the lights off before she went out. Nerves on edge, she reaches for one of her mother's walking sticks from the umbrella stand and walks around the house checking behind curtains and doors. There's no one there. She releases her breath, leans the stick against the wall in the kitchen and tears open a sachet of cat food, then freezes when she sees Frank's bowl. There are scraps of dry food in it, and they most definitely weren't there this morning. His water bowl is full to the brim as well, and she distinctly remembers wondering whether she should top it up before she left and deciding there was plenty to last him a few hours. She checks the dustbin and counts the empty sachets. There are two where there should only be one.

Her skin crawls. She checks all the rooms again. Nothing has been disturbed as far as she can see, nothing taken. But perhaps they didn't need to; they would have known that the simple act of feeding the cat was enough to make her feel unsafe. Coming so soon after the fire, this scares the crap out of her.

It's two hours before a pair of constables turn up, and when they do, it's abundantly clear from their expressions and tone that they know exactly who Claudia is and don't feel any need to be respectful. They are in their thirties, female, and both have brown hair tied back, but there the resemblance ends. One is small and stocky, the other average, forgettable until she turns startling black-rimmed blue eyes on Claudia.

'Why don't you tell me what happened, Mrs Hartman?' She manages to imbue the *Mrs Hartman* with disgruntled displeasure, as if she's been dragged out of her warm and comfortable squad car to see to a drunk lying in a puddle of his own vomit.

'Someone came in and fed the cat while I was out.'

The woman barely refrains from rolling her eyes. 'Could it have been a neighbour, someone your parents arranged it with before they went away? Who holds the keys?'

'Their cleaner. And no, it wasn't Eva; I have her set, but I checked anyway. And the arrangement was always for me to feed him. Someone wants to intimidate me.'

'Have you any reason to believe that?'

Claudia reacts impatiently. 'Everyone knows where I live and no one wants me here. My flat burned down last night. What more do you want?'

'Are you accusing anyone in particular?' the smaller officer asks.

'No.' There are too many to count. 'Perhaps you could take fingerprints from the packets?'

'Are you asking me to fingerprint your neighbours? I hardly think that's going to endear you to them.'

Claudia has an image in her head of Charles Roache pressing fat fingers onto the ink pad. 'No.'

'Then what do you expect us to do if you haven't been physically threatened and there's no sign of a break-in?'

'Trespassing is still a crime, isn't it?'

'Yes, it is,' Blue Eyes says. 'We'll be sure to put it at the top of our agenda.'

'Someone's trying to frighten me. I'm a threat to them.'

'Why would you be a threat?'

Claudia meets her eyes. She can see what this is about. They want her to say that someone else is guilty of taking Tilly so they can lock her up again. She is not falling into that trap. 'I don't know.'

The officer gives her a humourless smile. 'You see our problem here, Mrs Hartman. You have form for making stuff like this up.'

She sees the face of the judge, with his yellowing wig and raw red nose, his mouth thinning with distaste. *You lied … You lied … You lied*. They think she killed her baby, they think she should never have been freed, they may well have small children themselves. There's no pity in their faces. She chills them.

'I'm sorry to have wasted your time. I'm not going to take this any further.'

Tilly is crying. Claudia grumbles, turning over and reaching for Joe. It's 2.17 by the digital clock. He isn't there, so she pulls the pillow over her head and tries to go back to sleep. He's always been good at settling their daughter. But the crying goes on, cutting through the night. Maybe Tilly's running a temperature, or teething. She'd better go and take over, otherwise Joe will be exhausted at work.

Grumbling, she sits up and drops her feet off the side of the bed, but as her eyes adjust, she realises this isn't the bedroom she shared with Joe in Culloden Road. She's in the spare room in Shires Close. The sound must be the wind, or a fox. She gets up, staggers across the room and opens the window. A movement in the shadows makes her start, but it's only Frank returning from one of his nocturnal adventures. The sound is coming from inside the house.

Fear makes her ears ring so loudly they almost drown the wailing out, and suddenly she's not sure whether she's hearing it or dreaming. She goes out onto the landing and runs downstairs flicking switches, illuminating the stairwell, the wide front hall, the kitchen. The crying echoes off the walls, then suddenly it's gone. She finds herself standing in her bare feet in the middle of the kitchen, and she no longer knows what's happened.

She used to sleepwalk when she was a teenager, and it started again after she had Tilly. Occasionally, in prison, she would wake to find herself standing right up against the door to her cell, nose pressed to cold steel, her breath reflected back at her. With the abrupt change in her life, it's only natural that it should happen again. Comforted by the thought that it will at least give her something to talk to the psychiatrist about, she goes back to bed and buries herself under the duvet.

In the morning, the first thing she does is look for photographs of Tilly to replace the ones destroyed in the fire, the ones she had kept with her in prison. They've always been displayed in the front room, but when Claudia goes to look for them, they've been swapped for ones of Jason and his family. Before she went to prison, there was one on the mantelpiece of Claudia and Tilly with Louisa. Also missing is a photograph of her holding her baby half-brother on her lap, beaming with pride.

She opens the cupboards under the bookshelves. Stacks of old DVDs nobody watches crowd one of them, board games the other. In the kitchen, she rummages in the Welsh dresser, but by this time she almost hopes she doesn't find anything, that her desolation and sense of being cancelled by the family is validated. Who took the decision to strip the house of reminders of her? She assumes it was Robert. Her stepfather would have been ashamed to invite friends into a house where photographs of his notorious stepdaughter were displayed alongside ones of his irreproachable son. Perhaps he hoped that by banishing her image, she'd fade from memory. But you'd have thought they'd have kept the ones of Tilly.

Her mother should have stood up to him. She sniffs back a sob and stiffens her resolve. She will find out the truth, no matter what.

Chapter 17

CLAUDIA

When Claudia leaves the house, the neighbour's front door opens and two teenagers step out. A girl of about fifteen and a younger boy. The boy is wearing tracksuit trousers and a hoodie, the girl a quilted jacket, skinny black jeans and chunky lace-up boots. She looks Claudia up and down with an affected insolence before sauntering off. Claudia gives them time to get well ahead of her. Anna is outside too, dressing gown flapping in the wind, holding two bottles of milk and talking to Margery Roache. They stop speaking, and as Claudia walks away, she feels the force of their combined glare boring into her. It occurs to her the residents might have got together, might even have held a meeting, and are conspiring to get rid of her. Someone apart from Eva must have a copy of the key. Someone her mother gave it to so long ago she's forgotten. Someone like her old friend Frances Holt. She considers asking Frances, but she's hardly likely to admit it.

And anyway, one mission at a time. She's already planned her morning.

Just for a second, Claudia is thrown. The lavender which used to bloom behind the low white wall outside number 26 Culloden Road has been replaced by a row of olive trees designed to screen the bay window. The hall light is on; the stained glass in the front door with its birds on branches laden with blossom is aglow. Tilly loved to touch those birds.

She shouldn't have come, but as long as no one sees her, it can't hurt. Obviously she's not going to ring the doorbell.

A light goes on upstairs, and she's treated to a partial view of the bedroom she and Joe once shared. It's been redecorated in a neutral colour; Claudia had painted it blue. They didn't have much money at the time – two teachers, a baby on the way and a large mortgage – so she'd done most of the decorating herself, Joe being useless at that kind of thing. She wonders what they've done to Tilly's bedroom; whether Joe dismantled it long before Sara came on the scene, or whether he kept it as it had been when they were all together and Tilly was safe. His new wife would have dealt with that pretty swiftly, she reckons.

She mentally walks herself around the nursery, item-ising every carefully chosen item: the pretty stencilling, the white cot and changing table set Joe's older brother donated, the musical mobile with the little rabbits that played Brahms' Lullaby. She closes her eyes and makes herself hear Joe. He's calling up to them, telling them he's home, when they already know because he makes enough noise. And the smell: baby shampoo, talc and Sudocrem, and Tilly's deliciously scented skin.

Sara Hartman appears in the window, holding her baby. Claudia shrinks back. She finds it extraordinary that this woman is inside her house while she is outside looking in, exiled. She accepts Joe's right to be happy, but the sight is yet another punch to the gut. Sara is living Claudia's life, but a better version. She grits her teeth. Despite having spent the most terrifying time of her life inside those walls, it's still home, still where she loved and was loved, still where she spun dreams for the child in her arms.

A wave of bitterness rolls over her. No doubt Sara has put her baby down for the same nursery Claudia put Tilly down for; no doubt she's friends with the neighbours Claudia struggled to form bonds with. Apart from Kate and Paul, none of them liked her very much – too challenging, with her sharp face, deep, shadowed eyes and slash of red lipstick. Sara would have fitted in better. The dinner party circuit would have scarcely missed a beat.

The window is empty again. Claudia waits a few more minutes, but Sara doesn't reappear. Her fingers are tingling with cold, but just as she's made up her mind to go home, the door opens and Sara comes out, pushing a buggy. The baby is wrapped up warm, a pink woolly hat under the hood of her white all-in-one, fingers in thick mittens, feet in little pink snow boots with sheepskin lining poking out of the top. Claudia drinks in the sight of her, eyes stinging. She waits for Sara to double-check the contents of a quilted baby bag, then follows at a distance, pretty sure she knows where her replacement is headed.

Claudia reaches Canbury Gardens and hides near the tennis courts. She watches Sara wave a greeting to another mother. This woman has a Jack Russell, which she ties by its lead to a post outside the playground. They push their prams through the gate. The other woman laughs at something Sara says, then bends to unstrap her child. She lifts him up, kisses his nose, then places him on the ground. He immediately leans in to Joe's baby, who is struggling against her straps while Sara removes her gloves. Freed, the babies toddle off. Claudia can't help remembering a time when she and Kate Shaw would pause on their walks and count the months before their babies could join in the fun.

She walks down the path, past the playground, pausing casually beside a bench, pretending to check her phone, peering at Sara from under her lashes. She must be giving off an odd vibe, because Sara's friend glances curiously at her. There's no spark of recognition. The terrier bares its sharp teeth and yaps loudly, pulling on its lead. Claudia starts back, but it's too late. Sara has seen her. She says something to her friend before marching out of the playground. Claudia turns on her heel and bolts.

Half an hour after she arrives home, the doorbell rings hard, three times.

Chapter 18

CLAUDIA

'Claudia! I know you're in there. Open the door.'

It feels as though she's deep underwater, breathing into a mask. She can't move.

'I'm not going away,' Sara shouts. 'Let me in, or I'll tell the police you've been stalking me. I took a picture.'

Claudia snaps out of it and opens the door a crack. Sara gives it a shove. She has parked her car behind Robert's. She must have gone back for it. Her baby is asleep in her arms. With her long lashes, the curls peeking out from under her hat, the dimple in her chin, she reminds Claudia of Tilly. She reaches to stroke her cheek.

'Don't touch her.' Sara picks the car seat up and pushes past Claudia, looking around before heading into the kitchen. She lays the baby on her back on the sofa.

Claudia follows her, her arms wrapped tight around her chest, trying to stem the tide of jealousy and anger. The presence of Joe's little girl in her house has a physical effect on her. It is heart-splitting, rage-inducing, massive. She quells her emotions with difficulty and takes in the mother. The wife.

Claudia is bewildered. Sara is nothing special. She supposes she can understand why Joe might have fallen for her if she caught him at exactly the right moment, but it's weird. How come this short, rather overweight woman got to keep him?

Sara is looking round, critically. Claudia hasn't cleared up her breakfast things, let alone last night's microwaved supper.

'I wasn't going to approach you,' Claudia says. 'I just wanted to look at the house, and then you came out.'

'And you couldn't help yourself, I suppose.'

'No, I couldn't.'

'Give me one good reason why I shouldn't go to the police?'

'I won't do it again.'

'Not good enough.'

Sara takes her phone out of her pocket and Claudia winces. She can grovel, she knows how to do that. It's yet another of those essential skills you learn behind bars.

'I'm sorry. I don't know what came over me. I needed to see the house, just once. And then you were there, with your baby, and I... I just kept walking. I wasn't going to approach you, but I needed to see what you were like, who Joe had chosen. You'd have done the same in my place.'

Sara mulls this over, then nods. 'Although I wouldn't have been stupid enough to get caught.'

Claudia breathes a little easier. 'Would you like coffee?'

Sara accepts. She says nothing while Claudia gets down mugs and heats milk in the microwave, but Claudia can tell she is as curious about her as she is about Sara. Maybe more so, given her predecessor's notoriety. She brings the cafetière to the table and pushes the plunger down.

'You must hate me,' Sara says. 'I'd understand, you know. You have a right to be resentful.'

'I'm not. If it hadn't been you, Joe would have found someone else. I don't like it, but I honestly don't have the energy to get worked up about it. I'm no threat to you.'

'I don't feel threatened.'

Claudia suspects she's lying. She doesn't want Joe back, because that would never work, but she does desire him, in the most basic sense. She imagines Sara can smell it on her. The silence grows so large, she can hear Frank licking himself in the corner.

'Is there anything I can do to help you?' Sara finally asks.

'Why would you want to help me?'

'Because the sooner you're settled, the sooner Joe and I can regain some normality.'

'All right then. You can help me find out what happened.'

'I meant starting over, or whatever. Not feeding your delusions.'

'So not actually helping at all, just making sure I'm out of your life?' She wonders how badly Sara Hartman wants that. Enough to set fire to her flat? Intuition suggests not. A young mother. A devoted wife. She isn't the right demographic.

'What is it exactly you think I can do?' Sara asks.

'Joe was having an affair and for ages I thought it was Kate. If I was wrong, then I need to know who it was.'

'There was no one, Claudia. I think it's been established that you were paranoid.'

'There was an element of paranoia, but that doesn't mean it wasn't true.'

She had ignored Joe's reassurances, had ignored everyone, caught up in her fixation. But still . . . there had been signs, subtle but unmistakable to someone on the lookout for them: a hesitation in his voice when he told her he'd be late home; catching him watching her face when he thought she didn't notice. And, so unsubtle as to be almost comic, bringing her flowers when there was no occasion for them.

'If there was someone,' she says, 'then it's important. It may be why Tilly was abducted.'

She hadn't been in control of her mind back then, she concedes that: first mugged by the antidepressants, then, when she secretly came off them, so tangled up in the agonising bondage of suspicion and jealousy that she was unable to handle anyone else's point of view.

'When Joe denied it and they couldn't find evidence, I didn't take it any further. To keep insisting on something when everyone thinks you're mentally unwell is self-defeating. The more you argue, the more they're convinced they're right.'

'Why didn't you tell them you'd stopped taking the pills?'

Claudia smiles, but it's a grimace really. 'Because I was deluded. Because I thought everyone was whispering behind my back. Because I thought they wanted me chemically coshed. That's the way delusions work. But Joe was definitely involved with someone, and it must have been more than a misguided fling with a colleague or a friend for him to have been too scared to admit to it during the investigation.'

Sara's eyes narrow. 'Listen, if you're implying something . . .'

'That it was a pupil?'

'Don't be so ridiculous.' Maeve's arms spring up, starfish-like, and Sara lowers her voice. 'You know Joe as well as I do, and you know he wouldn't have done something like that. You can't be married to someone and not know.'

'Why the hell can't it be true? I fell in love with Joe when I was sixteen.'

'But nothing happened between you.' Sara looks as though she's sucking lemons, her mouth pursed, nose wrinkled. 'My husband is a man of principle. What you're suggesting is disgusting.'

'Do we ever really know anyone?'

'You're barking up the wrong tree,' Sara says brusquely. 'There is nothing weird or pervy about Joe. He never behaves inappropriately with the pupils at his school. He doesn't try to be their friend or offer one-to-one counselling with troubled girls. He's just Joe. They love him at Overhill, but not in the way you're talking about. He's charismatic and fun and he cares. He knows every single one of those eighteen hundred pupils by name.'

'Yeah, okay. You've made your point. But what else would be so life-destroying you'd sacrifice your wife rather than be caught?'

'Nothing. Joe wasn't . . .' Sara takes a breath. 'He isn't hiding a guilty secret. It's all in your head.'

Claudia thinks about Anna at that age. Anna's inner light used to switch on whenever Joe entered the room. She remembers feeling a niggle of unease late one night when Joe ran her home after she'd babysat for them.

Any woman connected with Joe is of interest. But Anna? Would there have been something gauchely appealing about her to a man like Joe? Claudia has always believed that their ages were irrelevant when she and Joe fell in love; that it was just one of those things; a bolt of lightning. She refuses to believe that her schoolgirl status had been the thing that first drew him to her.

'It could have been someone with a crush on Joe,' Sara says. 'You hear about crimes committed because of obsessive love. He might not have known anything about it. Did the police talk to the pupils at his school?'

'Yes, of course they did. Nothing came of it.'

'There you are then.'

'*Where* am I? There must have been a reason Joe wouldn't admit to an affair.'

'Yes.' Sara sounds exasperated. 'Because there wasn't one.'

Claudia realises she's in danger of alienating the one person who could actually help her and softens her tone.

'I know how much you must love him, because I did too, but he isn't perfect. He has a weakness for women. If he was having an affair when Tilly was taken, I want to know who it was with, because the woman who abducted my child did not come out of nowhere.'

'If you think he would behave so despicably, then you never really knew him.'

Claudia shrugs. 'I was unreachable, and he looked for solace elsewhere.'

'If what you're saying is true, he didn't only sacrifice you, he also sacrificed his daughter. I refuse to believe he'd do that.' Sara jumps up and pulls on her coat, her movements jerky, anger pulsing off her.

'Wait.' Claudia stands up too. 'There is one other thing.

A girl at my school committed suicide. She lived in Shires Close and her family are still there. I... Well, I didn't behave particularly kindly towards her, and they found out about it years later; actually on the day Tilly went missing. She had a younger sister, Anna. Anna was the one who was meant to babysit for us that evening. Her mother claimed she was ill, but it was obviously a lie. It's always felt like too big a coincidence. I know she had a crush on Joe too.'

Sara frowned. 'If you're implying there was something going on—'

'I'm not implying anything, but a lot of things happened that day and I've never been able to connect the dots. I think she's worth talking to, but I can't get near her.'

'And you think I can? Why would I?'

'Aren't you curious? Anna has a baby,' she adds, glancing at Sara's daughter. 'A boy. She takes him to a yoga class in the church hall on the market square in Kingston. Tuesdays, three o'clock.'

'Fine. Give me your phone number. I'll be in touch. I'll give you mine in case you think of anything else.'

Claudia is thoughtful as she watches Sara's car drive away. She almost wishes she could call her back, tell her to leave Anna alone; but this is what she wants, isn't it? Someone to tread where she can't. At any rate, she doubts Sara will follow through; there is little in it for her. Unless what Claudia said has hit home. Sara was quick to protest Joe's innocence, but then again, she would be; she's his wife. Claudia doesn't trust her; she doesn't trust anyone apart from her mother. Kate, Joe, Anna, Sara: everyone has an agenda, and they all want her out of their lives one way or another. She is their worst nightmare.

Chapter 19

SARA

Curled up on the sofa with Joe, catching up with *University Challenge*, Sara studied her husband's profile: his slightly protuberant forehead, large nose and hard chin. She was nervous, had butterflies in her stomach. For the first time since they'd become a couple, she'd felt the earth shift beneath her feet.

Overall, though, she was glad she had that encounter with Claudia, if only because it gave her a chance to assess whether she was going to be a problem. Claudia wasn't much to look at, except for those strange dark-rimmed grey-blue irises. They had riveted Sara. She hoped they hadn't riveted Joe on Tuesday afternoon. She wasn't being horrible, she just needed to feel safe, and Claudia having clandestine meetings with Joe did not make Sara feel safe. Joe was hers, but she wasn't a fool; she accepted that a small part of him would forever belong to his ex.

'What?' Joe asked, sensing her gaze on him.

'Can't I look at my gorgeous husband?'

He raised his eyebrows. 'Bit scary.'

Sara laughed and turned away, back to the television and the competition that never failed to make her feel inadequate. Unlike Joe, Kate and Claudia, she hadn't been to university.

When the credits rolled, she switched off the television, took a deep breath and spoke.

'I saw Claudia today.'

His stillness could have meant anything. Surprise, shock, displeasure, disbelief. 'Please tell me that's not true.'

'Why would I make up something like that?'

'Where did you see her? She didn't come here, did she?'

'She followed me to the playground this morning. We spoke. She hasn't got over you. I don't think she's going to do anything, but perhaps be on your guard.'

Joe bent over, his head in his hands, turning to look at her through his fingers. 'I am so sorry. I'll call her and tell her she mustn't do it again.'

'I don't want you to call her. I don't want you communicating with her at all.'

'Okay. I won't. Michael can speak to her lawyer.'

Sara drew up her knees and hugged her shins. 'She's still banging on about you being unfaithful to her. She thought it was Kate, but apparently she's changed her mind about that.'

'Does she have a list of candidates?' Joe snorted. 'I hope you didn't believe her.'

'Of course I didn't.'

He leant back into the corner of the sofa. The light was dim, softening his face. She tried to read him. This was the man who swore she could trust him, who told her that he had moved on from Claudia, if not from Tilly. She had accepted that qualifier. But yesterday Claudia and Joe had sat in his car when he ought to have been at work.

'It isn't true. I promise.'

He took Sara's hand and looked into her eyes. She wanted to believe him.

'I'm a monogamist,' he said. 'A boring monogamist who likes to come home to his wife and child. I wouldn't swap what I have with you for an affair. Not in a million years. I'm not that shallow. I hope the same goes for you. You and Maeve are all I need.'

'You're not boring,' she mumbled.

'I love you.' He held her face between his large hands and brought their foreheads so close together she could feel his warm breath on her skin.

He was hers. She should know that. Besides, he was besotted with Maeve. There was no way he'd risk wrecking his relationship with his daughter by betraying Sara with his battered and broken ex. If he told her now about meeting Claudia, she would forgive him. It wasn't too late. If he didn't, she would have to tread carefully, be strategic. It would be a war fought in darkness.

'Why do you never talk to me about what happened in your marriage?' she asked.

He let her go and steepled his fingers against his mouth. 'I'm sorry. I know I haven't been fair, but I suppose I haven't really dealt with it properly. Her breakdown was the hardest thing I have ever had to go through, and it was partly my fault. I got complacent after she was put on medication, and I missed things I shouldn't have missed. I was working hard. I'd heard my deputy head was retiring and I wanted the job, so I was doing everything I could to make it happen, and it meant that Claudia was on her own with Tilly too much.' He sighed and took Sara's hand again, playing absently with her fingers. 'I didn't tell you about the problems between Claudia and Kate because I didn't want it to affect our friendship with the Shaws.'

'You shouldn't have kept it from me.'

Joe drew in a long breath. 'I don't like revisiting those weeks. They were extremely difficult. I blame myself for neglecting Claudia and expecting the pills to do all the work. After Tilly's disappearance, she had some weird episodes. There was one time she turned up at the school all done up like she was going to a party: backless black dress, high heels, lots of make-up. Lisa had the sense to keep her in the office, but half the school must have heard her screaming at me. And then when she stopped ranting, she was all over me. It was confusing, I didn't know what to believe. She was a mess, but there was something calculated about it.'

'Did you tell the police?'

'No. I couldn't have done that. Pretence or not, she clearly wasn't well. Someone else told them.'

'Lisa.' Sara disliked that woman.

'Probably. I want to show you something. Wait here.' He jumped up and ran upstairs, bounding down again with a brown envelope. He sat down and placed it on his lap, his hand splayed on top. 'I scanned these before I gave the originals to the police.'

Sara held out her hand and he gave her the envelope. She ran her thumb under the lip and slid out a thin stack of paper. They were photocopies from the pages of a spiral-bound notebook. She squinted to read the handwriting. Joe stretched across her and switched on the side light, then got up and propped himself against the window, his long fingers wrapped around the edge of the sill.

Sara felt his eyes on her as she read Claudia's unhinged, sometimes illegible scrawl. It appeared to be a stream of consciousness, with scratchings-out, capitalised words, a lot of exclamation marks, and underlining so heavy the scores were visible even on a copy. It made little sense, but the theme was obvious: her obsession with Joe and his perceived infidelities. Some of it was obscene, some of it merely sad. Kate Shaw featured in a big way.

She handed the pages back to Joe with a shudder of revulsion. 'Oh my God. That's terrifying.'

'Yup. But the thing is, the notebook turned up, conveniently, after she realised she was a suspect. I found it under a book in her bedside cabinet, and I think she meant me to, because she'd asked me to fetch a pack of painkillers from the drawer. It was while we still believed her story about the mystery woman pretending to be the babysitter. After that, her witness statement fell apart. She couldn't describe the woman, and when she was challenged, she stopped making sense and would fly off the handle at even the most innocent questions. She couldn't cope with anyone doubting her word. I'm so sorry, Sara. Claudia can be convincing, but you do understand that she was manipulating you, don't you? She's doing her best to manipulate me as well.'

Sara darted a glance at him. Was he finally going to confess to meeting her? 'How? Has she been in contact?'

Joe hesitated, rubbing the lines between his brows with his middle finger, a nervous habit. 'No. I mean through the sale of the house. She knows I have an emotional attachment to it. I don't think she's in love with me any more. She's just sad. She won't do us any harm.'

Chapter 20

SARA

Sara parked Maeve's buggy with the others in the foyer of the church hall and lifted her daughter out, opening the swing doors to a large room with an apex ceiling, white walls and a polished wood floor.

This morning she'd woken thinking she couldn't go through with it, it was too risky. It had been an impulse; she had seen a route into Claudia's paranoid world and had grabbed it without thinking it through. If Joe hadn't shown her those papers, she might have been taken in by Claudia's story about his infidelity. There had been something in her eyes; an almost manic determination to be believed.

She had seen that before, hadn't she? If you deliberately disbelieved someone and made them doubt themselves because it suited you to do so, things could go very, very wrong. Everyone had their limits. She couldn't afford to sympathise with Claudia, but it would have been inhumane not to have felt a scrap of pity.

She must be mad to even consider going anywhere near Anna, especially with the risks involved, but there was an

105

argument for it. Gain a grounded person's trust and they became reasonably cooperative; gain a damaged person's and they were yours. Anna was damaged; why else would she push the entire blame for her sister's death onto someone else's shoulders? She was another person who couldn't cope with having a mirror held up in front of her. And Sara couldn't deny it: she was curious.

There were a dozen or so women in the hall with their small children. There were toddlers everywhere, and two newborns sleeping in their car seats at the side of the room. A woman pulling yoga blocks out of a cupboard turned and smiled.

'You must be Sara,' she said when Sara wandered over. She had a bouncy ponytail and was wearing top-to-toe greenish-blue Lululemon. 'I'm Gillian. We spoke on the phone? I'm so pleased you've decided to give it a whirl. You'll love it. Everyone's really friendly. And this must be Maeve.'

'Is Anna here?' Sara asked. 'Only a mutual friend knows she does this class and said to say hello.'

'Anna Pemberton?' Gillian looked around. 'Not yet, but I expect she'll be here soon. She never misses a week.'

Sara lowered herself onto a mat, taking her cue from the other women. Maeve immediately toddled off to see what was happening elsewhere, showing no sign of self-consciousness as she sized up the other children, which pleased Sara immensely, since several remained glued to their mothers.

Gillian took her place at the head of the room and sat cross-legged, her posture perfect, shoulders back, neck straight, stomach in. Sara copied her. She'd practised yoga sporadically over the years and was confident that she would be able to keep up. She was good enough for this lot anyway, she thought, looking around at the various shapes and sizes, the wobbly tummies and full thighs, relieved she wasn't the only person in the room who wasn't thin. Maeve returned from her expedition and planted herself on Sara's lap.

The door swung open and a woman breezed in, and Sara suddenly had no idea what to do with her limbs or the muscles in her face. It had to be Anna. Sara's body was so racked with tension, it was all she could do not to scoop Maeve up and leave. Claudia's neighbour was petite and slender. She wore an acid-green top and black yoga pants and was carrying a little boy who had his arms wrapped around her neck. She seemed to know everyone, judging by the smiles she was throwing around.

'I'm so sorry I'm late. This one decided to do a poo just as we were leaving.'

'Good morning, Anna,' Gillian said. 'And good morning, Max. Get yourselves settled quickly.'

The mat next to Sara was free. Anna sat down and glanced Sara's way before contorting her legs into an impressive lotus. Sara detected no more than a natural curiosity, and some of the tension left her shoulders. Anna's son had no interest in sitting still and crawled towards Maeve. Anna smiled at Sara and Sara smiled back, relieved to have coasted the first hurdle.

As soon as the session started, Sara could see it was going to be chaos – a sheepdog would have had trouble keeping this lot corralled. There were tears, giggles, the patter of little feet running across the floor, a tussle over a toy truck. The sun streaming through the windows caused two tots and one exhausted mother to doze off. It was all very silly, making shapes to songs about caterpillars while the babies didn't take a blind bit of notice.

At the end of the hour, as the women chatted while pulling on their trainers, wrestling wriggling toddlers into snow-suits and scooping up woolly hats and stray mittens, Sara made sure she was close to Anna.

She was always surprised at how easy it was, how well the formula worked; how merely having a baby and dressing the right way gave you instant access to another woman's space. As long as your child didn't bite theirs, as long as you were personable and willing to share some-thing of your life, you were welcome.

'How old is he?' she asked, pushing Maeve's feet into her fleece-lined booties.

'Eighteen months. I'm sorry, have we met before? You seem familiar.'

'I don't think so.'

'Oh, well. I'm Anna.'

'Sara.' She smiled. One mother to another, no agenda.

'Did you enjoy the class?'

'Yes. I'm rusty, but that doesn't seem to matter here.'

Anna laughed. 'Yeah, it's all about the social interaction really. For us mums as well as the kids. Your little girl is adorable. What's her name?'

As they pushed their prams outside, Sara asked Anna if she fancied a cup of tea. Anna agreed, and they set off past the food stalls and through Bishops Hall to the riverfront, the air crisp and cold against their cheeks. The water was sparkling, swans drifted by, and steam rose from a scruffy houseboat. On the far side, the trees along the riverbank were reflected in the water.

'Whereabouts do you live?' Anna asked once they'd sat down and ordered.

'Not far from here. Kingston Gate. Near the park.'

'Ooh. Very smart.'

Sara laughed, but she felt she had gone up a notch in Anna's estimation, passed some kind of test. 'I don't know about that. What about you?'

'Long Ditton.'

'I know it. It's where my husband's first wife lives. God, sorry. That sounds stalkery.'

'It does a little.' Anna chuckled, her eyes rapacious for gossip. 'Is it difficult?'

The waiter brought their order. Sara took a packet of dried mango out of her bag and handed a slice to Maeve. She had limited time before her daughter got antsy. Right now, their prams pushed close together, the two children were happy enough babbling nonsense at each other, but Maeve could turn on a sixpence.

She sighed heavily to signpost that she had something interesting to impart. 'You could say that. She was recently released from prison.'

'Shit,' Anna said, slowly putting her cup down on its saucer. 'What's her name?'

'Why?'

'Because the woman in the house opposite has just been released. Claudia Hartman.' Anna lifted her chin as she said the name.

'Bloody hell,' Sara said in a hushed whisper. 'Yes, that's her. Joe's ex-wife. I can't believe it.'

'You're married to Joe Hartman? God. What are the chances?' Anna shook her head in disbelief. 'He used to teach me.'

'Small world,' Sara said. 'So what can you tell me about Claudia? Only I'm curious; Joe never talks about her.'

'I know a fair bit. Her family have lived in the close even longer than mine. Since we were children. Everyone's really pissed off that she's there. It's horrible. She shouldn't have been released.'

Sara raised her eyebrows.

'I don't mean to be unkind – I'm sure she's suffered for what she did – but I have to consider Max. Also, it's so depressing. She's a wreck, sloping out of the house when she thinks no one's looking. If I was in her shoes, I'd have gone somewhere no one knows me.'

'I'm not sure that place exists for Claudia. The case was pretty notorious.'

'That's her problem. We've had the press camped on our doorstep. Honestly, it's like she's a celebrity. And she managed to burn down the garage conversion. It looks awful.'

Sara could almost feel sorry for poor beleaguered Claudia. 'It won't be for long. Our house is on the market and we've already had three viewings. Two of them are coming back for a second viewing on Saturday. Claudia will get half the proceeds and then she'll be out of your hair.' She was not going to tell Anna how upset she was about having to sell up.

'It'll be a huge relief. Owen, my husband, thinks she's devaluing the close. It's put him in a filthy mood.'

'The whole thing has been a nightmare, to be honest. I'm constantly on edge.'

'I'm not surprised. I caught her staring at Max the other day. It gave me the creeps. She has those weird eyes. They're far too intense.'

Sara widened her own eyes. 'You must have got to know her well over the years.'

'Not all that well.' Anna went pink. 'Our mothers were good friends once, but I was a lot younger than Claudia. Joe taught English at my school,' she added wistfully. 'I remember he was always great fun in class, so entertaining and charismatic. But you know what I mean.' Something oddly like pain flashed across her features; Sara caught it and mentally filed it away to think about later.

'I know exactly.'

'I used to babysit for them, and Joe was different at home. I did notice that.'

'In what way different?'

'It was like he was weary; like he was carrying something heavy on his shoulders. I found out afterwards about Claudia's mental health problems, but I was a teenager and more worried about boys and how I looked than what the people I babysat for were going through. But I liked him. Everyone liked him.' Anna blushed again. 'Sorry. It's a bit of a cheek me explaining your husband to you.'

'No, it's interesting. Joe does turn it on for an audience. He's a youngest child, so I suppose it was his way of getting attention when he was growing up.' Sara smiled at Anna to reassure her. 'No performer can keep it up all day, and as you say, there was a lot of crazy stuff going on in that house.'

'I'm sure,' Anna said, sipping her mint tea. 'It was awful what happened to his little girl. I think it's amazing how well he's coped. It would have broken me and Owen. But that'll be down to you. He's lucky to have found you.'

Sara flushed, pleased, although it would be more accurate to say she had found Joe; found him, ensnared him, married him. Anxious to get off the subject, she glanced at Max pointedly. 'You need to be careful. Claudia is delusional and has an overactive imagination. I would double-lock your doors at night. And keep your distance. Don't get involved. She can be persuasive.'

'But I already am involved.' Anna placed her hand protectively on her son's head. He pushed it off. 'I was a witness for the prosecution.'

'Wow. Why was that?'

'Because of an incident when I was babysitting. Claudia badly overreacted to something.' She spiralled her finger against her temple. 'Loony tunes, if you know what I mean. Screaming and ranting. All I did was try on one of her evening dresses. She shouldn't have come home early. Joe said I looked nice and that went down like a ton of bricks. It was only a few weeks before I found out what she did to my sister.'

'Your sister?'

Anna folded and refolded a paper napkin as she spoke, describing her sister's death and the part Claudia had played in it. Sara was no apologist for Claudia, but it astounded her how Anna and her family literally took no responsibility; how they piled all the blame onto a teenage girl who had been inarguably insensitive and cruel, but not culpable. It was as though they were entirely without sin.

She decided to play along, nodding vigorously. 'The thing with Claudia is she never takes the blame. It's always someone else's fault.'

'Exactly. She refuses to acknowledge her part in what happened, or apologise. She never deserved Joe. Oh God, it's so nice to have met you, Sara. There's no one I can talk to about this. Owen doesn't want to hear about it, and my parents don't want to be reminded.'

Relaxed, they chatted about life, about their husbands, and the minutes rushed by.

'Will you come to the class next week?' Anna asked when it was time to go.

Sara sensed neediness and homed in on it. 'Oh, definitely! It was fun, and Maeve loved it. And I've met you.'

'Come back to mine afterwards. I'll sell you on my patch.'

'What if Claudia sees me?'

Anna shrugged. 'So what if she does? Let her be the one who feels threatened for a change.'

Sara thought it was highly unlikely that Claudia didn't already feel that way, and that Anna had to be one of the least empathetic women she'd ever met, but she smiled and exchanged phone numbers.

'I'd love to see Joe again,' Anna said. 'Though I don't suppose he'd want to see me. He probably hates me for the things I said at the trial, but it was only because the truth is important to me. I couldn't lie.'

She suddenly looked very young. Sara decided to humour her. She realised that, despite her denials, she needed to watch Anna and Joe together.

113

'I'm sure he doesn't hate you. You must meet up.'

'Do you think that's a good idea? Wouldn't he prefer not to be reminded of that time?'

'I don't think he associates you with it, Anna. To be honest, he's never actually mentioned you to me.'

'I suppose he just wants to forget.'

'I expect so. But don't worry. He won't have a problem meeting you.' Sara wrinkled her forehead. 'Perhaps it would be better to keep it casual, though.'

'What about fireworks night?' Anna brightened. 'There's a big one near us. They're having it on Saturday. It's a community event. You can have a look at our area. You might like Long Ditton. What do you think?'

'I think it's a brilliant idea.'

Sara was fairly certain it wasn't and felt a slight wobble. She looked at Anna's face, at her clear blue eyes and wide mouth, the bouncy blonde hair tied up in a high ponytail. This was a woman, after all, who had played a part in Tilly's abduction by cancelling her babysitting commitment. Joe was unlikely to want to renew the acquaintance. Still, she knew how to get round her husband, most of the time.

'Let me talk to Joe. I'll let you know tomorrow.'

'Sure.' Anna wound her pale blue scarf around her neck. 'Halloween tonight,' she added. 'I'd better get home and put the pumpkin out before it gets dark.'

Chapter 21

ANNA

Well, that was interesting. Sara is so different from Claudia, so much easier to talk to. But she's not that attractive. Perhaps Joe just wanted a boring woman and a peaceful life.

I get Max out of his pram and into the car. He reaches for his truck and sits back with it gripped between his mittened hands. I shouldn't have invited them to fireworks night, I should be sensible and keep my distance. But I've dreamt of running into Joe again for so long.

He used to come to Shires Close regularly, before. He and Claudia would drop in on Louisa and Robert when I was still living at home and our mothers were still best friends. Sometimes I'd be outside at the front when they left, and Joe would always give me a wave before getting into the car.

The first time I babysat for them, it was in Louisa's house. They went out for a family meal. I was fourteen, but it was okay, because Mum and Dad were across the close. Once I was fifteen, I went to Culloden Road to babysit from time to time. I liked exploring it, seeing photographs of my teacher, sniffing his clothes. One time I even lay down on his side of the bed and buried my nose in his pillow. That was when I started seeing Joe as a human being, his teacher cloak stripped away. There was even a photograph in their bedroom of him in a pair of swim shorts on the beach. In it his hair was untidy and he was grinning. He has a funny face, almost like rubber it's so mobile, but that was when I saw his beauty. I took a picture of that one.

Claudia wasn't nearly as friendly. She was polite but stand-offish. I thought it was because I was young and therefore of no importance. I only learned later what it was really about. Guilt. She couldn't look me in the eye without being reminded of what she did to my sister.

I don't know how I feel about Joe now. I only know that as soon as I realised who Sara was, my heart literally flung itself against my ribcage. What are the chances? Actually, it's not that crazy that we ended up in the same class: there are only so many places between here and Culloden Road where mothers congregate with their babies, and baby yoga is always popular. She looks like she needs the exercise.

I expect Joe will say no to fireworks, which will translate as no to meeting me again. I'm the last person on earth he'll want to see. It'll be disappointing, but perhaps it's for the best.

It's dark. I light the candle in the pumpkin, and take it outside. Max is too young for it, but he'll enjoy seeing the older children all dressed up and bouncing with excitement. I glance at Claudia's house. There's a light on. I wonder if she even knows it's Halloween. I doubt anyone will knock on her door. No one wants their children coming into contact with real nastiness.

Chapter 22

CLAUDIA

'So,' Sara says. 'What do you want me to do?'

Claudia is in the front room with the curtains closed, the lights dimmed, her phone pressed to her ear, a glass of red wine and a bowl of salted nuts within easy reach. Frank is on the sofa beside her, his paws hanging over the edge. She strokes him as she thinks.

'You know,' she says, 'I've thought a lot about Anna's reaction to me, both at the time and since I came out, and it's way over the top. And that makes me wonder.'

'If she's protesting too much?'

'Exactly. Even Frances hasn't been as vitriolic; she's just been cold. I know Joe will probably refuse to join them for fireworks night, but if you did manage to persuade him, you could see how she behaves.'

Sara mulls this over in silence. Claudia can hear her breathing. She isn't sure it's a good idea, but she's vowed to push at any chink just to see what light might be let in. Anna is a chink.

'I don't know,' Sara says.

'I think she's scared of me. If she sees you as an ally – you could hint that you've as much reason to be threatened as she does – she might...'

Children's voices bring her to the front window. She moves the curtain aside to see a crowd of little ones, parents in tow, dressed as witches, mummies, ghosts and super-heroes. Is that what day it is? She's lost all sense of time.

'She might what?' Sara asks.

'She might betray herself in some way. I think she knows something; why else would she be so vile? She can't really believe I'm responsible for her sister's death. Yes, I was unkind, but how was I to guess Megan was so unhappy? We weren't friends. She was two years younger than me. It's something else; it has to be. You said Anna was excited when she realised who you were. What if this is about Joe?'

'Don't start that again, Claudia. I'm warning you, I won't help if you say a word against him. Christ knows why I let myself get involved. I have nothing to gain from you being exonerated; I don't even believe you should be.'

Claudia swallows. 'I've asked myself that. I think you're doing it because you're curious. You know what they say? Keep your enemies close. And despite what you say, you aren't one hundred per cent certain of Joe. Listen, go if you can get him to agree. That would be interesting in itself, wouldn't it? Then find out something, anything, about the times she babysat.'

Claudia watches the children knock on doors, sweetly confident of a friendly reception, and wonders whether they'll knock on hers, in which case she's in trouble, because she has no treats for them. But they don't. They avoid number 7. It's as if she's the monster.

Another family group is doing the rounds. They stare at the house, their eyes narrowing as they try to see if she's there. She turns away, grabs the remote and puts the television on, turning up the volume to drown out the fun.

There's a thud. Claudia mutes the TV and listens, nerve ends prickling. It happens again; three thuds in quick succession. She sprints out into the hall and yanks open the door. Three people in hooded sweatshirts run away and disappear out of the close. The paving at her feet is wet and covered in eggshell. Yellow gloop dribbles down the paintwork. She closes the door quickly and sinks onto her haunches.

Crouched on the floor with her arms around her knees, her face pressed into them, she can smell stale wine on her breath. Her breathing is laboured; she thinks she might be having an asthma attack, although she's never been asthmatic. She squeezes her eyes tight shut and pretends she's locked in her cell.

Chapter 23

SARA

Joe walked into the bedroom in his pale blue boxers, pulling a white T-shirt over his head.

'You remember her then?' Sara said, resting her book against her raised knees and resuming the conversation they'd been having before he went off to brush his teeth.

'Of course I remember Anna.' Joe switched out the overhead light, pulled up the duvet and climbed into bed beside her. 'I'm staying well clear of that family.'

'I like her. We got on really well.'

'She's very young,' Joe commented. 'She must be at least ten years younger than you.'

'Eight years, actually, and so what? We're both mothers. She said we should consider Long Ditton. I wouldn't mind. I'd rather there than further out.'

'You've only just met the woman and you're thinking of moving close to her?'

She bats his comment away with a dismissive wave of her hand. 'I told her we're on the lookout for somewhere to move to, and we got talking about her area. If we're going to have to go halves with Claudia, we can get a decent-sized property there. Claudia will be gone by the time we move. What possible objection can you have?'

'What do you think? It's where my ex-in-laws live, and for all we know, Claudia might choose to settle round there eventually. That makes it a little too close to home for me.'

It rankled that he could say this after he'd actually met up with Claudia, but Sara kept her cool. It wasn't the right time to bring that up.

'I don't mean buy in Shires Close. I've looked on the property portals and there are some perfectly nice places we can afford. You don't have anything against the rest of her family, do you?'

'No,' he reluctantly conceded. 'I'm fond of Louisa Myhill, but it's difficult. She and Robert are not people I want to be bumping into all the time.'

'You won't have to. They're a different generation. We need to make a plan, Joe. I can't not know where we're going to be in a few months' time, so let's have a look round and go to the fireworks with Anna and her husband and see how you feel then. There's no harm in that, surely.'

'It sounds like my idea of hell. Standing around with a tired toddler on a freezing playing field with a bunch of people I don't know. Come on, Sara. We've got enough friends here. I'm sure Kate and Paul will be up for fireworks.'

'Of course they will, but they'll be going to the Haileycroft one, and they know everyone there. We won't see them for dust.'

Joe switched off his bedside light with an air of finality. 'I do not want to spend an evening with Anna Holt.'

'Pemberton now. You don't have to speak to her if you don't want to. You can just talk to her husband. If we don't go after I said we would, it'll feel like a snub. And it's only an hour.'

'If Anna hadn't been ill that day, none of this would have happened.'

'That is so unfair. It wasn't her fault.' She turned off her own light, moved down in the bed and stroked his stomach; still gratifyingly firm for a man in his mid forties. 'Don't be mean-spirited, darling. It'll do us good. Maeve adores Anna's little boy.' This was a slight exaggeration, given they'd only met once. 'Anyway, Anna's moved on. She's happily married. She doesn't dwell on the past.'

'She didn't lose her baby,' he said stiffly. 'So excuse me if I find it hard not to.'

'Oh, Joe. I didn't mean that. I'm sorry if I'm being insensitive. Look, why don't we go along, and if you feel uncomfortable, we'll tell them Maeve doesn't like the noise and slip away.' She moved her hand down and Joe began to respond. 'Please,' she wheedled. 'You want me to get used to the idea of a new place, don't you? Having a friend somewhere would really help me.'

'Somewhere, yes. But not Long Ditton.' But his hand was on her breast, his mouth buried in the crook of her shoulder.

She arched her back. 'Fine,' she gasped. 'We can move to Timbuktu if it makes you happy. But we are going to that fireworks display. If not, I'm going to start a rumour about subsidence in this road.'

Joe didn't laugh. There was a distance to him that worried her; he was holding her, touching her, but it felt like he was going through the motions. She drew back from him and searched his face.

'What is it?'

He shook himself. 'Nothing. All right, my stubborn, spoilt wife. Have it your way. I'll admire the bonfire, watch the sodding fireworks, be polite to my ex-babysitter and her husband. But that's it.'

Chapter 24

Saturday 4 November

SARA

Sara watched Joe meet Anna for the first time in maybe nine years in the queue to show their tickets. Joe was a social chameleon, a natural actor, able to dial up energy at the flick of a switch. Sara had often seen it: the way a fire would be lit from within, the timbre of his voice changing along with the set of his shoulders, his eyebrows taking on a life of their own, his face creasing round an irresistible smile, hands gesticulating as he spoke. It often happened when he met someone new, but it didn't happen here. She was aware of him holding back, almost as though he was waiting for his cue.

Anna behaved with grace, holding out her hand to take his. 'It's been so long, Joe,' she said. 'It's wonderful to see you again. This is Owen. My husband.'

Owen was confident, good-looking, though a good four inches shorter than Joe. He shook Joe's hand vigorously. 'Heard a lot about you, mate. Apparently you were inspirational.' He laughed loudly. 'I'm keen to hear what exactly you inspired.' Then he winked. 'And you're Sara. My wife was full of you last week. Sara this and Sara that. Couldn't shut her up.'

Sara smiled. 'We hit it off.' She thought he was a bit of a prat, and she could see Joe thought the same. She sighed inwardly. Never mind. The object here was not for Joe to acquire a bosom buddy.

They showed their tickets to a steward and walked on to the field, where a large crowd had already gathered. Sara found herself wishing they had gone to Haileycroft School's display with the Shaws. She was anxious. If Anna and Owen left them to talk to acquaintances, she'd feel like a lemon. Maeve was enjoying the experience, her eyes wide as she gazed about her from the lofty heights of her father's shoulders. Max was even more animated, pointing at everything, drunk on euphoria, cheeks pink and eyes bright. Sara told herself to relax.

The music was loud, making it hard to be heard. Their faces glowed with the heat from the fire. Sparks lifted and swirled around them, blown by a light breeze. Anna leaned against Sara's shoulder, speaking into her ear.

'That was so weird. I felt like I was back at school. I almost called him Mr Hartman when he shook my hand.' She giggled.

Joe and Owen had gone to get mulled wine and were in the scrum around the makeshift bar. Sara turned to look for them. Joe was talking to a big man with a beard, Owen to a woman. The way she shook her hair and rocked her head back when she laughed made Sara's antennae twitch. She turned to see how Anna was taking it, but Anna didn't appear to have noticed, or if she had, she chose to ignore it.

'Did you have to twist Joe's arm to get him here? I bet you did. You can be honest, I won't be hurt.'

Should she come clean or bluff? She decided on somewhere in between. 'He was wary. He's always set his sights forward rather than back.'

Anna squeezed her arm. 'I totally understand. It must be so painful for him. But once he's got to know us, hopefully he'll stop associating me with that time. I'm a different person. I look different, don't I?'

Sara laughed. 'I don't know what you looked like back then.'

'Oh, I was a real ugly duckling.'

'I'm sure only you thought that.'

'Does Joe mind us being friends?'

'Of course not, why would he?'

Tired of Anna's irritating insecurities, Sara surveyed the crowd. Small groups mingled, children weaving between them. A man raised his young daughter onto his shoulders while he talked to a friend, and close by, someone laughed so loudly it could be heard above the music. The fire grew hotter, and they moved back a couple of feet. Joe and Owen were on their way over, arms clamped round small legs. Joe caught Sara's eye with a broad grin, and some of the tension inside her unwound. She took the drinks to free his hands. The mulled wine, with its heat and sweet, spicy fragrance, relaxed her.

She had no idea how Joe was really feeling and wouldn't until they were on their way home. He hid things so well, was so considerate and friendly, that no one ever suspected he sometimes struggled. But this was his kind of event; he infinitely preferred a noisy crowd to a supper party. He had a horror of someone asking him intrusive questions under the guise of sympathy.

Anna had a smile plastered on her face. She stood between Joe and Owen, looking like a child at her own birthday party. At one point she shook her hair back, her face full of laughter. She was flirting.

The fireworks were spectacular, fifteen minutes of explosions against a background of thumping pop songs that hampered any attempt to hold a conversation. Something Sara was thankful for. Afterwards, they tramped back up the lane and out into the high street, where they stopped in front of an estate agent's window.

'Look, Joe,' Anna said. 'Detached house, large garden. Very swanky.'

'Nice.' Joe's tone was non-committal.

'I know it hasn't got the kudos of where you are now, but it's much closer to Overhill. You'd get home earlier. You wouldn't have Richmond Park on your doorstep, but Ditton Hill is very nice, and ten minutes' walk away, and Bushy Park is only a short drive.'

'It's got off-street parking,' Owen said. 'You could have an electric car. Listen, why don't you come back to ours for a bowl of chilli? There's loads. And there're potatoes baking in the oven. I made extra just in case.'

Torn, Sara glanced at Joe. She worried he would feel trapped into doing something he didn't want to do, even suspect her of orchestrating it. She hadn't, but on the other hand, this was precisely the kind of opportunity Claudia would want her to exploit. And what she wanted too, even though it felt like she was picking at a scab. Joe had lied to her about seeing Claudia. What else might he have lied about? She did want to see Joe and Anna together. In a crowd, juggling babies and glasses of mulled wine while fireworks screamed overhead, didn't count.

'Owen, you're being insensitive,' Anna said. 'I doubt Joe wants to go anywhere near Shires Close. Not while *she's* there.' She then spoilt the gesture by looking to Joe for approbation.

What did she want? Sara wondered. A medal? Still, she had made the decision for her and given Joe an out. They wouldn't be going.

'Shit. Sorry, mate. Forgot.'

'What do you want to do?' Joe asked, to Sara's surprise. 'I'm happy to drop in briefly if you are.'

'Really?' Sara searched his eyes for the truth. He had done enough by coming; she didn't want to push it. He smiled at her, and she was reassured. If he was that relaxed, then Claudia was wrong. 'Okay, then. Yes. But we won't stay long, because Maeve won't last.' Maeve was already drooping, her head on Joe's shoulder. 'Chilli sounds perfect, though.'

'There's a travel cot,' Anna said. 'You can put her down for a little while.'

Chapter 25

SARA

Joe drove round to Shires Close. They waited in the car for Anna and Owen to arrive on foot. The radio was on. Sara switched it off.

'Why did you agree to supper?'

Joe screwed up his face. 'I don't know. Curiosity perhaps. It's so long since I've set foot here, I wanted to see how it would feel.'

'How *does* it feel?'

'Strange.'

'Just strange?'

He turned to her, hooded eyes clouding. 'No, not just strange. Awful. Empty. Claustrophobic. I never liked this place, or the people who live here. It's that intrusive interest. They come out of their doors at exactly the right time, as if they've been watching. I don't know how Louisa Myhill has stood it so long.'

'Perhaps it suits her. How did Claudia feel about it?'

He leant back in his seat. 'She always said it was a lovely place to be a child, a nightmare as a teenager.'

Sara peered out of the window into the bulb of the close, at the houses angled so that they had a front seat on everyone else's lives. In the bland red-brick block of flats where she'd grown up, no one had cared what anyone else did. She doubted anyone noticed when she and her mother left. Which was why, on balance, she'd rather like to live somewhere like this. Her mother's loneliness had been painful and embarrassing to witness for a child. Sara had been obsessed by *Neighbours* and had yearned for a life where people wandered into each other's homes uninvited, sure of a warm welcome.

'They're here.' She opened the door and got out. Joe followed suit.

'What a mess,' he said, tipping his head in the direction of the burnt-out shell of Claudia's home.

Anna wandered over. 'I know. Poor thing. I do feel a little sorry for her, despite everything.'

Sara assumed this volte-face was for Joe's benefit.

'Stupid cow,' Owen said. 'Serves the Myhills right for letting her use it. It's fucking outrageous.'

'She's their daughter,' Joe said. 'What did you expect them to do?'

There was a moment when Sara thought it was all going to go horribly wrong, that Joe was going to drag her off and that would be that. But Owen surprised her.

'You're right. That was bang out of order. Sorry, mate.'

'It's okay. I get it.'

Sparkling fountains and shooting stars briefly illuminated the rooftops. Somewhere nearby, a dog barked. Behind the house next door to Claudia's, young voices shrieked and howled with laughter, the sound echoing in the night.

'Their parents are away,' Anna said sniffily.

Joe got Maeve out of the car. She slumped against his

shoulder as he took her inside. Anna and Owen's house gleamed with mirrors and chandeliers. Sara pulled off her boots and sank gratefully into a huge plum-coloured sofa while Joe and Owen went upstairs with the children and Anna checked on the baked potatoes.

'Thank God for that,' Anna said, walking in with a bottle of red wine, two glasses hanging between her fingers from delicate stems. 'I was worried it was going to be burnt offerings.' She set the glasses down on the mottled-silver coffee table and undid the screw top, holding the bottle up and glancing at Sara.

Sara laughed. 'Go on then. We can get a cab home and pick the car up in the morning.'

'Fab.'

Anna fetched cold beers for the men, then sat down beside Sara and pulled her legs into a half-lotus, giving an *mmm* of contentment as she relaxed back into the corner of the sofa.

'So where did you two meet?' Anna asked.

'I was in a pub with friends and he was there with a woman. I knew who he was as soon as I saw him. There'd been so much in the media, the poor man couldn't avoid being recognised wherever he went. He told me afterwards the woman was his cousin. He said he barely went out, and never dated.' Sara sighed. 'It was almost five years since he'd lost his daughter, but he was still raw, and terribly lonely. Bereavement is isolating, even more so when there's no real closure.'

'Because Tilly was declared dead but never found?'

'Yes.' She paused, looked down at her hands, catching her bottom lip between her teeth. 'Nothing happened that evening. I didn't even think he'd noticed me. The next time was in the street. He was looking at a display of glassware in an antiques shop window. I went inside. I thought: if he comes in, it's fate; if he doesn't, that's how it's meant to be.

'Anyway, he did come in. I was so nervous I knocked a vase off the table and broke it. The shopkeeper came rushing over, but Joe picked up the pieces and read the price tag. He said, "Forty quid? That's daylight robbery."' Sara smiled at the memory. 'He took out his wallet and handed the man his debit card. When I protested, he said I could buy him lunch at the sandwich bar opposite. So I did.' She smirked. 'And we've never looked back.'

'That's so sweet,' Anna said. 'Just like a romcom. So, have you always lived in Kingston?'

She recalled Anna asking if they'd met before, and wondered how much of this was casual interest, how much a test. 'Only as a child,' she said without a flicker. She didn't owe this nosy woman the unvarnished truth. 'We moved to Bristol when I was eleven. I wasn't academic at all, so I'd been put in one of the lower streams at school and Mum was worried I'd be led astray by the naughtier kids. She thought if we got out of London things would be different.'

'Bit of a long way to go, wasn't it?'

'Not that far for a larger flat with a beautiful garden, and a better work–life balance for Mum.'

A plaintive wail from one of the kids brought an end to what was beginning to feel like an interrogation. A door closed upstairs, and Owen and Joe walked into the sitting room, looking pleased with themselves.

'These for us?' Owen handed one of the bottles to Joe. 'Sit down, Joe. Make yourself at home.'

Joe sat opposite Anna, stretching out his long legs. Owen lit the gas fire and dimmed the lights. Sara watched Joe as he peeled off his jumper, showing a triangle of flat stomach where his shirt had come untucked, and pushed up his sleeves. Anna glanced surreptitiously at his forearms.

Owen raised his bottle. 'Cheers. What shall we drink to?'

'To new friends,' Anna said, smiling at Sara. She unfolded her legs and put her socked feet on the floor. Sara couldn't help noticing how close to Joe's she had placed them.

'So, Joe, you taught my missus at Overhill. What was she like?'

Sara caught Joe's eye. He seemed startled by the question.

A small smile played on Anna's lips. 'He wouldn't have noticed me. I was a plain Jane back then.'

Joe stepped up chivalrously. 'Well, you've turned into a swan.'

'You haven't aged so badly yourself, Mr Hartman.'

Sara glanced at Owen. Owen didn't bat an eyelid, but what he said next seemed designed to cause tension.

'And you taught Megan before that. At Lady Eden's.' A statement, not a question.

'That's right. A long time ago.'

'What was it like teaching in an all-girls school?'

Joe pulled his sweater off and bunched it up. 'It had its challenges.' There was a light in his eyes, like he'd seen the enemy. Sara tried to think of something to say to head off the conversation, but Owen was intent.

'How did you deal with crushes? Were you ever tempted? Teenage girls can be a handful.'

'I wouldn't know,' Joe said coldly. 'I was doing my job.'

Owen mulled this over. 'You can't tell me it didn't happen. You married one of them.'

'Thus proving it wasn't a crush.'

'You left soon after Megan died, didn't you? Lady Eden's get too hot for you? Just kidding. I'm sure you behaved with complete propriety.'

'Owen,' Anna interrupted. 'Don't be a jerk.'

'Joe doesn't mind, do you, mate? It's just a bit of friendly banter. You must be used to it.'

Sara watched Joe clock Anna's mortified expression and held her breath.

'To be honest,' he said, evidently choosing to take Owen's intrusive questions at face value, 'it was uncomfortable. I was a young man, and I hadn't really thought it through when I accepted the job. You could ask any teacher, male or female, working in secondary education, and find that a lot of them have experienced a pupil's fixation, whether romantic or the opposite. It's marginally easier in a co-ed school. I haven't had a problem with it since I became management. It's easier to maintain a distance.'

'You must have some tales to tell,' Owen said.

'So, tell me about primary schools round here,' Sara said, steering the conversation from what felt like quicksand. 'Are they oversubscribed? Only with Haileycroft, where we'd want Maeve to go if we stayed in north Kingston, you practically have to live next door to get in.'

Anna dragged her gaze away from her husband. 'It's like anywhere really. You just have to cross your fingers. Is everyone ready to eat?'

*

The baby monitor crackled, and one of them, Sara thought it was Max, started crying.

Anna picked up the monitor and switched it off. 'Can you see to him, darling?'

'Sure.'

Sara got to her feet. 'I'll go too. It might be Maeve.'

She followed Owen upstairs and into a large room that smelled of babies. A soft light glowed from a globe. She leant over the travel cot while Owen picked Max up. Maeve was stirring, but she settled when Max stopped crying.

'I'll stay here till he goes back down,' Owen said, rocking his son. 'All right, little man?'

Sara nodded and tiptoed out. As she came downstairs, she could hear Anna's voice. She sounded upset. When she opened the door, they stopped talking.

'All well?' Joe asked.

'Yes. Fine. What were you talking about?'

'The good old days,' Anna said. 'I tell you what, it feels weird having an adult conversation with someone who taught you. I've definitely regressed.'

'Very weird,' Sara agreed, looking from one to the other and wondering exactly what she'd interrupted. Joe's wry smile didn't particularly reassure her.

Owen reappeared with a snotty-nosed, red-cheeked Max in his arms. Max gulped back a sob and clung to his father's neck.

'Teething,' Owen said.

'Why did you bring him down?' Anna asked. 'He'll never settle now.'

She moved towards him, holding out her arms. Owen tried to pass Max over, but the little boy lashed out at his mother, smacking at her hands and screaming, 'No, Mama!' before tucking his head under his father's chin.

'Just give him to me,' Anna snapped.

Owen shrugged and unpeeled the child, handing him over. Max fought like a cat as Anna left the room.

'He's just overtired,' Owen told Sara and Joe. 'His first time at the fireworks. It was too much for him.'

'I need a pee,' Sara said. She had seen what no one else appeared to have seen. Anna surreptitiously switching off the baby monitor.

'Door across the hall.'

She ignored Owen's instructions and padded back upstairs in her socked feet. The bedroom door was closed, and from behind it she could hear Max protesting. Thankfully, there was no sound from Maeve. She was about to leave when she heard Anna's voice, not crooning her son to sleep as she would have expected, but an angry hiss.

'You little shit.'

There was a sound like a light slap; not meant to cause harm, Sara thought, but more like a reminder, if Max could understand that, of who was boss round here. It startled her, because it smacked of Anna knowing exactly what she was doing, the subliminal threat her child would feel. It evidently had the desired effect, because Max sobbed as though his heart would break. Anna's voice flowed like warm honey now that she'd got what she wanted.

'There, there. Mummy didn't mean it. You're my good boy. There, sweetie. You go to sleep now.'

Chapter 26

SARA

Sara didn't wait to hear any more; she ran downstairs, shut herself in the cloakroom and took a steadying breath. She counted slowly to ten, then flushed the loo, adjusted her face and went back to the sitting room. When Anna joined them a minute or two later, she gave Sara a quick, rueful smile.

'I can't believe Maeve slept through that.'

Butter wouldn't melt, Sara thought, smiling back. 'Oh, Maeve will sleep through anything.' This wasn't strictly true, but what else was she supposed to say? She was in shock.

'How's the sale going?' Owen asked. 'Any interest? I'll be fucking delighted when you sell. The quicker we're shot of your ex, the better.'

'Owen,' Anna said. 'What did I tell you? Joe does not want to talk about Claudia.'

Owen patted his wife's knee and jumped up. 'Another beer, Joe?'

'One of the houses in the close is about to come onto the market,' Anna said. 'The old lady who lived there died about three weeks ago. I didn't think to mention it before, but it's unmodernised and would be worth a lot more done up and extended.'

Owen turned as he opened the fridge. 'It's in reasonably good nick, all things considered.'

'Which one is it?' Sara asked.

Anna put her glass down. 'Next door. Number 14. I used to look in on Jocelyn from time to time. The place is a time warp.'

'I'm surprised you aren't going for it, Owen,' Joe said. 'Right on your doorstep.'

Owen handed him a fresh bottle and sat down. 'I would have, mate, but I've got too many irons in the fire right now.'

'It's not for us,' Joe said.

'Not even worth a look?'

'I wouldn't mind having a nose,' Sara said. 'We have to start somewhere, and I like the area. It doesn't have to be in Shires Close, obviously, but it would give us something to compare other houses with.'

'I'll come with you,' Anna said. 'There are nets in the front windows, but not in the back. There's an alley running behind the houses. We can get into Jocelyn's garden through that.'

'We'd be trespassing,' Joe said.

'Don't be such a stick-in-the-mud. No one's going to know.'

'I'll know.'

Anna cocked her head. 'So what are you going to do, Mr Hartman? Put us all in detention?'

Listening to this coy flirtation, Sara watched Owen's face. He was irritated, his smile fixed. She tapped his knee in an effort to distract him.

'So you think it would be a good investment?'

'I wouldn't have bought this place if I didn't. I wasn't

particularly keen on living next door to my in-laws, but as it is, it's worked out great because they babysit all the time.'

'Louisa and Robert are hardly going to offer to babysit Maeve,' Joe said.

'True. Well, it's up to you.' Owen stood up unsteadily and hooked an arm around Anna's waist. 'Lead on.'

'I'll pass,' Joe said. 'You take a look if you really want to, Sara. I'll stay with the kids.'

'We'll only be a minute or two,' Anna said. 'Do come.'

Joe's eyes flicked to Sara's face. He shook his head.

'Well, if you're not going, I might as well stay and clear up supper. Owen can take Sara. He's more knowledgeable.'

'No problemo,' Owen said.

Sara had to give Anna credit. She was an excellent strategist.

Sara trotted after Owen. They left through the back gate and walked along the narrow track, using the torches on their phones to avoid the brambles arching over from the gardens butting onto it. It smelled unpleasantly foxy.

Owen opened the next gate along, and as they went in, a rocket screamed into the sky above them, spouting a thousand stars. For a few short seconds, Sara could clearly see the crazy-paving patio, the overgrown lawn with its apple tree and washing line, the windows looking down at them. She felt someone walk over her grave, and shuddered.

Owen put his hand on her shoulder, startling her. 'You thinking about Maeve and Max playing out here together?'

She stepped away and put on a bright smile. 'No. It's a lovely space, but Joe's right. Too many bad associations.'

'Big, though, yeah? First thing I'd do?' He indicated the

shed crouching darkly in the corner to her left. 'Take that pile of shit down and replace it with a garden office.'

Sara wandered up to the house and cupped her hands around her face against the window of the sitting room.

'Of course, you'd knock this through to the kitchen.' Owen seemed determined to fix himself in her headspace. 'And build a fuck-off extension. Planning won't be a problem. These houses were built in the eighties, so no one cares what you do to them.'

She didn't answer.

'And don't worry about your other half,' Owen said. 'When a man marries a younger woman, he basically knows he's going to have to say yes to everything.'

'Joe's not like that.'

'Wanna bet?'

Not really, Sara thought.

'Anna seems to like him.' He was fiddling with a leaf on an overgrown shrub and not looking at her.

'Joe's easy to like.'

'You're not jealous?'

'Not at all.' She moved back from the window. 'Is something bothering you?'

'No, but there are some teachers you never forget, aren't there? I get the feeling your husband is one of them.'

Sara shrugged. 'Safety in numbers. If Anna had a bit of a crush, so did all her friends. I wouldn't worry about it.'

'I'm not worried.' Owen stomped back to the gate and held it open for her. 'Nice place, isn't it? Someone's going to make a pile.'

Chapter 27

ANNA

It is terrifying and exhilarating being alone with Joe. There are so many things I want to say but can't. I loved and hated him so much when I was at Overhill, and it broke me having to shut all that down. I was a pressure cooker for so long, and it seems I still am, because I badly want to touch him.

I've been so good, so restrained. I haven't stalked him or bugged him. I've literally only seen him once since everything fell apart. It was a July weekend about six months after Claudia went to prison. I was walking home from the shops and he was dropping off boxes and suitcases of Claudia's stuff in the close. Louisa really flipped. She screamed at him that he had let her daughter down. Then she slammed the door, leaving all the stuff on the front path. Joe looked as though he'd been slapped.

I called out, wanting to help him, but something in his face stopped me from approaching, reminding me of the danger, of my promise. I lifted a hand and sort of waved, and he paused, then gave me a regretful smile, got in his car and drove off. And that was it, I swear. Although I might have walked past the school once or twice.

He has kept a careful distance all evening, but I saw his dismay when I offered to stay with him just now. He's scared, and possibly feeling a little humiliated. They're going to struggle financially once they've bought Claudia off, and Owen is so obviously more successful. And he's younger. Age suits Joe, though. I love the lines on his face. I'd like to kiss them right now.

He piles the empty plates up and takes them to the sink. I rinse them and put them in the dishwasher. The atmosphere keeps snagging. I should have put music on. The silence is so fraught I can barely look at him.

'I want you to stay away from Sara,' he says.

So this is how he's going to play it. 'I didn't orchestrate the meeting, and neither did she.'

'I'm not saying you did. I'm merely asking you to walk away from whatever this is. She's not going to be your friend.'

'We're adults,' I hiss at him. 'We met with our little ones. This has nothing do with the past.'

'Everything's to do with the past.'

'That's your problem, not mine.'

'Yes. You're right.' He seems to recollect himself. He's a guest in my house after all. 'This is not your fault. I get paranoid sometimes. People's motives aren't always clear, you know.'

'I understand. But I'm not that girl any more. I've grown up, worked for my living, got married and started a family. I don't feel the same way I did when you were my teacher.' I risk a smile. 'Your problem is you're too vain. What do you think? That there are legions of women still carrying a torch for you from their school days? Get over yourself.'

He laughs, and it feels extraordinarily intimate.

'Are you okay?' I ask.

142

'Yes, of course.'

'Is it very hard having Claudia around?'

He picks up a pan and starts drying it, then can't find anywhere to put it. I take it from him and our fingers briefly touch. He looks horrified. Honestly, men are such cowards. I pretend not to have noticed.

'I want to ignore her,' he says after a minute. 'But I can't. I don't want to make another terrible mistake.'

'You worry about losing Maeve?'

He doesn't answer, but I can see from his eyes that that is precisely what he means.

'Oh, Joe. That must be awful. Have you told Sara how you feel?'

'No, I don't want to worry her.'

The back door opens and Owen and Sara come in, pink-cheeked from the cold.

'So what did you think?' I ask.

Sara glances at Joe. 'It's a great property, but probably not for us.'

Chapter 28

SARA

Sara looked from Anna to Joe as she took off her coat. Joe was standing with a dishcloth in his hand, Anna was at the sink. There was something in the air; a serious conversation interrupted. Or was she reading too much into it? Of course they'd been talking, but it was probably about Max and Maeve. Still, perhaps she should have been firmer, not allowed Anna to move the three of them around like pieces on a chessboard. She had been so adroit about it.

'Joe,' Anna said. 'Can I ask you something?'

'Sure.' He put the dishcloth down and moved away from her, back to the sofa.

'I'm thinking about retraining as a teacher and wondered if I could pick your brains.'

Primary school, Sara assumed.

'Tell them what your subject is.' Owen had a *wait for it* look on his face; a magician about to pull a rabbit out of a hat.

'Secondary school maths,' Anna said, and Sara swiftly reversed her original appraisal. Another high achiever to make her feel inadequate.

'In that case,' Joe said, 'of course. Maths teachers are like hen's teeth.'

'That surprised you, didn't it?' Owen said. 'The wife's not just a pretty face.'

'I did maths and accountancy at uni,' Anna explained as Sara arranged her expression into one of polite interest. 'I worked for PWC and then for myself. Then Owen and I got married and Max came along a couple of years earlier than we'd planned. It's made me think about a change of direction once I'm ready to go back to work.'

'What did you do before you had Maeve?' Owen asked Sara as the four of them sat down again.

'I had several jobs.' Put on the spot, Sara blushed. 'I never really knew what I wanted to do. I still don't.' She turned to Anna. 'I envy you your certainty.'

'Sara is doing herself a disservice,' Joe said. 'She's made me extremely happy after everything that happened, and that, I can tell you, is quite a feat. She put me back together.' He cast Sara a rueful smile and she smiled back. 'I honestly don't know where I'd be without you, darling. I owe you everything.'

She didn't know what to say, and after an awkward pause, Owen reached for one of the empty glasses and raised it.

'To men who are big enough to wear their hearts on their sleeves.'

'Yeah, well, enough of that.'

Joe had leaned back into the cushions. In his sloppy shirt, black jeans and socked feet, he looked perfectly at home and rather louche. Sara glanced at Anna to see how she was taking it. Anna was watching him sleepily, fiddling with a lock of her hair. The atmosphere was cashmere soft and almost tangible.

'We should go, darling,' Sara said. She found the cab app on her phone. 'Before you fall asleep.'

Obedient, Joe pulled his sweater on. 'It's been great.' He directed his smile at Owen, which Sara thought was so like him. He didn't bear grudges.

'Give me your number,' Owen said. 'If you find somewhere you like, I'll take a squint at it. I have a lot of contacts round here.'

Sara noticed Joe's hesitation, but Owen had his phone in his hand and was waiting, so Joe reeled it off.

'Can I come to Overhill?' Anna asked. 'I'd love to chat some more about my options.'

'Sure. Speak to Lisa, my PA. She'll find a time for you.'

She beamed. 'Thanks, Joe. I'll keep you to that. I'd love to see the place again.'

'Happy memories?' Sara asked.

Anna was still looking at Joe. It made Sara's skin prickle. Owen was eyeing his wife.

'Mixed. There were some hiccups, but I wouldn't change a thing. It was my teenage years that made me.'

'It wasn't that long ago you were there, love, was it?' Owen put an arm around her shoulder and drew her close, kissing her hard on the lips. When he turned his back on her to speak to Joe, she surreptitiously wiped her mouth.

Chapter 29

CLAUDIA

The fireworks don't bother Claudia. She is used to noise, used to banging and shouting, and after the silence of the past couple of weeks, she's grateful for it. She watches them from her bedroom, Frank on the bed, burrowed under the duvet. She glances at Anna's house. She saw the family leave earlier, Max on Owen's shoulders, Anna laughing. According to Sara, she and Joe are meeting them there. Claudia had been convinced Sara would fail to persuade him. The weirdest thing is, she feels left out. She wants to be there, a witness to their conversations, intuiting what is left unsaid, watching for non-verbal clues.

When the public displays that lit up the sky over Kingston and Hampton Court have finished, she goes down to the kitchen, shadowed by Frank, pours herself a glass of wine, selects a tagliatelle from the freezer and puts it in the microwave.

Apart from redecoration, number 7 Shires Close is very much the house Claudia grew up in. There are four bedrooms, one of which is Robert's study, a large kitchen cum sitting room at the back, and the more formal sitting room where the TV lives at the front. Robert doesn't hold with televisions in the kitchen.

Surely by the time they get back from South Africa, the sale of Culloden Road will be well under way and she'll be ready to buy somewhere. She has a mental picture of what she wants: to stay in London, because there's more chance of anonymity, but in a different borough, east or south-east, somewhere people are too busy keeping the hamster wheel moving to obsess about her like they do here. She craves bustle and noise, neighbours who keep themselves to themselves, builders and night workers, nurses and teachers, people who don't have the luxury of time to pry.

A sharp crack and a burst of hysterical laughter make her nerves prickle. The next explosion is so close it might have been in the garden. She goes to the bifold doors, stares out into the night. A firecracker leaps the fence and lands next to the greenhouse, the noise amplified by a yipping howl. Her heart races. There's another bang, a stuttering series of reports, like a machine gun being fired, but she can't see anything. It must be far away. It's weird how sound carries in the night.

A boy yells, 'Aim for the house, moron. She's in there.'

They are baiting her.

Claudia runs up to her bedroom and peers into next door's garden, where half a dozen teenagers are now milling round. One of them sets off a firework, angled towards her house. She steps back in alarm, watches its tail spark before it shoots over the fence. It goes wide, spinning wildly and landing amongst the ruins of the studio.

The kids shriek with laughter and tumble inside. Minutes pass. Peace returns. Any fireworks are further away, receding into the background. Occasionally a loud one makes her jerk her shoulders. Five minutes later, next

148

door are at it again but this time the noises are coming from the close, catcalls bouncing off brick and glass. She dashes across the landing into Robert's study. A boy peels away from the group and swaggers up to her door, bends down and shouts through the letter box, his voice taunting.

'Hey, Claudia. Did you enjoy the show?'

A girl pushes him out of the way. The flap clatters. 'Come on out. We're only being friendly.'

Claudia's eyes dart to the trio standing near Robert's car. One of them leans nonchalantly against it, vaping.

'Anyone need to take a dump?' a tall youth asks. 'We can post it through the letter box. Just make it a solid one.'

'It's either that or a Molotov cocktail,' his friend says.

A flurry of fireworks go off in the distance. The kids confer. A boy gets a key out of his pocket, and Claudia watches in horror as he goes to scrape it along the side of Robert's car. There's a scuffle as one of his friends tries to stop him. They mock-wrestle, but to Claudia it isn't a joke. They are overexcited, high on alcohol and adrenaline and God knows what else. They are unpredictable. There's a fine line between friendly joshing and harm. She runs downstairs, grabs one of Louisa's walking sticks and opens the door.

'What the hell do you think you're doing? Don't you dare touch that car.'

'Whoa!' one of them says. 'Easy, tiger.'

The key is scraped noisily along the bodywork, and Claudia stifles a sob with her fist. The neighbour's daughter steps forward. She has long glossy blonde hair and is extremely pretty, her face as delicate as a flower. She sashays up to Claudia in her torn jeans, clumpy black boots and padded bomber jacket. Claudia notices her earrings: tiny

149

butterflies with enamelled wings in a shade of blue that matches her eyes. She waits, half expecting a de-escalation, an apology, but unsure. The girl comes to within a foot and a half of her, smiling sweetly, and then draws her head back and spits in her face.

'That's for Mr Hartman's baby.'

With a howl of fury, Claudia lashes out with the walking stick, but in her left hand its force is ineffective. The girl wrenches it from her grasp and flings it onto the tarmac.

'She was my baby too,' Claudia whispers, wiping her sleeve across her cheek.

And then someone sprints towards them from across the road, a familiar figure, and her heart leaps. Joe shoves one of the boys in the chest so hard he staggers backwards.

'What the hell do you think you're doing, Matthew? And the rest of you?'

There's a collective sagging of shoulders, a shuffling of feet.

'Sorry, Mr Hartman. We'll pay for the damage. We didn't mean anything.'

'Didn't you? I'm going to be speaking to your parents about this.' He turns to the girl, bearing down on her. 'Rosie Mitchell, I thought better of you.'

'She had a weapon,' Rosie complains. 'She physically assaulted me.'

A firework goes off so loudly, Claudia jumps out of her skin.

'It was a misunderstanding,' she says. 'I overreacted because I felt threatened, but they were only messing around. It's just ... in prison, you know ...'

Joe waits for more, but Claudia forces a smile and a

shrug. He pauses, seems to recollect something and turns to the kids. 'What damage are you talking about?'

'It was only my top,' Claudia says quickly. 'It's ancient. It really doesn't matter.'

She can get the car fixed. Robert need never know.

'Are you sure?'

'I'm sure.'

She is good. She doesn't hold his gaze too long or attempt to communicate subliminally. She steels herself against the lure of him, the comfort. She wants to be hugged, but hugs are out of the question. The only person likely to hug her again is her mother.

'Apologise,' he tells the kids, his voice dripping with distaste.

'Sorry, Mr Hartman.'

'Not to me, you plonker. To her. And you can all come and see me in my office at lunchtime on Monday.'

Claudia notices he doesn't use her name, and neither do they. A chorus of mumbled *sorrys* floats on the night air before they slope away, scraping the soles of their shoes on the paving slabs.

Only once they've gone does Claudia notice Anna and her husband and Sara standing outside Anna's house, where there's a minicab waiting. Sara is holding her little girl asleep on her shoulder, her face like thunder. The hostility coming from the Pembertons is palpable.

'Thank you,' she murmurs. 'Everything's fine. You can go.'

'Claudia . . .'

His eyes fix hers. She remembers that expression so well. When Joe Hartman goes still, when he corrals the

151

ever-present energy, when he looks at you properly, the world can empty.

She moves her head a fraction, an almost imperceptible shake, but he sees it. He puts a hand on her shoulder, gives it a squeeze, then turns on his heel and walks back to his family.

In front of the cloakroom mirror, Claudia scrubs dry spittle from her face, scrubs so hard her cheek stings and starts to bleed. She sees herself through Joe's eyes: ugly, sexless, desperate. She needs to stop this, needs to show some bottle. She wrinkles her nose at her reflection and turns away.

She remembers her mother's walking stick lying on the tarmac, and not wanting to give her neighbours more cause for complaint, she goes out to get it. The air smells of spent fireworks. She hears raised voices coming from Anna and Owen's house. She stands very still, transfixed; the words are indistinguishable, but not the tone. So the perfect couple aren't so perfect after all. It's interesting coming so soon after Sara and Joe have left their house.

The Pembertons' front door opens. It's too late to turn tail and go inside, so she stands her ground. Owen strides over to his car, clicks the fob and wrenches open the door.

'What the fuck are you looking at?' he snarls.

'I'm not looking at anything. I was just picking up my stick.'

'You'll stay out of my sight if you know what's good for you.' He gets into the car, screeches into reverse, then accelerates out of the close.

*

152

That night, she hears the baby crying again. It's so real, she can't be imagining it. She drags herself out of bed and walks the house trying to pinpoint the source. On the landing there is a square hatch set into the ceiling. She grabs the hooked stick from the airing cupboard and pulls it open. The steps clatter as she drags them down. Inside the attic it is dry, warm and odd-smelling – the sweet odour of fibreglass insulation. She feels for the light switch and a single bare bulb goes on, the old-fashioned incandescent kind that heats the dust around it. The space is well organised, the floor boarded over, boxes stacked under the eaves.

The crying stops, and she feels a little foolish, standing half in, half out in a pair of briefs and a faded T-shirt. The ridged metal rungs hurt her insteps. She climbs down, closes the hatch and goes back to bed, but sleep eludes her. This is all so familiar: seeing and hearing things that aren't there; believing in her own irrational thoughts.

She swears under her breath. She doesn't want to start taking antidepressants again, at least not until this is over, but neither can she afford to ignore the warning signs. She ought to talk to Dr Ellis, but she's only seen the psychiatrist twice since she's been out, and both times has been left feeling as though the virtual meetings are a waste of time, an exercise in speaking in half-truths. To tell the undiluted truth is impossible, and he knows that as well as she does.

In fact, Dr Ellis has only been good for one thing: getting her released by assuring the parole board that he would supervise her, that the maintenance dose of antidepressants he prescribed would give her a measure of reassurance that would enable a gradual return to normal life. He committed to seeing her once a week for the first three months of her release and once a fortnight for the next six, at which point there would be a review. At no time would she be left to flounder on her own. It went down well.

If she's careful, if she monitors herself, keeps rationalising, then she'll be okay. She needs more time to get to the truth. After that, she doesn't care. She'll take whatever she's given.

Chapter 30

Sunday 5 November

SARA

In the cold light of day, the lumpen ruin of Claudia Hartman's temporary home looked so much worse. Sara got as close as she could without crossing the police tape. The smell was acrid even after a week and a half. It was horrific, of course it was, but she couldn't help regretting that it hadn't killed Claudia. Joe had lied to her because of that woman. She hated her for exposing her husband's cowardice.

She walked up the path to number 7 and rang the doorbell. There was no reply. She banged the knocker, took a step back and peered up at the windows. The curtains were closed. The house looked dead.

Around the close, residents were stirring. An elderly man came out of his house and glared at her before getting into his car. He honked his horn and his wife came dashing out. He slowed as he drove past Sara and wound down the window.

'Are you press or a gawper?'

Sara stepped back in alarm. 'Neither.'

'Friend of hers from prison, are you?'

'What? No!'

Behind her a door closed, and she turned away from the man with relief. A woman had come out of the house next door to Anna's.

'Are you looking for someone?' she called.

'I'm a friend of the Pembertons.'

'They aren't at home, I'm afraid. Shall I tell them you were here? I'm Anna's mother.' She started to move towards her.

Sara fished in her bag for her fob. 'Don't worry. I've only come to pick up my car. I knew they wouldn't be in.'

'You were outside number 7.'

'Yes, I was. Claudia Hartman used to be married to my husband. There was a bit of trouble here last night; I wanted to check she was okay.'

The woman frowned. 'Have we met before?'

'I don't think so. I just have one of those faces. People often think they've met me. Well, it was nice speaking to you.'

As she pressed the fob and opened the door, her hands were shaking. She could feel the woman's scrutiny.

'She's in.'

Sara closed the car door again, eyebrows raised.

'Claudia. She's in. I saw the curtains twitch.'

'Claudia? It's Sara. I need to speak to you.'

Her feet had grown cold in her trainers. She stamped them as she waited. Moments later, a light went on and Claudia opened the door. She wrapped her arms round her thin body.

'I'm sorry about what happened last night,' Sara said. 'Owen told me those kids have been a pain in the arse for the last couple of years. They go to Joe's school.'

'I could have dealt with them myself. I didn't need his help.'

'I'm sure you didn't. Can I come in?'

Claudia pushed back a hank of unwashed hair and opened the door wider.

It looked as though she'd interrupted Claudia's breakfast. There was half a slice of toast on a plate, and a cafetière of coffee on a plugged-in warmer. Nothing wrong with that, except last night's supper hadn't been cleared away; the warped plastic tray it had been microwaved in was still on the draining board.

Sara sat down, and after hesitating, Claudia joined her, cradling her injured hand.

'You don't look well,' Sara said.

Claudia shrugged. A cat approached and she picked it up. It squirmed aggressively, baring its claws. She put it down again, her cheeks pink.

'So what happened?' she asked.

'First you agree to stay away from Joe. I know you met him the day after the fire. I saw you.'

'It was you in the car park watching us?'

'Yup. I wanted to see it with my own eyes. I also saw the way he looked at you last night, when those kids were bothering you. I don't blame him. He likes to play the knight in shining armour, but I know what you're up to and I won't have it. Do you understand me?'

'I don't want him, Sara.'

'Do we have an agreement or not?'

Claudia sighed. 'If you have information that might help me, then I want to hear it. I'm not going to come after Joe; all that was over a long time ago. He let me down when he should have stepped up for me, and I'll never forgive him for that.'

Sara waited for her to say something like *you're welcome to him*, but she didn't. She sat there sipping her coffee, peering at Sara over the rim of the mug. It occurred to her that Claudia must have developed a hard core in prison and that she'd do well not to underestimate her. Just because she looked like she might break into pieces didn't mean she would.

'Fine. All I wanted to say was that Anna was weird around Joe last night. It was all a bit uncomfortable. A shade too intense, if you know what I mean.'

'Women find him attractive. It's nothing new.'

'It was more than that,' Sara pressed. What had happened to Claudia's fabled jealousy? The woman's equanimity was disappointing. 'She focused her attention on him, got all coy. It was really bugging her husband. And me too, for that matter. I think you could be right about her having a crush, but not about Joe reciprocating. There's no way ... Is there any coffee left in that pot? I can pour if it hurts your hand.'

Claudia jumped up. 'I can manage.'

'I can cope with her flirting with Joe,' Sara said to Claudia's back. 'What scares me is the way she treats her little boy.'

Claudia swung round. 'What do you mean?'

Sara described what she'd witnessed. 'She was drunk, I think, but Max rejecting her in front of us seriously pissed her off. She smacked him. And then she came down and was all sweetness and light.'

'They rowed after you'd gone,' Claudia said, frowning. 'Owen went off in a huff.'

'It must have been to do with her behaviour. He's an arsehole, but she's toxic.'

'It doesn't prove she had anything to do with what happened to Tilly, though.'

'Maybe not. I'm just reporting what I saw. It's up to you what you do with the information. Anna is a complex character, don't you think? Sometimes children can feel forgotten in the aftermath of the death of a family member, especially if they're not the sort to give any trouble. It's just a theory, but let's say she bottled up her feelings round the loss of her big sister for years, and on the day your daughter vanished, it all changed. She had a focus for her rage. If she could blame you, then her family, particularly her mother, was less guilty.'

For the first time since Sara arrived, Claudia's eyes showed signs of life. There was hope in them, hope that somehow, miraculously, Sara would have the answer. Sara pitied her. She was so desperate for an ally she was willing to put herself into the hands of the enemy. Sara would not allow Claudia to destroy the life she had built with Joe. He was weak when it came to damsels in distress, and she knew, deep in her heart, that if she wasn't there, he would get sucked back in. She hadn't missed the expression of pure fury when he saw what those kids were doing to Claudia last night. There had been a tightening in the atmosphere when he put his hand on his ex-wife's shoulder. Sara had felt sick to her stomach.

'In her eyes, you tipped Megan over the edge. After the memorial service she got herself all worked up. She made avenging her sister her mission. She wanted to destroy you but didn't have a plan. And then you handed over your baby and took a call from Joe, and she ran.'

Claudia wrinkled her nose and shook her head. 'I'd have recognised her.'

'There was a storm, you were distracted, the woman had her hood up. Can you honestly swear it wasn't her? And knowing what we do now, that she has a vicious streak, surely it's worth considering.'

'Maybe, but I still think I'd have known.'

'You were expecting a stranger, so a stranger was what you saw.'

'Tilly would have been too heavy for Anna to have got far, and someone would have noticed a woman carrying a baby. It would have seemed odd that she wasn't in a pram.'

'Well, I don't know. Perhaps she left her somewhere safe and dry, hoping she'd be quickly found and returned. When that didn't happen, she must have been terrified. Put yourself in her shoes. She was a teenage girl who'd done something impulsive and stupid and wanted to make it all go away. It makes sense that she would have left Tilly somewhere she'd be found, then returned home to wait for the ring on the doorbell, the police stamping into the house.'

'But the police didn't come,' Claudia continued for her. 'And bar a cursory interview because of their connection to the family, Anna wasn't properly interrogated. She was never a suspect. I remember she was there the next morning, helping with the search.'

'Exactly! Perpetrators often go back to the scene of

their crime. She was already screwed up by her sister's suicide; taking Tilly would have been the final straw. She's damaged, Claudia, and I worry that she might be dangerous. She has a huge amount to lose by you being out. Think how easy it would have been for her to start that fire.'

Claudia pulled her coat from the back of her chair and threw it on over her dressing gown.

'What are you doing?'

'I've got to make Anna talk to me.' Her eyes were distracted. 'Don't you understand? If she left Tilly in a public place, someone might have seen her without realising it.'

'You're not thinking straight.' Sara beat her to the kitchen door and blocked it with her body. Claudia the loose cannon was not what she needed right now. 'Anna isn't at home. I might be wrong. It might still have been you. And you're not sure either, are you? So please do not go over there.'

'I can't ignore this.'

'Claudia! Wake up, for God's sake. If I'm right, you're going to have to be extremely careful. If I'm wrong, you're going to make things a hell of a lot worse for yourself by throwing accusations around. You don't want to go back inside, do you? What I've said is just a theory. Something for you to think about. I don't actually know if it was Anna, or you, or someone else.' She paused. 'I'd better go. Joe will be wondering where I've got to. But let me work on this business with Anna. She seems to like me. If I can find evidence, that's when we approach the police. You don't want to waste their goodwill, do you?'

Claudia sagged. 'What goodwill?'

Chapter 31

Monday 6 November

SARA

Woken by Maeve, Sara opened bleary eyes and flung the duvet back with a groan. Joe touched her shoulder.

'Don't worry, I'll go. I was awake anyway.'

'What time is it?'

'Two. Go back to sleep.'

She shut her eyes gratefully. She felt the mattress move as Joe got up and heard the swish of door against carpet. The next time she woke, it was a quarter to five. She moved her hand over the empty space beside her and raised herself up on her elbow. The sheet was cool. Joe hadn't come back to bed. He'd fallen asleep on the rocking chair in Maeve's room more than once, waking cold and achy the next morning. She reluctantly got out of bed.

He wasn't in Maeve's room. Sara checked her daughter. She was sound asleep, her thumb in her mouth, her fine hair a halo of curls. Sara pulled the blanket up to her chin and left the room.

Downstairs was in darkness but for the pale electronic light of a mobile phone shining through the crack in the kitchen door. Sara peered in. Joe was sitting at the table, his phone in his hand, his face ghoul-like in its glow. She crept upstairs and came back down, this time treading heavily enough for him to hear. The light went out, and by the time she opened the kitchen door, his phone was lying face down on the tabletop and he had his arms crossed, his chin on his chest.

'Joe?'

He looked at her as though he didn't know who she was, then blinked and shook his head. 'Oh hell. I must have fallen asleep.'

'What are you doing down here?'

'I was wide awake after Maeve went off, so I came down rather than disturb you. I was only going to be ten minutes.' He rubbed his neck. 'What woke you up?'

'I was cold.'

Sara reached for a sweater of Joe's that he'd slung over the back of a chair and pulled it on over her vest top. The heating didn't come on until six, and the kitchen felt like a morgue. She wandered over to the sink and poured water into the kettle.

'I'll make coffee. I'm not going back to sleep now.' She glanced at him over her shoulder. 'What kept you awake? Was it Claudia?' What she really wanted to ask was if it was Anna.

Joe stretched his arms behind his head and yawned so widely his jaw clicked. 'No,' he replied, a tad belligerently. 'Not Claudia. At least not in the way you mean.' He hesitated, then shrugged, as if he'd won an argument with himself. 'We've had an offer on the house. Asking price.'

Sara took two mugs down from the cupboard, then

opened the tin of coffee grounds and scooped some into the cafetière.

'Sara?'

She turned round. 'That was quick.'

'I know. It was the couple with the twins. They want Haileycroft School. If we accept it, it would mean we don't have to have any more people tramping around the house.'

'When did you hear?'

'Saturday afternoon.'

'And you kept it to yourself all weekend? Why?'

'I don't know. I was processing it, I suppose. I've lived here for twelve years, and so much has happened. I told the agent I'd speak to you and give him an answer today. And don't worry, I've already said there's no way we'll agree to be out before Christmas. I suggested February half-term.'

Sara pulled a chair out and sat down heavily. Joe reached for her hand and kissed her knuckles, his stubble grazing her fingers.

'I am sorry. I really am. This is all my fault. I should have sold the house as soon as Claudia and I divorced. Keeping it was idiotic. Tilly is never going to come home.'

'No,' she said gently. 'No, she isn't. It's time to go.' Suddenly she wanted shot of Culloden Road, shot of the house, the neighbours, everything. 'I'll find us somewhere better; we'll start again. It isn't healthy for Maeve to grow up in this place knowing her half-sister used to live here. I'd never want her to feel second best.' She smiled at him. 'Why don't you get a shower? I'll bring your coffee upstairs.'

He wiped his nose on the back of his hand, his face so crumpled and exhausted she wanted to wrap him in her arms and let him go back to sleep on her breast.

'I'm sorry I didn't tell you sooner. I had to get my head round it.'

'I know.'

'We're both going to be hopeless today.'

'Scrambled brains,' Sara said. 'I'm used to it. I love you.'

'I love you too.'

As soon as he'd left the room, she stretched across the table and picked up his phone. She held it in the palm of her hand, staring at the blank screen. They trusted each other, but she had broken that trust once before, and invading his privacy already felt like a compulsion. She keyed in his password and checked his messages. The last exchange was between him and Anna Pemberton at 10.15, after Sara had gone to bed. Anna's opening text was almost innocent, but not quite. Sara sensed the thought that had gone into every word.

Just wanted to say how lovely it was to see you again after all this time. It brought so many memories back. A x

Good to see you too. Stay in touch.

Half an hour ago, Anna had responded.

It was nice to have a chance to talk. I hope we can be friends.

Sara dropped the phone and snatched her hand away from it. How dare she? How the hell did she even have his number? Then she remembered Owen asking Joe for it. She picked it up again and reread the exchange. Joe's tone was reassuringly uneffusive, but Anna had clearly missed the subtext. *Leave me alone.* She swiped out of messages and returned the phone to its original spot. She had zero qualms about using Anna to undermine Claudia now.

She poured Joe a coffee and took it upstairs. From the bedroom she could hear the shower, and pop music on the radio, turned up loud. An unusual choice for Joe, who normally caught up on current affairs. She opened the door a couple of inches, watched him as he soaped his crotch, one hand pressed against the tiles. Even through the billowing steam she could tell he wasn't washing, that his face was pulled into a rictus of concentration. She knew that look. She shut the door quietly and leant against it, her eyes wide with shock.

But she couldn't think about that now; there was something else on her mind. Yet another thing to deal with. Pulling herself together, she ran downstairs and googled the estate agent dealing with Jocelyn's executors. Anna had given her the name; it was the same agency she and Owen had bought their own house through. She opened the contact box and started to type.

Dear Sir/Madam,

Re: 14 Shires Close

I understand from my friend Anna Pemberton that this property will be coming up for sale in the near future and I'd like to express a keen interest now. We have accepted an offer on our own property and are in a good position financially.

She added, because she wanted them on her side:

I would be incredibly grateful if you could keep me updated. We would absolutely love to live in Shires Close. Our daughter frequently plays with the Pembertons' little boy. They are great friends and we look forward to them attending the same school and having the run of each other's houses.

Yours sincerely,
Sara Hartman

Whatever happened, she had to have that house. At ten o'clock, a reply dropped into her inbox.

Dear Mrs Hartman,

Re: 14 Shires Close

Thank you for your interest in this property. As you will be aware, the estate is currently in probate. We have already had a great deal of interest and will add you to the list. While I don't want to discourage you, I do have to let you know that it is very likely that it will go to sealed bids.

I will be in touch as soon as the house is ready to go on the market. I can tell you that the valuation will be in the region of £800,000, to reflect its unmodernised state, but I fully expect it to go for more than that, given the enthusiasm.

Kind regards,
Lia Cockburn

Chapter 32

CLAUDIA

The family snaps of her and Tilly must be somewhere. Her mother would never have allowed Robert to throw them away. Claudia has searched the entire house, apart from the loft. She opens the hatch with the brass-hooked pole, releases the ladder, climbs up and feels around for the light switch. The space is huge, stretching from one side of the house to the other, and surprisingly clean, the air warm and stale. The rafters are neatly stuffed with insulation, the floor boarded with particle board. Boxes are arranged neatly in the eaves.

Each box has been carefully labelled with a black marker pen, so it doesn't take Claudia long to locate what she's looking for amongst Jason's university papers, old family accounts and Robert's archives from his days as a marketing man.

There are three boxes marked *Claudia Culloden Road*, this time in Joe's loopy handwriting, sitting here since he purged the house of her bits and pieces. She can hardly bear to open those, with their physical reminders of her former life, but she forces herself to rifle through them. There is make-up, books, contracts, school admin, favourite mug, hair accessories and gloves – random stuff but no photographs. Was that deliberate on Joe's part?

Another box is marked *CLAUDIA MISC* in untidy capital letters. Her mother. She drags it under the light, removes the lid and rummages inside. She finds the photographs and sighs with relief. Putting them to one side, she goes through the rest of the contents. It's mostly old reports and other school-related paperwork, but there is a blue manila file with her name on it. She takes it out and opens it.

The top sheet is a letter from the Department of Child and Adolescent Psychiatry at Kingston Hospital, dated 1995. She frowns, scanning the contents. This is not something she remembers anything about. She reads it with growing horror. How could she have forgotten something like this?

Dear Mrs Myhill,

Re: Claudia Simone Myhill DOB 03.06.1989

Thank you for bringing Claudia to see me. I very much enjoyed chatting to her. She is a delightful, engaged little girl. Claudia was referred to me by your GP because you were worried about an incident in which her one-year-old half-brother needed to be taken to Accident & Emergency. He sustained bruises, a cut to his forehead and concussion, but fortunately nothing was broken and there are unlikely to be lasting effects from the head injury. You explained that Claudia had pushed Jason down a flight of stairs in the family home. It is not unusual for a child to be jealous of a sibling and I do not see anything to be overly concerned about. It seems to me that Claudia understands what she has done and what the implications would have been if indeed Jason's injuries had been more serious. She is an intelligent child, but she is sensitive and needs to be handled carefully.

As we discussed, my advice to you would be that you don't take this any further and that Claudia isn't made to feel responsible. In my opinion, regular visits to a psychiatrist would risk leading to feelings of alienation within the family.

Please do get in touch if you have any further worries, but as I said, I really don't think you should make more of this than you have done already. It's best that the incident isn't mentioned in her hearing and that she is allowed to forget all about it and enjoy being a child. However, for the time being, I'd caution against leaving her alone with her brother.

Yours sincerely,
Dr Frances Holt MD

cc: Dr Piper, Manville Road Surgery

At the bottom, Frances has scrawled in biro: *Between you and me, Louisa, there is nothing wrong with Claudia, and I don't want you to worry about it. I've seen a lot worse! Frances x*

Stapled to the letter is the referral request from Louisa's then GP.

Dear Dr Holt,

Re: Claudia Simone Myhill DOB 03.06.1989

I would be grateful if you could see my patient, Claudia Myhill, aged six years and three months. Claudia recently pushed her one-year-old half-brother down the stairs.

Claudia is an intelligent child who shows signs of emotional fragility. At the age of three, her father died in a car crash and her mother was badly injured. Claudia, though travelling with them, wasn't hurt, but she has some behavioural issues that could be linked to losing her father and being parted from her mother for the six weeks Louisa Myhill was in hospital. Before the incident with her half-brother, there had been nothing that would have occasioned any worry about Claudia's attitude towards Jason; in fact, Mrs Myhill described her daughter as doting on him. I have not referred this case to social services. Louisa has been my patient for ten years, and I know her as a woman of common sense and empathy.

Yours sincerely,
Dr Jessica Piper

cc: Mrs Louisa Myhill

'Fuck,' Claudia murmurs. She doesn't know what to make of it. No one has ever mentioned the incident to her, not her mother, not Frances. Not even Robert. She wonders what pressure Louisa brought to bear on him. No wonder he dislikes her so much. No wonder he believes her capable of inflicting harm on her own child.

Was she really calculating enough to give her resented little brother a shove? She imagines Jason tumbling, the noise he would have made, her mother screaming. If she was capable of that at such a young age, what might she have been capable of at twenty-four and in the grip of psychosis?

Everything Claudia thought she knew about herself, her certainty that whatever happened to Tilly, it couldn't possibly have had anything to do with her, all of it dissolves, leaving her standing in a puddle of her own delusions. Her instinct is to call Jason, but what would be the point? He couldn't have been told either, otherwise he would have mentioned it.

Without the certainty that she'd never hurt a fly, who is she? What is she?

Something else occurs to her. Does Anna know? Could Frances have told her what happened, told her to be careful, that Claudia was dangerous?

There's a sound from downstairs and her heart jolts. She crawls across the boarding and looks through the opening, but all she can see is the ladder and the carpeted floor. Her awareness is heightened, almost as though her senses have commandeered her body. There it is again, a light shunting noise as though someone is trying to move a piece of furniture without being heard. She reaches for the switch and turns the light off. She can hear voices but too indistinctly to make out what they are saying. She stays very still and waits; the voices continue but no one comes upstairs.

One of them is definitely a woman and the tone is cheerful. Maybe Robert has sent round his golf buddies to check on her. What a cheek to just let themselves in. Or did she miss the doorbell? She can't stay here for ever. She'll have to face them, whoever they are.

Aching from her crouched position, she turns herself round and lowers her feet. The ladder creaks and she goes still, holding her breath. No one comes. She climbs down and peers over the banister. The front door is closed, and Frank is sitting at the bottom of the stairs looking up at her.

'Who's there?' she shouts. 'Eva?'

No reply. She comes slowly downstairs, darts over to the door and grabs the walking stick.

The voices are coming from the sitting room. She pushes the door open as someone laughs, and lets go of her breath. The television is on. She must have knocked the controls when she was dusting. She goes to turn it off, then realises that what she's looking at is not a daytime soap, it's her. Her younger, happier self turns to the camera and pulls a face. 'Daddy's being silly!' she says. She's holding Tilly. She presses her nose against her baby's cheek. Behind her, Kate Shaw bends into frame and waves before turning away.

Claudia drops the stick and grabs the controls, manically pushing the buttons until the television switches itself off. She grabs the phone from its cradle and calls Detective Sergeant Ward.

'No one here, Mrs Hartman,' DS Ward says after searching the house. 'Could your cat have sat on the controls and switched it on by mistake?'

'Yes,' Claudia says patiently. 'It's possible. But he didn't take the DVD out of its case and put it in the player, and neither did I.'

'The house belongs to your parents, doesn't it? Perhaps that DVD was the last thing they watched before they went on holiday.'

'I...I don't know.' Could it have been her mother? Knowing she wasn't going to be there when Claudia was released, she might conceivably have played the video. 'It's possible,' she says carefully.

'No sign of a break-in. You didn't hear footsteps, or smell anything?'

'I did hear something. Like a soft shunting sound.'

The officer picks up the controls and rewinds the video to the beginning. It starts with the camera on Joe. He's bouncing Tilly in his arms. Claudia stares at her daughter, biting down on her thumb knuckle to stop herself crying. There are lots of noises. A champagne cork being popped. Paul Shaw clinking his glass against her mother's. Robert full of bonhomie. A shriek of laughter. It goes black, and there's a bit of white noise before filming starts again, the camera's eye on Claudia and Tilly.

'Lots going on there,' DS Ward comments. 'Listening from upstairs, you could have caught any of it.'

'I suppose so.'

'You need to calm down. No one's been in the house. You're safe.'

She follows him to the door. 'And what about the fire? Do you know what started it yet?'

'The report should be ready tomorrow. Someone will drop by.'

Chapter 33

CLAUDIA

'Was it you, Frank?'

Claudia would love to scoop him up and bury her face in his fur, be comforted by his warmth, but Frank only enjoys attention on his own terms. Instead she picks up the remote control and turns it round in her hand. Does she remember seeing it on the sofa, on the side Frank seems to favour? Try as she might to picture the room, she really can't say one way or the other. It makes sense that it was the cat, or even that her mother had been watching the video, but that doesn't make her feel any better. She's still afraid.

She double-locks the front door and puts the chain on, then fetches the blue folder from the loft and reads the letters again. Child or not, it was a horrible thing to do, and she can understand why she subconsciously suppressed the memory. She debates asking her mother about it, but she knows that if Louisa sees the house number come up on caller display, she'll think there's been another crisis, and Robert will get his knickers in a twist. God, she detests that man; she will never understand why her mother married him.

Outside, Rosie Mitchell and her brother leave for school,

heavy rucksacks pulling on their backs. They are dressed in the Overhill uniform: a black blazer and blue and black tartan skirt for Rosie, her brother in the saggy-kneed trousers of schoolboys everywhere, his blazer rumpled. Rosie is walking fast, on her phone already, as though she doesn't want to be seen with him.

Later, Claudia forces herself outside and walks into Surbiton, where she picks up her replacement prescription then goes for a walk along the river. Killing time again. A car draws onto the drive outside Jocelyn's house as she arrives home. A middle-aged couple get out, remove what look like bags of cleaning gear from the back seat, and go inside. Jocelyn's daughter and her husband, she guesses.

From Robert's desk, she watches the comings and goings in the close. Up near the entrance, a woman leaves her house and returns half an hour later with a little girl. The girl is talking nineteen to the dozen, her mother smiling down at her, responding as she fishes in her bag for her keys. Claudia smiles. She used to be that child.

Jocelyn's relatives leave the house and load bags of rubbish into the boot of their car. They go back in and come out with pictures under their arms. Then they leave. Watching has become weirdly addictive. She can't seem to drag herself out of the room.

Twilight falls. A splash hits the window, then another, and another. At six o'clock, Frances Holt comes out of number 12, pulls her coat collar over her head and runs next door. Claudia sits up straight. She realises this is what it is all about; she's been waiting for a glimpse of Anna.

Owen arrives ten minutes later, sweeping onto the forecourt in his flashy white car. At seven, he and Anna step out. Anna is wearing skinny black-and-white animal-print trousers, and a cream ski jacket with a fur-lined hood. She looks fabulous. Claudia shifts her gaze to Owen. He's dapper in a narrow-legged, slim-waisted suit. Half hidden by the door, Frances is holding the little boy, and Anna leans in for a kiss. Claudia picks up her phone and sets it to camera. The baby grips Anna's hair, and she laughs as she disentangles it. She does not look like a mother who resents her child, but who knows what that kind of mother looks like? Anna pulls her hood over her head and trots to the car. Claudia snaps picture after picture.

The headlights flare and they're off. Claudia scrolls through the pictures and finds the least blurry. She zooms in with her fingers, but there's no spark of recognition, no gut punch. The conditions are right – the dark street, the rain, the hooded coat – but Anna in no way resembles the woman she handed her baby to on that terrible day.

But then they've all changed, haven't they? Anna has become a mother and has acquired poise; Claudia has done the opposite. The transformation they've both undergone in the last ten years is immense. She looks again, trying to recognise something, anything that would mean she could absolve herself from blame, but she's clutching at straws. So that leads back to her. The child who tried to kill her baby brother, the teenager with emotional problems, the adult so paranoid and deluded that she accused her best friend of having an affair with her husband and alienated those who might have helped her. Instead, she was told over and over again that she was either imagining it or making it up. That crushed her spirit before and during the trial.

*

On the other side of the close, Frances brings Max to the window. She's singing to him, her body gently swaying. Every so often she touches his head with her lips, and Claudia's heart contracts. She leans over the desk, puts her hand on the glass, and the movement catches Frances's eye. She looks straight at Claudia. Claudia lurches back, rolls off the chair and scuttles out of the room on her hands and knees. Downstairs, a glass of Robert's finest claret hits the mark, loosening her.

The clock says it's a quarter past six. Claudia wishes it was ten and time to go to bed. She longs to speak to another human being, to hear her own voice without it echoing round an empty room. She doesn't want to worry her mother or irritate her stepfather any more than she has done already, and she doesn't dare call Joe, so that leaves Sara. But when she calls, Sara is at her mother's house and Maeve is having a tantrum in the background.

'Sorry,' she says. 'It's pandemonium here. I'll call you when I can. Was it anything important?'

'No. Nothing.'

Claudia moves the kitchen chairs and crawls under the table. She used to do this as a child, when Robert was in a bad mood, sitting cross-legged while her mother cooked, telling stories to herself or singing something she'd learned in school. Once she's pulled the chairs back into place, she breathes easier. The legs are like the bars in her cell window. Ridiculous behaviour, but no one is watching.

She crawls out when she starts getting cramp. Crossing the hall, she sees an envelope sticking through the letter box, caught by the flap. It's addressed to her. She opens it and gingerly slides the letter out. The message is printed at the top of the sheet.

You know what to do if you don't want to die.

Oddly, it doesn't scare her half as much as coming home to find Frank had been fed. She rereads it, thinking. Joe might be more inclined to take her seriously if he sees it, and with Sara and Maeve out for the evening, he's on his own. Her breath shortens at the thought of seeing him. The way he looked at her when he raced across the close to lay into those kids had reminded her of what they once were to each other. He wouldn't have done that if he didn't care. She picks up the phone, hands shaking.

'What do you want, Claudia?' Joe's tone is curt, but she anticipated that.

'Can you come over?'

He doesn't reply immediately. She imagines him pinching the bridge of his nose below his spectacles. 'You know that's impossible.'

She can hear him banging around. Perhaps he's making his supper, the phone caught between his ear and his shoulder.

'Sara's with her mother, isn't she?'

'How do you know that?'

'I bumped into her yesterday when she came to pick up your car.' She lies so easily these days. 'We got chatting and she told me she was going.'

'That doesn't sound like Sara.' Joe says. 'But I'll take your word for it.'

'So will you come? I need to see you.'

'Claudia.' He sounds tired.

'I've had another death threat,' she blurts out. 'And it's not just that. I've found something out about myself and

179

now I'm not sure if my memories are real. I need to speak to someone who knows me properly.'

'I thought you had a psychiatrist.' There is no sign of affection in his voice. It's stripped of emotion, as dry as summer soil. He must have given himself a stern talking-to since fireworks night. Or perhaps Sara did.

'Yes, but I can't tell him the things I want to tell you. Please, Joe.'

'Christ. Okay. Give me half an hour. But if I come, you have to promise me you won't make a scene. I don't want an emotional tsunami.'

Claudia closes her eyes tight. 'I don't want that either. I just need you to listen.'

Chapter 34

CLAUDIA

'Do you want a drink?' Claudia asks, coming back from the loo. She's a bundle of nerves, fingers plucking at her sleeves, a tic flickering under her right eye. 'There's beer and wine. Or spirits. Whatever you like.'

'A beer will be fine.'

She pulls one from the fridge, prises it open, then hands it to him. He's leaning against the counter, watching her.

'We've had an offer on the house.'

Her mouth hangs open. She knew it was coming, but not so soon.

'It's the best thing for all of us,' he says.

'Yes. I just . . . um.' She takes a swig of her wine. 'It's fine. It's good. I need to get away from the close.'

'You sure you're okay?'

'Yes.' She thrusts the anonymous note at him. 'And there's this as well.' She unfolds Frances Holt's letter to Louisa.

Joe puts the beer down, swaps his glasses for the pair in his shirt pocket and reads both sheets. 'Have you shown the note to the police?'

'Not yet.'

'You should. It's probably just malice, someone wanting

181

you out of here, but you might as well log everything. As for this.' He taps Frances's letter. 'It's not such a big deal. Children do that kind of thing.'

'Most children don't go on to be accused of killing their own child.' She pours herself another glass of wine. She isn't an alcoholic; she has a temporary need to dull the accusatory voices. She rubs nervously at her neck with the cuff of her jumper. 'I don't remember it happening, I don't remember talking to Frances about it, and it makes me look like a psycho.'

'Hardly. You were six years old.'

'But this gives me a history, doesn't it?'

'Frances didn't mention it at the time of your trial, so she evidently didn't think it was relevant, or more likely had forgotten all about it. She must have seen a lot worse over the years.'

'I suppose so.'

'You're going to be all right.'

'I don't know.' She sighs heavily. 'I still can't believe that this is my life now. All I wanted was to be married to you, to have babies and teach. They aren't big things, are they? Just ordinary life stuff. But it's all been ripped away and I'm back to square one.'

'What do you want me to say? I can't bring any of that back.'

'Do you love Sara as much as you loved me?'

Joe groans. 'Claudia, there are different times for different people. Sara suits me now. And yes, I do love her as much as I loved you, I wouldn't have married her if I didn't. But that doesn't devalue what I felt for you.'

'Then how can you think the way you do about me? I

182

get that you've had to believe the worst of me in order to move on, but I can't accept that you think I could have hurt our little girl. You didn't look me in the eye when the guilty verdict was announced, you didn't speak to me afterwards. You allowed me to go to prison without a murmur of protest. I would have appealed if I'd had you behind me.'

'I was barely thinking straight.'

'That isn't good enough, Joe. You allowed me to be trapped in the system. You know as well as I do that it was a Catch-22 situation. Plead guilty and eventually be eligible for parole, or tell the truth and spend a lifetime banging against a brick wall. The system would never have let me go without me saying the unsayable. But I did. I said I killed Tilly, and now I'm free, but I might as well be locked up because I'm not allowed to say I lied. Do you have any idea what it's like to live like this?'

'I can imagine.'

'Good, then you'll have no trouble imagining this: the only credible reason for someone to be threatening me is because they're scared they'll get found out.' She pauses, searches his face and frowns. 'But you don't want to see that, do you? Because it makes you uncomfortable.'

'I've never been afraid of the truth.'

'How pat. Avoiding the truth is what keeps your life on track. Why can't you admit it?'

He straightens up. 'Enough. I don't have time for this. What exactly do you want?'

'I want you to tell me about Anna.'

'Anna?' He manages to inject such incredulity into the word that she almost laughs. He's normally so much better at acting than this.

'Yes. Anna Pemberton. Our old babysitter.'

'Why?'

'You told me you could always tell when a pupil had a crush on you. I remember you saying there were particular things they did that made your heart sink. The hungry way they looked at you when you were teaching, the way the shyer ones would go bright red when you spoke to them. The way the confident ones touched their hair and widened their eyes and stood too close.'

'It's a downside to the job, but it's reality and it's been going on for as long as there have been teachers and pupils. You deal with it or you get out. What's this got to do with anything?'

'On the day our daughter was taken, Anna was angry and overwrought. She wanted me to feel pain. If it was her at our door that afternoon, she'd be terrified now, right?'

Joe presses his fingers against his forehead. 'You have got to be kidding.'

'Did she have a crush on you?'

Joe reaches behind his neck and scratches the space between his shoulder blades. 'Not as far as I know.'

'I think she did. She used to talk to you more than me when she came round to babysit. I'd be putting Tilly down, and you'd let her in and chat to her while you waited for me. Once or twice I remember you driving her home late at night. If I hadn't been struggling, I might have been suspicious, but I was fixated with Kate. If Anna did fancy you, she may have misinterpreted your friendly interest, like Megan did.'

Joe's nostrils flare. 'I did nothing to encourage Megan. I had literally no idea how she felt until she made that accusation. Why bring that up? She never took it any further.'

'Because she killed herself.'

'No. Because she finally understood it was a fantasy.' He mashes his fingers through his hair. 'I feel bad for that family, but I cannot be expected to police every adolescent girl's emotions. You're grasping at straws.'

'Am I?' She gives a groan of frustration. 'You're not listening. How many women are there out there who had a motive to take our child? It wasn't me, so who does that leave? A besotted teenager who thought her sister had been driven over the line by the wife of the man she imagined herself in love with. And now she's worried she's going to be found out. It would have been easy for her to set fire to my flat when everyone else in the close was asleep. There've been other things too, weird things that can be explained if it was her, because she's right at my doorstep. I hear a baby crying almost every night. Someone's been in and fed the cat while I wasn't here. Someone . . .' She trails off. If she mentions the DVD, she'll lose him altogether.

'For Christ's sake, this whole conversation is nuts.' He picks up Frances's letter, taps it with his knuckles. 'You blanked this incident. Whether subconsciously or consciously, you've always used temporary amnesia as a convenient excuse for poor behaviour. You are an unreliable witness to your own actions. You need to bear that in mind before you go accusing Anna of something so vile.'

'I'm just trying to make sense of this. So would you if you were in my shoes.'

'I'd better go,' he says. 'This has achieved nothing. I can't help you if I don't know what you need.'

'In that case, I'll tell you. I need you to have a conversation with Anna. I need to know if she had feelings for you back then, and if she still does now.'

'That's the most ridiculous suggestion I've ever heard. If you're that interested, ask her yourself.'

'I can't. She's too antagonistic and she'll deny it. You can tease it out of her.'

'You have a very high opinion of my abilities.'

'That's because I know you.'

'Not any more you don't. I'm sorry, Claudia, but I can't get involved.'

She sets her chin. 'If you refuse, the Holts are going to be told the real reason Megan killed herself. You'll be suspended at the very least.'

Joe pales. 'You know perfectly well that I didn't touch that girl.'

'Oh, absolutely. But these days you only have to be accused to be found guilty in the court of social media.'

'You're drunk. I can't talk to you when you're like this.'

'Like what? Inconveniently confrontational? Honest? I'm running out of options, Joe.'

'What's happened to you?'

'What hasn't?' she counters fiercely. 'Just do it, or your career is over.'

Joe puts his head in his hands. His elbow knocks the open laptop, and Claudia's last email cancelling her psychiatrist flashes up.

Anxious to close it, she pulls the mouse across the mat and the cursor blinks over a minimised document. It fills the screen for a fraction of a second. Joe takes the mouse from her and clicks. He jerks his head round.

'What is this, Claudia?'

She frowns, and as she reads, a chill settles over her shoulders.

You know what to do if you don't want to die.

'I don't understand. I didn't type that.'

'You're pathetic. Stay away from me and stay away from my family.'

He pushes her out of the way and she stumbles, her head swimming as she rights herself.

'Joe, wait.'

But he's already out of the house, striding down the front path. She runs after him, the shock of cold paving slabs through her thin socks making her wince.

'Don't underestimate me,' she says. 'I will talk to the police about Megan Holt.'

Joe shakes his head and unlocks his car. On the other side of the turning circle, Frances is watching their exchange from a window. Claudia goes back inside and slams the door. She walks around the house holding the walking stick, throwing open cupboards and checking behind curtains. She double-locks the front and back doors, then goes to bed with a kitchen knife under her pillow.

Chapter 35

Wednesday 8 November

SARA

Anna Pemberton was a scheming cow. Carrying Maeve, Sara rang the bell. She might have felt bad about using her, but not any more. It was obvious she was trying to lure Joe into an affair, her schoolgirl infatuation still an itch that needed scratching. Joe must have understood what those text messages hinted at. He hadn't bitten, but it didn't mean he wouldn't if she carried on.

Anna opened the door, fresh and elegant in wide-leg jeans, white jumper and long camel coat, Max on her hip. The smell of coffee and toast wafted out. They air-kissed and the children stretched for each other.

'All ready?'

Sara nodded. A gust of wind tore at her hair, and she pulled it back behind her ears, plastering a smile on her face.

'Everything okay?'

'Fine. Just got a lot on my mind.'

'Buying a new house is one of the most stressful things you can do. But you didn't have to buy Culloden Road, did you? So you haven't been through it before. It must have been weird, Joe not wanting to leave that house but still wanting to start a new life with you. I wouldn't have put up with it.'

'It was something he had to work through,' Sara said.

'You must be very forgiving. I'm surprised you let him go round to see Claudia.'

'What?'

'Oh God, I'm so sorry. I assumed you knew. Mum saw Joe coming out of the Myhills' house. Apparently he looked furious. Sorry, I probably shouldn't have said anything.'

Sara refused to rise to the bait. 'Don't worry. I'm glad you did. Claudia's a bit loopy these days. I expect she cried wolf and got Joe to come over.' She stopped. 'Damn.'

'What is it?'

'I told her I wasn't at home. She knew exactly what she was doing.'

'Mum told me you had been round to see Claudia.' Anna looked suspicious. 'I didn't realise you two were close.'

'We're not.' Sara pulled herself up. She couldn't afford careless mistakes. 'I had to call her about the sale. And I looked in on her because I was worried about what happened on fireworks night; with Joe, I mean.' She blushed. 'I ... um ... didn't like the way she looked at him. I wanted to warn her off.'

'Oh.' Anna thought for a moment. 'Well, if I was you, I'd ignore that sort of behaviour. You'll only make her think you don't trust your husband.'

'I know. I knee-jerked. It was stupid of me.'

'Will you say anything to Joe about my mum? Only I don't want him to think we're spying on him.'

'Don't worry.' She heard the sound of a car slowing and

189

glanced round with relief. 'Here's the agent.'

The car pulled up, the driver's door opened and a woman in her thirties got out, her sharp blonde bob swinging as she moved. She seemed familiar, but Sara couldn't place her.

'Hi, I'm Lia. You must be Mrs Hartman.'

Sara mustered a smile, driving away the enormity of what she'd learned. Joe had gone to his ex behind her back again. 'That's me. You know Anna.'

'I do indeed. Your little ones are the same age. How gorgeous!' Lia cooed at Max and Maeve. 'Shall we go in?'

Sara's eyes shifted to number 7, where lights were on in the hall and the upstairs rooms. Could she live here if Joe could be persuaded? Even if Claudia had gone by the time they moved in, she would visit her parents. Was it worth it? Maybe there was another, less extreme way of solving her problems.

Lia fiddled with the lock, issuing a hiss of frustration, then the key turned and the door swung open.

'I adore the smell of a project,' Anna said as Lia stooped to pick up the post.

Sara didn't. The place smelled of neglect, old skin cells, mice and some weird musk. It reminded her of the elderly childminder her mum used to leave her with.

They moved into the back room, which was dominated by a dusky pink velour sofa and armchair set. There were dark patches on the walls where pictures had once hung.

'Come and look at the garden,' Lia said, sliding open the aluminium doors. 'The space is fantastic, and it's so mature. You can tell the owner cared about it.'

They left the children inside and followed her out.

Autumn leaves lay scattered on the damp lawn and

190

clumped against the edges of the path. There was a stone birdbath and rockery, a greenhouse and the shed. At the end, a clothesline stretched between two poles, a forgotten tea towel hanging from it. The three women breathed clouds of mist.

Megan had brought Sara here once. She had taken her along the narrow passageway at the back where Owen had led her on Fireworks night, and through the gate. She had used her mother's set of keys to get into the house, where they'd stolen cigarettes left lying on the table and smoked them behind the shed with only Jocelyn's cat as witness.

'What do you think?' Anna whispered.

Sara almost jumped out of her skin. 'It's perfect.'

'Don't tell Lia that.'

Lia already knew. Sara looked back at the house. The two toddlers were at the window, palms and noses pressed against the glass, like dogs waiting for their owners to come home. Lia picked her way across the grass.

'There's plenty of room to extend,' she said. 'If you don't mind doing a bit of work.'

Sara nodded. 'It's definitely the kind of thing we're looking for. We're a little pushed for space where we live now, and it might get even more crowded soon.' She noted the look of dismay on Anna's face, swiftly concealed. She knew it. Anna had feelings for Joe.

Anna was eyeing Sara's stomach. 'Are you pregnant?'

'Not yet. But we're trying.'

In fact, Joe, forty-three this year, didn't want to expand their family, but Sara didn't see that as an insurmountable problem.

'We are too,' Anna said, collecting herself. 'Wouldn't it

be fantastic if we had our babies at the same time?'

If Anna hadn't looked so put out a moment ago, Sara would have believed in her enthusiasm, but she allowed the fantasy to play out. Two kids knocking on each other's back doors. She'd never had that growing up.

She turned to Lia. 'I'd like to make an offer now.'

Anna's jaw dropped.

'Wow, that's decisive!' Lia clapped her hands. 'But don't you want your husband to see it first?'

'He's super busy right now, and I don't want to miss out. Owen warned me that unmodernised houses here get snapped up really quickly.'

'They do, and often before they come on the market. As I said in my letter, there's been a lot of interest.'

Sara felt a surge of panic and almost grabbed the woman by her silk lapels. 'Is this all done under the table, between you and preferred buyers?'

Lia looked a little less friendly. 'Absolutely not. That would be in breach of the code of practice.'

'Sorry, I didn't mean to imply anything. But what can I do to secure it?'

'Offer more than the asking price. But even then there are no guarantees.'

As Lia drove off, Anna turned to Sara, eyebrows raised. 'You were fibbing, weren't you? There's no way Joe is going to roll over that easily.'

'I have ways and means.' Sara moved to her car, clicking the fob.

'Why do you want the place so badly?'

'When something is right, it's right.' Sara winked at her, and at the same moment, a car turned into Shires Close.

Chapter 36

ANNA

The car stops outside number 7 and a tall man gets out.

'Police,' Sara murmurs, bending to strap Maeve into her car seat.

She gets in and moves off, and I stay where I am, watching for Claudia. Claudia opens her front door, says something to the detective, then glances over at me. I keep staring at her until they've gone inside.

More interesting than Claudia receiving a visit from the police is Sara's behaviour. Why on earth has she offered on number 14 without Joe seeing it, when he's so obviously against the idea of living there? She has to want it badly. I mean, it's true, it's a developer's holy grail – the worst house in the best street – but Sara is not a developer, and I can't see her living through the stress of restoring the place. And yet there was a light in her eyes just now. Real fervour. Perhaps she's caught the bug off Owen. Or is there something else going on? Does she actually want to live opposite Claudia's parents? Maybe she wants to become like a daughter to them. Another stealth attack on Claudia's life.

I allow myself to contemplate the idea of having Joe Hartman as a neighbour and feel a frisson at the prospect. They say you never forget your first love.

Chapter 37

CLAUDIA

Claudia closes the door behind DS Ward. Frank slinks out of the kitchen, curls over himself and proceeds to lick his hindquarters.

'We've had the fire investigation report,' Ward says. 'I thought I'd drop in and tell you myself.'

'What did it say?'

'Arson. Traces of accelerant were found where the burn marks suggest the fire started, inside the front door, so that implies something was pushed through the letter box.'

She puts her hand to her throat, makes an effort to breathe and coughs convulsively. DS Ward waits. His expression isn't unkind.

'If you can think of any reason why someone might have done this, now is your chance to tell me.'

'The kids next door. On fireworks night they were joking about throwing a Molotov cocktail at the house. I don't think they would have actually done it, though. They just thought they were funny. I'm sure it wasn't them.'

'Names?'

She might have been able to overlook the scratch on Robert's car, but not arson.

'Their surname is Mitchell. They moved here while I was away, but the kids go to Overhill School. The daughter's called Rosie.'

'Right, we'll have a chat.' His eyes scan her face. Looking for what? It occurs to her that she is in the frame for this as well. 'Shall we sit down?'

'Yes, of course.'

She shows him into the front room because she doesn't want him to see the messy kitchen. He takes a notebook and biro out of his pocket while Claudia perches on the edge of the armchair. Her burnt hand begins to pulse, as if this reminder of what happened has switched the pain back on. She clasps it in her lap.

'This puts a slightly different complexion on the other incidents you've reported,' Ward says. 'Does anyone else have a key?'

'Not that I've been told, but it's possible.'

'Where do your parents keep their spare keys?'

'In a drawer in the kitchen.'

'Perhaps you could show me.'

Claudia nods and gets up. She feels so much tension in her body that she's convinced it's coming off her in waves. In the kitchen she opens the drawer where her parents keep a collection of keys, many of which she suspects are defunct.

'Don't touch them,' Ward says. 'Just point them out.'

She indicates a Yale key with a green plastic tag fed through the ring. Her mother has written *SPARE No,7* on the cardboard insert. Ward pulls on a pair of latex gloves and puts the key in an evidence bag.

Does he believe her now? She waits for him to speak.

It feels as though they've turned a corner. If he agrees that she's being threatened, then he'll believe she isn't responsible for what happened to Tilly.

Ward folds his arms. 'Claudia, did you start the fire yourself? It's important you tell the truth.'

Her heart sinks 'No. Why would I destroy my own home?'

He taps his pen against the edge of the dresser. 'The home intrusions. If someone is trying to terrorise you, what are they doing it for? You'll be gone soon.'

'Because—' She stops short, and clamps her mouth shut. She's not going to say it. People have strong feelings about her release. He may seem nice and kind, but he might be trying to trick her into getting herself recalled. She knows that game and she's not falling for it. 'I don't know.'

She looks directly at him, trying to gauge what he's up to. His gaze is speculative. Does he want her to say it? Is that what this is about. Or is she being paranoid? It's clear to her what's happening; someone thinks she'll find out what they did. But is it clear to him?

'You're understandably on edge,' he goes on when she doesn't speak. 'It's a shame your parents went away. It isn't good for you to be on your own so much. It's easy to build things out of proportion when you have no one to let off steam to. Personally, if I didn't have my wife, I think I'd go crazy. Stress can do that to you.'

The latest death threat is in her pocket. Her fingers itch to take it out, but she can't show it to him. She wouldn't be able to lie. It would destroy any credibility she has left if Joe were to tell him he'd seen the original on her laptop.

'Right. Well, if you think of something, call me.' He does

up his coat. 'If it wasn't you, then it's possible someone else accessed this house with another set of keys. Do you know who that might be?'

'You could ask Frances Holt at number 12. She used to have a key. Maybe she forgot to give it back after she and my mum fell out. Or maybe her daughter knows about it.'

'Anna Pemberton?'

'Why not? She's made it clear she hates my guts.'

'And why would that be?'

Claudia explains her history with the Holt family, careful not to link it to Tilly's abduction. DS Ward listens just as carefully, occasionally jotting down a note. She doesn't tell him she thought Anna had been trying to steal Joe from her, because she knows full well what kind of reaction that would provoke.

'Will you question them?'

'I will, yes. I should warn you, though. It's extremely difficult to prove who set a fire like that. Your other issue will be with the insurance claim. It depends on whether arson is covered. I'll be in touch.'

She shows him to the door and notices a locksmith's van on the forecourt of number 14. The place is being secured. She contemplates nipping across the close and asking him to change the locks on her house, but the idea of explaining to Robert that she's taken it upon herself to do that is too much. It's a good idea though. She'll bring it up next time her mother calls.

Chapter 38

Thursday 9 November

CLAUDIA

That night the baby cries again, but she doesn't get out of bed. She pulls the duvet over her head and hums to drown it out. When it eventually stops, she drifts into a fitful sleep, waking as the dawn light filters through the curtains. She gets up and looks out. The grass in the central circle is white with frost.

She goes downstairs, makes coffee and takes it up to the study, cradling its warmth in her hands. She can't think of anything to do except watch the comings and goings opposite and speculate about what is going through the heads of the Holts and the Pembertons. That her presence has set them on edge is understandable; it's the reasons for it that are hard to pin down. Is it guilt, hatred or shame?

Later that morning, a scruffy hatchback turns into the close and pulls in behind Robert's car. Claudia recognises it and melts into the shadows. The doorbell rings. She goes halfway down the stairs and peers at the figure visible through the obscure glass panes. It rings again.

'It's Greg Davies, Mrs Hartman. I have information for you.'

'You can tell me through the door.'

'I'm freezing my bollocks off out here. Come on. You're going to want to hear what I have to say.'

Claudia clings to the banister, feeling light-headed. She hasn't had breakfast, has barely felt like eating since fireworks night. 'I'm not letting you in unless you tell me what this is about.'

He bends and speaks through the letter box. 'I've been having a look at Joe's second wife. I've found something.'

She crosses the hall, undoes the bolts at the top and bottom and unhooks the chain before pulling the latch.

'Sorry,' he says, taking in her dishevelled appearance. 'I should have called first.'

'Just say what you have to and go.'

'Busy, are you?'

He grins at her as he divests himself of his thick woollen scarf. He keeps his brown leather coat on. Last time she saw him, when he drove her away from the mob, she was rude to him. He must have a thick skin.

'I'm busy minding my own business.'

'And I'm doing my job.'

'Why are you so interested in Sara? All she did was marry Joe.'

'Exactly. She knows him; she may even know him better than you. Understanding the wife helps flesh the husband out.' He curls his lip. 'Plus I don't like the woman. When I tried to interview her about your release, she tore up my card and told me to get lost.'

Claudia raises her eyebrows. 'Sensitive.'

199

'Irritable.'

That makes her lips twitch. 'So, what have you found out?'

'Did you know she was at Lady Eden's?'

'No she wasn't.'

The shock confuses her. She finds herself leading him to the kitchen when she hadn't meant to allow him any further than the hall.

He hangs his scarf over the back of a chair. 'Her maiden name was Massey. Ring any bells? She was only there for her GCSE years, but you crossed over between September 2004 and June 2006.'

'I don't remember her.'

Sara at Lady Eden's? Why didn't she know that? Claudia racks her brains, but she had very little to do with the girls in the years below her.

Greg hands her a copy of a playbill for a school production of *Romeo and Juliet*. The years roll back, and she's sitting in the audience with her mother, unable to stop smiling, bursting with her secret.

'Where did you get this?'

'From a friend of my sister-in-law who teaches there.'

'You're a family man.' She finds it oddly reassuring.

'I'm divorced,' he says shortly.

Thinking it doesn't necessarily follow, she frowns as she runs her eyes down the cast list. *Sara Massey: Malvolio*. The summer play was one of the few opportunities for different year groups to mix. Joe had suggested she get involved behind the scenes, but although sorely tempted by the prospect of spending time with him, she'd been sensible and refused. It was too dangerous. It had given her a frisson when he came up on the stage at the end to take a bow. The girls had mobbed him. He'd caught her eye and she'd been hard put not to giggle, especially with her mum beside her going on about how marvellous he was. She glances at the next page and sees Megan's name. *Stagehand*. She points to it.

'This girl is important too. She killed herself a few days after the performance.'

'Megan Holt. I remember the case. Tragic.'

'She lived in the close. She became fixated on Joe that summer term.' She sees Greg's expression and shakes her head. 'He did nothing to encourage her, but she made him uncomfortable. Firing up every time he looked her way. Then it got unpleasant. She hung around waiting for him outside the school. Joe was used to girls having crushes, but this was different. She was stalking him. Eventually it got better, and he relaxed, but then . . .'

Greg nods and strokes his thumb over the list of names. 'And now here we are, seventeen years later, and Sara Massey has Joe. The competition has been dealt with. Megan Holt is dead, and you've been convicted.'

'I don't think . . .' She frowns.

'Yeah, it's a stretch. To take it that far, so many years later . . .' He scratches his head. 'If you want someone else's husband, you seduce them with your womanly wiles, you don't steal their child.'

Claudia flinches and Greg's smirk vanishes.

'Sorry. I didn't mean to be offensive. Sometimes I can be a bit of a twat.'

'I think you've proved that.' She picks at a mark on the table.

'It's very difficult for you at the moment, I imagine.' His voice is gruff.

She raises her head and finds him looking straight at her. She's suddenly aware of everything, the untidy kitchen, her badly cut hair and bitten fingernails.

'Things have happened here since the fire. Weird things.'

'Such as?'

She feels heat rise to her face as she briefly outlines what's happened. She adds, with a wry smile, 'The police have come up with a rational explanation for all of it, even the arson. It's all me. There's this as well.' She pulls the anonymous note out of her pocket and hands it to him. 'But I haven't shown it to them yet.'

Greg scratches his stubble. 'Okay,' he says slowly. 'Why not?'

'I was intending to, and then I found something else.' She swivels the laptop and shows him the document. 'This proves that someone's been in the house, because I didn't type it.'

'When did it come?'

She's grateful to him for not questioning her story. 'On Monday. I'm taking it at face value. It means I'll have to act fast if I'm going to have any chance of finding out what happened to Tilly.' She pauses, weighing her words, wondering how much more trouble she can get herself into, because everything has consequences. She decides to take the risk. 'If you help me, I'll give you an exclusive.'

'You don't need to bribe me. I'd help you anyway.'

She glances at him, surprised. 'Thanks. The message says I know what to do. I think what it means is that I have to start running around shouting that I'm innocent so that

I get recalled. Whoever it is wants me safely back behind bars. They don't want to kill me.'

'The fire?'

'I don't think it's the same person. Whoever sent this,' she touches the sheet of paper, 'they're too squeamish to kill. Basically, they want me to do what I always do.'

'And what's that?'

She wrinkles her nose. 'Be my own worst enemy. Look, do you think you can buy me the weekend? *London News* is online, isn't it? Could you hint that you have a scoop? You can't say I'm going to make a statement, because that would get me into trouble, but say enough that whoever wrote the note will think I'm going to. If there is someone else, someone prepared to get their hands bloody, it might bring them out of the woodwork too.'

He folds his arms and tilts his head, like a bird appraising a worm. 'Do you want to make yourself bait?'

'If necessary. Yes.'

'How's this?' Greg turns his laptop round to show her what he's written. He's used a picture of Claudia looking distraught outside the courtroom. She tries not to look too closely at her own face; it tells too painful a story.

Next week we reveal astonishing new developments in the case of Tilly Hartman. Claudia Hartman has been found guilty in a court of law, but the court did not have all the information. Almost a decade on from the tragedy, we take a close look at the people involved and the exclusive private school they once had in common. Things weren't as innocent as they seemed at £24,000-a-year Lady Eden's, where

Claudia Myhill first laid eyes on the charismatic English teacher who years later would become her husband. But it turns out Claudia was not the only schoolgirl to fall under Hartman's spell. Read the full story in this column next week.

'What do you think?' Greg asks. 'It's vague enough that the police aren't going to come after you for it, and specific enough to keep your anonymous correspondent happy over the weekend.'

'Do you have to write all that about Joe? It could be very damaging.'

Greg rolls his eyes. 'He knew Sara and they kept that quiet. He groomed you, and possibly even Megan Holt.'

'I told you, Joe did not encourage Megan. It all came from her.' Claudia believes Joe absolutely on that one. 'And as for me, it wasn't grooming. Far from it.'

'Is that what you believe? Don't look at me like that. It may have been benign; he probably wouldn't have used those words – he'd have told himself it was love – but it was grooming.' He picks up the playbill. 'To quote the author, "a rose by any other name would smell as sweet".'

'I wasn't stupid or naïve, if you don't mind. I knew exactly what I was doing. And Joe behaved like a gentleman.'

Greg laughs, and she wants to punch him.

'Do you have to be so cynical?'

'I don't write about old ladies leaving their money to cats' homes. I write about people who do horrible things to other people. I understand conflict, and I've got a nose for a bastard.'

'I don't want you to bring Joe into it,' she says.

'Then what the hell do you want me to write?'

She doesn't know. She sits silently.

'Sorry,' Greg mumbles.

'It doesn't matter.'

'It does. You're going to have to trust me. Whatever happens, Joe is unlikely to come out of this whiter-than-white, and you are not going to be able to protect him. And Christ, you don't owe him protection. He didn't exactly fight your corner during your trial.'

She can't argue with that, but this is different. He's implying that what happened at Lady Eden's was somehow dirty. She'd loved Joe and he'd loved her. He'd waited for her, hadn't he? She glares sullenly at Greg.

'Good,' he says, ignoring her expression and taking her silence as consent. 'Before we post this, you do understand that we can't leave it hanging, don't you? I'll put it off for as long as I can, but at some point next week you're going to have to tell your story whether you want to or not. I can't do it without that assurance. I'd lose readers' trust, not to mention my editor's.'

'You'll get the story. Nothing is going to happen unless I do something extreme.' Then she covers the mouse with her hand, takes a deep breath, and clicks. 'Gone.'

'Okay. Now we await developments.' He rubs his face.

'They might not even read it.'

'They will.' He pauses. 'Claudia, whatever we do, whatever I write, however sympathetically I try to couch it, it's going to get ugly. It's going to remind readers who you are and what you were in prison for.'

She starts to feel sick. Her fingers go to her singed brows. 'Do you believe in coincidences?'

205

Why hadn't she thought? Lack of food and too much alcohol has made her slow. A little kindness and she's fallen for his schtick. And now it's too late.

'Nope. Why?'

'Funny how you keep turning up just after I receive a threatening note.' She laughs. 'God, you nearly had me there. No wonder it feels like there's more than one person out to get me.'

He cocks his head. 'We established that the first time couldn't have been me. Do you think I broke in and used your laptop? Because of course I have a key *and* I know your password. Even if that wasn't a ridiculous idea, I would never stoop to using scare tactics to get copy. I don't prey on vulnerable women. If I want something, I ask for it. I'm a determined little bugger, so I usually get what I want in the end. You would have given in with or without the note.'

'I would not,' she says, mustering some dignity. She feels ridiculous. Of course he couldn't have done it.

He sits back and rakes his fingers through his wiry hair. 'For fuck's sake.'

'Okay, okay. I was wrong. I'm sorry. Let's start again. Can you give me a lift to the school? I want to see what Joe has to say for himself.'

The irritation leaves his face. He rolls the tension out of his shoulders. 'Sure. I'll be your chauffeur if you have something to eat first. And maybe get dressed. We don't want you fainting in your pyjamas.'

Upstairs, hurriedly sprucing herself up, she becomes aware of an odd sensation in her facial muscles and touches her mouth. She's smiling.

Chapter 39

ANNA

'Oh, Anna dear!' Lisa says. 'How nice to see you. Joe's expecting you. He's just finishing up on a call.'

I remember Lisa Haskell. She was a mixed bag: funny and sweet with the kids one moment, sharp-tongued the next. You crossed her at your peril.

'Ah, there we are. He's free. Just let me tell him you're here.'

She beams at me approvingly as she calls through. But then I was never a difficult pupil, or not in the sense she would recognise. My difficulties were internalised. Only Joe had any idea what I was going through.

'Joe will come and find you. Can I make you a cup of tea?'

I play with the idea of saying yes, just to annoy her, but I don't want the interruption so I shake my head. 'That's very kind, but no thank you.'

Joe pushes open the door, a harried look on his face, but he smiles and meets my eyes properly. I follow him along the corridor, trying to think like a mother, not a teenage pupil with a massive crush on her teacher. He's the head now, a whole different ballgame.

He wouldn't have made it this far if I hadn't kept my

mouth shut. I glance at him as he ushers me into his office. My palms are sweaty. I take a seat on the sofa, cross one leg over the other and brush my fingers through my hair. Joe swivels his black leather chair round and folds his long body onto it.

'So,' he says. 'You want to be a teacher.'

'You know that isn't why I'm here.'

He takes a breath, starts to say something, stops and picks up his pen, for no reason other than to occupy his hands. I go hot under his gaze, my fingers trembling. I tell myself I'm not that needy teenager now; I'm an attractive, sophisticated woman. I am Anna Pemberton and I hold all the cards.

'I don't understand what you want,' he says. 'You have a good life. You have a baby, a husband, a lovely house; choices. So what are you doing here?'

'Perhaps I feel guilty.'

His eyebrows buckle. 'About what?'

'About your ex-wife. About Claudia. What if you had told the truth?'

'It wouldn't have made any difference. It wouldn't have brought Tilly home.'

'How do you know that?'

'Anna.' He lowers his voice. 'Claudia killed our daughter. She would have done that with or without you reporting our relationship.'

'Our relationship?' I laugh. 'Is that what it was?'

'I'm talking about what you believed back then. Not what I knew was true.'

'You would have been arrested, Joe. Your life would have been over. I saved you.'

He sits back and folds his arms. 'Is that why you're here? To exact your price?'

'No. I—'

'Listen to me. What happened all those years ago was a mistake on both our parts. I was having a difficult time of it with Claudia. I honestly didn't know up from down.'

'Or right from wrong.'

'Yes.' He drops his head into his hands, his hair flopping forward. 'If I could go back now and change things, I would. I am truly sorry, Anna. I'm sorry you got dragged into my mess, I'm sorry I took advantage of you. I behaved like a shit and used you, and I've regretted it ever since.'

'You could make it right.'

'What do you mean?' He looks up, his gaze sweeping me back to the thrill of that summer night. I can taste his lips on mine, feel his hand on my breast.

'I'm still in love with you. I knew as soon as I saw you on Saturday night.' I reach over and weave my fingers into his. 'I'm an adult now. I can make these decisions for myself. We can be together.'

Joe laughs and peels my fingers away. 'Don't be ridiculous.'

I fumble in my bag on the off chance there's a tissue in there, and find one of Max's muslins. I blow my nose into it before I speak.

'I could report you.'

It's satisfying to watch his face go sheet white. He eyes me with the cornered look of a caged animal.

'I didn't know you felt so strongly.'

I smile. 'Are you scared of me, Joe?'

'If you destroy my life, I'll destroy yours. I'll tell the

police what Sara told me. She witnessed you hitting your child.'

'That's not true.'

He slams his hand down on the desk. 'Fireworks night, Anna. And whatever, I don't give a shit about true. Mud sticks. Do you want to risk losing Max?'

'Your wife is lying. You can't do anything.'

'Don't underestimate me.'

And that's when I lose it, when years of suppressing the hurt boil over and I'm like a child, dashing tears from my eyes and telling him I hate him. Hate him. I storm out of his office, ignoring Lisa. I need to get away from him, I never thought it would be this bad.

Chapter 40

CLAUDIA

The school, three storeys of grey brick and glass, is on a road with commercial buildings on one side, common land on the other. The playground is protected by chain-link wire and dense shrubs.

'I must be mad bringing you here,' Greg says. 'You do realise they'll have been warned about you? The secretary probably has a photo of you pinned up on her corkboard. Do not approach this woman.'

Claudia refuses to laugh at his clumsy attempt at humour, his olive branch. She hasn't forgiven him for what he said about Joe grooming her. She doesn't need to be told she was wrong. She doesn't need to be made to feel stupid.

'I should have time before the alarm's raised. If you do your part.'

'And what part would that be?'

She swivels round in her seat. 'Pretend we have an appointment to see round the school, then distract them.'

'I'm up for that.' He reaches back through the seats, grabs a scruffy fleece beanie and pulls it on, wraps his scarf around his neck, covering his chin. 'They know me from when I doorstepped Joe here recently,' he explains.

Claudia contemplates telling him what she thinks of

that behaviour, but she's impatient to get going. It's still lunchtime, and unless he has a meeting, Joe will be doing the rounds, interacting with pupils, talking to staff. She knows how he operates. He makes himself available to everyone. She needs to catch him before the bell rings at one.

She takes a deep breath and gets out of the car, sending Greg a nervous smile. The cold wind blasts her.

'Here goes.' He tweaks the scarf up.

The gate opens before he can press the buzzer, and Anna rushes out and collides with him. She apologises, and then sees Claudia and recoils.

'Mrs Pemberton, isn't it?' Greg says.

Anna turns on him. 'You're a journalist. I've seen you hanging around the close. What the fuck are you doing with her?' Her eyes are red and swimming with tears. 'Then again, why not? A marriage made in heaven.'

Claudia steps forward. 'I know you hate me—'

'Of course I bloody hate you.'

She is half inclined to laugh. There's no one who doesn't hate her, it seems, apart from a dodgy journalist and her mother. 'I know you've made friends with Sara. But there are things you don't know about her.'

'There are things I don't know about a lot of people. I like to give them the benefit of the doubt.'

Not in Claudia's experience, but she refrains from voicing the thought.

'Good. But you should know she hasn't come out of nowhere.'

'What do you mean?'

'Sara was at Lady Eden's with Megan.'

Anna's mouth opens but no sound comes out, and Claudia presses home her advantage.

'She was in your sister's class. If you don't believe me . . .' She holds out the playbill, jabbing her finger against Sara's name.

Anna casts her eye over it. 'It isn't necessarily the same Sara.' But she doesn't sound sure.

'Of course it is. It checks out. If it makes you feel any better, I didn't know until today. Otherwise I wouldn't have enlisted her help with you.'

'I don't understand.'

'It was no coincidence that she joined your yoga class. I sent her. She told me she wanted to help me. So I asked her to find out what you knew.'

Anna's eyes flash. 'You asked her to spy on me?'

'You wouldn't talk to me,' Claudia replies bluntly. 'I didn't have a choice.'

'So what did she say about me?'

'She said you were flirtatious with Joe on fireworks night. She implied you came on a bit strong.'

Anna colours up. 'Oh yuck. No. He's practically old enough to be my father.'

'Then why have you been crying?'

She flicks a hand, dismissing what Claudia has said as trivial. 'That is nothing to do with you.' She gets into her car, closes the door and winds down her window. 'How many more lives do you have to ruin, Claudia?' She drives off with a screech of tyres.

Greg's eyebrows shoot up. 'Interesting.'

Claudia is thoughtful. She didn't divulge that Sara had witnessed her smack her child. Perhaps she should have.

She isn't sure, but Anna already had that cornered look about her. She shakes herself and follows Greg to the gate.

Claudia turns her back on the camera while Greg presses the buzzer. She has no idea what he's going to say, doesn't like to ask in case she bottles it. She's chosen to trust this man, which is odd, seeing she doesn't trust her own judgement most of the time.

'Hi,' Greg says. 'It's Mr and Mrs Smith.'

Claudia opens her mouth, then clamps it shut.

'We have a meeting with Mr Hartman at ten past one.'

'Smith?' Claudia hisses at him as the buzzer sounds.

She imagines the school secretary going into a panic, checking Joe's diary, wondering if she forgot to log the appointment. She'll dispatch an assistant to track Joe down. She hopes Lisa Haskell doesn't still work here. Claudia had been in a dreadful state the last time she came to the school, mortifying Joe and ruining any chance she had of convincing a jury she was a reliable character. Lisa had witnessed the whole sorry episode. Though of course, during the trial, it was alleged that Claudia had been putting on an act. Not being believed can make you spiral, especially if you're exhausted and questioning your own fitness to be a mother. But she hadn't been acting. The psychotic episode had been real.

She stiffens her resolve. The list of things she is forbidden from saying out loud is an increasingly heavy burden, but one day she is going to say it all.

Greg approaches the office window, blowing his nose into a hanky, while Claudia hovers behind him and keeps her face averted. Fortunately, it isn't Lisa; it's someone she doesn't know.

'Mr Hartman's PA has gone to track him down,' the secretary says. 'If you'd like to sign in and take a seat in the waiting room, he won't be long. Can I offer you something to drink?'

'Oh no, we're fine,' Greg says smoothly.

'You'll find prospectuses on the coffee table – if you haven't already had one.' She hands over visitor lanyards, catches Claudia's eye and frowns.

Claudia quickly scribbles *Mr and Mrs Smith* and the time in the visitors' book. Greg holds the door to the waiting room open for her. When it closes behind them, she whispers, 'I think she recognised me.'

'What do you want to do?'

'You stall her. I'll look for Joe.'

The bell rings as Claudia walks into the corridor and kids start pouring in from the playground. They surge towards the stairs, forcing her to keep to the wall. She covers her bad hand protectively.

It's a long time since she's been here, but she remembers the layout. Overhill is a modern school, designed by an architect in the 1990s. Its blocky L shape hugs a large playground marked out for sports. There's a light-filled central stairwell and wide corridors going off to the left and right.

She moves along, peering through doors. No one questions her presence, but in her experience kids don't notice adults unless they're being addressed directly, up to no good or need something. They are sprawling, running and pushing, throwing arms around each other's shoulders, messaging frantically on their phones. Claudia can smell the kitchens, something meaty, something boiled. The bombardment of noise, the bang of doors, the loud laughter and shouts, the drum of rubber soles against lino is an unwelcome reminder of prison but she clings to the idea of Joe and keeps moving, keeps searching until she sees him.

He's taller than the biggest kids, and rangier. He can make himself heard too, his voice a boom that stops people in their tracks.

'Into your classrooms, now. Liam, tuck your shirt in.'

Claudia hangs back. Someone bumps her with their elbow; a girl stares hard at her as she twists her hair up and secures an elastic. Joe feels her eyes on him and turns his head, his brow furrowing.

Chapter 41

CLAUDIA

Joe pulls her into an empty classroom. Oddly, since she's in trouble, she feels exhilarated, her sense of panic slipping away.

'What the hell are you doing here?'

She is surprised by the force of his anger, but then remembers Anna's face. Whatever was said between them, it's bled into his mood, but she can't go into that now. She slaps the dog-eared *Romeo and Juliet* playbill against his chest.

'You knew your wife back then.'

He shrugs. 'Not knew in the sense you're implying. Sara was just another pupil.'

'Really?' She hopes she sounds as sceptical as she feels.

He takes the playbill out of her hand, glances at it casually. 'I can't even remember which part she played.' He runs his eyes down the cast list. 'Malvolio.'

He evidently hasn't seen Greg's post, and there's no reason why he should have, though no doubt the staff will spot it soon enough, if they haven't already. She's relieved that she doesn't have to deal with the fallout from that decision yet.

'Why did you never mention that Sara was at Lady Eden's?' she asks.

'Why would I tell you anything about my wife?'

'Because it's relevant.' She lowers her voice. 'There must have been something to make her come after you all those years later.'

'She didn't come after me. It was pure coincidence that we bumped into each other.'

'Yeah, I'll bet.'

Beyond the door, the corridor has emptied and the clamour has died down.

'I trusted you, Joe. You had us wrapped around your little finger, but I thought I was special. I thought I was the one. When you were directing *Romeo and Juliet* with your little groupies, did you take your pick? Was that why it was so easy to keep your hands off me?'

Joe is rigid with anger. 'Stop it,' he says through clenched teeth. 'Stop being mad. You are poisoning my life and damaging my marriage and you're doing your best to damage an innocent woman as well. Why don't you calm down and accept what has happened before you go too far?'

'I just saw Anna leaving the school. She'd been crying. Did you do what I said?'

'She was here to talk about teaching,' Joe snaps. 'Anna was not and is not in love with me. I have no idea why she was crying, but it has nothing to do with me.'

'Of course it does.'

Twin spots flare on his cheeks, and Claudia narrows her eyes. She knows him. He doesn't flush easily. When he does, it's generally because he's lying.

'Oh, for Christ's sake,' he explodes. 'What is it?'

The door has opened. Lisa Haskell comes bustling in, fluffed up with indignation.

'I am *so* sorry, Joe. Mary didn't realise who it was. I've called the police.'

'That was unnecessary.'

Lisa sends a ferocious glance Claudia's way, as if it's Claudia's fault that she's displeased her boss.

'She's not allowed near children. There was a memo saying to call the authorities immediately if she came on to the premises.'

'She's no danger to this lot,' Joe says wearily. 'You should have asked me first.'

'She might have a weapon.'

'Lisa.' He sounds exhausted. 'Please give us some privacy.'

Lisa breathes in sharply, which has the comical effect of lifting her breasts. 'Of course.'

Claudia can hear the wail of sirens, then above it, Greg calling her name. She barges past Lisa and runs out of the room ignoring Joe's shout. She can't be caught here; it'll ruin everything.

Greg belts up the corridor, reaches her and bends double, dragging in a breath. 'You've been rumbled. Let's go.'

Joe steps between them, a beanpole blocking her from a bulldog. 'What are you doing here?'

Greg squares his shoulders. 'I'm here to support Mrs Hartman.'

'Claudia?' Joe turns to her, raising one eyebrow.

Claudia shrugs. 'I can't do this on my own.'

'But you chose *him* as your knight in shining armour?'

She shakes her head slowly, then turns to Greg. He nods and she follows him back along the corridor and down the stairs to the front hall. They run across the empty playground and through the gate, just as a squad car swings into the kerb. Two officers jump out. Claudia backs away, turning to Greg in alarm.

'Don't worry,' he says. 'It's all cool.'

'Really?' Her voice reaches an unnatural pitch.

'Claudia Hartman? You're under arrest for breaking the conditions of your parole.'

The officer takes her by the arm, swings her round and, ignoring her yelp of pain, locks a pair of handcuffs round her wrists. She's so thin, they hang like heavy bangles above the knuckles of her thumbs, the edge of one of them pressing into a blister. The pain is excruciating, and tears spring from her eyes.

'Oh, come on,' Greg says. 'You don't have to do that. Can't you see she has burns?'

'Mr Davies. What are you doing here?'

They sit in Joe's office. Two policemen on the sofa, Claudia on the matching armchair, Joe on his office chair and Greg on a child's stool brought in from the assembly hall. Claudia's handcuffs have been removed at Joe's request.

'So what exactly are you saying?'

'That Mrs Hartman didn't come here of her own accord,' Greg responds. 'I coerced her. She's vulnerable and I took advantage.'

'Mr Hartman?'

Claudia looks straight into Joe's eyes, pinning him with her gaze, needing him to understand that she is pleading;

that she would get down on her knees if she could. He can't let them recall her. Not when she's inching closer to the truth.

Joe hesitates, then nods, his jaw tight. 'It's what Claudia told me, and I've no reason to disbelieve her. Look at her. She's clearly not well, and that bastard knows it. All he wants is a story. Can't you make an exception this time? I'm not making a complaint.'

The older of the two officers stands up. 'Can I have a private word, Mr Hartman? Won't take a moment.' He leads Joe out into the corridor. Claudia watches through the small window in the door as they confer. When they come back, the officer nods at his colleague.

'She can go. Last chance, though. This happens again and there will be consequences.'

Claudia turns to Joe when they've gone. 'What did he say to you?'

'His daughter started at Overhill in September. He wants her moved into a different class next term. He doesn't like the kids she's hanging out with. I think we're quits now, don't you?'

She nods, dry-mouthed. Joe puts his hand on her shoulder for a fraction of a second. He's being kind, but his kindness is tinged with sorrow, as if he knows he's helping someone who cannot be helped. She has an odd feeling that this is the last time she'll ever see him.

Chapter 42

SARA

Sara was sitting on the bedroom floor, surrounded by piles of clothes pulled out of drawers and wardrobes, when her mobile phone rang. She reached for it. Anna. She wasn't in the mood. She didn't like the woman and was almost sorry she'd ever got involved. She sighed and tapped accept.

'Hi.'

'Hey. What are you up to?'

'Going through our stuff for the move. I thought I'd make a start on my clothes while Maeve's having her nap.'

'Can I come over? I'm going stir crazy here. Max is so clingy at the moment. He's teething.'

Sara wasn't sure, but instinct told her there was an off note, and her instincts were usually right. It felt as though the three of them, she, Anna and Claudia, were constantly trying to second-guess each other. She had to be on her toes.

'Actually,' she said, 'that would be lovely. I've no idea whether half this stuff suits me any more. Most of it I haven't worn since before I was pregnant.'

'Amazing. I can help you decide what to keep and what to chuck. I'm good at that.'

Dropping the phone on the carpet beside her, Sara

shook her head and got back to work. Now that they had made the decision to leave, it felt as though the house was turning its back on her. It was hardly surprising. This was where Tilly Hartman had lived, where Claudia and Joe had loved each other. The devastation that 26 Culloden Road had borne witness to was appalling. Once she had the house in Shires Close, she would be able to breathe easy again. Start over. There was just the small matter of getting round Joe. There was so much riding on this, she sometimes found it hard to breathe.

Sara held a blotchy-faced Max, who immediately pushed his sticky fingers into her hair, while Anna removed her coat and scarf and hung them over the bottom of the banisters.

'Here, give him to me. He's making a mess of you. Had me up half the night, didn't you, my little soldier?'

Sara set her teeth as she handed Max over. Anna was sugary sweet, but Sara knew what she was capable of. She couldn't bring herself to respond.

'I've dosed him up on Calpol, so he should be okay for an hour.' Anna raised a rueful eyebrow. 'My mother thinks I've taken him to one of my NCT friends. I thought I'd better not mention I was coming here. Anyone connected to Claudia is a no-no in our house. You're all bad news as far as she's concerned.'

'It's a shame she feels that way, especially since we might be moving to the close.'

Sara saw a shadow pass across Anna's face and was puzzled. She'd thought Anna wanted her to move there. Had she changed her mind?

'Joe's agreed then?' Anna asked.

'I'm not there yet, but since there's very little else on the market, he might give up and let it happen. *Voilà.*' Sara opened the bedroom door with a flourish. She would act her way through the afternoon. She was good at that.

The bed was heaped high with clothes, the floor with smaller piles. Wardrobe doors were open, three quarters of the hangers bare. Anna set Max down beside a basket of Maeve's toys and plunged in. She pulled out an emerald-green dress and held it up in front of Sara, tilting her head as she considered the effect. Sara forced herself to look, to react positively, despite the odd atmosphere.

'I went to see your delightful husband this morning,' Anna said. 'To talk about teaching assistant opportunities at Overhill. Did he tell you?'

'I haven't spoken to him yet.' Sara stood in front of the mirror and held a cream silk shirt to her body. 'But that's great. I'm so pleased he's helping you.'

'Apparently one of the assistants who support children with learning difficulties is leaving at the end of next term, so Joe said if I wanted to, I could do the summer term. It will be invaluable experience. Hopefully I'll be pregnant by then, have the baby at Christmas and apply for a PGCE for the start of the following autumn term.'

'You are organised. Won't it be terribly demanding?'

Anna nodded. 'Yeah, Joe was worried I wouldn't hack it. Not that I told him about the baby plans. Just because I have no experience. It's only for a term, though.' She opened her eyes wide. 'What could possibly go wrong?'

'What couldn't in that place? So you're serious? You really do want to teach?' There was an odd pitch to Anna's voice that set her teeth on edge. She had no clue what Anna was here for, just a sense that it wasn't for the love of her company.

'Absolutely. I'm enjoying motherhood, but I'm not the stay-at-home type. I mean, I respect anyone who wants to do that, but it's not for me. And teaching is a pragmatic decision as well as an emotional one. I need a career where the holidays work round being a mother.'

'I'm not sure staying at home is for me either. What do you think of this?' Sara offered up a short black dress with a beaded scoop neckline and three-quarter-length sleeves with beads at their cuffs. The beads were black too.

'Bit young?'

She dropped it on the charity pile. Anna picked it up.

'I might nick it, if you don't mind.'

'Go right ahead,' Sara said drily.

'Thanks.' Anna folded it and put it to one side. 'Listen, there's another reason I wanted to see you. It's about Jocelyn's house.' Her face was a picture of guilt, her lips drawn between her teeth. Max lost interest in the toys and crawled over to a pile of clothes, which he started systematically dismantling, until Anna pulled him away.

'Let him,' Sara said, a shade too quickly. 'I don't mind.'

Anna's eyes narrowed, and Sara felt a jolt of electricity in her solar plexus. Had Joe told Anna what she had witnessed? He wouldn't be so stupid, surely? If he had, then as far as Anna was concerned, Sara was the enemy. In which case, what the hell was her agenda today?

'This is really awkward,' Anna said. 'But Owen's changed his mind. He said he couldn't pass up the opportunity. I'm so sorry, Sara, but he's put in an offer as well.'

225

And there's your answer, Sara thought. Spiteful revenge. Anna had wanted to see Sara's face when she told her. 'Right.'

'I know how emotive house-buying can be, especially when you really fall in love with a place, but Owen is a businessman. He said we'd be mad not to buy it. It's nothing personal.'

'I suppose it depends who makes the highest bid, though, doesn't it?'

Anna looked at her pityingly. Sara had a flash of memory, a blonde woman laughing at something Owen was saying at the fireworks. That was where she'd remembered Lia from. The estate agent was in Owen's pocket.

'It's fine,' she said. 'Joe wouldn't have gone for it anyway. It was pie in the sky.'

'True. It was always going to be tricky for you two moving into the close.'

'Yup.'

What the hell was she going to do? Was this what her life was going to be like? Constantly troubleshooting, plugging gaps, looking over her shoulder?

'Are you sure you're okay?' Anna persisted. 'Only I don't want it to affect our friendship.'

Sara gritted her teeth. Anna was enjoying this. She felt such bitter hatred and fury it took every ounce of willpower to hide it.

'It is absolutely fine. I promise.'

'I bumped into Jocelyn's daughter outside the house yesterday. She was there to check there was nothing left she wanted before the house clearance people come on Monday. Everything is going to be stripped out, and the

226

garden too. The shed's going, and the greenhouse, so we'll be able to get a better idea of how much needs to be done. I have to say, I'm quite excited.'

'I think Maeve's woken up,' Sara said abruptly.

'I didn't hear anything.'

'I'd better check.'

Sara went into the nursery, where her daughter was still sound asleep, and closed the door. There was a strange electricity surrounding Anna. It was as if she knew, or sensed something. What was going on? What exactly did she want from Sara? Somewhere along the line, Sara must have made a mistake. She'd been too eager to buy number 14, despite Joe's perfectly understandable objections. That had to have something to do with it. Or perhaps she was overthinking and it was less complicated than that. Perhaps it was simply that she knew too much about Anna.

Anna turned when Sara walked back in. For a fraction of a second, she looked flustered. Sara logged that and asked casually if she had seen anything of Claudia.

'Not really.'

'It must so difficult for you all.'

'It's been terrible.' Anna gave a wan smile. Max tottered over and wrapped his arms around her leg. She scooped him into her arms and yawned. 'God. I need some fresh air. I can't keep my eyes open.' She gave Sara a kiss on the cheek. 'See you soon, okay?' And then she was gone.

Sara went to the window and watched her cross the road to her car and strap Max into his seat. When she turned back, her eye was caught by the half-open wardrobe. She moved the chair from her dressing table, climbed onto it and reached into the top shelf. From inside an envelope she removed the playbill for *Romeo and Juliet*, taking it into the bathroom and setting fire to it with a match from the box she kept there to light her scented candles. She watched the flame eat Joe's words. They could be easily misconstrued.

You have restored my faith in women, Sara Massey. I hope you know how incredible you are. Joe x

Then she lay down on the bed, grabbed a rejected shirt and, crumpling it in her fist, crammed it against her mouth and screamed.

Chapter 43

SARA

Sara's stomach churned; she didn't want to quarrel with Joe, but if he'd told Anna what Sara had told him in confidence – because you should be able to tell your husband everything – then he needed to know she was livid. When she heard his key in the lock, she braced herself. He walked into the kitchen with a face like thunder, forestalling her.

'Have you seen this?' He handed her his phone.

Sara read the short piece and raised her eyes to Joe's face. He looked like he had aged ten years, his eyes shadowed, the vertical lines between his brows deeper and darker. His mouth was tight. She gave him the phone back. She wouldn't say anything about Anna.

'She must be mad. Or desperate. This is a big risk.'

'Never mind *her* risk. She knows what an insinuation like that can do to me. She came to see me today. Why the hell didn't she mention it?' He struck his fist down on the counter.

'Have you asked her?'

'No, because I've no doubt that's what she wants. I've called Michael. I'm going to meet him tomorrow.'

Sara nodded. It seemed like the sensible thing to do, and no doubt Michael would agree; getting into a row with Claudia about it would only make things worse. She glanced at him.

'Why did Claudia come to see you?'

'Yeah, well, that's the other thing. She's found out you were at Lady Eden's.'

Sara pressed her forehead into her palm. 'Great.'

'It was going to happen eventually, I suppose, but coming at the same time as this . . . I imagine it's what prompted her.'

Sara couldn't look at him. He wanted her to be strong, like she had been in the past, and she wasn't sure she had it in her.

He seemed to sense her holding back. 'We've never lied about it, Sara, we just haven't talked about it. The worst is going to be a bit of embarrassment, but with any luck it'll be short-lived and we can move on. Michael's going to get on to the editor today, see if he can't put a spanner in the works.'

Sara pulled herself together. 'Claudia has one agenda, Joe, and you know it's not about embarrassing you or getting your attention. She wants to clear her name, and if that means using a tabloid journalist to deflect attention to you, or even me, that's what she'll do. But the police aren't stupid, and it isn't going to work; because we're innocent and she's guilty.'

Joe massaged an eyebrow. 'You're right. I shouldn't let her wind me up. Of course she's desperate. Let's not talk about it any more.' He sighed heavily, then shrugged his suit jacket off and hung it over the back of a chair. 'I need to get changed. What time is Elektra coming?'

Shit. She'd forgotten they were going to Kate and Paul's.

They did this every year around the anniversary of Tilly's disappearance, a tradition that had begun long before Sara came on the scene and an annual duty she found almost intolerable, fond though she was of their friends. Of course she felt for Joe, and understood that it helped him, but frankly, to have to sit and listen to another child and another time being eulogised for an entire evening, well, she could do without it. Could this day get any worse?

She knew Joe wasn't going to like this, but she had no choice. 'Darling, would you mind terribly if I didn't come?'

Joe's face fell. 'Why?'

'I don't feel up to it.'

'You can make the effort for one evening, can't you? We haven't had a night out for ages. I need this.'

'I'm sorry.' She drew a breath. 'It's just that I haven't been seeing as much of Kate recently, and I feel like it's coming from her.'

'Don't be silly. Kate loves you.'

There was a hint of impatience in his voice, but she steeled herself.

'I don't want to go.' Her fists were clenched at her sides, her nails biting into her palms. 'This is about you and Tilly, it has nothing to do with me. Paul and Kate won't care whether I'm there or not. Kate's never cared about me the way she cared about Claudia. It isn't a real friendship. It never has been.'

'They weren't getting on at the end, you know that.'

'Yes, and I also know how much it hurt Kate. If *I* fell out with her, she'd shrug it off. It wouldn't touch her in the same way.' She was getting heated. She took a breath and dialled it down a notch. 'You'd have a much better time without me. They're your friends, and you can talk more freely if I'm not there. Claudia's release has been extremely stressful for me too and the house move isn't helping.'

'That's not my fault.'

'Well then whose fault is it? You should have sold up the moment you divorced her.'

Joe's face stiffened. He looked battered and angry, but she couldn't stop.

'And now that bloody piece online.'

'You should come precisely because of that! We need to present a united front, act normally.'

'I don't want to have to pretend things are normal when they aren't.'

'What do you think I have to do every day of my life?'

The silence rang with their anger. She glared at him and he glared back.

'This is about me, not you,' she said through gritted teeth. 'I don't want to have to sit around feeling like a lemon while you three get all deep and meaningful about a time I wasn't part of. It always makes me feel like I don't exist.'

'What the fuck is it with you? Don't you think I've been under a lot of strain too? It's ten years since someone took my baby, and nine since my wife went to prison. The Shaws have been incredibly supportive, and this annual supper is the one time I'm still allowed to talk about what happened and openly grieve without people wondering why I can't get over it. You're my wife, Sara. You are part of this whether you like it or not. If you stay away, then you're not with me, you're not on my side.'

Sara felt as though she'd been battered by a gale. She

had gone too far. She started crying, letting the tears fall because she had nothing left in her armoury.

For once, it didn't work.

'You do what you like,' he said stiffly. 'I'll be going across the road in half an hour. If you're not coming, I suggest you think very hard about your commitment to our marriage, because I'm not sure it's going to survive this.'

She wiped at her eyes. 'Joe. Please.'

He glared at her. 'This is about love and friendship, and if you can't understand that, what are you even doing here?'

Chapter 44

SARA

Kate's delight at seeing them both felt genuine. She hugged Sara with warmth and pulled her inside, and Joe gave her a look as if to say, *See? You built it all out of proportion.* Sara felt almost stupefied by anxiety and impatience. But it wasn't Claudia she was worried about. It was Anna. Had she known what she was doing when she told Sara about the immediate plans for number 14? No, she couldn't have. There was nothing Sara could do, not now. She was trapped.

'So, do we mention the elephant in the room?' Kate asked, holding Joe's hands in hers.

Joe rolled his eyes. He threw himself down on their voluptuous old sofa, pulled a crumpled gilet from behind his back and hung it over the arm.

'Not much to say, is there?' His mouth pulled to one side. 'Claudia is rattling my cage.'

Sara sat beside him. Paul propped up the wall by the door and Kate stood over them with her arms folded.

'It'll blow over,' Kate said.

'Will it?'

'It was bound to come out,' Paul said. 'With the press

interest in Claudia rekindled, they're all looking for an angle.'

'But why pick on me?' Sara asked.

Kate wrinkled her nose. 'I don't think she is. You're just collateral damage. Let's get some drinks down us, then we can relax.' She left the room.

'So what do you think this is about, Paul?' Joe asked.

Paul was a psychiatrist who specialised in treating people who'd been through trauma. He steepled his fingers against his face for a moment, then folded his arms. 'One, she's being manipulated by the journalist. I expect he's told her he can help her.'

Sara winced inwardly.

'Two. As someone who's been released because she's pleaded guilty, she is in an invidious position and she knows it. She needs to shift public perception in order to survive. It's basically Maslow's triangle.'

'It's what?' Sara asked.

Kate came back in and handed them their drinks. 'Your quick explanation, Paul darling. Dinner's almost ready.'

Paul lifted his beer bottle to his lips and took a swig. 'At the bottom of the triangle, you have your basic needs. First is food, water and shelter. Claudia has that sorted. It's all been done for her. Above that is security and safety. She doesn't have that, and no one can give it to her. If one of the two basic props of human life is stripped away, it leaves a huge gap when it comes to building and sustaining the three above them: the ability to form relationships and friendships, followed by self esteem, the need to feel a sense of accomplishment, and finally self-fulfilment. Maslow believed that without the lower levels, humans can't deal with their needs higher up. Claudia can only focus on her security now. She can't move on until she feels safe. Everything she does is fundamentally in pursuit of that. She may dress it up as the search for the truth about Tilly, but it's about survival. Bottom line.'

'So do you think that by making other people feel unsafe, namely me and Sara, she's simply bolstering her own sense of security?'

'Yes, I do. It makes her feel better when the public's focus shifts to you and whatever you may have done. Having a relationship with another ex-pupil, in this case.' He flashed Sara a rueful smile. 'Sorry.'

Sara shook herself. She had been thinking that the Maz-whatever triangle applied as much to her as to Claudia. 'Don't worry about me. Thick skin.'

'Marrying another ex-pupil, never mind that it was years later, isn't a good look. People will be interested in that; more interested, perhaps, than in a woman who has already been tried and sentenced.'

Beside her, Sara felt Joe bridle.

'You can't help who you fall in love with,' he said.

'I'm not getting at you. You asked me what I think this is about, and I'm being honest. You need to prepare yourself for further revelations. Get ahead of Claudia. Tell your side of the story and don't let her steer the narrative.'

'I am fucked, aren't I?'

Sara rubbed his back. 'No you're not. It'll be fine. Like you said, a bit of embarrassment. People will forget pretty quickly, especially if Claudia gets herself recalled because of it.'

'That's right,' Kate said soothingly. 'Claudia is very close to overstepping the mark. Stay strong, darling. You'll get through this. Let's eat.'

Following Kate's broad back into the kitchen, Sara frowned. Kate did call Joe darling from time to time, but right now, when Joe was so low, well, she shouldn't have.

For supper, Kate had made a venison stew. There were candles on the table, curtains closed against the night. After they had eaten, they raised their glasses to Tilly and, as was traditional, Joe stood up to say a few words.

'Thank you so much for this delicious supper, you two, and for your incredible hospitality.' He gave them a crooked smile. 'It's been a weird few weeks, as I'm sure you're aware, but strangely enough, seeing Claudia has been cathartic.'

Sara shot him a look. If only he knew what she was going through, he wouldn't say things like that.

'Since her conviction, I've only ever thought of Claudia as a monster, as someone for me to focus my anger on, but in reality she's a pathetic creature, in need of help more than anything else. That help cannot come from me, but I don't wish ill on her now, despite her recent behaviour.' He raised his glass to his lips and swallowed a mouthful of wine. 'I forgive her for Tilly. I can't forget, but I can stop poisoning myself with toxic thoughts, because I'm not the only one I'm hurting: I'm also hurting my family. If I can forgive Claudia, then I can be more present for Sara and Maeve, and for you two.' He tipped his glass towards Paul and Kate. 'I don't know what I would have done without you. You have saved me from despair time and time again.'

Kate, who was gazing at him with rapt attention, briefly touched his hand, and Sara tensed. She hoped no one could

237

see the bitterness she felt. If anyone had saved Joe from despair, it was her.

'You two have filled the gaping hole in my heart,' Joe went on. 'You've protected me and have stepped up and told me when I'm in the wrong. You've counselled me when I've been about to make a mistake.'

Why did Kate glance at Sara at that particular moment? Did she consider *her* a mistake? Sara wondered whether the Shaws had advised Joe against marrying her. Kate had only committed to their friendship once Sara and Joe were married and there was no getting rid of her.

She remembered being introduced to them for the first time. The couple had been friendly enough, but they were there to get her measure. She didn't mind. It was only natural. What she had minded was Kate talking about Joe as if he belonged to them. As if however wonderful she was, they were Joe's safe place, they had history. She had been direct about it.

'We'll always be there for him,' she'd told Sara. 'He's part of the family. You mustn't feel threatened.'

Sara had had to bite her tongue in order not to come back with a sharp riposte. Why did people assume she felt threatened? The journalist had said the same thing. It was demeaning. Was she that much less attractive than Joe?

Paul was hanging on Joe's every word with dog-like devotion. Sara felt shut out of their friendship, their tight triangle. She wished she hadn't waited for as long as she had to approach Joe, but she couldn't just step into the shoes Claudia had left behind. The press would have been on her like leeches. Instead, she'd immersed herself in her job and her social life and put up with a second-rate relationship until she deemed it safe. She had made it her business to bump into him. Kate didn't know that.

After supper, they moved to the sitting room, where Paul served them glasses of grappa. Sara let the sweet liquor rest on her tongue. Paul stoked up the fire, then promptly fell asleep on the sofa. He always did that, and Kate always pretended not to notice. Sara felt sleepy herself, but there was no way she was leaving Kate and Joe as good as alone, so she stayed awake and contributed to the conversation as best she could. Out of consideration for her, Kate steered clear of Claudia and Tilly, and instead talked about the houses she and Joe might consider, scrolling through Rightmove on her phone and sending links to Sara. She seemed to assume they'd be staying in Kingston, just downsizing. Had Joe given her that idea, or was she being hopeful? Living opposite Joe meant a lot to Kate, that much was clear.

Sara was tired, the room was warm and the grappa sense-deadening. She was so worried and preoccupied she could barely focus. She said less and less, and as she became quieter, Kate and Joe slipped into talking about old times. Joe recalled some long-ago party at a neighbour's house where Paul got so pissed he vomited in the flower bed, and how for ages afterwards the hostess would mention it, and Kate and Paul would feign indignation on her behalf and join in the speculation as to who the culprit had been. When she laughed, Kate rested her head against Joe's shoulder.

*

The mumbling of voices woke her and her eyes flickered. Paul wasn't snoozing beside her any more. Judging by the sounds coming from the kitchen, he was cleaning up. Kate and Joe seemed to have forgotten her, and she closed her eyes again, the better to hear. Joe was whispering.

'When I didn't have to see her, I could believe in her guilt. But it's much harder now. I keep telling myself she's guilty, but Kate, I'm not convinced she did it.'

'You can't say that now,' Kate replied. 'You're torturing yourself.'

'No. I'm torturing *her*. I feel like a bully. I keep insisting that it's her doing everything, that she's making up the home intrusions to get attention, or she's imagining them because her mental health isn't great. That's gaslighting, isn't it? Shit. I don't recognise myself. Maybe if I hadn't done that, she wouldn't be going out of her way to cause me problems now. I can't win.'

'Joe . . .'

'It's my fault. I closed the door on that part of my life even before the sentencing. I just wanted her locked up and out of sight because I thought that way I'd be able to move on. I know she was convicted, I know she admitted to what she'd done, but I'm not one hundred per cent certain. She swears it was the only way to get out and get to the truth. It's tearing me up. What if we were all wrong? What if by doing this we are pushing her back into psychosis?'

'We weren't wrong. And you have moved on. You have Sara and Maeve.'

He sighed. Sara peeked through her lashes. He was hunched over, and Kate's hand was resting lightly on his

240

back. 'It isn't the same. Sara is very different from Claudia. She's quite self-centred.'

'She's got a lot to live up to. It's hard for her.'

'But that's it. I don't think it is. I don't think Sara feels things the way other people do. I love her, but I've noticed that if it isn't about her, she isn't interested.'

'Oh, Joe. Listen, I know what you mean. I've noticed that too, but it doesn't mean she's a bad person, or can't be a great wife and mother. She's both those things. You hang on in there.'

Sara seethed with fury. How dare Kate defend her? She peeked again and saw Kate briefly touch Joe's knee. Fuck that. She made a soft grunting noise and shifted her shoulders. The atmosphere changed instantly. Joe and Kate stopped talking in whispers, Joe saying loudly, 'Time to go, I think. The wife's had it.'

He nudged Sara's foot with his, then stood up and held out his hand. She let him pull her up.

'You were out for the count.'

'A full stomach and a good red wine will do that.' She smiled sleepily at Kate. 'Thank you for a delicious dinner.'

'You're absolutely welcome.'

Paul came in and gave Joe a manly hug, while Sara picked up two coffee mugs and took them into the kitchen. She waited for Kate to follow her, then shut the door.

'I heard what you and Joe said about me just now.'

'Oh, Sara, I'm sorry. But you should have let us know you were awake.'

'Why do you behave like that?'

'Like what?'

'Wedging yourself into my marriage. Having private

little tête-à-têtes with my husband. Making me feel like an interloper. You've known him longer than me, but that does not give you ownership rights.'

Kate raised herself to her full height. A bulky woman, she could be quite intimidating. 'I assure you, that is not the case, and if you weren't so insecure, you'd understand.'

'I might be insecure, but you're jealous. I bet you were pissed off when Joe married me. You can't bear him not to need you, so you constantly undermine me. Well, I've put up with this shit long enough. You can back off and keep your nose out of our business, or once we've left Culloden Road, you won't find a welcome. I can do without your sort of friendship.'

'My sort of friendship?'

'That's right, Kate. You're friends with me because it's the price you have to pay to stay close to my husband.'

'Nice to know where I stand,' Kate said. 'I didn't realise you were brooding over all this. Perhaps you should have said something earlier. I didn't know there was this agenda. And if we're being honest, of course I befriended you for Joe's sake. I would have been a pretty cold person not to have done. You are my best friend's wife. In another world, if we had met at work or whatever, we probably wouldn't have been friends, but we met in circumstances where it was only right I made an effort. I enjoy your company and I thought you enjoyed mine. But you do what you like. As you say, Joe is your husband. I'd like very much to put this behind us and move on, but in the end it's up to you.'

She stalked out of the room, leaving the door open behind her so Sara could see her brushing off their argument, putting her arm around Paul's waist and saying something to make Joe grin. Sara gritted her teeth and walked into the hall, all smiles. She thanked Paul a little more profusely than Kate, then followed Joe into the night. She thought about the night ahead and her chest felt tight with anxiety.

Chapter 45

Friday 10 November

CLAUDIA

Claudia waits for Owen to leave for work, hoping for a glimpse of the family, but Anna doesn't come to the door to kiss him goodbye. Are they still pissed off with each other? Frances appears and goes into number 13, emerging half an hour later with Max on her hip, followed by Anna. Even from a distance, Claudia can see Anna's face is blotchy, her movements brittle. All is not well in Paradise. Perhaps the police interest has jolted her out of her complacency. If she has done something terrible of course she'll be in a state of fear. Claudia knows exactly what it's like in prison if you're believed to have hurt a child. Anna would never survive it. Claudia almost didn't; she still can't be certain she has.

Frances holds out her free arm, and Anna hesitates before she allows herself to be hugged. And her mother really does hug her, as if she never wants to let her go. Anna breaks away and Frances says something. Anna nods frigidly, then goes back inside. Frances stares at the closed door before letting herself into her own house.

Claudia's phone rings, making her jump.

'How dare you.'

It's Sara.

'I'm sorry?'

'After everything I've done for you, how could you go after us in such an underhand way? I would never have offered to help if I'd known you were going to twist what Joe and I have together just to take the focus off your own guilt. It's pathetic.'

'You only helped me because you wanted to keep an eye on me. You should have told me about the school; not left me to find out from Greg.'

'Your pet hack? You're deluded if you think he's on your side. Do you really think he's going to look out for you if you're recalled?'

'I haven't done anything. It's Greg's story, not mine.'

'As if you didn't have something to do with it. You've gone after Joe, and when you go after him, you go after me. I'm going to make life extremely difficult for you. Stupid bitch.' The line goes dead.

Claudia lets the silence envelop her, sitting absolutely still. After a few minutes, Frank pads over and jumps up onto her knee. She rubs the space between his ears and he purrs.

That afternoon, she has a video call with Dr Ellis. She doesn't mention the altercation with Sara. The baby cried again last night, so instead she tells him about that. He suggests she wrap up warm, get outside and walk; perhaps go to the river or the park and focus on the natural world. He's right. She has become lodged in her spiral of anxiety, spent a lot of time jumping out of her skin at every bump and creak, unable to sleep for more than an hour at a time. She has forgotten that the world is still turning. She'll walk to Kingston Cemetery and find Tilly's plaque. Perhaps there'll be some measure of peace to be found there.

She enters the cemetery through one of the smaller entrances, studies the map and doglegs along the foot-paths. There are grassy paths and places left to grow wild, birdsong and rustlings in the overgrown area. Apart from two gardeners chatting beside their van and a skinny young man strolling with his Jack Russell on a leash, his baby strapped to his front, she has the place to herself. She has a fantasy that when she finds the children's ceme-tery, Joe will be there; that they will stand by Tilly's plaque and remember their daughter together, perhaps even hold hands.

Joe isn't there. Of course he isn't. As she searches for the plaque, she reads inscriptions to lost babies and children and is nearly driven to tears by the legion of broken hearts. And then there it is, a square of granite at her feet. It reads: *Matilda Josephine Hartman, 'Tilly', born 8 March 2013. All our love*. She kneels, tucking her hair behind her ears. She's touched that Joe used *our*, not *my*, and there is no mention of death. Perhaps he isn't as certain as he says he is.

Many of the graves have little ornaments around them: a snow globe, a china teddy bear, a porcelain bell with Father Christmas's face on it, plastic windmills. A solitary helium balloon with *Happy Birthday!* in silver letters makes her particularly sad. She has nothing to put on Tilly's tiny patch, nothing in her bag except her phone, a pen, and a wallet with a little cash in it; nothing personal. She pulls her hair out of its ponytail, then digs in the ground with her fingers, tearing at the soil until she's created a small dip. She teases out hairs that have become trapped in the elastic and drops them in before covering them up. She presses her fingers into the soil to leave their imprint and then sits on a nearby bench and forces herself to call up memories of her daughter, her muscles creaking from lack of use because she's kept the images locked away for so long. She sees Tilly nose to nose with Joe, holding his ears, her concentration on her father fierce.

'Tilly.' Her voice is lost in the freezing mist.

She brushes the dirt from her hands as best she can. It doesn't matter what stupid ritual she carries out here; she will not accept that Tilly has gone for good, not without irrefutable proof.

Someone is guilty, and she's almost sure it's Anna, although discovering that Sara was at Lady Eden's has called her story into question. Claudia accepts Sara has a perfectly reasonable excuse for concealing the truth about her relationship with Joe; she was protecting his reputation. His self-appointed guardian. But what if there's a greater connection? She dismisses the thought. What possible reason could Sara have had for stealing her and Joe's baby? Even if she was in love with Joe, she wouldn't do that. As Greg so crassly put it: *If you want someone else's husband, you seduce them with your womanly wiles, you don't steal their child.*

She is shivering, her bones trembling beneath her skin, and she wishes she had worn gloves. She tugs the cashmere cuffs of her mother's cardigan out from under her coat sleeves and curls her fingers into them, then draws her feet up onto the bench and tucks her knees under her coat. She can feel the cold seeping in.

It all comes down to the same thing. Whichever of them abducted Tilly that afternoon, the threats have come from them. Greg's article will have shaken Anna as well as Sara, even without mentioning names. Both women stand to lose their husband, their child, their freedom. Terrified people make mistakes.

For Joe's sake, she hopes it was Anna who walked off with Tilly that day, not Sara. Whatever. Both women will surely be waiting in fear for Greg's follow-up and what it will reveal, whether guilty or not.

She imagines fifteen-year-old Anna Holt deciding that Claudia had to lose something precious to her, even if only for a few hours. She remembers what it was like to be fifteen, to have that raging hormonal anger, to lose any sense of reason, to be obsessed, fixated and misunderstood. And then somehow or other, everything had gone wrong. It wasn't a case of best-laid plans, it was a case of no plan at all.

Anna's life is on a settled trajectory, hitting the traditional milestones. But what if someone attempts to ruin everything for her? What then? If Claudia's theory is true, Anna watched while Claudia was blamed, vilified and incarcerated, stayed silent while she was branded the lowest of the low, a mother who had killed her own child. Even if Claudia is ultimately vindicated and her conviction quashed, it will be hard to come back from that. Nobody wants that whiff of evil in their lives.

Anna has felt safe for so long, she made the mistake of assuming she always would be, and failed to anticipate a scenario where Claudia was released early and creating waves. For the first time it occurs to Claudia that Anna, now she's a mother, must be able to feel what she put Claudia through. If she's guilty, then how can she sleep at night? But that is a big if, because Anna's guilt is not a settled thing.

If. If. If.

If she tries to explain this to the police, they'll send her back inside, and only her mother will object. To everyone else it'll be a case of good riddance.

The sky is dimming, twilight creeping in. Claudia looks up with a start. There's a child on one of the benches, a pale stone slab held each end by a stone rabbit. She's wearing a blue coat and white trainers and she's watching Claudia. Claudia looks around for the parents, but she can't see any adults. On impulse, she stands up, but as she approaches, the girl jumps off the bench and runs away. Claudia strides after her. Gripped by a stitch, she bends double, digging her fingers into the muscle above her right hip. When it fades, she unfolds herself and holds her hands out, sees smoke drifting from fingertips burning with cold and curls them into fists. She is hallucinating. She tells herself this over and over again, and after a while she hears birdsong and her mind settles. The child doesn't exist, never existed.

She retraces her steps to Tilly's plaque and drops exhausted and miserable onto the bench. What good is any of this doing? She's about to tear Joe's life apart, which will mean his little girl will suffer, and for what? It won't bring Tilly back. It won't make the pain go away. Claudia won't walk into a brand-new life, find a fulfilling job and form

249

new friendships, meet someone and have a relationship. None of that is for her.

Something hits the back of her hand, and she looks down as a snowflake melts. More float towards her, a loose flurry on the breeze. She watches fascinated as each flake dissolves into her lap. She picks one out of her hair, pinching it between her fingers as it turns to water.

It feels too much, too complicated. Why ruin everyone else's lives when her own isn't worth living? She's so tired, her body so heavy. The dream child has upset her because of her age, and the way she looked. Like she can imagine Tilly would have looked aged ten. She pulls her hood over her head and hunches over her knees. Would it be such a terrible thing if she lay down here and never woke? She's read somewhere that hypothermia is painless. When she told Joe that she'd kill herself if she didn't succeed, it had been an impulse, but as soon as the words were out of her mouth, she had known they were true, that it was the only way. She could join Tilly, be the mother she should have been and look after her in the next life the way she failed to in this one. All she has to do is let go. The man with the baby and the dog is nowhere to be seen, and the gardeners have driven away. There is no one else around and the wind is bitterly cold. A hot tear cools against her cheek. She closes her eyes.

Chapter 46

CLAUDIA

As Claudia begins to drift, her phone rings in her coat pocket. Her fingers are numb, and so clumsy that she drops it, and by the time she's fished it out of the icy dirt, it's rung out. She checks the call list. Greg.

'Hey,' he says when she calls him back. 'Are you all right?'

She starts to move, stamping her feet to get some life back into them. 'Fine. Why wouldn't I be?'

'No reason. I just had a weird feeling. Like someone walked over my grave.'

Claudia looks round and swallows. Her throat feels scratchy. 'I've heard from Sara. She's furious about the post, but I think it's more about the damage to Joe's reputation than anything else.'

'Joe couldn't speak for himself?'

'Evidently not.'

'What about Anna?'

'I haven't heard from her.'

'When do you want to go with part two? Monday?'

'No,' she says. 'Let's let them stew a little longer.' She needs time to think it through, to make sure she's doing the right thing, that it's worth it. She knows she'll piss him off if she says she's unsure, so she keeps quiet about her qualms.

'All right. I've got my boys for the weekend. I'll catch up with you on Monday. Just be careful.'

The snow swirls around Claudia, starburst flakes that no longer melt as they hit the ground, her feet sinking as she walks. She doesn't think there's an inch of her that's properly dry. She hunches her shoulders and presses on. The snow attaches itself to the fur lining of her hood and melted flakes trickle down her neck, catching in her clavicle. By the time she reaches Shires Close, she's having an out-of-body experience. She seems to float, as if she'd died amongst the graves and is now a ghost, haunting the places she knew as a child. She can't make up her mind whether to be thankful to Greg for snapping her out of it or not. She'd hoped for oblivion, only to be brought back to this.

At home, she will shut out the blizzard, switch on the lights and turn the heating up. She'll make herself a hot chocolate. At that point she starts imagining the underside of the kitchen table, the chair leg bars, and closes the image down. She is not doing that. She'll do what normal people do to distract themselves and watch television.

Shires Close is already covered in a layer of white. Garden paths sparkle under street lights, snow lounges along the branches of trees and smothers cars. The scene is so complete, so perfect, she can imagine she's under a globe. In the grass turning circle some of the younger residents are building a snowman, and she's about to smile when she realises the two teenagers helping them are her neighbours. They barely glance at her.

She is trembling so violently that she struggles to fit the key in the lock. In the kitchen, she cuts a slice of Cheddar, but after only two mouthfuls, a wave of nausea sends her stumbling to the sink. Sweat is pouring off her. She pulls out the drawer where Louisa keeps over-the-counter headache and cold remedies and pounces on the Lemon Flu Relief. She pours the powder into a mug, fills the kettle.

Clicks the switch.

Nothing happens. She tries it again, then sees that the plug has been pulled out of the socket. Her ears start to ring. She last used the kettle before she went to the cemetery, and she knows she didn't take the plug out, because it isn't something she does. She stands very still, listening, but the house is quiet.

This is Anna's doing. It has to be. Claudia lets herself out, crosses over to the Pembertons' house and rings the bell. When no one comes, she goes next door.

Frances yells, 'Can you get that, darling? It's only Anna.'

The door opens, and Patrick Holt greets her with a smile that instantly slips. Drawing his shoulders back, increasing the space he takes up, he looks as though he's prepared to protect his family from marauding Vikings rather than the pathetic specimen of humanity that Claudia presents.

'Yes?' he says.

When she was young, Claudia had adored Patrick, secretly preferring him to Robert. If they bumped into him, he always made an effort to speak to her, to ask her something she had to give more than a one-word answer to. And whatever answer she gave, he would look as though she was the most interesting creature in the world and she would glow under his approbation. Things are different now. She must be such a disappointment to him.

'Is Anna here?'

'She isn't, I'm afraid.' He starts to edge the door shut. Beyond him, the house looks warm and inviting.

Frances comes downstairs carrying the little boy wrapped in a towel. His cheeks are rosy, his blue eyes wide open. He tries to grab Frances's glasses, but she intercepts his hand, kissing his pudgy knuckles. Her smile vanishes when she sees Claudia, who is holding herself so rigid she thinks she might snap.

'Oh. I thought it would be Anna. What is it you want, Claudia?'

'Actually, I was looking for Anna, but could I have a word? It won't take long.' She lifts her chin before adding, 'It's important.'

'Not to me it isn't.'

Claudia doesn't move. Neither does Frances.

'Why don't I read Max his story?' Patrick suggests, reaching for his grandson.

Frances reluctantly hands him over. Snow gusts in, swirling around Claudia's feet before settling on the coir mat.

'You'd better come in.' Frances turns her back and marches into the kitchen. She pours herself a glass of red wine but doesn't offer Claudia one.

'Can I sit down?' Claudia feels as weak as a kitten.

Frances nods, and Claudia sinks onto a chair with relief. The kitchen is overheated and she's drowsy; only her increased heart rate keeps her alert.

'You've never liked me, have you?' she says.

'Was there something specific you wanted to say?'

'What happened after you left Miss Colville's memorial service?'

Frances looks at her blankly. 'What on earth has that got to do with anything?'

'A lot, since it was the day Tilly was abducted. Where did Anna go afterwards?'

'Anna? You're accusing Anna of taking Tilly?' She laughs like it's the funniest thing she's ever heard, but her eyes are like stones.

'I haven't accused her of anything. I'm asking you to account for her whereabouts that evening. Unless there's some reason you don't want to tell me.'

'Anna started to feel ill during the service, so I cancelled her babysitting, as you know. She spent the evening at home, in her bedroom.'

'But she didn't feel ill, did she? It was an excuse, because you were furious with me. I understand why you were angry, I understand why you shifted the blame for Megan's death from your own shoulders onto mine, but Anna was with you when you found out about that conversation. She would have held a grudge against me as well.'

'This is old news. I don't see how any of it's relevant.'

'What's relevant is your family's opinion of me even before that happened. I found a letter you wrote to my mother. It was an official letter, as a child psychiatrist. You talked to me after an incident that happened with Jason.'

Frances moves away from the counter and, after a second of indecision, sits down. She taps the table with her fingernails. 'You say I didn't like you, and that's perfectly true. You were a sly little girl who wasn't averse to being mean to Megan when no one was looking. And before you tell me I should have been aware of that, I had my own struggles. I'd had three miscarriages and was barely holding it together. But I don't suppose you knew that.'

Claudia is burning up. She wipes her brow. 'No, I didn't.'

'You made Megan feel small when she was having a difficult time. She killed herself two hours after that conversation with you.'

'But there had to be something there already. I said the wrong thing at the wrong time and I'm sorry for that, but the rest of it . . . well, that wasn't down to me, was it, Frances? How good a psychiatrist were you if you didn't recognise depression in your own daughter? How good a mother were you?'

Frances draws herself up like a snake ready to strike, but Patrick pops his head round the door and she leaves the words unspoken. The silent vitriol streaming from her whips round Claudia like the cold wind had earlier.

'I don't know what's keeping Anna,' Patrick says. 'I've tried to call her mobile, but she's not picking up.'

'I'm sure she'll be back any minute,' Frances says impatiently.

'I've put Max down in the travel cot. He can always stay the night here if they don't want to move him.' He closes the door quietly.

'Did you ever discuss the incident with Jason in front of Anna?' Claudia asks.

'Of course not. Anna wasn't even born when it happened.'

'No, she wasn't. But when she was a baby, I was never left alone with her. When I was a teenager, I was never asked to babysit. Did you ever talk about it to Patrick?'

'It's extremely unlikely. I wouldn't be so unprofessional.'

'But hypothetically. Anna may have picked up on your attitude over the years. She would have been predisposed to distrust me, possibly even fear me, if she'd overheard you bitching about me.'

Frances presses the flats of her hands down on the tabletop. 'I know what you're implying, but you're wrong.'

'Your daughter is aware of my history. If you didn't talk about me, others in the close probably did. My anger issues at school, those were well known.'

'You had lost your father in an accident and your mother was hospitalised for weeks. That would have had a lasting effect.'

'And you understood that because it was your job to. But you still disliked and judged me.'

The doorbell rings and Frances jumps up. 'Thank goodness.'

Claudia takes the hint and follows her out of the kitchen. Patrick reaches the door first, but it isn't Anna, it's Owen.

'The wife with you?' he asks, looking beyond Patrick and clocking Claudia. He frowns. 'What's she doing here?'

'She's leaving. Haven't you heard from Anna?'

'No. I called her on my way home, but her phone went straight to voicemail. Where's the little man?'

'In the spare bedroom. He might be asleep by now. I'm sure she'll be back any minute.'

Claudia tries to pass Patrick, but Owen gets in her way. There's something overly macho about him: a cock puffing his chest out.

'You any closer to moving yet?' he asks.

She is in no mood to be apologetic. 'None of your business.'

Owen steps to one side and Claudia stalks out, and it occurs to her that even the most pristine snow can't conceal the dirt underneath for long.

Chapter 47

CLAUDIA

Claudia shoves the kettle plug back into the socket. She puts the chain on the front door, rams the top and bottom bolts into their catches and goes up to bed, lying awake for a long time, staring into the darkness, her fingers on the knife under her pillow.

She wakes to the sound of car doors closing. Blue lights pulse through the curtains. She feels rough, and her pillowcase and the edge of the duvet cover are soaked with sweat. She drags herself to the window and pulls the curtains. A squad car is parked outside Anna's house; two officers leave footprints in the snow. Owen opens the front door, and light floods out before he closes it behind the officers. She glances at the time. It's a quarter past eleven. Ten minutes later, Frances and Patrick come out of number 12 and enter Anna's house.

She throws the damp pillow onto the floor and plumps the rest up against the headboard. She sinks back against them, hugging her knees. The snow is still falling, but it's lighter, less dramatic. She closes her eyes and allows herself to drift.

When the knock comes, she isn't ready. It never

occurred to her that the police might want to speak to her. She becomes tangled in the duvet getting out of bed, catches her foot in its buttoned opening and hits the floor. She scrambles up and throws on a dressing gown.

Downstairs, her wet boots are still lying cock-eyed where they landed, next to the dark, damp pile of her coat. She slides open the bolts but leaves the chain on before she pulls the latch.

'It's me, Mrs Hartman. Detective Sergeant Ward. Sorry to alarm you. Can I come in?'

She closes the door and undoes the chain. 'What's happened?' Her throat sears.

Instead of answering, he clumps his feet on the doormat, knocking snow off his shoes. Claudia leads him into the kitchen, takes the kettle off its stand and fills it. It's such an effort to speak, she holds it up, raising her eyebrows. Frank looks up at Ward, then lowers his head and closes his eyes.

'Nothing for me, thanks.'

Claudia follows his curious gaze as he takes stock of the mess: the bottles clustered together like penguins, the overflowing bin, the dirty spatters on the floor. She's too ill to care.

'How well do you know the owners of number 13?'

'I know Anna,' she croaks. 'I've seen her husband, but we haven't been introduced.' She feels Owen's breath on her face, the snide tone of his voice. *You any closer to moving yet?*

'When was the last time you saw Mrs Pemberton?'

'This morning, about nine.' She swallows. 'She came out of the house with her mother.'

'Did you speak to her?'

260

'No. I was inside.'

'What was she wearing?'

Claudia closes her eyes and concentrates. 'Grey coat. Pale blue scarf. That's all I can remember.' She hesitates. He'll find out soon enough, so there's no point lying. 'I bumped into her outside Overhill School on Thursday, though.' A fit of coughing causes tears to squeeze from her eyes.

'Was that before or after you paid a visit to your ex-husband?'

'Before.'

'What time was this?'

'About ten to one. The bell went after I went in.'

'Bit risky, wasn't it? When you could be sent back inside?'

She doesn't answer, because there isn't any point. She's more worried that he'll read her convulsive trembling as a sign of a guilty conscience.

'How did Mrs Pemberton seem?'

'She was upset.' She remembers the look on Anna's face when she told her about Sara. Her mind swiftly calculating the double betrayal. She had been made a fool of by both Joe and Sara. Should she mention what Greg had uncovered? Ward was looking at her enquiringly. No. Not yet. He would only slap her down.

'Why do you think that was?' he asks.

She gives him a look. 'Why are you asking me to speculate?'

'Did you have a conversation with her, Claudia?'

'Not really. She just asked me what I was doing with Greg Davies.'

261

'The journalist who's about to run a scoop on your case.' The detective writes something in his notebook, then looks up. 'What *are* you doing with him?'

'He's the only person who doesn't treat me like a pariah.'

'How did you respond to Anna?'

'I didn't feel I needed to. She and her family have been unpleasant since I moved in here.'

'Bit of a coincidence, wasn't it? Both of you visiting Joe.'

'I suppose it was.'

Ward looks sceptical. 'Frances Holt, Anna's mother—'

'I know who she is.'

'She says you've been harassing them. According to her, you came storming round earlier this evening and accused Anna of stealing your baby.'

'I didn't *storm* round, and I didn't accuse Anna. I politely asked Frances where Anna had been when Tilly was stolen.'

'You were granted parole because you admitted guilt. You're on shaky ground.'

'I'm well aware of that.'

She tries to sustain eye contact, to show mettle, to give him a look that says, *What of it?* But she thinks she's going to collapse. She grabs a chair before her knees give out.

'Are you all right?'

'Not really.'

'I won't keep you much longer.' He waits while she sits down. 'What can you tell me about Owen and Anna Pemberton's relationship?'

'I don't know anything about it, except that I heard them having a row on fireworks night, then Owen left in his car.'

'What was the row about?'

'I've no idea, I only heard raised voices.' She swallows painfully, her hand on her throat.

'Thank you. That's very useful.' He goes to the tap and runs a glass of water for her. 'Here. This might help. Are you able to talk me through your movements earlier today?'

She drinks some of the water. 'I had a video call with my psychiatrist in the morning, and after that I went to Kingston Cemetery. There's a plaque in memory of my daughter there. I wanted to visit it. It's as close as I can get until she's found.'

He leaves a respectful pause before he asks his next question.

'What time would that have been?'

'Between two and four thirty.'

He raises his eyebrows. 'I'm not surprised you're sick. Why did you stay so long? It's arctic out there.'

'I don't know.' She glances at him, hoping he'll understand. 'I thought about dying... You know, falling asleep and not waking up.'

'I'm sorry. You must be going through hell.' He gazes back at her, curious. 'I'm glad you changed your mind.' He snaps his notebook shut. 'Just one last thing, then I'll let you be. What was the nature of your ex-husband's relationship with Anna around the time Tilly went missing?'

Claudia feels the skin on the back of her neck prickle. 'She was our babysitter.'

'Was he ever alone with her?'

'He drove her home once or twice. Not regularly. I know what you're implying, Detective, but Anna was not exactly ... well, she wasn't what she's like now. She was quite affected and rather insecure. The type who's always asking what someone's said about them. It's only the truth.'

'Are you saying that if she had been less affected and less insecure, Joe might have been interested? Like he was interested in you?'

Despite everything, she does not want Joe's reputation blackened, not unless she's absolutely sure, and she isn't. 'No. Just because he and I met when I was sixteen does not mean he was interested in young girls. We fell in love. That's very different.'

It *was* different. Joe had waited for her. She hangs on to that like a drowning man hangs on to a piece of disintegrating driftwood, knowing that it's only a matter of time.

'Look, it's late, I'm not well, so if you don't have any more questions, I'd like to go back to bed.'

'Of course.' Ward moves towards the door. 'Have a good night's sleep, Mrs Hartman. And promise me you'll talk to someone about the suicidal thoughts.'

When, at 2.17 a.m., the baby starts to cry, she rolls onto her back and stares at the ceiling. After a while, she gets up and opens the door. She can feel the creep of anxiety, her racing pulse, the ache around her diaphragm, the lead forming in her legs, but she won't let it overwhelm her. There is no baby. Like this afternoon, in the cemetery, this is a hallucination, albeit an audible one. When it stops, she drags in a huge breath and closes the bedroom door. She's shivering violently as she gets back into bed and pulls the duvet over her. Perhaps when she finds out the truth, it will stop for good.

Chapter 48

Saturday 11 November

CLAUDIA

Claudia comes downstairs at six, dragging the duvet with her. She curls up on the sofa. Frank jumps up beside her and pours himself against her thigh. She strokes him absently, still brooding on her conversation with the detective. The one thing she's clung to all these years is that what she and Joe felt for each other was true and good. If she doesn't have that, then the frame her life is hinged on is warped, and nothing is as she thought it was.

She sighs with frustration. Why can't she look at this full on; why does she feel like she's peeking at it through her fingers like a terrified child watching *Doctor Who*? She needs to ask the question, look Joe in the eye and say, 'Did you touch our babysitter?' If he did, that might go some way to explain Anna's extreme behaviour.

She's reached the point where taking a risk is the only way to move this sluggish juggernaut forward. Joe is likely to be at home on a Saturday morning. She will ask him straight out and gauge his reaction, because she knows every tic, every muscle, every movement of his mouth. He won't fool her. Not again.

If she goes, she will be playing into Sara's hands, because Sara would like nothing better than for Claudia to be recalled to prison and won't give her another chance. It will mean long hours waiting in a cell, visits from lawyers and the probation officer whose sympathy she's made zero attempt to elicit. Then the ride back to the prison, the derision of guards and inmates. The spittle in her food, the covert assaults and overt hostility.

She can't go back. Can she? It has to be worth it. The provocative teaser Greg wrote has put Joe and Sara on their guard. But Joe might be anxious to keep her sweet, to persuade her to pull the second part. He has to be forced to confront his own behaviour and stop hiding behind women.

She tries to doze off on the sofa, but an hour passes and she's still awake, the pain in her throat monstrous. She drags herself up and goes to the cupboard where Robert keeps his spirits. She gargles a mouthful of expensive Macallan, anaesthetising the pain before swallowing. It burns like hell, but she pours another finger and it does the trick: she sleeps for three hours solidly. When she wakes up, she comes to a decision. She has a Lemon Flu Relief and gargles with more of Robert's precious Scotch.

Bundled in warm clothes, wearing Louisa's sheepskin-lined boots, Claudia leaves the house. The snow has crisped to ice on the footpath and she almost goes flying. As she rights herself, she notices that the snowman has acquired props overnight. She tilts her head, trying to work it out, and gasps in dismay.

On its front, a chrysalis-shaped bulge has raisin eyes and a carrot-disc mouth. A snow baby. A spade leans against it, and to her feverish imagination it looks as if it's been brought along to dig a grave. She marches over, grabs the spade and destroys the snowman. Then she walks quickly away, exhausted by the exertion, hoping no one saw.

On the bus, she draws disapproving stares from some passengers, while others avert their gaze. She's trying not to cough, gives up and bunches her scarf over her mouth. Her eyes stream. Someone tuts, memories of the pandemic still raw.

Claudia loiters behind a van on the other side of Culloden Road. She's about to cross over and knock when Sara comes out and dumps two bags into the boot of her car. She has her hand on the door to the boot, ready to close it, when her phone rings.

'Hi, darling. Did you forget something? Okay. Hang on. I'll see if it's in the kitchen.' She turns and goes back into the house.

So, Joe isn't home.

Claudia is turning to go when she realises Sara hasn't closed the front door properly. She eyes it cautiously. She's been looking for opportunities, hasn't she? It would be wrong to ignore the first decent one she's been given. She hesitates, then steps off the kerb and crosses the road, glancing into Sara's car as she slides between it and the car behind. The bags are stuffed with clothes. Something snags, but there's no time to linger.

Standing in the doorway, she can hear Sara's voice.

'Found it. Do you want me to open it? . . . Okay. Hang on a mo.'

Entering the house is like ripping the plaster off an open sore. Claudia slips off the snow-encrusted boots and, holding onto them, darts upstairs and shuts herself in Joe's study, and is immediately disorientated. The room is stuffy and dark, and smells of baby. Her eyes slowly adjust to the light. Maeve is standing up in her cot, clutching the wooden bars, her hair tousled. Transfixed, Claudia steps towards her. Maeve holds out a hand and Claudia presses her palm lightly against it.

A sound makes her lurch away. Sara is coming upstairs. The room is small and there is nowhere to hide. Claudia braces for an explosion. Maeve burbles excitedly; she's heard her mother's step.

Chapter 49

SARA

'Mummy's here.' Sara pushed the bedroom door, jumping out of her skin when the doorbell rang and a deep voice called out.

'Hello!'

'Hold on, sweetie.' She ran back downstairs to answer it. The door was wide open, a man standing outside on the tessellated path. He had solemn eyes. In his black overcoat and scarf, he could have been a funeral director.

'Can I help you?'

He held up his ID. 'Sara Hartman?'

'Yes, that's me.'

'My name is Detective Sergeant Simon Ward. I'm concerned about the whereabouts of a friend of yours and wondered if you'd seen her. Anna Pemberton? Have you spoken to her recently?'

'Anna? I saw her on Thursday. She came here.'

'What time would that have been?'

'Oh, I don't know. Early afternoon, because I'd had lunch. Two o'clock maybe? Half past at the latest.'

'What kind of mood was she in?'

Sara's forehead buckled. 'I don't know her very well, but I thought she seemed pensive.'

'Did she mention any difficulties at home? Strained relations between her and her husband, perhaps?'

'No, but it wouldn't surprise me. He was obnoxious to Joe, my husband, when we were round at theirs on fireworks night. But he was drunk, and I don't think he meant any of it. Anna was furious.'

Ward made a note. 'That's very interesting. Thank you. Why was Mr Pemberton being obnoxious, do you think?'

'I'm not sure. He hadn't met Joe before, and I think it was just a man thing. They're very different. Owen's a bit pleased with himself to be honest, and Joe was tired. I'm sorry I can't tell you anything else. We don't know them very well.' She paused. 'What do you mean, Anna's whereabouts? Is she missing?'

'She hasn't been seen since yesterday morning, and her family are concerned for her safety, as am I.'

'Oh my God. Poor Owen, he must be frantic. And her parents. Sorry, don't stand out there in the cold. Come in.' She ushered him through the door and into the kitchen.

'Is your husband here? Perhaps I could have a chat with him too.'

'No, he's out.' He had gone to meet Michael Chancellor. Upstairs, Maeve was bleating. 'Give me one minute, I need to get my little one out of her cot before she screams the house down.'

'No hurry. You do what you have to, Mrs Hartman.'

Sara pulled the curtains and raised the blackout blind. There was a distinct smell of Lemon Flu Relief in the room. Joe must have had one before he went to meet Michael, though he hadn't mentioned feeling unwell. He was under so much strain. She would cook him something lovely and nourishing for supper. Comfort food. She could do with some of that herself. She sniffed at the air and frowned, then carried Maeve into her bedroom. She could smell it here too, although it was much fainter. She stood very still, her skin prickling. Then she swore under her breath and left the room, calling out as she ran downstairs.

'I just need to close the car boot.'

Without waiting for an answer, she hurried into the street, heart thumping. The bags were as she'd left them. Shifting Maeve to her hip, she slammed the door down.

She found the detective hovering in the kitchen, flicking through a pile of Joe's papers. He dropped his hand when Sara coughed.

'I'm sorry about the chaos,' she said. 'We're moving house and I've been turning out cupboards. In fact, I was just on my way to a charity shop with a load of clothes.'

'I won't keep you long.'

She lifted the kettle off its stand. DS Ward took it from her.

'Why don't I do that? You see to your baby.'

'Thanks so much. The mugs are in the cupboard above, and there's tea, herbal and instant coffee in those jars.'

She took a pint of milk from the fridge, poured some into a beaker for Maeve and gave it to her. Maeve sucked greedily. When her daughter was content, Sara felt less harassed, more in control. This was her house, her territory. She could handle herself.

'Did Owen tell you about me?' she said over her shoulder.

'He mentioned you and your husband, yes. I'm here

because Mrs Pemberton's phone records show that she called your number on Friday.'

Sara felt something squirm in the pit of her stomach. She smiled at the detective. 'Yes, that's right. She did. It was just baby chat. God, I can't believe she's missing. That's horrific.'

He narrowed his eyes. 'Can you remember more detail about what was said? It's all helpful.'

She ran her tongue over her lips. 'Let me see. To be honest, I was a bit distracted. Maeve was whining. Anna said she'd been doing Owen's bookkeeping and that between that and her little boy, it was doing her head in. I sympathised.'

'Did you make an arrangement?' He cocked his head. 'I know when my wife gets on the phone to one of her friends, they usually finish up by agreeing to meet for a coffee or something like that.'

Sara put Maeve down on the floor to avoid looking at him. 'We made some vague plans. Nothing concrete. It's hard for me at the moment. I have to be here for Joe. He's been really rattled by Claudia.'

'I understand. Tell me about your relationship with Mrs Pemberton.'

Would the man never let up? She spoke patiently. 'I've only recently met her, but our little ones are the same age, so obviously we have plenty in common. Joe and I have been round to theirs once, after the fireworks, as I said, and I've had a cup of tea with her. And that's it. I'm sure she has better friends than me to talk to if she needs a friendly ear.'

Maeve toddled across the kitchen, swinging her

beaker, spraying droplets of milk across DS Ward's legs. Sara jumped up and prised the cup out of her hand.

'Sorry.' She could tell the poor man was fastidious by the tension in his jaw as he wiped the milk off his trousers.

'Not a problem.'

She took a clean tea towel out of the drawer, ran it under the tap and squeezed it out. 'Here, use this.'

While he dabbed at his trouser legs, DS Ward said, 'Did Mrs Pemberton say anything that surprised or worried you?'

Sara hauled Maeve onto her knee. 'No, not at all. It was just baby chat.'

'Earlier you said she was pensive?'

'Yes, but like I say, I don't know her particularly well. She did seem quiet, but there could have been any number of reasons for that. She could have had a bad night with Max. He's teething.'

Ward put the cloth down and made a note. 'Right, thank you for your time, Mrs Hartman.' He pulled a card out of his top pocket and handed it to her. 'If you think of anything else, or if Mrs Pemberton gets in touch, could you call me immediately?'

'Of course.'

'Before I leave you in peace, have you had any trouble with Claudia Hartman since her release?'

'A bit. She has a journalist in her pocket.'

'He made some interesting remarks in that piece of his,' Ward said.

Sara took a breath. Control the narrative, Paul had said. 'He was referring to the fact that I was taught by Joe for a short time.' She looked into his eyes steadily. 'There

273

was nothing going on. For one thing, he was involved with Claudia. I met him again years later, quite by chance, and we fell in love. But the press will twist that for sensation. Joe and I are seeking advice – that's where he is now; with his lawyer – and we'll just have to deal with whatever she flings at us. This has nothing to do with Anna Pemberton. It's an entirely separate issue.'

Chapter 50

CLAUDIA

Claudia steps out of Sara's wardrobe when the front door closes. She is overcome by a fit of coughing that rocks her so hard she can feel her bones rattling. When it's over she moves to the window and is just in time to see Sara's car turn the corner. She should leave, but being alone in her old home, the temptation to poke around is too much. Sara has secrets, and if Sara does, then it's possible Joe does too.

She searches the bedroom, trying not to be distracted by the memories it brings. At least they bought a new bed. To hide inside the wardrobe she'd first had to move shoeboxes to make space to stand. Now she opens each one. Disappointingly, they all contain shoes. She steps back and contemplates the cupboards above before moving the chair over from Sara's dressing table.

Inside she finds a hat made of straw, the kind you buy on holiday, and a well-loved teddy bear with a bald patch on his tummy where he must have been nuzzled by a child. Sara is sentimental, then. There are photo albums containing snaps of Sara growing up, and her wedding album.

Claudia can't resist taking a peek. Standing outside the registry office, Sara looks beautiful, her curvaceous figure complemented by a dress with a fitted lace top and flared net skirt that reaches her ankles. Her hair is caught up by a floral coronet, with a stray lock artfully drifting across her cheek. She is beaming, alight with a love tinged with triumph. She has her man. Joe's smile is broad as he gazes at his new wife, but examining the familiar details of his face, Claudia tells herself he's playing a part. He more than anyone would have known that happy-ever-after isn't guaranteed. He wouldn't have wanted Sara to sense his cynicism. She remembers her own wedding, looking up into his face and seeing the pure joy, the light in his eyes, the smile he couldn't contain. That's missing in this photograph, and she allows herself her own momentary triumph.

She and Joe were married in church and had their reception at the golf club where Robert is a member. They'd argued for something quieter, less public, but Louisa had insisted. She said if they kept it low-key, people would say they were ashamed. They needed to hold their heads up if they were going to rise above the gossip and innuendo. She had been right. At the wedding, no one mentioned their history, and once Tilly was born, it seemed as though everyone had forgotten that Mrs Hartman had once been Joe's pupil. They only remembered it again when everything went wrong.

She snaps the album shut and replaces it, then reaches to the back of the cupboard and pulls a tube towards her. The Lady Eden's school photograph. She teases it out, unrolls it on the floor and searches for Sara. She finds her in the fourth row. How could she have missed her?

Because she hadn't been looking for her. She'd only been interested in Joe. And Megan Holt.

Sara and Megan are sitting nowhere near each other,

but that means nothing. They still could have been friends. Could Joe have asked Sara to help him out with Megan? From what she's seen of Sara, it's plausible. She remembers how distressed Joe had been, a young man at the beginning of his teaching career, when Megan Holt's harmless adoration had become toxic. And then Megan died. It was a tragedy, but it meant the threat had gone away.

Horrified at the turn her thoughts have taken, she rolls the photograph, returns it to its container and shoves it into the back of the wardrobe. It hadn't been Joe's fault any more than it had been hers. Feeling around, she finds an envelope. She shakes it, and Miss Colville's order of service slides out. Claudia feels a bolt of excitement. Sara was there that day as well. On the front there's a photograph of the head teacher, with her icy smile and her thick grey hair sprayed into its familiar bouffant style. She still makes Claudia shudder. On the back, below the lyrics to 'Abide With Me', someone has scrawled a phone number and a message.

Great to see you again. Give me a call. Jenny.

On impulse, she pulls out her phone and calls the number.

'Yes?'

'Is this Jenny?'

'Where are you calling from?'

'This isn't a cold call. I'm calling about Sara ...' She hesitates. What had Greg said her surname was? 'Sara Massey. You were at Lady Eden's together, I understand.'

'Yes, I knew Sara.' Her voice is friendlier. 'What's this about?'

'I was a pupil there too. A couple of years above you.'

'How did you get my number?'

'You wrote it down on Miss Colville's order of service.'

There's a long pause. 'You haven't told me who you are.'

Claudia takes a deep breath. 'My name is Claudia Hartman. Sara is married to my ex-husband. I need to know what you talked about when you met her.'

'I'm sorry, but this is outrageous. How dare you call me and demand information about my friends.'

'So you are friends with her?'

Jenny disconnects, and when Claudia tries to call back, she finds she's been blocked. She could kick herself. She should have waited and thought this through. She's wasted an opportunity.

She slips the order of service into her bag, then puts everything else back as close to where she found it as possible and moves into the spare room. This is where Tilly used to sleep. It seems odd that Joe swapped the rooms, considering their relative sizes, but perhaps he couldn't bear the thought of the new baby sleeping with the ghost of her predecessor. His guitar is in here, propped in the corner, and she can't resist. She picks it up and strums a note. She used to love listening to him, when they were happy, but he had played it a lot in the weeks leading up to her trial, and in the end she'd thought she might go mad if he didn't stop. She leans it back against the wall and turns to the window.

The garden isn't as well kept as it used to be, and some old friends have gone. The cherry tree has been cut down, along with the rose that clambered through it. In spring, the pink blossom and yellow rosebuds against a blue sky had been exquisite. There's new trellising, the rough pine still orange, with an immature clematis trained up it; a small plastic slide and a covered sandpit. She moves away and tips her head up. If she ignores the new furniture and the different colours on the walls and fixes her gaze on the familiar cracks in the ceiling, she can almost pretend 26 Culloden Road is still her home, that Tilly is asleep behind her in her cot, her little panda sitting in the corner. That her world never fell apart.

Her nose is streaming. She takes an already soggy tissue out of her pocket and blows into it. Joe's desk drawer is a muddle of envelopes and old invoices, receipts and blocks of Post-it notes, pens and paper clips. Beneath it the cabinet is stuffed with suspension files thick with folders, labels in Joe's handwriting in their clear plastic tabs.

Claudia shuts down her emotions and goes through them. One contains passports, birth and marriage certificates; another documents to do with the sale of the house. There are three files stuffed with papers and newspaper clippings about Tilly's disappearance and Claudia's court case. She can hardly bring herself to look at those, let alone touch them, but she forces herself to do it and finds nothing she hasn't seen before. Other files contain financial matters, printed-out emails between him and Claudia's parents, paperwork for his mother's estate.

She pulls up a file labelled *Miscellaneous* and unfolds it on the desk. There are photographs of Tilly, a birthday card to Joe. Claudia remembers making it, pressing Tilly's tiny hand into the blue paint and then onto the white card, Tilly smearing the blue all over herself, her mother and the kitchen table. She puts it down, flicks through sheet after sheet, then she picks up a strip of photos taken in a booth and her breath shortens.

Anna Holt stares provocatively from the frame. Incongruously, she is wearing make-up with her school uniform. Why does Joe have this? She turns it over, checking the back for a message, but there's nothing.

She has to go. Sara could be back any minute. She slips the photographs back into the file and closes the cabinet.

She puts her boots back on and lets herself out, hood pulled down so low it covers her entire forehead, her coat collar flipped up. She thinks she's going to vomit and crushes her fist against her mouth.

Chapter 51

SARA

DS Ward returned in the early evening to speak to Joe. Sara asked him to wait in the front room. Joe was in the bathroom playing boats with Maeve, sleeves rolled up to reveal hairy forearms. Maeve was splitting her sides laughing as she tried to sink the plastic boats.

'Detective Ward's downstairs. He wants to talk to you. I'll take over.'

'Maeve's ready to get out. I've washed her hair.'

'I know. I heard the hullabaloo.'

'Best get it over with.'

'How are you feeling?'

'I'm fine. Why?'

'I thought you took a Lemon Flu Relief this morning.'

'Nope.'

Sara felt a prickle of unease.

Joe stood and she took his place. Maeve pulled herself up, so Sara grabbed her rosy-cheeked baby before she could slip, scooped her out of the sudsy water and wrapped her in a towel. She took her into her bedroom, got her into a nappy and a babygro and put her in her cot with a couple of toys and a fabric book.

'Be good, sweetie. I'll read to you in a minute. Mummy promises.'

Maeve looked at her with huge mournful eyes and opened her mouth, her chin wobbling. 'Na-na!'

Sara backed out and pulled the door to. She crept downstairs and stood listening from the hall, straining to tune in to the different voices. Joe couldn't help speaking clearly; it was part of the job. Less so the DS. She debated for a second, then went and stood right next to the door. She could hear clearly now.

'What did you talk about?' the detective asked.

'We discussed career options for her. I wanted to help. She's a friend of my wife's.'

'According to Mrs Pemberton's phone records, you exchanged four WhatsApp messages and you telephoned her. Why was there so much communication between the two of you?'

Sara didn't like the way he said *the two of you*, imbuing the phrase with innuendo. From the tone of his reply, Joe didn't much like it either. Had the journalist's scrap of non-news damaged him already? Even though it was vague, readers would pick up on the not-so-subtle implication that Joe couldn't be trusted with his teenage pupils.

'If you read the messages, you'd see we were just trying to fix a time,' Joe said. 'Making time at short notice is extremely difficult. My diary is packed. I have a raft of meetings every day, and in between those I squeeze in a couple of classes. I also factor in time to return calls from parents and to walk round the school during breaks so anyone who wants to speak to me can do so; particularly students who would shy away from knocking on my office door.'

'And yet you did make time for Mrs Pemberton, and then for your ex-wife.'

'Claudia turned up out of the blue. I didn't want a scene, so I took her into an empty classroom and had a quick chat, which your officers interrupted.'

'Busy day.' There was no mistaking the frostiness.

'It always is.'

'Can you describe Mrs Pemberton's mood?'

In the brief silence, Sara imagines Joe running his hand across his mouth.

'She was energetic and upbeat.'

'Your ex-wife says Anna was crying when she left the school.'

'I don't know anything about that, but then she was selling herself, so if she was angry or upset, she would have concealed it.'

'You didn't say anything to cause that upset?'

'Like what?' Joe was becoming defensive. Sara clenched her fists, willing him to ride it out. He understood the value of staying calm in a crisis. 'I barely know the woman.'

'Really? In spite of her attending Overhill and baby-sitting for you?'

'That was years ago.' Joe's voice was cold.

Maeve was crying. Sara closed her eyes and gritted her teeth. A few minutes more. She needed to listen to this.

To her relief, Joe tempered his tone. 'She seemed a nice enough kid.'

'How often did you drive her home after babysitting sessions?'

'I know what you're implying, officer, and the answer is rarely.'

'Why didn't you use someone who lived closer?'

'We did. We often used a neighbour's au pair. If she wasn't available, we used Anna because my ex-wife knew the family. We trusted her, Tilly adored her, and she adored Tilly. Sometimes it's worth paying a little more for peace of mind.'

'I'm sure it is. So there's nothing else you can tell me about Mrs Pemberton?'

'No.'

'Why were you delayed on the evening your daughter was abducted? I understand you were expected for an early supper at the home of Kate and Paul Shaw, but you phoned your wife to tell her you'd have to meet them at the theatre.'

'I don't understand; I thought we were talking about Anna's disappearance. That has nothing to do with what happened ten years ago.'

'We'll be the judge of that, Joe.'

Sara winced. There was such disrespect in the use of Joe's Christian name.

'I don't remember. I expect some emergency cropped up at the school. It often did. Staff and parents are a demanding bunch. I'll ask my PA if she remembers.'

'Well, let me know. Thank you for your time. You've been very helpful.'

Sara ran upstairs. Maeve was choking on her tears, her face red and wet. Sara scooped her up and held her tight, talking nonsense as she reached for a picture book from the shelf. She made herself comfortable on the little armchair, holding Maeve in the crook of her arm, the book with her hand, flipping it open with her thumb.

'Shall we see the owl?' she cooed.

Maeve bashed the book out of her hand and Sara left it lying on the floor, splayed open. She stood Maeve on her lap, hands under her armpits.

'I'm sorry, baby. I really am.'

She could hear them in the hall, voices polite but restrained, the front door closing, the brief, telling pause before Joe came up to find them. Maeve reached for her father and he took her. She burrowed into his jumper.

'What did they want?'

'To know about the meeting with Anna.' He yawned. 'I honestly don't know what's going on. I don't understand how life has become so complicated.'

'Nor me.' She looked him in the eye. 'Four WhatsApp messages and a phone call? It does seem over the top.'

'You were listening?'

She shrugged.

Joe shifted Maeve to his hip and heaved a sigh. 'There was nothing unusual about it. Anna sent me a message, we went to and fro trying to fix a time, and then I thought, sod it, it's easier to have a conversation. I called her and we worked it out. The police know there was nothing weird about the messages. You can see them if you like. I'll get my phone.'

'No, don't. I don't need to. I'm sorry. I'm just tired and pissed off.'

'You're not the only one. I'll get this one to bed, shall I?'

Sara left them and went downstairs. She caught her reflection in the darkened French windows, her face ghostly pale. Unnerved, she drew the curtains and looked around, a pit in her stomach. Change was coming.

She thought about Joe, about what made him tick. He had a gift for people-pleasing. He made others feel as though they were special to him and implied that he felt more himself when he was with them. She had been drawn into that beguiling narrative years ago at Lady Eden's. He'd needed her help with the Megan situation. Not that he'd asked for it; he'd merely confided in her when he was at his wits' end, and she'd lifted the problem off his shoulders and onto her own, and had felt so mature, almost older than him. The delight she'd felt in being needed was seductive, but it had led all the way to this.

When Megan finally caved in and admitted that she'd made it up, Joe had sought Sara out. He'd cupped her cheeks in his hands, looked deep into her eyes and told her he'd never known a girl her age to be so wise. She'd thought he was going to kiss her, had even raised her chin and parted her lips, but he had twisted a lock of hair behind her ear and moved away. Even so, that contact had been enough to nourish a fantasy that sustained her for years; those warm, long-fingered hands against her skin, the idea that he had touched her involuntarily, that his subconscious had made him lift his hands to her face. She convinced herself he'd fought the urge to kiss her because he was a decent man. He had written that note to her, that precious note that she had been forced by Anna's snooping to burn.

She sighed. But then Megan had taken her own life and it was partly Sara's fault. Whether her story was true or not, and Sara was convinced it wasn't, she had put unfair pressure on a vulnerable girl.

You imagined it, Megan, because you fancy him.

Mr Hartman wouldn't do that, Megan.

You're not his type, Megan.

I'm sorry, but you have to face it, Megan, you're just not pretty or interesting enough.

When Sara's mother told her she had given notice on the flat and they were moving to Bristol, Sara had been relieved to have the decision to leave Lady Eden's taken out of her hands. The thought of going back in September was too much, even though she had kept her brief friendship with Megan Holt a secret. She had no one to confide in, because the consequences of persuading an unhappy teenager that she'd imagined Mr Hartman making a pass at her, even though she definitely *had* imagined it, had been so shocking, so final. It left Sara feeling isolated, her self-confidence crushed. No wonder she had underachieved, no wonder she'd never had a proper career.

When Sara had told Joe she was leaving London, she had cried on his shoulder and he'd crooned into her hair: she was young, she had a lot of growing up to do, they would meet again.

She heard what she wanted to hear, infusing his words with meaning they didn't contain, and had done her growing-up a hundred miles away. She'd returned to the area a poised young woman, eager to prove she was worth waiting for, still blissfully ignorant. The invitation to the memorial service forwarded to her flat share by her mother and arriving on that very day had felt like serendipity. It never occurred to her that Joe wouldn't be there.

And now she and Joe were hiding things from each other. Were they going to start again in a new house on the back of those secrets? Was the rest of their life together to be tinged with distrust? It was unbearable, and yet she had to bear it, like she'd borne everything else. She had to get through this sticky period and she didn't see why she shouldn't. She had always got away with it. It was the way she looked, unthreateningly pretty, deceptively soft; the woman who had healed Joe Hartman, his patient and loving second wife.

Chapter 52

CLAUDIA

Police are increasingly concerned for the welfare of a Ditton woman missing for 24 hours. Thames Valley Police are appealing for help in tracing 25-year-old Anna Pemberton. Anna is 5' 4", with a slim build. She has blonde hair and blue eyes and on the day she went missing was wearing grey and pink tracksuit bottoms, a grey tracksuit top, blue Nike trainers and a grey coat with a pale blue scarf. Anna left home on foot. She has an 18-month-old son and her family have said her disappearance is completely out of character.

Anyone who may have seen Anna or who has any information on her whereabouts is urged to contact Thames Valley Police via 101 quoting incident number 4267.

Claudia expands the image on her phone and examines the picture beneath the appeal. It's a close-up head shot of Anna with Max. They have matching rosy cheeks, sparkling eyes, wide smiles and windswept hair, although Max's is more of a tousled tuft. Washed in sunshine, a beach stretches into the distance behind them. Claudia imagines Owen Pemberton framing his family, capturing the moment. She minimises the article and puts the phone down beside her just as the doorbell rings.

Whoever it is, she can't face them. It's six o'clock in the evening, and dark outside. Dark inside too, because the lights are off and the curtains closed. She's hardly moved from the sofa all day, sleeping on and off, still running a temperature, her throat still painful.

The letter box flaps.

'Claudia. Open up, will you? I know you're there.'

It's Kate. Claudia groans, but she gets up and opens the door, then clamps her hands under her armpits. Kate is child-free, dressed in her long coat, hair bundled onto her head. She steps inside, scuffing the soles of her boots on the mat. Claudia turns without a word and walks through to the kitchen.

'You look awful,' Kate says.

Claudia lifts a bottle of red wine, showing it to Kate, who nods. She takes down two glasses and fills them, spilling some. The atmosphere is odd. Kate seems less sure of herself, and Claudia is brittle. She's not sure she can take any more hurt. She forces down a mouthful of wine, wincing.

Kate frowns. 'Have you seen a doctor?'

'No.'

'Well you should. You might need antibiotics.'

'What are you here for, Kate?'

'I...um...' Kate pulls out a chair. 'I need to tell you something.'

Claudia remains standing, leaning against the counter. She waits, watching her old friend, so tense and anxious she thinks she might crack open.

'Won't you sit down?' Kate says.

Claudia hesitates, then comes forward and takes a chair. Kate draws a deep breath. She sets her glass down and rests her elbows on the table, her chin on her laced fingers. She looks away from Claudia, seems to be inspecting the room. She's been here before, for Tilly's christening and other family events. Claudia doesn't prompt her. She cannot think what she's come for, unless it's to apologise for being a fair-weather friend.

'On the morning Tilly disappeared, I met Joe for a chat.' Kate shifts her eyes back to Claudia's face. 'I wanted to talk to him about you. I told him I was worried, that your jealousy was affecting me and that I could see it was also affecting him. Joe was very kind about you. But I thought . . .' She takes a deep breath. 'You see, I was in love with him, or at least I thought I was. Nothing had happened or had even been said. I just longed for him. I told him and . . . and I made a pass.' She grimaces, her eyes fixed to Claudia's.

'Oh God,' Claudia says. 'I knew it.'

'No. You don't understand. Joe fended me off. It was all horribly awkward. The reason he said that he was delayed at work and would meet us at the theatre was because he couldn't bear the thought of an intimate dinner with the four of us. We never mentioned it again – obviously events overtook it. I really don't think this has any bearing on what happened, but I owe you the truth, and I'm sorry, I've been a crap friend. I want to be a better one, starting now— Jesus.' Someone has crashed their fist against the door. Kate's hand flies to her chest.

'They'll go away if we ignore them,' Claudia says. 'It's probably kids.'

Kate looks horrified. 'Do you get a lot of that?'

'No. Well, a bit. I'm the local Frankenstein's monster.'

'Claudia, I am so sorry.'

'Open the fucking door, Claudia, or I'll break it down.'

'It's Owen,' Claudia says. When Kate looks mystified, she adds, 'Anna Pemberton, the woman who's disappeared? It's her husband. I'd better see what he wants. Wait here.'

She drags herself into the hall and pulls the latch. Owen barges inside, trailing a potent waft of aftershave. Aggression pulsates off him.

'Why couldn't you mind your own business?'

'What?'

'I've just spent eight hours at the police station because of you.'

Claudia backs away from him. 'I have no idea what you're talking about.'

'You told the police we rowed, and now, thanks to you, I'm top of their list of suspects. You did it to deflect attention from the fact that you've been stalking my wife, watching our house. I've seen you up there in the window.'

'I can sit where I like.'

Owen sneers. 'Yeah. Of course you can, love. How do you think Anna's parents are feeling? They've already lost Megan, and now they're terrified they'll lose her as well. And what about my son? What about Max? He might have lost his mother. For fuck's sake, tell me what you know.'

Claudia feels dizzy and miserable. She needs to sit down, but she's not encouraging him deeper into the house. She moves back a few steps and rests her hand on the banister.

'You can believe what you like, but the last time I saw Anna was when she was talking to Frances outside your house on Friday morning. I can understand how incredibly anxious you are—'

'Can you?'

Claudia almost laughs. She stares at him for so long he flushes.

'You'd better watch your back,' he hisses, then turns on his heel. The house shakes when he slams the door.

Claudia drops down onto the stairs and puts her head in her hands. Kate squeezes into the space beside her and they sit in silence. After a while, Claudia leans her head against Kate's shoulder. Kate tilts hers against it briefly, then hauls herself up with a sigh.

'I'd better get back. I'm not sure it has any bearing on what happened, but if you want me to, I'll talk to the police.'

'Thank you for being honest.'

'It's about time, isn't it? But I'm afraid it took Sara being a complete bitch to make me realise where my loyalties lie. I was wrong about her. That woman is only really interested in herself. She's not a friend like you were.' She kisses Claudia's cheek. 'Take care, and call me if you need to. If I can help, I will.'

Chapter 53

Monday 13 November

SARA

Sara sat in her kitchen nibbling toast slathered with butter and marmalade, DS Ward's card beside her plate. He had said to phone him if anything, however small, occurred to her. Something had been bothering her since Saturday. She hadn't imagined the smell of Lemon Flu Relief. The question was, would reporting a possible intruder be a good thing or a bad thing? The answer was a resounding *good*, if what she imagined had happened really had; if Claudia had been in her house. If it was proven, that would be it, problem solved. If she was wrong, she would have wasted police time, but that wasn't the end of the world. The end of the world was letting Claudia continue to wreak havoc in her life. She typed Ward's mobile number into her phone. He picked up immediately.

'What can I do for you, Mrs Hartman?'

'Claudia was in my house on Saturday.'

'Right. What did she want?'

'I didn't actually see her. I smelled Lemon Flu Relief in

our bedroom, and in Maeve's room. I thought Joe must have made himself one in the morning, but I asked him and he said he hadn't. I know that doesn't sound like much, but it's odd, don't you think?'

'Odd, yes, but I don't understand why you would jump to the conclusion that it was Claudia.'

'We haven't had any visitors, apart from you, over the weekend. It had to be her.'

'Mrs Hartman, you can't go throwing accusations around.' There was something in his voice, though; he was uncertain. What she'd said had chimed in some way with him. 'Does she have a key?'

'Not as far as I know, but I suppose it's not impossible. Her mother may have kept a copy. But even if she didn't, I left the door open when I was loading the car. There was a phone call, it was literally only a couple of minutes, but if she'd been watching the house, she could have easily slipped inside.'

'I know you're jumpy,' Ward says. 'But it's unlikely she'd take such a huge risk, don't you think, given the consequences if she was caught?'

'There was a distinct smell of Lemon Flu Relief. I wasn't imagining it. I am sure she's been here. I want someone to check. I'm scared of what she could do. She's got to be desperate, hasn't she, to take the risks she's taking?'

'You seem very keen to get her back behind bars.'

Sara trips over her tongue. 'I . . . That's not what it is. Look, this isn't me being spiteful. It's just that from the moment she got out, she's been difficult. She's seen Joe behind my back, she's made accusations, she's made some sort of pact with a journalist. She's supposed to be keeping out of our lives, but she just won't stop, won't go away, and it's a strain.'

Sara showed the forensics officer upstairs, wondering if she'd done the right thing. But it was her right to feel safe in her own home, and she genuinely didn't. The officer politely rejected her offer of a cup of tea and spent two hours dusting the surfaces for prints while Sara sat downstairs listening to the floorboards creak overhead. As he left, she asked him how long before they got the results.

'Not sure, madam. Depends if it's marked urgent or not.'

Shortly after Joe returned home from work, DS Ward appeared. Sara hadn't had a chance to tell Joe what she'd done and had to hurriedly explain as she showed the detective into the kitchen. Joe frowned, but he didn't comment.

'It seems you were right, Mrs Hartman. Claudia's fingerprints have been found on the banisters and the wardrobe doors, inside the wardrobe, and on the desk and filing cabinet in the spare bedroom.' The detective paused. 'And on the side of Maeve's cot.'

'Oh shit,' Sara said.

Joe's face went slack with shock. 'Where was Maeve when all this was going on? Please tell me she was with you.'

'She was in her cot.' There was no easy way of saying it, no way of making her seem anything other than grossly negligent.

'You're joking. How could you have let that happen?'

'I didn't let it happen. She just sneaked in.'

Ward scratched his chin. 'It's possible she was hiding

upstairs while I was in the kitchen talking to your wife. Since she's been through your filing cabinet, we can only assume she was searching for something. Do you have any idea what that might have been?'

'No,' Joe said. 'No idea at all.'

'I suggest you go through your files and see if anything is missing.'

'Jesus.' He raked his fingers through his hair. 'I persuaded your colleague not to arrest her after she turned up at the school. What are you going to do?'

'We'll bring her in for questioning.'

'You're not sending her straight back to prison?' Sara said. 'That's what we were given to understand would happen.'

Ward's appraising gaze seemed to crawl under Sara's skin. 'It's likely she'll be recalled, but we don't want her back inside just yet. It'll only give us more hoops to jump through when we need to question her. But don't worry. Claudia Hartman won't be free for much longer.'

She breathed a sigh of relief. 'Thank God for that. We'll be able to get back to normal.'

She showed the detective out of the house. When she came back, Joe was sitting at the kitchen table with his head in his hands. She touched his shoulder and he looked up.

'Do you still love me?' he said.

'Of course I do.'

'I'm so sorry I brought all this down on you.'

'Don't be. How was your day?'

'It was shit. That bloody article has caused quite a stir. I'm just hoping it doesn't get me suspended.'

'It won't, will it?' Sara was horrified.

'I hope not, but when you lose the respect of the kids and their parents, it makes running the place much harder. I've got a meeting with the chair of governors tomorrow. With any luck it'll blow over, but they may make me take a week or two off to recover,' – he made quotation marks with his fingers – '"stress". They'll put it like that, I expect. To spare my dignity.'

Chapter 54

CLAUDIA

Claudia's phone rings as she's putting her supper on. Pasta with pesto. She's run out of fresh food. The call is international. She answers reluctantly. She can't keep ignoring her mother.

'Where've you been?' Louisa asks. 'I was beginning to worry.'

'Sorry. I've been busy with appointments.'

'In the evening?'

'No,' Claudia says shortly. 'But I go for walks after dark.'

There's a pause while Louisa digests this information. 'Okay. I suppose I can understand that, but I don't like the idea of you wandering round on your own. What if someone attacks you?'

'Mum, please.' Claudia rubs her forehead. 'Long Ditton isn't exactly a hive of criminal activity.'

'I saw the news,' Louisa says. 'About Anna. That's so awful. Have they found her?'

'Not as far as I know, but they're hardly likely to come over and tell me if they do.'

'Don't be sharp with me. I'm concerned about you. If there's someone out there attacking young women . . .'

'I don't think it's that.'

'Poor Frances and Patrick. They must be so worried.'

'Why are you bothered about them? They've been horrible to you.'

'That doesn't mean I can't feel sorry for them. Are you looking after yourself, darling? You sound bunged up.'

'It's just a cold.'

'I've had an email from the insurers. They have a couple of questions I can't answer. Can I forward it to you?'

'Sure.'

'Thank you. Have you made a start with your house hunting? Robert called the agents. Apparently Culloden Road is under offer.'

'I've looked online and walked round some areas that might work.' She's sure her mother can smell the lie. She hasn't done anything about it. She dips her head, as though Louisa can see her expression. 'Anyway, I'd rather wait till you're back. I'm not sure I'll be able to do the viewings. No one will want me in their house.'

To her consternation, Louisa starts to cry.

'Oh, Mum, don't. Please. I'll survive. Don't make me worry about you as well as everything else.'

Louisa sniffles and blows her nose. 'But it's so unfair. You've done nothing wrong.'

'I think you're the only one who believes that now.'

'I knew it was a mistake to leave you alone. I'll come back; Robert will be fine without me. He's got his family and a queue of old friends wanting to see him. I'm surplus to requirements. I can book a flight and be home in two or three days. I hate thinking about you dealing with all this on your own.'

Claudia is tempted to say yes, yes. Come home now. But

she doesn't want to see the wreck of herself reflected in her mother's eyes. The last time she looked in the mirror, she'd been dismayed at the way her collarbone jutted out and her hair hung lank against her scalp.

'You've only been gone three weeks. It'll cost you a fortune to change your return flight.'

'I don't care about the money; I care about you.'

'Don't come back, Mum. Please don't. I don't think I could bear it. If I really need you, I'll ask. I promise.'

There's a shadow at the door. Claudia had been preparing for a night in front of the TV and has already changed into pyjama bottoms and a long-sleeved T-shirt belonging to Louisa, one of Robert's sweaters and a pair of fluffy socks.

Detective Sergeant Ward is accompanied by a female police officer who he introduces as Police Constable Miranda Pett.

'Apologies for disrupting your evening, Mrs Hartman. May we come in?'

Claudia nods. She goes ahead of them into the kitchen and leans against the counter.

The detective and the officer hover beside the table, which she hasn't yet cleared. Her smeared plate, knife and fork and a drained wine glass sit there like an accusation.

'Mrs Hartman, we have evidence that proves you entered 26 Culloden Road without permission on Saturday. Your fingerprints have been found on several surfaces in the upstairs rooms, including on the baby's cot.'

Oh God. Not yet. Please not yet. It's warm in the kitchen, but she feels fingers of cold grubbing around inside her. 'Are you recalling me?'

'It depends. We'll give you a chance to explain yourself down at the station.'

She panics. 'Can't we do it here?' Once she's there, she fears she might never get out again.

'Not this time, I'm afraid. Things are a little more serious.'

Patrick and Frances Holt are standing outside with Owen, watching as she leaves, as still and expressionless as mannequins. Claudia isn't under arrest, so she's been spared the indignity of being cuffed, but that's small consolation. She looks away, directing her gaze towards the back of DS Ward's head. His hair is dense, straight and short. This has happened once before, although last time it was Culloden Road she was taken from, and it was in broad daylight. She particularly remembers Kate looking at her. And Joe's eyes had clung to hers with a desperation that cut her to the quick. Why couldn't he have looked at her like that when it mattered? Before it was too late.

Chapter 55

CLAUDIA

'Do I need a lawyer?' Claudia asks as she's shown into an interview room.

'It's up to you,' DS Ward says. 'If you feel uncomfortable at any point, we can stop the interview and you can either call your own lawyer or we'll organise a duty solicitor. It will all take time, though. I'd like to do this quickly and get you home.'

He's being polite, almost solicitous, opening doors for her, pulling out a chair, but she knows what this is leading to. Sara has succeeded and it's Claudia's own fault. She made the decision to enter the house.

'Would you like a hot drink?' PC Pett asks. 'It's out of a machine, but it's drinkable.'

'No thank you. But could I have a box of tissues, please?'

Pett nods at a waiting constable.

DS Ward rests his elbows on the table. 'Why don't you begin by explaining what you were doing in 26 Culloden Road on the morning of Saturday the eleventh of November?'

'I needed to talk to Joe. I know I shouldn't have done it, but I was running a temperature and I wasn't thinking

303

straight. When I got to Culloden Road, the front door was wide open and Sara was on the phone in the kitchen. I went in on impulse. Joe wasn't home.'

'Are you jealous of Sara Hartman?' Pett suddenly asks, and Claudia's gaze darts from Ward's face to hers.

'No.'

'But she has your husband and your house and to all intents and purposes is living the life that once belonged to you.'

'It doesn't make me happy, but I'm not jealous. It's not like that. I've accepted that I've lost everything. I've made my peace with what my life is now.'

'Is that right?' Pett says. 'It doesn't look like it from where I'm standing. Why did you touch Joe and Sara's baby daughter?'

Claudia drags in a sharp breath. 'I didn't touch her.'

'You were in that room, all alone, and there she was. Did she remind you of Tilly? Did you think about taking her from her mother?'

'Why would I put another woman through that?'

There's a knock on the door, the constable enters and puts a box of tissues down in front of Claudia. She pulls several out and blows her nose.

'Because you've been unwell. You're not in your right mind. Calling the police because you think someone's fed the cat and because of a DVD? What was that all about? The Holt family have said you've been behaving increasingly erratically since you moved into Shires Close. They've been particularly concerned about the threatening way you've been watching their homes.'

Claudia crosses her arms. 'I haven't been behaving

erratically. I've watched them consistently. And they've watched me.'

'Can I show you a piece of film one of your neighbours sent us?'

Pett slides an iPad out from under a manila folder, swipes it and swivels it round. In the film, taken on a phone through a window, Claudia grabs a spade, arcs it round and smacks it into the snowman. She does it again and again until there's nothing there but a pile of snow.

'You're not as weak as you look, are you?'

'It was adrenaline.'

'It got you riled, did it? The snowman.'

'It upset me.' She's mortified but adamant. 'It was a message.'

'A message?' Pett says. 'Somebody builds a snowman, and that's a message for you? Any chance it could just have been a snowman?'

'It was holding a baby and a spade, implying that I buried my daughter.'

Pett rolls her eyes. 'That's what you read into it, because you were overwrought. Whichever child built it, I expect they left the spade there. You know what kids are like.'

'It was deliberate,' Claudia insists as heat creeps up her neck. 'It's a campaign. I've had eggs thrown at my door, there've been threats, and someone spat in my face. My flat was burned to the ground.' Her knee won't stop jiggling. She presses her hand on her thigh. 'I lost my temper. I haven't been well.'

'Did you intend to harm or abduct Maeve Hartman?' DS Ward asks.

'No!'

'Then what were you doing in her bedroom?'

'I thought it was Joe's study. It used to be when I lived there. The lights were out and the blackout blinds were down, so I didn't realise until she made a noise. She was standing in her cot and she held out her hand. I touched our palms together, that's all. Then your lot arrived and I slipped out and hid in the wardrobe in Sara and Joe's bedroom. Of course I wouldn't have hurt her.'

'What was so important that you'd risk your freedom by entering the Hartmans' house?'

She wraps her hand around the back of her neck. She's tired of being the monster. It's time Joe shouldered some of the burden. 'Because I suspected Joe of having had some kind of affair with Anna Pemberton, when she was our babysitter.'

'You thought you'd carry out your own investigation?'

She looks directly into the detective's eyes. 'No one else was going to do it.'

'Did you find anything?'

'Yes, I did. Joe has photographs of Anna in his desk.'

DS Ward and PC Pett share a glance. 'What kind of photographs?' Ward asks.

'A strip of four from a photo booth.'

'Is she fully dressed in the pictures?'

'Yes. It's only head and shoulders, but it looks like she's wearing her school blazer. Her expression is provocative. In 2013, when I said he was having an affair, he denied it and he was believed. But if he lied to protect himself, because it was with a pupil, then it makes sense.'

'Why didn't you come straight to us?'

'I've told you. It was a shock and I wanted to think about it.'

'Or you kept it quiet because you thought you might need leverage with Joe.'

'Maybe that too.'

'Because he was turning out not to be the man you thought he was?'

'Yup.'

'Where are the photographs?'

'Still in his desk. In a file labelled "Miscellaneous".'

Ward gives her a stern look. 'If you're accusing Joe of inappropriate behaviour with a minor, that's going to have serious repercussions. Given that you're basing it on speculation rather than evidence, are you sure you want to proceed with it? It smacks of shifting the blame by destroying someone else's life.'

'I'm not doing that. I'm simply suggesting that Joe may have had good reason to lie, and he's probably worried. What if Anna's been thinking about their relationship in a different light, post Me Too? She left a meeting with him in tears. What if she's tackled him about it?' She can hear her voice rising, knows she shouldn't say any more but her mouth has taken over. 'What if he groomed her?'

What if he groomed *me*? she thinks. What if Greg was right?

'Whoa. Let's stop right there,' Ward says, raising his palms towards her. 'That is an extremely serious accusation. Unless you have evidence, I'd suggest you keep your hunches to yourself.'

'But I do. The photographs.'

'There could be any number of reasons they're there.

307

Rest assured, we will ask him. Frankly, I cannot believe Davies has allowed you to take it this far. Whatever he's paying you, it isn't worth it.'

Claudia flushes. 'He isn't paying me. I asked him to write that piece. I wanted to rattle cages.'

'Davies could be sued for defamation. Joe has already been to see his lawyer. What the hell was he thinking? What were *you* thinking? Do you want to destroy his career as well as Joe's?'

'No,' she says desperately. 'I'm sorry. I was clutching at straws.'

'But you've promised him an exclusive, am I right? He scratches your back, you scratch his.'

Claudia feels her cheeks redden.

'Is that why you didn't tell us about it immediately? You've been saving it for Mr Davies.'

'No! I wasn't sure I wanted to put Joe through that. I wanted to think about it first. Maybe talk to him.'

'Very magnanimous of you, I'm sure.' He doesn't believe her. 'Do you think that article might be behind Anna's disappearance?'

Claudia can't look at him. 'I don't know. I hope not.'

'Well, if I was you, I'd get straight on to Mr Davies and tell him to take it down and issue an apology. If it's not too late. The Hartmans have put up with your behaviour up until now, and we've been lenient, but you've crossed a line. I suggest you keep an extremely low profile from now on.'

A wave of anger replaces her fear and she leans forward, pressing her forearms into the table.

'I have nothing to lose, since you're going to recall me

anyway, so I'll be clear. I did not hurt my child. I lied to get out of prison. I've done the best I can and I only enlisted Greg Davies's help because I was running out of options. So get this on tape. Claudia Hartman categorically denies causing harm to Tilly Hartman. She did not abduct her, and the statement she made admitting to manslaughter is a tissue of lies.' She sits back and wipes her nose.

'Look at it from our point of view, Claudia,' Ward says patiently. 'You're released from prison, and three weeks later the woman who was meant to be babysitting for you on the day your daughter disappeared goes missing and you conveniently find photographs of Anna Pemberton in your ex-husband's desk. Not very subtle, is it?'

'Do you think I hurt her?' Claudia clasps her hands around her scalp. She's sick with exhaustion. 'I don't have the strength to hurt anyone.'

'Mrs Hartman, please cooperate,' PC Pett says. 'Everyone is extremely anxious about Anna. You need to tell us what's been going on.'

'We know what you're trying to do,' Ward adds.

'What am I trying to do?'

'To cast doubt on your conviction, by shifting suspicion onto Sara Hartman and Anna Pemberton. You can't do this, you can't get your case reopened. It's over. I think you know that, or you wouldn't be talking to a journalist. But Davies can't help you. He won't be allowed to post another article. It's libel. He should know better.' He pauses. 'Perhaps he does know. Perhaps he's stringing you along.'

'He isn't like that.' She has to believe in Greg, because there is no one else.

Ward shakes his head slowly, then he slaps his hands

down on the table. 'Thank you for your time,' he says. 'I think we have enough. You're free to go.'

'I'm not going back to prison?'

'Not yet, but I'd prepare myself if I were you.'

Claudia does just that. She prepares herself by calling Greg.

Chapter 56

Tuesday 14 November

SARA

A 34-year-old woman has been released after helping police with their enquiries. No arrest has been made. The search for missing Long Ditton mother Anna Pemberton continues.

Sara swore under her breath, put her phone down, pinched a lock of hair and ran it through her lips. Maeve's mouth and hands were smeared with strawberry yoghurt. Sara wiped them clean with a damp muslin, then lifted her daughter out of her high chair, picked up the remote control and switched the television on. Together they watched an episode of *Bluey*. Maeve's belly laugh was the best medicine.

The detective had let Claudia go. What did that mean? That she was free to carry on poking the hornets' nest? That she was free to continue turning Sara's life upside down? Sara stroked Maeve's hair and pulled her closer. She had screwed up, but all was not lost. The main thing was, Claudia must go back to prison. Everything Sara did now was to further that aim.

She heard Joe's key in the lock and stood up. He could only have been at school for an hour or so. How odd. He was speaking to someone, and she assumed he was on his phone, but when she met him in the hall, he was accompanied by Detective Sergeant Ward. Joe was using the social voice he saved for school events; a tone that implied everything was all right because he was in charge, but rather than reassure her, it hit a false note and made her nervous.

'What's going on?'

'Sorry, darling. I should have phoned first. I need to nip up to my study with the detective. We'll only be a minute, then we'll be out of your hair.'

DS Ward nodded a greeting.

'I hear you let Claudia go,' Sara said.

He paused, one foot on the bottom stair, his hand curling round the banister. 'Don't worry, we have her in our sights.' He looked at her with such sympathetic understanding that she went pink.

After a while, Maeve rolled onto her tummy, slid to the floor and toddled over. Sara picked her up and kissed her. Maeve wriggled, and she put her down, watched her return to the sofa, lift one leg on, her joints supple as a ballerina's, and pull herself up. She was getting bigger and stronger by the day.

In the garden, a squirrel scurried along the fence and disappeared into the tree at the end. When she heard the men coming downstairs, Sara darted out into the hall.

'Stay a minute, Joe.'

'I can't.'

He stared at her, and she tried to work out what message

he was trying to convey. She wanted to cling to him, but she kept her hands by her sides.

'Is everything okay?' She stopped short of demanding to know what they were looking for. Not with DS Ward listening.

Joe squeezed her elbow and kissed her cheek. 'Everything's fine. It's just Claudia being Claudia. The detective rightly had to check his facts. I'll explain later.'

'You really needn't worry, Mrs Hartman,' DS Ward said. 'We're following up a piece of information Claudia Hartman gave us. It's pretty clear she made it up to deflect attention, but I'm sure you understand we need to tick all the boxes.'

She went with them as far as the door and watched Joe getting into the back of DS Ward's car. Despite his willingness to cooperate and his relaxed body language, it seemed ignominious, and she scanned the street to reassure herself no one was watching.

Whatever DS Ward had expected to find, it had evidently not been there. She wondered what it was, her sense of unease deepening. Far from being hog-tied by the rules, Claudia was finding myriad ways to bypass her restrictions and make a nuisance of herself, no doubt aided and abetted by that bloody journalist.

Claudia didn't move aside or invite Sara into the house. She was shifty, glancing behind her as she blocked the door. Was there someone with her? Was it Joe? Her nostrils were red, her face gaunt, her wrists and hands so bony they looked as though they would rattle if Sara shook her. She had never been beautiful, but she'd had something. Now she was just plain ugly. No man in his right mind would want her. The thought gave Sara some satisfaction but did little to assuage her sense of being hard done by.

'What did you tell the police?' she demanded. 'I've had them at the house searching through Joe's things.'

'Did they find anything?'

'No, they did not. Why are you ruining my life when I've done nothing wrong? All I did was fall in love with a man who'd been put through hell by his wife.'

'You shouldn't protect him.'

'Protect him from what?'

Claudia made no attempt to soften the blow. 'I found photographs of Anna in his desk. They were taken about ten years ago. She was still in school uniform.'

Sara stalled. 'Right . . . well they didn't find anything like that, so you were either mistaken or lying. If you think you can change people's minds about you by making other people look bad and smearing their names, I can tell you it's not working.'

'Why would I lie? I'd look pretty stupid if they weren't there.'

'Well, they weren't. If they existed outside your imagination, DS Ward would have found them.'

Claudia shrugged. 'I expect Joe destroyed them when he realised I'd been in his study.'

'There's always an explanation with you, isn't there? You can't bear that I've got Joe, you can't bear that he's happy with me and that we have Maeve. You are fixated with what I have and you're incapable of taking the blame for losing it all. What do you even know?'

'What I know,' Claudia responded, taking a step forward

so that Sara was forced to take one back, 'is that you're not what you seem. What is it you want? To protect your marriage from me? Or to make sure no one sees you for what you really are? How well does Joe know you? How well does Kate? Not very well, I suspect.'

'Oh, Christ,' Sara spat. 'You are a screwed-up, vindictive bitch who can't tell up from down. Everyone thinks you're nuts and nothing you've done since you've been out has made them change their minds. Kate thinks you're a joke.'

'That's not the impression I got when she came round to apologise.'

Sara spun on her heel and marched back to her car. Claudia was still standing there as she drove away, fizzing with anger.

Chapter 57

CLAUDIA

'It's debatable which of you is the more deranged,' Greg says, grinning at Claudia when she comes back into the kitchen.

She offers him a dry smile in response. She can't believe he's being so good-humoured about everything. Unlikely though it seems, she gets a sense that he finds her attractive, and she doesn't know how she feels about that. Greg is so different from Joe, a strange mixture of spiky and thick-skinned, yet there is an appeal. Perhaps it's a knight-in-shining-armour thing. It'll wear off once she's either exonerated or back behind bars. She doubts he'll visit.

Perversely, although she's determined never to put herself in a position where she's reliant on a man again, part of her yearns for someone to lean on.

'You've scared her,' he says.

'Mm.' Claudia sits down and picks up her mug, cradling it as she thinks over her conversation with Sara. 'She wouldn't have come otherwise. I wonder whether she's frightened for herself or for Joe.'

'Both, by the sounds of it.'

'I'm sorry if I've got you in the shit with your editor.'

'It won't be the first time, and it's my fault, not yours.

I didn't think it through. I wanted to help. Anyway, I kept him sweet by promising an exclusive once the truth comes out.'

'Do you think it will?'

'You can count on it.' His confidence reassures her. 'It might have been a mistake, but it's had its effect. Ward might say he isn't interested in pursuing Joe for historical abuse, but it's in his head. He knows full well that Anna's disappearance has nothing to do with you. You have no car, no strength, no place to hide her. If he seriously thought you had something to do with it, he'd have a warrant to search your house by now. No, I reckon he's scratching his head as we speak.'

'Do you think Joe's killed her?'

'I don't think she's alive.'

'This is my fault for encouraging Sara to make friends with her. I should have stayed out of it.'

'Good point. You should have stayed in prison. Then everyone would be able to live happily ever after, including me. Right. What's next on the agenda?'

She smiles. 'Jenny Buckland.'

'Give us her number.'

Claudia has tracked down Jenny's surname through the Lady Eden's alumni Facebook page. She hands over her phone with Jenny's contact details displayed. Greg keys the number into his own phone, then holds her gaze while he listens to it ring.

'Jenny? I hope I'm not disturbing you. This will only take a minute. My name is Greg Davies and I'm a journalist ... No. Not at all. Please don't hang up.' He jumps up and walks out of the room, resting a clenched fist against the banisters. 'There are lives at stake and you may be able to help. I assume you've heard about the missing woman. It's been all over the press. Anna Pemberton? . . . Yes, that's right . . . No, I'm sure, but there is a connection . . . Claudia Hartman? Yes . . . I'm not on anyone's side, I try to take an unbiased view. Can I persuade you to meet me? It's urgent.' He screws up his face while he listens to her response, then gives Claudia a thumbs-up. 'That's extremely kind of you. I'll be there.'

'She's agreed to meet us.' Claudia grins. It's the first piece of positive news she's heard for a long time.

'She's agreed to meet *me*. I didn't want to push it. Unfortunately, she's on a course today, so I'm seeing her in the morning. I'll report back.'

'I'm coming with you.'

'You're not well enough. You shouldn't be trailing your germs across London.'

'I'm on the mend and I'm not staying here.' She does feel a little better. Her voice is still hoarse and her throat is sore, but her fever has broken. 'I'll wrap up warm.'

'I'm not really a team player,' Greg grumbles.

'I beg your pardon. What are we exactly?'

'You are in distress. I'm helping you out.'

'You want me to believe this is altruism? You're here for the story.'

'Jesus, woman.' He rolls his eyes. 'Okay. I'll pick you up at nine. Try and stay out of trouble in the meantime.'

Chapter 58

SARA

Sara marched into the school and demanded to see Joe. Lisa, looking harried, showed her into his office.

'He's in a meeting with the chair of governors. I don't think they'll be much longer. Can I make you a cup of tea?'

Sara parked the buggy in the corner. She was worried. Lisa had been avoiding eye contact. 'No thank you. I'm sorry, Lisa, but this is an emergency. Would you ask him to come immediately.' She had never liked Joe's PA, always felt judged by her, so if she was coming across entitled, she couldn't have cared less. She was the headmaster's wife, after all. There had to be some perks.

'Well, I—'

'Just get him, please.'

She sat on the small sofa and picked up a copy of *Education Today*, ignoring Lisa, who was hovering uncertainly.

'I'm sorry. Can I give him a clue as to what it's about?'

'No.'

Sara stood in Joe's office, fingers wrapped so tight around the shoulder strap of her bag her knuckles were white. 'Sorry to interrupt your meeting.'

'It was over anyway. I've been asked to take a couple of weeks off. They've been kind and are calling it compassionate leave, but it's about those insinuations. They want to give it a chance to blow over. I'm writing to the parents today.'

'What are you going to say?'

He curled his lip. 'Due to stress, et cetera . . .'

'Oh, Joe.'

'I don't want to talk about it now. Why are you here?'

She took a deep breath. This was obviously the worst possible time for the conversation, but she needed to have it. 'Claudia told me she found photographs of Anna in your desk. Was that what Ward was looking for?'

Joe's face lost colour so fast she thought he was going to faint. 'Claudia is lying. She doesn't have many weapons at her disposal, so she's stooping to making up stories.'

She might have believed him once, but she didn't any more. In fact, even though she loved him as much as ever, she was beginning to believe that his reputation as a charismatic educator who had a way with troubled teenagers, who was one hundred per cent trustworthy with the girls who adored him and obsessed about him, was a construct. She examined his face. He looked older, and lately his fabled charisma had been in short supply. She could bring it back if only she could sort this mess out, but to do that she needed to know what was in his head.

'Did you remove them when you heard she'd been in your desk?'

'I didn't know anything about them.'

'If you have any respect for me, you'll tell me the truth.'

'It was you who invited Anna into our lives and gave her the opportunity to make trouble.'

'That's not fair. If you'd been honest with me from the off...'

'Alright! I rejected her when she came to the school, and I assume planting photographs of herself in my house was her way of paying me back.'

That rocked her certainty. It explained why Anna had phoned out of the blue on Thursday asking if she could come round. It was possible that she'd dashed into Joe's study when Sara was seeing to Maeve, and slipped the photographs into the filing cabinet, but was it likely? Knowing the Holts, it was. Look at the way they'd treated Claudia and her mother over the years. They were horrible people.

Joe doubled down. 'For God's sake, why would I keep something like that? I don't lock my filing cabinet; you know my phone passcode. I have nothing to hide.'

'Has something happened between you?'

'No.' He spoke forcefully. 'Absolutely not. She came on to me. I said no.'

Sara leapt on that. 'Then something did happen.'

'You're splitting hairs, but I suppose so. I said I wasn't interested. End of story.'

He'd raised his voice. She glared at him, then glanced at Maeve. Joe grimaced an apology, rubbing at the grooves in his brow with his fingertips. He was stressed, but so was she.

'Why would she do that? Why would she risk her marriage, risk humiliating herself? There has to be more to it.'

'There isn't. She's obsessed with me and it isn't reciprocated. I hoped I'd made that clear to her.'

Someone knocked on the door.

'What is it?' Joe barked.

Lisa popped her head round. 'Sorry to disturb you, but I have Robbie Merchant's father on the phone.'

'I'll call him back.'

'Fine, but it's almost time for—'

'Go away!'

Lisa's face fell. She stepped backwards into the corridor and closed the door.

'This is a nightmare,' Joe said.

Sara wasn't about to disagree. 'I promise you, I am not going to stick around unless you tell me what's going on. I'll take Maeve and go and stay at Mum's. It's all getting too much. First I have to deal with your neurotic ex, and now this. Anna, for Christ's sake. Is there something wrong with you? I'm beginning to have some sympathy for Claudia. Does it make you happy, being the cockerel in the henhouse? Manipulating all of us.'

That she was the one doing the manipulating didn't bother her. She'd do what she needed to.

Joe started pacing the room. Sara watched him, then shook her head and reached for her handbag.

'Call me if you change your mind. Otherwise, leave me alone.'

He blocked the door. 'Don't go. I'll tell you the truth about Anna.'

'All right. I'm listening.'

Chapter 59

SARA

Joe took a deep breath. 'We'd been invited to a party in Fulham. Claudia didn't want to go, but I persuaded her. I said I was sick to death of being stuck in every night with the baby. Anyway, by the time she agreed, it was too late to get one of the local au pairs to babysit, so we used Anna. I was driving, because I knew it'd be difficult to get a taxi to take us home at that time on a Saturday night, so I only had a couple of beers. Claudia wasn't meant to drink on her medication, but she did, and it was probably my fault for being so hard on her. She fell asleep in the car on the way back and went straight to bed when we got home. I tried to book an Uber for Anna, but I was being quoted forty-five minutes at the earliest, so I gave her a lift.'

'Oh, Joe,' Sara groaned. 'Really?'

'You said you would listen,' he snapped.

She clamped her mouth shut.

'On a normal night it would have been a ten-minute drive, but there'd been an accident under the railway bridge, so ten minutes turned into half an hour. We chatted and I didn't think anything was going on. It was stilted, but I assumed that was because she felt awkward having to make conversation with her teacher. She asked me to park outside the entrance to Shires Close. I thought it was an odd request, but since we were right there and no harm was going to come to her, I pulled in round the corner. I turned to thank her, expecting her to get out, and when she didn't, I leant across her to open the door, and that was when she made a pass.'

'What kind of pass?' Sara's heart beat so fast she thought she would have a heart attack. She had been so hoping to be proved wrong.

'She turned her head so that her lips grazed my cheek.'

'Are you certain you didn't misunderstand? It might have been accidental.'

'It wasn't,' he said grimly. 'My instincts were clearly off. I don't know what was going on in her head, but I lost mine. It was a moment of madness.'

'What did you do?'

'I kissed her.'

'A peck on the cheek? Open mouths?'

'Don't. I feel bad enough as it is. It's something I've done my best to forget.'

'You don't have that luxury, I'm afraid. Tell me.'

'Open mouths. Is that what you want to hear?'

'And touching?'

'I don't like this side of you.'

'Tough.'

Joe pinched his lips together, then released a long breath. 'There was some touching before I came to my senses and hustled her out of the car. I apologised immediately, of course.'

'Did you sleep with her?'

'No!'

'Are you sure?'

'What do you think I am?'

His facial muscles were so taut she could see a nerve tic beneath his eye. She badly wanted to believe him.

'It was still assault,' she said.

'Do you think I don't know that?'

'And afterwards?'

'Afterwards nothing. I tried to shrug it off and get on with my life, and I had plenty to distract me. Claudia's behaviour had deteriorated. Home was pretty unpleasant by that time.'

'You selfish bastard.'

He raised his eyes to her face. They were filled with sorrow. 'You're not telling me anything I haven't told myself.'

'That doesn't exonerate you. Did you use Anna to babysit again?'

'We didn't need to. I made sure that on the rare occasions we went out in the evening, we used a local babysitter. Generally, though, if we did socialise, it was kitchen suppers with Paul and Kate and we always brought Tilly with us. And even those outings fell away because of Claudia's obsession with Kate and me. I'd see Anna round the school, but I genuinely thought she was over it. I didn't understand how powerful an infatuation like that can be.'

'Come on, Joe. You knew exactly what it was like. You saw enough of it.'

'I assumed she would snap out of it, get bored or fixate on somebody else.'

'Have you never felt like that?' When he didn't answer, she let the question dissolve into the air and changed tack. 'What happened on the day Tilly went missing?'

He raked his fingers into his hair. 'It was the end of the school day and it was tipping down. There were a lot of people milling around in the hall waiting for the rain to let up. Anna wasn't in school; she'd got permission to go to Miss Colville's memorial service with her parents.'

'Why? She didn't go to Lady Eden's.'

'I thought it was odd too, but apparently her mother wanted her to be there because it was all part of getting closure for her sister's death. Frances is a psychiatrist, which I suppose is why they did this whole thing of facing up to Megan's death and forgiving the school for failing her. You have to understand, with the Holts, nothing is ever their fault.'

'They didn't extend that forgiveness to Claudia.'

His mouth thinned. 'No. Anyway, Anna came into school and walked into my classroom. She was angry and tearful. She told me what they'd heard; about what Claudia said to Megan. Anna demanded I make Claudia admit that her sister's suicide was her fault. I tried to reason with her, but the situation became surreal. She put her arms around my neck and told me that if I loved her, I'd leave Claudia. Except she said, "that cow" and called her evil. Then she tried to kiss me. I told her not to be ridiculous and not to come anywhere near me again. She started crying, and it dawned on me that in her head we were in a relationship. I knew I had grossly mismanaged a volatile situation. I apologised for giving a mistaken impression and tried to smooth things over, but she stormed out. I was going to go after her, but I got cornered by another member of staff.'

Sara put her head in her hands. So that explained

Joe's mood. It had little in fact to do with Claudia. With historical rapes and assaults seemingly being reported every day, he was terrified that he'd lose his career and his reputation.

She glanced up. 'So last week, when Anna came to see you about teaching, did she threaten you?'

'Not as such. But we came to an understanding.'

'Exactly what did you say to her?'

'I persuaded her it was in her best interests to keep quiet. I told her I knew she hit Max. But her disappearance has nothing to do with me, I swear.'

'The police are interested in you, though. They might not have found anything, but they're suspicious.'

'I was at school all that day, I can prove it. But Sara—'

She stopped him there. 'Let me think. Who might need to shut Anna up if it wasn't you? There is no one else. Unless . . .' She couldn't believe she was saying this. 'Unless it was Anna and not Claudia who took Tilly. I'm just speculating here, but if Claudia was getting close to the truth, Anna would have acted, don't you think? What if she tried to kill Claudia, but Claudia fought back? She was in prison for nine years; she'll be a hell of a lot tougher than Anna. I bet she can fight like a cat if she wants to. Maybe she accidentally killed her.'

'There's no way. She isn't that strong.'

She thought quickly. Joe had let her down, like he'd let so many women down, but if he faced charges, chances were Sara herself would come under scrutiny. She wasn't going to let that happen. It was up to her to keep her family safe.

'True. But it's amazing how people can find reserves

when they're on the edge of a precipice. Think, Joe. Is there any way Claudia could be innocent and Anna guilty?'

Joe stared at her. He closed his eyes briefly, then opened them and nodded. 'Yes. Yes, it's possible.'

Chapter 60

CLAUDIA

Greg has gone home. There was a moment, before Claudia closed the door on him, when she was tempted to ask him to stay. What stopped her wasn't the fear of getting into something that might turn out to be a messy mistake, it was the fear of seeing the look of horror in his eyes at the prospect of intimacy. She craves physical contact, that's the trouble. Even Frank ignores her most of the time, slipping through her hands like a fish when she tries to scoop him up, hoping to cradle his warm body against her.

She closes the curtains on the deep blackness of the garden – she's seen enough films where the victim doesn't – and takes another microwave meal out of the fridge, this time a portion of chicken in white wine sauce. She heats it up and slides it out onto a plate. It smells good but reminds her of the mono-coloured fare she was provided with in prison. She can't be bothered to cook greens and picks through it without much enthusiasm. Tomorrow she will meet Jenny Buckland and will hopefully be a step closer to the truth. For the police it was simple: the mentally unwell mother did it. Lock her up. Job done. But it's clear it was anything but.

Why did no one look deeper into Sara's past, for instance? The question is easily answered: because she came into the picture almost four years after the crime was committed. Only it turns out that wasn't true. She had been to the same school as Claudia, had been in the same class as Megan Holt and, years later, had showed up at the memorial service for their headmistress. Basically, the police hadn't done their homework, because they were convinced of Claudia's guilt.

And as for Joe, the grieving father. Although it causes her immense pain, she has accepted that their love affair wasn't the pure thing she had considered it, that there had been something dubious about the way he'd sucked her into his world. Of course she had fallen in love with him; how could she not have? She had never felt like a victim, never wanted to see herself that way, but if Tilly had been allowed to grow up, if she had been seventeen and in thrall to a charismatic teacher, Claudia would have removed her from the school. Even if he didn't see it like that at the time, even if the girls were willing and eager, even if they did the chasing, he must know by now that his career will end. She wishes her mother had spotted her infatuation, but she was good at hiding it.

She watches television and dozes off, but once she's in bed, she's no longer sleepy. She lies on her side listening to the sounds of the close. She's so used to them by now, she can tell whose car is pulling onto a forecourt and recognise voices. She closes her eyes and starts to list names of people she used to know, an A to Z of lost friends. She falls asleep at K for Kate Shaw.

When she wakes up, she is on high alert, heart racing,

the sound of blood pulsing in her ears. Even the muscles around her stomach ache with tension. She had been dreaming she was with her mother and Joe, talking about Jason of all people, but then someone had started lobbing snowballs at the house. And that had woken her.

Sliding her hand under the pillow she feels for the knife she's kept there since the day the video played of its own accord, yelping when she nicks her little finger on the blade. She sucks a drop of blood from the wound, then curls her fingers around the hilt, and winces as the burned skin stretches across the back of her hand. She gets out of bed and silently eases the door open. Someone is moving around downstairs.

She checks outside, peeking through a gap in the curtains. The close is completely still, no fox leaving prints in the snow, no local cat scouting their territory.

Claudia lets the curtain drop and leaves the room. She moves silently down to the hall, then into the kitchen. Her skin feels alive, her nerve endings thrumming, her ears ringing as she strains to hear. It seems darker than usual, and she realises the gadget lights are off, the glow from the microwave clock extinguished, the internet router no longer flashing its green column. Nothing happens when she presses the light switch.

Gripping the knife, she pushes open the door to the utility room and feels her way to the cupboard. Inside it a torch hangs from a hook. She takes it and switches it on. The first thing she notices as she moves the beam around the room is that the washing machine has been shifted an inch or two and is sticking out at an angle. She crouches and shines the torch into the cavity, sees something and stretches in up to her shoulder, her fingers delving into the narrowing wedge at the back.

She's reached it, almost hooked her fingers round it, when she's grabbed from behind and screams. She smells something sweet before she blacks out.

Claudia opens her eyes. She props herself up on her elbows and looks around. Daylight is filtering through the curtains; the digital clock reads 8.17. She blinks to focus. Did she dream last night? She lifts her pillow. The knife is still there. The last thing she remembers is being pulled against someone's body. She doesn't remember going back to bed. Was she sleepwalking? Or did someone want her to think she was? Not many people know it was a problem when she was a child. Frances, because Louisa used to tell her everything, and Joe. Even though it was rare after she reached adulthood, it had happened two or three times while they were together.

The electricity is back on. Claudia doesn't remember flicking the switches up on the fuse box under the stairs. She's confused, unsure whether to trust her instincts.

Her little finger stings. She inspects it, finds a smear of blood, and her memory comes back in a rush. She cut herself on the knife; she came downstairs and went into the utility room to get the torch; the washing machine had been moved.

She runs barefoot to the utility room. The torch is hanging from its hook, the washing machine sitting square in its slot. She shifts it, gets down on her knees and squints into the gap, but all she can see is dusty skirting and the two sockets, one of which the washing machine is plugged into, the other empty. Maybe she dreamt it after all.

Except.

She looks again. On the wall, close to the skirting, there's a tiny smear of blood. She sits back on her heels. She didn't imagine it, and now she remembers what she was trying to reach: a thin white cable, pushed right to the back. It's no longer there.

Chapter 61

Wednesday 15 November

CLAUDIA

Greg is waiting for her in his car. Claudia wraps herself into a quilted coat with a belted waist and is pleased at the way it disguises her extreme thinness. She looks as good as she can, considering the challenges. She's even drawn in her eyebrows. They're not straight, but they're better than the sparse hairs that have begun growing back.

She checks her bag for her phone and glances round for the keys. She can't stop thinking about last night. Whoever she'd interrupted, they had been removing something plugged in behind the washing machine, and she thinks that what she saw in the torch beam was a phone cable. She also knows, having just googled it, that you can buy sounds, like a baby crying, and set an iPhone to play them at regular intervals, and that the sound can be somehow magically synced through Robert's speaker system. So she isn't going mad, or probably isn't. Last night, for whatever reason, whoever it was decided it had to stop – either it had served its purpose, or they had reason to believe the phone might be found. And that someone had a key to her house.

Frances might still have a copy, and Anna could have taken it. But Anna has disappeared, so that leaves Sara or Joe. Her nerves prickle. Or even Frances. Frances hates Claudia because she reminds her that she failed Megan. There's Owen too, although that's really unlikely. He's obsessed with the effect she's having on property values in the close, but he knows she'll be gone soon enough.

Stepping outside, she sees Frances coming out of her son-in-law's house. Her hair is pulled back in a tight pony-tail and she looks drained. Signalling to Greg to hang on, Claudia approaches her.

'Frances.'

'I don't want to speak to you.'

'I just wanted to say I'm so sorry about what's happened. I know how you must be feeling. If there's anything I can do to help ...'

Frances takes a step towards her. 'You can tell me where my daughter is.'

'I promise you, I don't know.'

Frances turns on her heel.

'Wait. Don't go. I need to ask you something. Do you still have a key to our house?'

The venomous look in Frances's eyes as she swings round reminds Claudia of Miss Colville's expression that afternoon she caught Joe kissing her. Pure disgust.

'How dare you?' Frances says, pushing Claudia's shoulder with the flat of her hand. 'We were all right before you came back. And now look at us.'

'I know, and I'm sorry. But the key ...'

Frances pushes her again. 'I do not have it. Now get out of my sight.'

At the second shove, Claudia is back in Bronzefield, being manhandled by a fellow inmate. She shoves back, and Frances grapples with her coat, screaming into her face.

'Go on. Get out of here. Go back to prison where you belong.'

'Oi!'

Greg bolts across the close and hauls Claudia away. She struggles against him, her feet kicking out in the slush as Frances keeps coming, keeps yelling. Patrick runs out of the house, takes hold of his wife's arm and pulls her sobbing against his chest. He glares at Claudia over Frances's shoulder.

'Just leave us alone.'

Claudia's heart is racing. She pushes Greg's arms down and brushes herself off, then turns and walks with dignity to the car.

'You okay?' Greg asks, getting in beside her.

She scowls as she discovers a tear in Louisa's coat. 'Yes. Let's go.'

Claudia nibbles at a fingernail as they drive, occasionally casting glances Greg's way. She notices the car has had a tidy-up – he's even hoovered – and she can't help wondering if the effort was for her.

'Who was the unnamed source?' she asks.

Greg turns his head briefly. 'Sorry?'

'In the article you wrote after I was sentenced. The anonymous person who told you they thought I was jealous of Joe's relationship with Tilly.'

'You know I can't tell you that.'

'Was it Anna?'

He sighs. 'No.'

'Female?'

'Yes.'

She feels sick and lowers her window an inch. The cold wind catches at her hair, flicking it across her mouth. She pulls it away. 'It was Frances.'

'I couldn't possibly comment.'

'You don't have to. I'm sorry about what she's going through, especially if it's connected to anything we've done. But even if she was angry with me back then, she shouldn't have said that. It was pure malice.' She hesitates. 'Unless she knew something?'

Greg nods. 'I think you're right. Let's go see Jenny, tick that box, then I'll come back and talk to Frances.'

'Good luck with that.'

The café in Vauxhall is Italian, its glass door splashed with flyers advertising local art exhibitions and gigs. Inside, Claudia is hit by a headily fragrant waft of coffee and freshly baked pastries. Jenny is at the back, easily spotted because she's looking right at them. She's wearing a trim suit jacket with a cream silk shirt, and her brown bob is brushed neatly behind her ears. There are gold knots in her lobes. She looks neat and professional, which makes Claudia painfully aware that her efforts aren't good enough.

Greg introduces himself and shakes her hand. Jenny eyes Claudia, and Claudia tentatively smiles before sitting down. Greg asks what she's having and goes to the counter to order their drinks. The silence is awkward, and Claudia trawls her mind for a harmless topic, darting glances Greg's way, as if her impatience will speed up the process.

'So do you work locally?' she asks in desperation.

Jenny puts down the phone she's been fiddling with and gives a thin smile. 'Yes.'

'Right,' Greg says, setting steaming mugs down in front of them. 'First of all, thank you for agreeing to meet us.'

'I didn't realise you were going to bring *her*.'

'We felt it was important for Claudia to be part of this.'

He takes the folded order of service out of his pocket and lays it on the table between them, pushing it towards Jenny with his fingertips. 'You bumped into Sara Hartman that day. She was still Sara Massey then.'

Jenny glances at her handwritten note. 'I remember giving this to her. Can I ask how you got hold of it?'

'I was given it—'

Claudia interrupts. 'I stole it.'

'When was the last time you'd had any contact with Sara?' Greg says quickly. 'Before this, I mean?'

Jenny drags her eyes from Claudia's face. 'Oh God, years before. She left Lady Eden's in 2006.'

'You didn't stay in touch?'

'Nope. Sara neglected to tell any of us she wasn't coming back. I didn't find out until halfway through the summer holidays.'

'Did you try to contact her?'

'I didn't get very far. When she didn't return my calls, I went to her flat, but someone else was living there, so I gave up. I assumed she didn't want to know.'

'Were you close?'

Jenny makes a face. 'I thought we were. She was a bit off with our group that term and I hardly saw her outside school. It was weird.'

'You must have been hurt.'

'A little.'

'So, after Megan Holt kills herself, Sara Massey leaves the school without telling anyone she isn't coming back and drops all her friends, then reappears seven years later at a memorial service for the headmistress. She must have been very fond of Miss Colville.'

Jenny laughs. 'You're joking. Everyone hated her. That woman had the emotional range of a gnat.'

'If that's the case, why did Sara come?'

'The same reason most of us did, I presume. It was an excuse for a reunion.'

Greg nods. 'I get it. You want to know what everybody's up to, compare your lives. I've been to two. They're a mixture of fun and toe-curling embarrassment.'

'Exactly.' Jenny turns to Claudia. 'Why weren't you and Mr Hartman there?'

'Personal reasons.'

Claudia still feels uncomfortable about that decision. Miss Colville had taken pleasure in making them squirm all those years before. Maybe she's looking down at them now and laughing – *I warn you, nothing good will come of it*. She may have been right: if they had gone to the service, things might have turned out differently. It was possible they would still be a family. She swallows hard. She mustn't go down the *what if* road.

'So you spoke to Sara,' Greg says.

'Yes. It was before the service. She was standing outside on her own, sheltering from the rain under a tree. I recognised her and walked over.'

'That was friendly in the circumstances.'

Claudia's phone vibrates. She glances at the screen, sees DS Ward's name and rejects the call. Jenny looks at her in surprise, as if she's forgotten she's there. Such is Greg's animal magnetism, Claudia thinks.

Jenny shrugs. 'Life's too short to bear grudges. Sometimes we need to reinvent ourselves. I wasn't going to hold it against her. It wasn't easy for her at Lady Eden's.'

'Why was that?'

'Because she was there on a bursary. It was supposed to be confidential, but everyone knew. She was the only girl living in a housing authority flat, for one thing. It didn't make any difference to me, but she was sensitive about it.'

'What did you talk about?' Claudia asks.

'We talked about you. Well, you and Mr Hartman. I'd already heard he wasn't coming, because I'd been chatting to Megan Holt's mum.'

'How did *she* know?'

'Because your mother told her. At least that's what I remember. You're neighbours, aren't you? People who had been at the school during Mr Hartman's time there always remembered him. I told Sara it was probably because of his relationship with you. There was a lot of gossip when he didn't come back to the school in September. Joe Hartman leaving would have been a big thing. He was so popular. The fact that he kind of slunk away with no fanfare, no speeches; well, you know what schoolgirls are like. Then someone saw the two of you together at Heathrow airport. You were saying goodbye to each other and kissing like mad. Of course, the news swept round after that.'

Claudia winces.

'Sorry. I don't know how Sara missed it, but she'd left

a few days before it all blew up, so I suppose she was busy starting her new life. She had no idea Joe had married you, or that he was married at all. Though why she would think for one moment he wouldn't be, I have no idea. Wishful thinking, probably. Well, she's got him now. Funny how things turn out.'

'What exactly did you tell her?'

'That you and Joe had been in love since he started teaching there; that it had been the school's best-kept secret. Literally no one knew.'

'How did she react?'

'She seemed a little crushed, then she kind of picked up. She said she was surprised she hadn't heard about it, but I reminded her that she'd deliberately lost touch with us all. I wrote that note, then we went into the church. It was packed, so we couldn't sit together and had to squeeze onto the end of separate aisles. I didn't see her leave because I had to dash. For a while I thought she would call, because she was so friendly, but then she didn't and I thought, well, that's Sara for you. Listen, I'm sorry, but I should really get back to work.'

She reaches round for her coat and pushes her arms into the sleeves.

'Did you see who Sara sat next to?' Claudia asks.

'Yes, as a matter of fact, I did. She sat next to Megan's mother.'

'Where was Megan's sister sitting?'

Jenny thought for a moment. 'If Anna was there, it would have been on the other side of her father, because Mr Massey was sitting next to his wife. But I can't actually remember seeing her, to be honest.'

'Right,' Claudia says, glancing at Greg. 'Thank you so much.'

Jenny looks at her as she shuffles out from behind the table. 'I'm sorry about what you've been through.'

'There's one more thing,' Greg says, sparing Claudia the necessity of responding. 'Was Sara friendly with Megan?'

Jenny hitches the strap of her bag over her head. 'It's a funny thing. Sara was very careful about her image. If she couldn't live in a big house, she could at least be super cool. You'd have thought she wouldn't have been seen dead with someone like Megan Holt. But I saw them together once, in Kingston. They were in Starbucks and talking really intensely. Megan was crying and Sara got up and came round and sat beside her. She put her arm round her. It was weird, because in school it was as if they weren't even on the same planet.'

'When was this?' Claudia asks.

'Summer. The day Megan killed herself.'

'Did you tell anyone?' Greg asks.

Jenny looks put out. 'Yeah, I did. I told the policewoman who came to the school to interview us. I assume they asked Sara about it, but nothing came of it. Maybe Sara denied it. She was always very persuasive.'

Chapter 62

CLAUDIA

Walking to the station, Claudia is reeling. For years she's felt guilty about Megan, but Sara was with her that day.

'My money is still on Anna, because I cannot believe Sara would take my child then five years later come back and embed herself in the same community. On the day Tilly was stolen she found out about me and Joe. She was angry and hurt and she got her revenge by whispering poison about me into Frances Holt's ear and destroying the relationship between our families. It was pure spite, because it could just as well have been her fault that Megan took her own life. I might not have helped, but I didn't know Megan was in that state, and evidently Sara did. I reckon she did the damage, then left. But Anna was younger, more volatile.'

'How would Sara have known about your families?'

'Through Megan presumably.'

'And Anna didn't recognise Sara later on?'

'I don't think so. She's a lot younger and wasn't sitting beside her. She may not have clocked Sara's face or been interested enough at the time to make a mental note or even listen to what was being said. I imagine they would have lowered their voices out of respect. Also, Anna may have been distracted by her phone, texting her friends or whatever. Her parents could have picked apart what Sara said on the way home. They would have been in shock. I was Frances's best friend's daughter. She and Patrick would have discussed what to say to my parents. I suspect Anna absorbed all that even if they weren't talking to her directly.'

She turns her head to sneeze into the crook of her arm. 'Let's look at this again. Whether it's deliberate or he's unaware that he's doing it, Joe uses women to create a protective ring round himself when he's in trouble of his own making. I think he used Sara to help him with Megan after he found out that my family had a close relationship with the Holts. Then when Sara had served her purpose, he distanced himself, but in such a way that she wouldn't come after him. He's very clever.' A bus roars by, drowning her out, and she repeats her words. 'He left her with hope, just like he left me with hope, and Anna also, I assume.'

'Then his child is taken,' Greg says. 'He thinks it may have been Anna but he doesn't know for sure; all he knows is that he could be in a great deal of trouble, so when the police make you their prime suspect, he goes along with that narrative even if he has to make you believe you're crazy.'

Claudia nods. 'I get released, and he's managing the situation reasonably well, although he never assumes he's safe, and then Anna becomes a threat and suddenly the stakes are sky high. Loss of everything.'

'He silences her?'

Claudia bites down on her lip, pushing away the image

of Joe with Anna, his hands around her neck. She was with him for four years, six if you count Lady Eden's. She knows him. There isn't a violent bone in his body. She turns to Greg. 'He wouldn't. Joe could never do anything like that.'

'I'm sorry, but he absolutely could if he was convinced she was responsible for what happened to Tilly. Years of bottling it plus his own culpability. It's a recipe for an explosion. You're going to have to face facts. Joe played his part in what happened to your daughter by staying silent. We need to establish whether it was inadvertent or deliberate. Whether he turned a blind eye or simply didn't see it. All right?'

'All right,' Claudia answers sullenly.

Greg takes a breath before he speaks again. 'So let's say we're right. You are out of prison and rocking the boat. Anna is threatening him. Sara?'

Cold, she pulls her coat collar together at her throat. 'Sara is protecting him. She is absolutely in his thrall. You only have to look at how she came back years later hoping to see him again, expecting something. And when his life fell apart, she bided her time before making herself indispensable to his emotional well-being.' She nods to herself. 'She cast herself as the perfect choice of partner: the reliable wife after the car crash of his previous marriage. But I don't think she's ever felt secure. Look at her reaction when I left prison. When she saw me following her, she didn't push me away, she did the opposite. She tried to get close to me. She'll see me go back to prison before she sees Joe destroyed. She might be misguided, but she's cunning. Oh God, I think it's her who's getting into the house.'

'Really?'

Her adrenaline is so high it feels like she's on fire. 'Yes! It would be just like her. Everything has been so subtle. I'm going to ask her. If we can tick that off, then we're getting somewhere.'

'She won't tell you anything. You'll only put her on her guard.'

'Maybe, but even if she refuses to answer, I should get some sense of how involved she is.'

'I'll come with you.'

She rolls her eyes. 'I can manage fine on my own.'

'I don't doubt it. But so far everything you've told the police they've either disbelieved or ignored. You need a witness.'

Claudia's phone vibrates as she and Greg walk into the station. The screen reads *Mum*, and her heart misses a beat. Surely it should say *International*.

'Darling,' Louisa breathes. 'Thank God.'

'Mum? What's going on? Where are you?'

'At home. I couldn't twiddle my thumbs while you were in trouble. I could tell things were bad.'

Claudia cringes. 'If I'd known you were coming, I would have tidied. And I've been borrowing your clothes. I'm really sorry. Oh God, and Robert's car. I was going to get that fixed. I can explain. Please don't tell him.'

'Claudia. Stop. None of that matters right now.' Louisa's voice lowers to a whisper. 'The police are searching the house. They've found something. A pale blue scarf. Wasn't that what they said Anna was wearing the last time she was seen?'

'I told them that.' Claudia puts a hand to her head. 'It wasn't me, Mum. I've done nothing wrong.'

'I know, darling. Oh Lord. The detective's coming over.'

Claudia hears Detective Sergeant Ward's voice before Louisa can cover the mouthpiece. Then he's in her ear and he doesn't sound happy.

'You've been ignoring my calls, Mrs Hartman. Where are you?'

'I'm in central London. Mum says you've found a scarf.'

'Anna's husband has confirmed it's hers.'

'And it was in my house?'

'In the garden.'

'Well, I didn't put it there. You won't find my DNA on it.'

Greg is staring at her, eyebrows raised.

'That's a funny thing to say. Why won't we? Did you wear gloves?'

'No. I mean I didn't need to because I haven't been anywhere near it or Anna.'

'I expect to see you at the police station in one hour. If you don't turn up, I'm afraid I'll be forced to instigate proceedings to have you recalled.'

Claudia disconnects and switches off her phone. She's shaking. 'They've found Anna's scarf. He wants me to turn myself in within the hour. I'm going to be arrested.'

'Not necessarily.' Greg smiles. 'Come on, chin up. You know how unreliable public transport can be. I'm sure the detective will understand if you're a little late.'

Chapter 63

SARA

Frances Holt was the last person Sara expected to see when she opened the door. She'd thought it was the detective, and had arranged her face accordingly. She wished Joe had come home with her, but he'd insisted on speaking to each of his management team face to face. He refused to sneak off ignominiously.

'Hello again.' She added an upward tilt to the greeting, as though Frances were a canvassing politician.

'I didn't realise you were Joe Hartman's wife.'

'Who told you?'

'The detective. Well, he didn't tell me exactly. It came up in conversation and he assumed I knew.'

Sara attempted a wry smile. 'It's not something we advertise. I'm so sorry about what's happened. Have you heard anything?'

'Can I come in?'

'Yes, of course. Sorry, you must be frozen.'

She opened the door wider and Frances walked in, bringing with her a perfume that Sara remembered from long ago. Megan had sprayed herself with it once. It had been incongruous; a sophisticated, citrusy scent on a lump of a girl like that. Frances stamped grey slush onto the mat.

Maeve came in search of her, toddling like a drunk. Sara scooped her up and led Frances into the kitchen, moving instinctively to the kettle, taking it off its stand and filling it under the tap, all one-handed. When she looked round, her uninvited guest was standing in the doorway, still bundled up in her coat. Sara tamped down the fear. Frances didn't know anything. How could she?

'I came here once, years ago,' Frances said.

'Oh?'

'Anna was babysitting for Joe and Claudia. I picked her up, I can't remember why, and Claudia invited me in.' Her voice trailed off, and she walked over to the French windows. The snow was still on the ground, the small snowman Joe had made with Maeve still standing, though its carrot nose drooped and one of its twig fingers had dropped off. 'You and Anna haven't been friends for long, have you?'

'I've only known her for three weeks. She's a lovely person, Mrs Holt. You must be very proud of her.' Maeve was wriggling and Sara put her down. She grabbed hold of a chair and gazed up at Frances.

'Is there anything you can tell me?' Frances said. 'Because I'm desperate. She would never have left Max. We are all at our wits' end. I came here because I thought she might have told you something about her state of mind.'

Sara set two cups of tea on the table and sat down. 'I'm sorry I can't help, but I really didn't know her all that well.'

'We had words, you know, before she went missing.'

'What kind of words?'

'It was a misunderstanding. Something she said years ago that I misinterpreted. I just thought she might have

349

confided in you. I'm clutching at straws.' Frances's eyes searched Sara's face, then she gathered herself, and Sara had a feeling that what she said next would be what she had come to say. The rest was window-dressing.

'Anna had an abortion in 2013, a few weeks before Tilly Hartman went missing.'

Sara stiffened. This she hadn't expected. 'She never mentioned it to me, but that isn't surprising. It takes years of friendship before you build up enough trust to share something so deeply personal and distressing. I'm very sorry for her, though. How awful.'

'I knew nothing about it until she told me last week. She tried to tell me at the time, but I didn't listen properly. I only heard one thing that afternoon. Do you want to know what it was?'

The question didn't require an answer, so Sara kept her mouth shut.

'She said, "I got rid of the baby." If she had said, "I got rid of *my* baby", things might have been different. Do you understand what I'm saying?'

PART TWO

Chapter 64

Six days earlier: Thursday 9 November

SARA

'Was it better with Kate?' Joe asked, as they shut the door on Maeve and crept into their own bedroom.

'Much better.'

'I'm sorry if it was difficult for you, and I apologise for earlier. I should have thought.'

'It doesn't matter. And I'm sorry I was grumpy. It was lovely. Really. They're good friends.'

Actually, they weren't. She didn't recognise the portrait of her that Kate had painted. Kate was nasty: coming on to Joe and siding with him against Sara. She'd always known Kate preferred him, had probably preferred him to Claudia as well. She was a man's woman. Sara was surrounded by enemies. She had felt safe all these years, but now she knew it had been false security. The trouble was, it felt as though for every leak she plugged, another spurted up elsewhere. She got into bed, so tense she thought she might snap, and tried to get some sleep.

*

Her phone vibrating under her pillow at 3 a.m. woke her. She fumbled for it and folded the duvet back. Joe grumbled and reached for her, wrapping his arm loosely round her hip. Her body screamed in protest, but she gritted her teeth and kept still, and within minutes his breathing deepened and she could ease herself out. She put on the black leggings and hoodie she had hidden in the wash basket earlier, slipped her feet into a pair of black ankle boots and left the house.

She parked at the end of the alley running behind the gardens on Anna's side of Shires Close. She grabbed a bag for life from the collection in the boot and stuffed it into her pocket, then made her way down the footpath. It was pitch dark. Long wet grass soaked the hem of her track-suit bottoms and her ankle boots. A security light came on and she stifled a scream when something brushed her legs before taking fright. It scrambled over a fence.

She used the torch on her phone to work out which was the gate to number 14, Jocelyn's house, but there was a keypad on it. She could have sworn there hadn't been one when Owen had taken her in on Fireworks night. The family must have secured the house. She contemplated the fence, but it was too high for her to climb over without something to stand on, and even if she was fit enough to make the attempt, it would make too much noise.

She retraced her footsteps to the road and assessed her options. The close was dimly lit, the lamps further apart than they would be on the main road. A couple of security lights flashed on as she passed, electrifying her, but she kept going and slipped into the gap between Anna and Owen's house and number 14 without a problem.

The side gate had a brand-new key pad too, but there was a black bin, and the bonus of a blue plastic recycling box. She turned that upside down to use as a step, grabbed the top of the gate and hauled herself over, dropping down onto the path with no more than a quiet thud. She waited in the passageway, to make sure, then ran across the garden and breathed a sigh of relief when she saw the shed didn't have a lock.

She recognised the smell as soon as she went in. Damp, creosote, oil, rotting wood. She turned on the torch on her phone and leaned it up against an old paint tin, then set the bag down on the floor, puffing it out with her hands so that it stood. Using a rusted chisel, she lifted one of the floorboards, the horror of it making her gag. She reached behind her for her phone, shut her eyes for a second, then swallowed hard and shone it in. The shallow grave she had so frantically dug in the dirt ten years ago was empty.

Chapter 65

Wednesday 15 November

SARA

Sara stared at Frances. 'Why are you telling me this?'

Frances finally removed her coat. She hung it over the back of the chair opposite Sara's and sat down. 'I've no idea. I haven't felt able to discuss it with my husband, so I suppose I'm thinking out loud. Do you mind?'

'I can't stop you.'

Frances lifted the corners of her lips. 'Louisa had come round earlier, while Anna was still out. She told me her granddaughter had gone missing. She was in a dreadful state. I wasn't in the mood to be helpful, because of what you'd told me at Miss Colville's memorial service – don't look so surprised. I knew we'd met before, but couldn't think where until today. You knew all about Megan. Quite a coincidence, isn't it? You befriend one of my children and she dies; you befriend another and she goes missing.'

'I didn't befriend Megan. I barely knew her.'

'You knew her well enough for her to tell you her secrets. How else would you have known how Claudia treated her that day? But I suppose you'd got bored of her by then. I expect the hero worship was flattering, but a bit tiresome after a while. I know what my daughter was like. Megan was prone to crushes on the classmates who rejected her. Why did you even make friends with her? Surely she didn't have anything you wanted?'

Sara sidestepped the question. 'You're reading too much into this. I barely knew Megan.'

'Don't lie to me or I'll go straight to the police. I need you to tell me what was going on that summer, and why my daughter died.'

'Does Anna's father know you're talking to me?'

'No. I didn't want to distress him unnecessarily, not before I'd spoken to you. When I get home, I'll explain.'

Sara mulled this over. Perhaps there was still time to repair the damage. 'Okay. We hung out for a few weeks while we were doing the play. Megan did tell me what happened with Claudia, but I thought she was just trying to make herself interesting, because you're right, she had become a little tiresome. As for Anna, when I met her a couple of weeks ago, I decided not to mention that I'd known Megan. It was a long time ago.'

Frances took a hanky out of her bag and blew her nose. 'Not that long. The reason I'm here, Sara, is because I think what happened back then and your behaviour at the memorial service is somehow linked to Tilly Hartman's disappearance.'

'I don't understand,' Sara said. Her mind was jumping ahead, trying to second-guess her unwanted visitor, to formulate her responses.

'Anna hadn't been listening in church, but she saw we

were distressed when we came out. Patrick and I told her what had happened, what you'd said about Claudia. Anna left the house soon after we got back. The weather was getting worse, so I tried to stop her. But you know fifteen-year-old girls. About half an hour after Louisa had been round, hysterical over Claudia and Joe's baby, Anna came back soaked to the skin and went straight up to her room. She looked extremely upset, so I followed her. I sat on her bed and put my arm around her, and she didn't shake me off. That in itself was unusual. And that's when she said it: "I got rid of the baby." I jumped to conclusions. I was terrified. I truly believed that she had taken revenge for Megan's death in the most appalling way. Then she said, "I don't want to talk about it, ever." And I said okay. What else could I have done? I wasn't going to turn her in. I got it so wrong.' She shrugged sadly. 'I'm a psychiatrist, and I failed both my daughters.'

This was so patently true, Sara could only nod.

'I remember Anna coming home from babysitting Tilly Hartman one night, and she was on a high. I was a little suspicious, but I knew Joe reasonably well because of his relationship to the Myhills, and because I'd known him as Megan's teacher at Lady Eden's and Anna's once he moved to Overhill. It honestly didn't occur to me that he'd take advantage. I thought maybe she'd snuck a boyfriend into the house.'

Sara felt tension invade her muscles and tighten around her head. Joe had made one stupid mistake, and not that she was in favour of victim-blaming, but it was Anna who had made the first move in the car that night. Anna who had been fantasising about her teacher, Anna who'd made a pass at a man staggering under the combined strain of caring for his mentally unwell wife and his baby. Whatever his failings, it had to be Joe. It was always Joe.

'Joe did not touch your daughter. If she said he did, she was lying. He wouldn't do something like that.'

'Are you certain?' Frances asked.

'Absolutely. He loved Claudia. There's no way he would have betrayed her with a fifteen-year-old girl. That's disgusting.'

It was only a kiss, she told herself. Only a kiss.

'But Claudia was a mess at the time,' Frances said. 'If he was tempted, who could blame him?'

'That would make him a paedophile and a rapist, Frances, so don't you dare accuse him.'

'Defend him all you like, but I believe my daughter.'

'You covered up for your daughter. You impeded the investigation. You could get in a lot of trouble for that.'

'But the facts are there. You were in Megan's class at Lady Eden's and she died. You made friends with Anna and she vanished.'

'Coincidence. Why would I hang out with someone like Megan?'

Frances flinched. 'Because you needed something from her. I believe what happened to Megan has a bearing on what's happened to Anna.'

Sara frowned. 'You thought it gave Anna a motive to kill Tilly Hartman. So you got rid of the evidence.'

'What else could I do after letting her down so badly? I'd already lost Megan. I wasn't losing another daughter. That night, Jocelyn called me because she thought she'd seen an intruder near her shed. I went out with a torch to investigate. I found a scrap of material caught between two floorboards, and when I tugged it, the boards moved.

Sara swallowed hard. 'What did you do with the body?'

Chapter 66

SARA

Perhaps she'd made a mistake, Sara thought as she quietly let herself into the house. Maybe Tilly's bones had shifted over the years. Maybe a fox had got under there. Her hands shook. Banished memories flooded back. She recalled her fear, her disbelief at the situation she'd found herself in. An impulse born of fury and hurt had led her to do something so stupid, so deeply unpleasant, it had destroyed lives. She had spent years regretting it, years trying to get past it. And all because she'd offered to help the man she was in love with: her teacher. But what good did dwelling on past mistakes ever do? She was here to ensure her family had a future.

With her in it.

There was a chance she was fussing over nothing, wasn't there? Perhaps the corpse had rotted away. It had been pitch dark in the shed, and hard to see even with the torch. And she'd been retching as she pulled up the loose board, her eyes wet and stinging.

So many maybes. She had to ignore them and face the facts.

She had placed Tilly Hartman's body in the gap under the floor of the shed in the garden of number 14 Shires Close.

Tilly's remains were no longer there.

Sara eased herself back into bed, careful not to touch Joe with her cold hands and feet. Anna had deliberately dangled Jocelyn's house in front of her. She had accompanied her when she went to view it, had watched her reaction, had told her when the house clearance firm would be coming. Could that be a coincidence? Sara didn't think so.

Chapter 67

Wednesday 15 November

SARA

'I put it in a sports bag with some old tools I found in the shed and dropped it into the Thames from Teddington footbridge,' Frances said.

Sara bit her lip, calculating. In that case, any DNA evidence would be too corrupted to use. She could still deny having anything to do with it.

Frances pressed her finger and thumb into her tear ducts and took a deep breath. 'Now I find out that Anna had nothing to do with Tilly's abduction, and she knows her mother believed her capable of a dreadful crime. I blame you for that.'

Sara stared at her as the truth dawned. 'It was you who set fire to Claudia's flat. You thought you were protecting Anna. How could you be so stupid?'

'It was the only way,' Frances answered. 'I thought I was saving Anna. You were wearing a dark quilted coat with a fur-lined hood in the church that day, weren't you? Like the kidnapper. I remember the fur brushing against my hand when I stood up just before you. Anna didn't own a coat like that. Where did you go after the service?'

'Home.'

'Funny that you have Joe now, isn't it? Anna told me you were interested in buying number 14. She couldn't understand it, given Joe's history with the Myhill family. She said you made an offer behind his back, that you seemed desperate to get it. I might be guilty of perverting the course of justice, but you? You're guilty of the abduction and murder of an innocent child. You are the monster, not Claudia. Not me. It's time for a reckoning, Sara.'

Sara was rigid, caught in the headlights, her mouth dry, her heart hammering. 'You can't go to the police. After what you did, concealing evidence and lying through your teeth, not to mention arson and trespassing. You'll be locked up too.'

'Oh my God. Do you think I care?'

Frances shoved her out of the way, and Sara lurched so hard against the dresser it rocked and a china plate fell and broke on the floor. She marched out of the room, leaving Sara reeling with shock. The front door opened, there was an *oof* sound, then Joe's voice.

'Frances. What are you doing here?'

364

Chapter 68

Five days earlier: Friday 10 November

SARA

Waking up the morning after Kate and Paul's dinner, Sara found earth beneath her fingernails and panicked, scrubbing them until they felt raw. She had lost control of the situation and she was scared. Word was getting round and soon everyone would know she'd been at Lady Eden's. She felt as though a great big finger was pointing at her everywhere she went. She was ill with anxiety, and the more she told herself not to lose it, the sicker she felt.

Anna knew something. It was that note in her voice when she'd relayed Owen's decision to buy number 14: triumph. As if she truly thought she had the advantage. Sara would talk to her again, try and assess what her agenda was. Thankfully, Kate's au pair had taken Maeve across the road to play, an arrangement made before she and Kate had fallen out.

She glanced out of the window. It was snowing heavily. She could be wrong, of course; she had barely slept, her thoughts on a reel. For the first time, she experienced something of what it must feel like to be Claudia, clinging to the edge of paranoia. She was unable to understand why things had panned out this way, why she was in so much trouble. Life had been good before Claudia left prison, and it would have continued to be good, because she'd never have met Anna.

She called Anna before she could change her mind.

'Do you fancy a walk? I'm desperate for fresh air and adult company.'

'I'm doing Owen's VAT,' Anna said. 'But sure. I could use a break.

'I'll meet you at the entrance to Ditton Hill.'

Anna kissed her on the cheek. 'I feel like I'm bunking off school. Mum doesn't know I'm out.'

Sara smiled. 'Same. Joe thinks I'm packing.'

They walked briskly along the by now almost invisible footpaths, Sara wittering nervously about their buyers, who had come round with their builder and interior decorator and basically poured scorn on all Sara and Joe's decorative decisions. They'd brought their two obnoxious sons, who had pounded up and down the stairs, yelling. Anna appeared to be listening, but Sara was doing most of the talking. Every so often she thought about last night and her stomach churned.

'Why didn't you tell me you were at Lady Eden's with my sister?' Anna asked.

Sara was ready for the question. She assumed everyone knew by now. 'Because it never came up.'

'I asked you where you went to school. You said Bristol.'

'What I remember is someone I'd only just met probing me for information. I thought you were trying to see if I was worth getting to know. I lied because I resented having to pass some kind of test.'

'I don't know why you should be so oversensitive.'

Anna pulled off her scarf, then rewound it so that it covered her chin, giving Sara a chance to recalibrate. Her mind was working through options like she was playing a game of chess. So much depended on what Anna's agenda was. There might be nothing sinister behind this. It might just be annoyance. Anna had shared things with her; why hadn't Sara shared back?

'I am oversensitive,' she said finally. 'I was made to feel less somehow at Lady Eden's because of my family circumstances. And I'm sorry I lied. I was chippy and defensive. I understand now that you were only being friendly.'

They walked along, feet crunching in the snow, a heaviness descending on them. Anna muttered something, and Sara wasn't sure she'd heard her right.

'What did you say?'

'I said, your husband had sex with me when I was fifteen.'

Chapter 69

Wednesday 15 November

SARA

Sara ran out into the hall and pulled Frances back by the shoulder. Frances turned on her in alarm.

'Get off me.'

Joe stood in the doorway, taking in the scene. 'What on earth is going on?'

'You'll have to ask your wife about that.' Frances did up the zip on the coat. 'Because I'm leaving.'

'Close the door, Joe. Don't let her out.'

'What are you talking about? Has everyone gone mad?'

'Your wife killed your daughter,' Frances said.

'I know that.'

'Not Claudia. This wife. I'm going to the police.'

Joe frowned. 'Okay, let's not do anything hasty. Sara didn't kill Tilly; she hasn't killed anyone. I know you're worried about Anna, but making mad accusations about my wife is not going to help find her.'

'Mad accusations? Your darling wife—'

'Shut up,' Sara said through her teeth. 'Or I'm going to tell him what you did.'

Frances laughed. 'By all means. Go ahead. I have nothing to lose now.'

Sara turned to Joe, her eyes imploring him to take her part. 'Frances has admitted to throwing Tilly into the Thames.'

'That is not what I said!'

'Shut up.' Joe was still blocking the front door. 'Sara?'

'I can explain. She's lying.'

'Please let me leave,' Frances said.

'Not until we've sorted this out.'

Joe marched both women into the kitchen, almost tripping over Maeve. He picked her up and cradled her, his hand curved protectively round her head.

'Right. Will someone tell me what the fuck is going on?'

'I thought Anna had done it,' Frances said. 'There was a misunderstanding.' She shot him a look filled with hate. 'She told me she got rid of the baby. It was just after I'd found out Tilly was missing, so I thought that was what she meant.'

The blood drained from Joe's face. 'I don't understand.'

'You got my daughter pregnant when she was a schoolgirl. She had an abortion.' She took a moment, then added, 'And don't you dare lie to me. If anything's happened to Anna, I'm laying it at your door. I can tell the police where to look for Tilly, but first you have to tell them where I can find Anna.'

His eyes pleaded with Sara. 'Why does she think it was you? Please tell me she's wrong.'

Sara held his gaze. 'She's wrong. She has no evidence, nothing. She wants you to suffer for what you did to Anna. She and Anna are exactly the same; always looking for

369

someone else to blame for their mistakes and failures. It's pretty sad.'

'Is this true, Frances?'

Frances raised her head. Her eyes were bloodshot. 'I can't prove it, but it wasn't Anna, and I don't think it was Claudia, not any more. I've made a mess of things and I'm prepared to accept the consequences, but one way or another the truth is going to come out and my daughter is going to be found. God knows I hope and pray she's alive, but if she isn't, I have no doubt that your wife's DNA will be all over her.'

Chapter 70

Five days earlier: Friday 10 November

SARA

Sara couldn't process this. Joe had said a kiss. Just a kiss. Ambushed by his infatuated babysitter. A mistake. On the green to their left, children pelted each other with snowballs; to the right, wooded paths created some shelter. Snow clung to Sara's fur-lined hood and settled on the toes of her stout walking boots.

'It isn't true.'

'I was in love with him,' Anna said. 'Joe was literally everything to me, and he knew it. When I met you that day and you told me you were married to him, I knew I had to see him again. I was going to look him in the eye.' She shrugged. 'But it was like he'd forgotten it ever happened.'

'Joe would never do that. He didn't touch Claudia when they were at Lady Eden's together.'

'That's only what they told you. I've never really believed it. I was their babysitter. He loved that. He couldn't keep his hands off me.'

'You're lying. Joe is not a sleaze.' Sara felt her certainty ebbing and knew it was detectable in her voice.

'That's the thing, though. It never felt sleazy. Anyway, it didn't last. He was already beginning to distance himself. He said things like I was too young, that he'd lose his career if we were discovered, and if that happened there would be no chance for us. I refused to read the writing on the wall and clung like a limpet. When I realised I was pregnant, I didn't tell him; I just went ahead and had an abortion. I went by myself; no one knew. It was awful.' Anna's face reddened. 'I went to see him after the memorial service. I was all worked up. I thought he would take my side, be as disgusted with Claudia as I was. When he was less than sympathetic, I started pushing. I told him about the pregnancy. I could tell he was terrified and wanted nothing to do with it or me. I was so embarrassed, so heartbroken and angry, I just left and went home and cried and cried. It was only when I saw the police in the close that I knew something had happened. I had no idea Mum thought it was me, but our relationship was weird after that.'

Sara was finding it hard not to scream. Anna was lying. She had to be.

'I never spoke up, never blamed Joe for anything. I got on with my life. I saw him from time to time going in and out of number 7, but he stopped visiting Shires Close when Claudia went to prison. When I finally met him at the fireworks, it was such a disappointment. I just thought, you're a sad middle-aged man. He even flirted with me. It was pathetic. Why would I look at him when I'm married to an alpha male like Owen?'

'Oh my God.' Sara stared at her. 'He rejected you. You went to Overhill to prove you were all grown up, not the silly little girl with a crush on her teacher, and he rejected you. You're just like Megan. A fantasist. I bet the pregnancy was a lie, thought up to emotionally blackmail him.'

'You're right about Megan, it was all fantasy. But I could have proved the pregnancy and abortion if I'd chosen to. It's too late now.'

'Why didn't you?'

'I still loved him. I thought about it when Me Too became a big thing, but by then he was already broken. He'd been punished enough.' She sighed. 'Once I've told the police what I know, they'll reopen Tilly's case. I hope you have a decent alibi. I'd better turn round soon. I can't leave Mum with Max for too long. He's a nightmare when he's tired. He had me up at two in the morning.'

'Poor you,' Sara said tonelessly.

'I know, right? For such a quiet little cul-de-sac, it's amazing how much activity there is at night. I've even seen badgers. So imagine my surprise when I looked out of Max's window and saw someone all dressed in black creeping across Jocelyn's garden. It gave me the fright of my life.'

'I bet it did,' Sara managed. She was thankful to be swaddled in thick winter outer wear. The layers disguised her trembling.

'They got into the shed. Odd, don't you think?'

'Very. I wonder what they wanted.'

'Oh, I don't know. Probably garden tools.'

'You should report it.'

Anna shrugged. 'Shall we stop playing games? I know it was you, I know what you were looking for and I know why you were so keen to buy a house that's patently unsuitable for your family. Your face when I told you Owen was going for it – utter horror.'

'That might be the way you interpreted it. I was naturally upset. You seemed to relish telling me.'

Anna smirked. 'That's true. I did enjoy the moment, but that's not what this is about. I don't know if it was deliberate or an accident, but I do know that what happened to Tilly Hartman was your fault.'

Chapter 71

SARA

Joe turned to Sara. The look on his face almost rent her in two. 'Is she telling the truth?'

'No! You have to believe me. I could never do something like that.'

'I'm calling the police.'

'Don't. Please, Joe. I can explain everything.'

'I don't want to hear it. You're disgusting.'

'You're as bad as each other,' Frances said. 'You're going to pay for what you've done to my family. I hope the pair of you rot in hell.'

There was a prolonged silence. Then Sara spoke up.

'It was Joe's fault that Megan killed herself, not mine. She was unhappy, and he talked to her, encouraged her to rely on him, maybe even cuddled her. Megan misinterpreted it. She thought he found her attractive, and then when he realised and tried to distance himself, she threatened to tell the head teacher that he'd sexually harassed her. You were scared, weren't you, Joe?'

Joe looked at her with mute appeal, but she couldn't stop now she'd started. She had to save herself.

'I offered to help him, Frances. I offered to convince Megan she'd imagined it. He shouldn't have involved me, but instead he encouraged me to gaslight a vulnerable girl.'

She couldn't meet his eyes. The betrayal on both sides was too great. Their marriage had crumpled so easily.

Frances's voice sliced through the tension. 'If you're not going to tell me where Anna is, then the police can deal with you.'

She pushed past Joe. Maeve let out a yell, and while Joe was distracted, Sara grabbed a knife.

Chapter 72

Five days earlier: Friday 10 November

SARA

The snow was falling hard. For a second Sara wished that Maeve and Joe were with her. What fun they would have had. But the chances of living that beautiful life were fast disappearing. 'I don't know where you got that idea from, but you've got your wires crossed. Tilly's death had nothing to do with me. I wasn't in the garden last night and you can't prove I was.'

'Did you know my sister used to visit Jocelyn?'

Sara frowned. 'What on earth has that got to do with me?'

'Megan hung out with an elderly lady because she didn't have friends her own age. Except perhaps the summer she took her own life. I'm right, aren't I? Megan wanted a friend badly, but unfortunately she found you.'

'I have literally no idea what you're talking about.'

Sara veered off the track, plunging into the woods, where the paths were less well defined. Anna caught her up.

'When I first met you, I had a feeling I'd seen you before somewhere. And I had, hadn't I? It was you at Miss

Colville's memorial service, sitting next to Mum. It was you who told her about Claudia and Megan. What made you do that? Spite?'

Sara remembered that day vividly. What Jenny Buckland had revealed had smashed the stuffing out of her. In the days running up to the service, she had fantasised about meeting Joe there, him seeing her for the first time as a woman, their instant connection. The gutting disappointment at his absence, and then the realisation that he and Claudia had used her, had upset her dreadfully. So when she spotted Frances Holt sitting at the end of a row, she hadn't been able to help herself. She politely asked if Frances could make space. She hadn't intended for the ramifications to be so far-reaching, obviously, but why shouldn't the Holts know what Claudia had said? She had done them a service.

'It's caught up with you now,' Anna said. 'You've had Joe for five years. I hope it was worth it, because you're going to be inside a lot longer than that.'

Sara turned on her. 'Do you think anyone's going to believe you, or even be interested? Someone breaks into a shed in a dead woman's garden? Wow. The police don't even pursue house burglaries these days. You're being ridiculous.'

'Am I? You're a manipulative bitch who preys on weaker women and will do anything to preserve your reputation. There was no way you were going to let the shed be pulled down before you removed Tilly's remains.'

Sara's breathing was ragged. She was aware of every pull and push of her lungs. It hung in the air, a thick mist that wetted her face under the hood.

'I've told you. You were mistaken. It wasn't me. I expect

it was someone who saw the death announcement and thought they'd try their luck.'

Anna's laugh was more of a sneer. 'So they broke into the shed rather than the house. Seriously? Not a very ambitious burglar, then. I presume it's where you hid Tilly's corpse. Forensics will still find evidence, you know. There'll be hair, or blood, or even skin cells. You do realise that, don't you? I'm going home now. I'll give you until this evening to walk into a police station and tell the truth. I might not be able to prove that I saw you last night, but I will tell them what Joe did to me. They'll soon figure out the rest.'

Sara refused to fall apart. Anna had nothing concrete on her. She wished she'd never listened to Claudia, never offered to contact Anna. She'd only done it to win Claudia's confidence; she'd never thought Anna would be a problem.

'You destroyed Claudia's life,' Anna said. 'Why did you come back for Joe? To revel in it?'

Sara stared at her. She felt a hot trickle on her cheek and realised she had started to cry. She couldn't breathe and her pulse was racing, her knees felt like jelly. She opened and shut her mouth like a fish. Nothing came out.

'Goodbye, Sara.'

They'd reached the edge of the park. Not the salubrious side bordered by expensive family homes, but the side that crept up against the dual carriageway where a stretch had been closed for repairs. The ground there was scrubby and uneven and an overgrown drainage ditch marked the territory. A culvert ran under the road. When Anna turned on her heel to walk away, Sara picked up a cement-encrusted brick and smashed it against her head. Anna dropped like a stone.

Chapter 73

Wednesday 15 November

CLAUDIA

On the train, she and Greg sit opposite each other, both lost in thought. She has the answer to the puzzle, now she only needs to prove it. Anna took Tilly on impulse because she was broken. Something happened – Claudia can't bear to speculate what that might be – and she panicked. Joe said nothing, even though he suspected it was Anna, because it would have damaged him so badly. Fast forward ten years to Claudia's release, and Anna is terrified. And then Sara gets involved. Sara wants Claudia back inside because she's terrified of losing Joe. Claudia isn't sure, but it seems likely that either she's convinced he's still in love with her, or she thinks he'll be charged with grooming and rape if Claudia starts overturning stones. Unbeknownst to them the two women have been working towards the same aim. She sits back, brooding. An end is in sight, but it's unlikely to bring her daughter home, and she knows that once she gets there, there will be no euphoria. She will still be grieving, still unable to hug and kiss her child.

She glances at Greg. He's scrolling through something

on his phone. The man is an enigma. He has made himself her friend, taken advantage of her situation, but she doesn't resent him for it, because she senses something else: a need for justice. He's out for what he can get, but he's on her side too. And that matters very much in a world where she can trust no one. She allows herself to imagine their friendship continuing after all this is over. If she goes back to prison, will he visit her? If she's freed and exonerated, will he move on to the next irresistible story? She'll be sad if he does distance himself. It's just one more reason why she won't relax her guard around him.

She thinks about her final summer at Lady Eden's. She wasn't at school much because she was revising for her A levels, so she wasn't aware anything was wrong until Joe confided in her. Megan Holt, a Year 11 girl who also happened to be the daughter of her mother's best friend and a neighbour, had threatened to report him to Miss Colville for sexual assault. Claudia knew Joe had done nothing wrong, that the girl had been so wrapped up in her dreams she actually thought there was a romance brewing between them, but she could see the danger he was in. He was a young man, at the beginning of his career, and an accusation of that nature could wreck his life. She had offered to talk to Megan. Joe had almost taken her up on it, until she told him that the Holts lived in Shires Close and knew her family well. He changed his mind after that and insisted he had things under control.

But she interfered anyway.

It's taken her a long time to admit that she was poisonous that day, that Megan's deep unhappiness and sense of betrayal may have been exacerbated by that nasty put-down. Even knowing Sara was involved, she doesn't let herself off the hook. She had been cruel and she profoundly regrets it.

What had Sara expected in return for saving Joe? And what did Megan's suicide do to her? Unless Sara is a psychopath, she must have felt partly responsible, and with no one to talk to about it, her anxiety would have been off the scale. Only one thing would have kept her going: the belief that Joe Hartman loved her. Had Joe said the same thing to her he'd said to Claudia? *You're so young; go out into the world and live a bit. I'll wait for you.*

Had he taken advantage of Sara's feelings to clear up a potentially career-sabotaging problem? Had he allowed Sara to think he had turned to her because she was special, that she was saving him, thus creating a problem that would reverberate down the years? But this is all speculation. There's no evidence of Sara and Joe having had any kind of relationship before Tilly was abducted. Just a part in a school play.

Claudia rubs the tiredness out of her eyes. *I'll wait for you.* He had waited for her, hadn't he? Or had she too heard only what she wanted to hear? When she'd finished her teacher training, she had called him, and he'd been delighted to hear from her, eager to meet, but now that she thinks back, she accepts there's something that she's blanked: a tiny hesitation after she said, 'Hi, Joe. It's Claudia,' imagining the look on his face. He'd been over-friendly afterwards, as if to make amends for his lapse of memory. She'd conveniently forgotten that, because it wasn't part of their love story. How could she have kidded herself for so long?

It's absurd, but then again, it isn't, not with hindsight. She didn't doubt that Joe had loved her, but if she hadn't turned up when he was between relationships, he probably wouldn't have given her a second thought. Had it been the same for Sara? For Anna? She sits up straighter.

Jesus, Joe.

Greg suddenly speaks. 'How did Sara do all this stuff when she had Maeve? Sneaking in and out of someone else's house requires planning. She would have needed to know when you were out. She would have had to arrange for Maeve to be looked after, she would've had to go at a time when she wouldn't be noticed. It does seem a bit improbable.'

Claudia's sense of possibility dims slightly. 'I suppose so. Whoever it was removed the iPhone cable from behind the washing machine, so there's no evidence.'

'Plus, it's highly unlikely Sara is strong enough to have carried you up to your bedroom. I know you're skinny, but you'd have been a dead weight.' He taps his fingers on his thigh. 'The person with the best opportunity would have been someone else in the close, wouldn't it? Someone who had a view of the house, who knew when you were coming and going. Someone with muscle. A man. What about Owen Pemberton?'

She thinks about it. 'No. He's brash and unpleasant, but I don't think so. He's happy to tell me what he thinks of me to my face, and he knows I'll be leaving soon. There was never a danger of me staying. Why would he bother? Joe, on the other hand,' she muses. 'It would have been easier for him. No baby to deal with. And he can slip away from Overhill pretty much any time it suits him. It's dark by four at the moment, so if he was careful, he could avoid being seen. He knows the house well, and he knows we have a back gate.'

Greg nods. 'Fucking creepy if it was him. What's his motive?'

'The fire made him realise he was on shaky ground. I might not be guilty. But...' she follows her chain of thought, 'he still wants me put away for life, because if I'm not, and the investigation is reopened, then everything falls apart. For once he can't use a woman to get him out of trouble. He has to deal with it himself. He needs to silence me because he's petrified his dubious relationships with his teenage pupils will come out. He will want to keep his new family out of it at all costs. Add Anna to the mix, and he's feeling the strain. Oh God. Do you think Joe is the reason Anna is missing?'

'Do you mean has he killed her?'

'I didn't say that.'

'But that's the implication, isn't it? Anna has been gone five days now. The chances of her being alive are slim. Hang on.' His phone is ringing.

When he answers the call, Claudia detects a flicker of excitement in his eyes.

'Right. Of course. I'll be there in an hour.' He pockets the phone.

'What is it?'

'A situation I've been following for a few weeks. There's a big celebrity involved. It looks like the boil is about to burst. I'm sorry, Claudia, but it's my job.'

She raises her eyebrows. 'Nice to know where I stand.' She's joking, but she feels a cold wind swirl around her; she's become accustomed to the warmth of his presence.

'Don't worry. I'll have a chat with Sara and catch up with you later.'

'No, don't. Go home, and I'll message you when I'm free. We'll beard her together.'

'I'll be fine, Greg. Really.'

He leans forward, hands clasped on his knees. 'But what if Joe is there? This guy's watched you being charged with the abduction and murder of your baby. He's watched your reputation being savaged by people like me, and he's said nothing. If you believe he killed Anna to keep the truth from coming out, then you have to believe him capable of anything.'

Claudia scowls at him. 'Joe won't be there. He'll be at work.'

'No he won't,' Greg says. 'He's taken temporary leave. I've a feeling it might be a kind way of saying he's being suspended.'

'What? How do you know? Oh, yeah.' She smiles. 'Your sister-in-law's friend.'

'Please don't go there. Wait for me.'

She huffs. 'Okay.'

'Good.' He sits back, relieved.

When they get off the train, she slips her phone into Greg's bag before they part company, Greg for the station car park where he left his car earlier, Claudia for the bus stop. She's not entirely sure of the physics regarding iPhones and the tracing of errant suspects, but obviously there's something in it, because it's often referred to in the crime dramas she's been watching. She does not want to be tracked to Sara's house by an impatient DS Ward.

Chapter 74

Five days earlier: Friday 10 November

SARA

The swiftness, the cool decisiveness with which she'd acted stunned her. She stared down at Anna, then dropped to her knees in the snow and pressed her fingers against Anna's neck. No pulse. Anna's flesh felt hot in contrast to the cold that gathered about them. Sara shuddered with horror. This was a deliberate kill, unlike the accident that had taken Tilly Hartman. A crow came down to land close by. It tilted its head, appearing to assess her. She swept out an arm and it flapped up into the air with a scolding caw.

She took Anna's phone out of her bag and put it in her pocket, then with gloved hands, she pulled brambles away from the entrance to the culvert. She grasped Anna's wrists, but her hands slipped on Anna's wet skin, so she was forced to bend into her, put her face close to Anna's, her hands under her arms, and drag her. The entrance was no more than two feet high, and narrow. If she pulled her in, she wouldn't be able to get out herself, not without cramming their bodies together. She folded Anna so that her head flopped down like a marionette with its strings cut, then stifled a visceral recoil and shunted the body into the culvert and crammed the bag in with it. She didn't allow herself time to catch her breath before pulling foliage and bracken over the entrance.

As she turned to go, she glimpsed something snagged against the fence. Anna's scarf. Hearing a rustle close by, she swiftly bundled it up and stuffed it into her pocket with the phone, then set off at a jog, blinded by the thickly falling snow. When she glanced back, her footprints had almost vanished.

The thought of the world discovering what she was, of Joe knowing what she'd done, of Maeve eventually finding out, threatened to entirely dismantle all the hard work she'd had to do on her mental health in order to live with the past. Years of training her mind to block it, years of trying to atone by giving Joe some vague shadow of what he'd lost, and what for?

No. It was impossible. Anna was gone and there was no evidence to suggest Sara had had anything to do with it. Claudia might be a threat to her, but it wouldn't occur to anyone that Anna Pemberton was. She choked on a sob as she pushed forward, hood up, chin tucked into her chest, back to her car, brushing dirt and leaves off her coat and picking brambles out of her woollen gloves. No one noticed her.

She swept a blanket of snow from her windscreen, thinking it was a blessing that Anna had arrived on foot and there wasn't the presence of her car to worry about, then drove away. At home, she stripped off her clothes, put everything into a hot wash, showered and blow-dried her hair. When she put on her coat to collect Maeve from the

Shaws, she found Anna's scarf and phone in her pocket and swore silently. She ran upstairs and pushed them deep into one of the charity bags. She'd think about what to do with them later.

Chapter 75

Wednesday 15 November

CLAUDIA

Claudia rings Sara's doorbell again. The baby is crying, and it sounds as though she has been for some time. She is becoming increasingly uneasy. She presses the base of her palm against the bell and keeps it there until she detects movement beyond the stained-glass windows.

Eventually, Sara opens the door. Bizarrely, since it's the middle of the day, she's wearing a dressing gown. Not that Claudia is judging; she used to do the same when she was ill. Sara isn't ill, though, or not as far as Claudia knows. She looks dishevelled.

'Sorry. Sorry. I was spark out on the sofa. Bad night.'

'Can I come in? I need to talk to you.'

When Sara lets her in, some instinct of self-preservation makes Claudia discreetly put the door on the latch before she closes it.

'Shouldn't you check she's okay?' she says, peering up the stairs to the closed door on the half-landing.

'Excuse me? I know what my own child needs.'

Sara turns and shuffles into the kitchen. Claudia

recognises her former self in that shuffle, and the feeling of dread, of something being out of kilter, deepens.

'A little accident,' Sara explains.

She follows Claudia's gaze to a scattering of broken china at the foot of the dresser.

Claudia's diaphragm contracts. She tells herself to keep calm. The baby is crying, so nothing has happened to her.

'Where's Joe?'

'At work.'

'I thought he'd taken some time off.'

'You've been misinformed.'

Claudia tries to be patient, to tread carefully. Sara is behaving like someone who's just woken from a horrific nightmare, something Claudia can empathise with. She wonders what's happened. 'Fine, but maybe we should call him.'

'Now why would we want to do that?'

'Because you're not well. Your baby is crying her eyes out and you're barely reacting.'

'So speaks the good mother.'

Claudia takes a deep breath, holds onto her nerve and doesn't react to the provocation. There's a weird smell, heavy and pungent, that she can't place. 'Surely you must know by now what he is, Sara.'

'I'm not sure what you're getting at, but what you and your seedy little friend insinuated was unforgivable. According to you, Joe never even touched you before the end of that summer. And he barely knew I existed. God, you are destructive.'

'You were in *Romeo and Juliet*, which Joe directed.'

'As were at least twenty other girls.'

390

'If it was so innocent, why did you keep it quiet?'

'Why are you here, Claudia?'

'Because I need to ask you if you've been in my house, moving things around.'

Sara tilts her head. 'No. What would I do that for?'

'To terrorise me. You're scared of what I could do to Joe. If the press find out about Megan they'll tear him apart. Even if he's innocent, it'll be a stain on him. You must see how it looks, how the police might construe it.'

Sara narrows her eyes. 'Are you threatening me?'

'No. I'm just trying to get to the bottom of this.'

'And I want the truth as much as you do but you've got it all wrong. Joe and I, we're not the enemy; the enemy is your mind. You think everyone's plotting against you, and I get that. Anyone who's been through what you have will have become a little distorted emotionally. I'm on your side.' Sara's wheedling tone is at odds with the angry light in her eyes. 'I want to be able to move on with my family. I want a quiet life.'

'You're more likely to get one than I am.'

'Do you always have to play that card? It isn't my fault you did time. You were found guilty in a court of law. I'm not perfect, I haven't always made the best decisions, but criticising me is not going to get you what you want. And luring my husband round when I'm out of sight won't either.'

'Oh,' Claudia says. 'I didn't—'

'He was seen leaving your house, so don't deny it.'

'I got spooked. I was scared and drunk and imagining all sorts. But I promise you, nothing happened.'

Sara's mouth twists. 'Of course nothing happened. You couldn't possibly imagine that he'd be interested in you now. I understand that you have unresolved issues, but you need to sort that out with a psychiatrist, not go behind my back, playing on my husband's good nature. Do you understand?'

Claudia nods. It isn't worth a battle. Sara starts dumping things in the sink. She turns on the taps and squeezes washing-up liquid into the bowl. Claudia spots a dustpan and brush lying in the corner and uses it to sweep up the broken china.

'Just leave it,' Sara snaps.

Claudia puts the pan down slowly. 'Would you like to know what I think?'

'Not particularly.'

'Joe will do anything, walk over anybody, including you, to make sure no one finds out what he really is. I think Anna may have threatened to report him, and that's why she's vanished. He groomed us all, and now he's scared that his luck has run out.'

'You have no idea what you're talking about.'

She decides to change tack. 'I've had a chat with Jenny Buckland. Remember her?'

'Vaguely.'

'She said you bumped into her at Miss Colville's memorial service.'

Sara shrugs. 'I might have done. There were a lot of people there.'

'Well, if you don't remember Jenny in particular, you might remember what she told you: that Joe had married me.'

'I don't listen to gossip.' Her eyes are shifty.

'Don't you? You were in love with him at Lady Eden's.

It's nothing to be ashamed of; a lot of the girls were. Joe thrived on the adulation. You left, but you never forgot him, and years later, you attended the memorial service in the hope of rekindling what you had thought was a love affair. But Joe wasn't there because we'd boycotted it. It must have been a shock to find out he had been involved with me all along. Then while you were still smarting over that, my child was abducted and once again you dropped off the radar. You still thought a relationship between the two of you was possible, but you didn't want to be associated with the crime, maybe even implicated. You were worried people would think you were a vulture, feeding off the carcass of my life. So you played the long game.'

Sara slowly shakes her head. 'You have a vivid imagination.'

'You're wrong about that. I don't have enough imagination.'

'You underestimate yourself.'

Claudia smiles. 'Well, possibly. But let me finish. We all thought Joe was a god back then, didn't we? What if he was just an egotistical wanker who enjoyed exerting power over gullible teenage girls? At best he was young and drunk on his power, but he was old enough to know better by the time Anna was babysitting for us. I expect he genuinely wanted to resist, but couldn't, not with her pushing for it. I think he went too far then dumped her at the worst possible time. I believe it tipped her over the edge. In her mind I had taken her sister from her and Joe had broken her heart and utterly humiliated her. I think she came to this house to tell me about the affair because she wanted to cause pain. When I took a phone call and left her with Tilly, she thought she'd teach us both a lesson. Only something went badly wrong. I think it's likely Joe suspected her but kept his mouth shut and fed me to the dogs because he's a coward.'

Sara's whole demeanour is taut with anger. 'What is it exactly that you want of me, Claudia? Do you want all this back?' She swings her arm, indicating the house. 'Is that it? Or is it revenge on me and Joe for being happy?'

'I want you to tell DS Ward that you removed those photographs of Anna from his desk.'

Sara looks surprised. 'I didn't even know they were there.'

'But you knew I'd been in his filing cabinet. I bet you went in to check what I might have seen as soon as the police told you where they found my fingerprints. Because you never have trusted Joe one hundred per cent, have you? This isn't the first time you've taken it upon yourself to protect him. There was Megan.'

Sara stood mouth agape and Claudia felt relief wash over her.

'I'm right, aren't I?'

'She would have destroyed him, and for what? Nothing. He gave her a hug when she was having a bad day and she misinterpreted it. All I did was help her see she was making something out of nothing, that she was hardly likely to be of interest to him. I didn't *do* anything to her.'

'You did Joe a favour while he kept me out of it. It must have been mortifying when you found out that he was using you to do his dirty work in order to protect his future with me.'

Sara hesitates for a fraction of a second. 'Where were

you when he was in bits over that stupid girl and her threats? You were keeping your distance while I smoothed things over. Yes, I worked on her until she doubted herself. I did all that because I was in love with him. If I'd had any idea you were waiting till it was all over so that you and he could ride off into the sunset with your reputations intact, I never would have got involved. When Jenny told me, it absolutely devastated me. I had compromised my future. I deserved that man. I only went after what I'd earned.' Sara lifts her chin. 'And I got him in the end.'

'Yes, you did. And all the baggage that comes with him. He doesn't know what you're capable of does he? Or how far you'd go to keep what you have. Or were you in league? Is that it? One of you set fire to my home, wrote threatening notes, rigged up the house to scare me.' She sees a flicker of confusion in Sara's eyes but presses on. 'Joe came to destroy the evidence on Saturday night. You must have known.'

'Neither of us had anything to do with it, although Joe had enough provocation. You tried to destroy him with those snaps of Anna. You made him feel like a creep. He's had enough of feeling threatened by the mistakes he made when he was young. He was only twenty-six, for fuck's sake, and the girls worshipped him.'

Above them, Maeve is screaming so loudly Claudia thinks the child might do herself an injury. She can't understand why Sara is unaffected. She doesn't so much as glance up at the ceiling. Claudia's heart has gone into overdrive in response.

'I'm going to check on Maeve.'

'Get out of my house.'

'It's half mine, actually. And I'm not leaving you alone with her.'

She walks to the stairs.

Sara comes after her and grabs her arm.

'Get out of here, Claudia. You don't know what you're doing.'

Claudia looks down at Sara's hand, and for the first time she notices a smear of red on the cuff of her sleeve, red trapped under a broken finger nail. She looks up into Sara's eyes, and the truth hits her like a brick. This isn't about Sara protecting the man she loves. She as good as told her. She was angry enough to lash out at her rival. She had failed in so many things, and it was always someone else's fault. Claudia has now been added to the list of people to blame. Sara is not going to lose this one last chance to be something; to be Joe's wife.

'What have you done, Sara?'

'I haven't done anything. Get out of here, before I call the police.'

She's protecting herself, Claudia realises. It wasn't Anna who took Tilly, it was Sara.

'Where is my daughter?'

Sara doesn't answer.

She screams the words. 'Where is my daughter?'

Sara lunges unexpectedly, but Claudia's reflexes are still sharp from being subjected to regular ambushes in prison, and she is able to block the attack. She spins Sara round and smacks her head hard against the door frame. Sara goes heavy in her arms, collapses to her knees and slumps over.

Chapter 76

CLAUDIA

The nursery curtains are open, winter light streaming in. Maeve is clinging to the bars, one foot stuffed through them, her face streaming with tears and snot. Claudia wants to call the police, but she can't bring herself to leave the child in this state. She'll get her clean and calmed down, then do it. She picks Maeve up and holds her, absorbing the jolting, gulping sobs into her own body. Maeve smells strongly of urine and her pyjama bottoms are soaked through, but Claudia doesn't care. When Maeve's body stops convulsing, it makes her feel like a mother again.

'Good girl,' she soothes. 'Let's get you changed. Mummy's having a little rest.'

She can't help pressing her lips against the child's sweaty forehead as she carries her into the bathroom and lays her on the changing station. She strokes damp curls away from Maeve's flushed face. The look the child gives her is full of trust and curiosity. It breaks her heart.

The weird smell is stronger up here, even with the stinking nappy. Claudia's nose twitches in disquiet, and she starts to take in her surroundings. The walnut vinyl flooring is splattered with blood. It's everywhere.

She can see a dark hump through the shower curtain.

She pulls it aside and screams. Frances is slumped in the bath, her arms draped over her chest. Incongruously, a yellow rubber duck has fallen between her ankles. She is fully dressed, her clothes soaked with blood. Claudia grabs Maeve, turns and skids. She's unable to break her fall and lands hard, jarring her coccyx and elbow and hitting the back of her head on the rim of the bath.

Holding Maeve's face against her shoulder to shield her from the carnage, she gets awkwardly to her feet. She touches Frances's neck but can't feel a pulse, even though she's warm. She backs out and glances towards the other rooms. Outside the bathroom there is blood on the wall and blood on the door frame, smears made by fingers trying to grasp it. Maeve shouts for her mother, pummelling her feet against the soft area under Claudia's ribcage, small hands pushing her jaw.

'It's okay, sweetie. It's okay. Shush now. Mummy will be with you in a minute.'

She needs to find a telephone, but first she takes Maeve back to her bedroom and lowers her into the cot. Maeve bellows with fury and immediately starts trying to climb out. Hating herself, Claudia turns to go, and stifles a yelp. Sara is standing in the doorway. There is a knife in her hand.

She forces herself not to show fear. 'Why did you kill her?'

'She was going to ruin everything.'

Her instinct is to shove past Sara and run, but she holds firm. Maeve is her priority now. 'What are you going to do?'

Sara shrugs. 'I honestly don't know. I want things to be good again. I like being Joe's wife and living in this house. I have everything I've ever wanted.'

'Sara, please.' Claudia looks around. The closest thing to a weapon in the room is a wooden xylophone with brightly coloured keys. 'You're scaring me. Put the knife down. Maeve needs you.'

'She's too young to remember any of this.' Sara gives the door a shove with her hip and leans against it.

'What happened to Tilly?' Claudia can barely breathe.

'I didn't plan any of it. I don't know what I was thinking coming to your house. I only wanted to see Joe. I needed to understand what had happened at the school years ago. And then there you were, and Joe obviously wasn't in. You barely looked at me; you assumed I was the babysitter and left me standing in the hall with Tilly. It was an impulse.'

'What did you do with her?'

'She's dead. I'm sorry.'

Claudia staggers, a moan spiralling up her throat. She sounds like an animal keening.

Sara's voice is high with stress. 'I only meant to keep her for half an hour, to punish you and Joe, but I panicked. I drove around the back streets for a while, and it was okay when she was asleep, but she woke up and started screaming. It distracted me, and then the idiot in front of me braked and I had to do an emergency stop. Tilly was thrown off the seat into the footwell. I was in such a state I just kept driving. I got to Ditton, and then I recognised Shires Close. I'd bunked off school with Megan one time when her parents were out at work, and she'd persuaded me to sneak into her neighbour's house and steal her cigarettes. So I knew I could let myself in through the back gate. I thought I would hide in the shed for a while, but Tilly was making so much noise. I couldn't believe how loudly a baby could scream and I was convinced the old lady would hear us. I'd meant to return her safe and sound, or at least leave her somewhere she'd be found quickly, but she just kept screaming and screaming. I thought she must have banged her head too hard. I thought she was badly hurt and I'd be blamed. There was a nasty lump on her forehead.'

'She'd got that earlier.' The waste and futility of it make Claudia wish the floor would swallow her whole. 'If she was screaming, then she was fine.'

'I knew nothing about babies then. I just needed her to be quiet. I put her inside my coat and turned her face into me, but I didn't realise how hard I was pressing.'

'You suffocated her.' Claudia takes a deep breath. 'You killed her.'

'It wasn't deliberate. I'd never deliberately hurt a baby. I'm sorry it ended the way it did. I only wanted you to feel something of what I felt when I found out about you and Joe. Because of what happened with Megan, I lost my confidence. I didn't go to university, I didn't have a career. And don't expect me to believe you didn't know what was going on, that you and Joe didn't talk about it. You must have congratulated yourselves on keeping him well away from the situation while I did all the work persuading her that nothing happened.'

'But nothing did happen. And that is not the kind of person I am.'

'It's exactly the kind of person you are. Nobody round here liked you, except maybe Kate, and that was only because she was secretly in love with Joe and felt guilty. He thinks I don't know, but I'm not blind.'

Claudia doesn't give a shit about any of this. Her face

is stiff with the effort of not wailing. 'Where is she?'

'I made a hole for her under the floorboards in Jocelyn's shed. I was sure she'd be found, I was waiting to hear about it on the news, but no one thought to look there, even though the police came to Shires Close to interview Anna.'

Claudia's stomach churns. She thinks she's going to be sick. 'Is she still there?'

'No. That's the thing. I went to get her because I found out the shed was going to be demolished, but the hole was empty. Frances had taken her years ago.'

For a moment Claudia is speechless. Her blood runs cold.

'Wha . . . Why on earth would Frances do that?'

'Because she believed Anna had abducted and killed Tilly and she was terrified you would somehow work it out. And now she's trying to get you recalled because she knows you aren't guilty, she knows you lied to get parole, so it's obvious you're going to go after the truth.'

Claudia crumples. The horror of it paralyses her and it's some time before she can speak again. When she does, her words are so measured, so calm, she hardly knows herself.

'And then you came back, married the man you'd all but destroyed, moved into the house he'd shared with me, had his baby, and all the time you were carrying this secret. How could you bear it? The strain must have been appalling.'

'I forgave him, and fell in love with him all over again.'

'But was it worth it?' Claudia eyes the knife. Sara seems to have forgotten she's holding it. 'The police are expecting me at the station. If I don't turn up in the next fifteen minutes, they're going to come looking for me.'

'I don't believe you.'

'Why not? I presume it was you who hid Anna's scarf in my garden. Well, they've found it. They want me, and they know I'm here, because they can trace my phone.' Sara won't question that she has it on her.

'Give it to me.'

'What's the point? I've been here half an hour. If the signal suddenly goes dead, they're going to be even more suspicious.'

Sara's eyes narrow. She raises the knife and Claudia freezes, but she stabs it into her own hand, then her upper arm, her face a rictus of agony.

'Stop it! For Christ's sake.'

Sara is breathless with the pain, her voice warped. 'I'll tell them you came here, that you found Frances with me and went crazy when she confessed to conspiring with Anna to conceal Tilly's body. I can tell them I got the cuts defending Frances.' She winces. 'They'll believe me when I explain that Frances did it to save Anna. They'll take my word over yours. I'm not the self-confessed killer.'

The door swings open behind Sara so suddenly that she turns away from Claudia. Greg grabs hold of her wrist, twists the knife out of her hand and pins her against the wall.

'I leave you alone for one minute,' he says, turning his head to look at Claudia.

'I had things under control.'

'So I see. Have you called the police?'

'I was about to.'

'Your phone's in my back pocket.'

*

402

Greg takes Sara downstairs while Claudia makes the call. She finds them in the kitchen. Sara is sitting on the sofa with Maeve on her knee. Her eyes are blank. She doesn't even look up when Claudia comes in.

'What're you doing here?' Claudia asks Greg.

'Finding your phone in my bag confirmed my suspicion that you hadn't taken my advice. It's not like you to give in so easily.'

She blushes. She likes the idea that he knows her. 'But what about your story?'

'Told my editor I had something better,' he says gruffly. 'Are you all right?'

'Yes.' She's about to tell him about Frances when something drips on her head. She touches her hair and looks up. Bright red blood has pooled in one of the spotlights.

'Oh fuck.' She holds her hand out; her fingertips are smeared with blood. Another drop falls as she lurches backwards. 'It must be Joe.'

Claudia bolts upstairs to Joe's study. He is on the floor, leaning against the side of the bed, his hand cradling his side, blood soaking into the carpet, his guitar smashed and lying in a tangle of splintered maple and steel string beside him. He opens his eyes a crack, then closes them again. His face is grey. Sirens wail as she grabs a blanket off the bed, drops down beside him and presses a wad of fabric against the wound.

Chapter 77

Three months later

CLAUDIA

Claudia works efficiently and with determination, scrubbing the insides of the cupboards whilst Louisa tackles the oven. She's half enjoying getting into the nooks and crannies of her old home, half hating it, but the focus on the physical helps her with the mental. She finds she can think about Tilly without breaking down if she's doing something. It's during the quiet hours, when she's trying to fall asleep, that she can't control the surges of emotion.

She is looking for a house to buy in Leyton, where she knows no one, and from September she will be back in the school environment she loves, supporting children with special educational needs. In the meantime, she's staying with Louisa in Shires Close. She's chosen life, angry but exhilarated after so many dead years.

Her friendship with Greg has deepened, but she's both wary of allowing herself to fall in love and scared of losing him, and that can make her difficult and brittle. Luckily he has a thick skin. They talk every day, either on the phone or on WhatsApp. They go for a coffee or an evening drink most weeks, though Greg will dump her for a story. He is a big hugger, and it's always there, that breath-shortening pull of attraction, that fine membrane between do and don't. She loves the smell of him.

Number 26 Culloden Road has been packed up, and the removal lorries are booked for midday tomorrow. There are new carpets and the rooms have been redecorated. You would never know that Joe's blood had come through to the kitchen, but even so, the buyers dropped their offer substantially. There were no other takers, which, given the publicity, isn't surprising. Claudia is philosophical about it.

Anna's body was quickly found after Sara confessed to her murder. Claudia can't bear to face Patrick. Grief and devastation have aged him ten years.

In Joe's statement, he described coming home to find Frances Holt and Sara having a violent row in the hallway. He endeavoured to calm the situation, but he soon discovered what sort of a woman his wife was. He was about to call the police, but Sara attacked him with a knife then ran upstairs with Maeve, screaming that she would kill her unless he helped her. Frances had gone up to reason with her: she was a psychiatrist after all. By the time Joe managed to get to them, Frances had been stabbed through the heart and Sara was waiting for him. Sara is now residing at Bronzefield Prison, where Claudia served so many years.

A mini-series will be streaming on Netflix next year, which, given the huge interest, infuriates but doesn't surprise Claudia. It's the perfect dark domestic drama: lies and betrayal hidden behind a veneer of middle-class respectability. Claudia has not contributed to the project and neither have Patrick Holt, Joe or the Shaws. Joe's PA, Lisa Haskell, recently retired, has been extremely helpful, as has the estate agent Lia Cockburn and, to a lesser extent, Owen Pemberton. As promised, Claudia has talked exclusively to Greg Davies.

Joe has gone to ground, nursing his shame. With no witnesses alive to report his behaviour, and a couple of dozen ex-pupils from both Lady Eden's and Overhill coming forward to say they never witnessed anything inappropriate, that he was an inspirational teacher and that Megan and Anna Holt were fantasists, there wasn't enough to convince the CPS that he should be taken to court.

As one woman gushingly put it, 'We absolutely adored Mr Hartman, and of course half of us had crushes on him, but he never overstepped. He was just so charismatic, and so much fun.'

Claudia doesn't blame the women – Jenny Buckland amongst them – who, faced with the truth, still put their faith in the memory of their favourite teacher; the one with the face made of rubber, whose mobile eyebrows were legendary, whose sense of humour and friendliness often blurred the lines. He was a genie back then, but now he's small, his humour gone. When she does speak to him, she senses that he feels hard done by, that he honestly doesn't think he did anything wrong. She believes he's telling the truth when he says he didn't touch Megan, because Megan wasn't his type. Too odd, too quiet. He liked the girls who gave it back to him, like she had. But Anna? He is still insisting that he didn't have sex with her, that the baby couldn't have been his. He doesn't understand that it's his dishonesty that is holding him back and making him bitter.

Claudia saved his life that day, but she cannot save his soul. It isn't her job.

Claudia met Kate Shaw, because that had to be done. She is finally putting her former life to bed. Saying goodbye to Kate was difficult, Kate's remorse hard to bear. It'll be easier with Joe. She disconnected from him long ago in order to survive, just as he did from her.

Contrary to what she'd told Sara, Frances didn't throw Tilly's body into the Thames. She hid it in a cardboard box in the loft, tucked into the eaves behind a black bin bag containing clothes that had once belonged to Megan. She'd swaddled the baby in the gossamer-soft christening blanket she'd been saving for her grandchildren. Patrick knew nothing about Anna's pregnancy; he only discovered the truth after the police turned up on his doorstep. In his statement, he denied that he and Frances knew that Megan was friends with Sara Massey, or that she had had an unhealthy obsession with her English teacher, but he had no trouble believing it.

Tilly's funeral was a quiet affair, just Joe and his immediate family, Claudia, Louisa and the Shaws. The police kept the press at bay. Greg didn't attend but waited for Claudia back at the house. Her half-brother and sister-in-law offered to come but were rebuffed. Robert didn't return from South Africa for it, a snub for which everyone was profoundly thankful. Louisa finally admitted what Claudia already suspected, that he wouldn't be back at all. Their marriage had ended. Louisa had put her daughter first.

The police tracked down the driver of the cab who'd picked Claudia up from the prison car park. Shown a photograph of Frances, he confirmed that she was the woman who had handed him the envelope to give to his fare. Frances hadn't sent the second threat; that had been Joe. He had typed it onto a document on the laptop when she went to the loo. When the fire happened and Claudia told him about the note, he had seen an opportunity. He had an alibi for the night of the fire, so why not make it seem as though the same person was trying to scare her off. He wanted her crazy, because in his heart, he knew it wasn't her, and he knew what her digging might reveal. It was Joe who'd let himself in and fed the cat, pulled the kettle plug out of its socket, put a home video in the recorder and started it playing; Joe who had set up the recordings that had plagued her at night. He knew the streets round there, knew the entrance to the back alley, even knew the combination to the lock on the gate. He had wanted her so stressed that she would break her parole conditions.

Anna's part in what happened will never be fully known, but it's assumed that on that afternoon in November 2013, she had run to Joe for comfort after the memorial service, and when she didn't get the reaction she expected, when he stood up for Claudia, she told him that she'd been pregnant and had aborted his baby. Even though he tried to let her down gently, the teenager understood she was being dismissed. It must have been devastating.

Claudia imagines Anna listening to Joe and not quite hearing what he was saying, because he was being so kind. She would have been seduced by the way he looked into her eyes, by the sympathetic curve of his lips, by the touch of his fingers on her wet cheek, but once she was out of the door, she would have experienced a cold realisation.

By that time the storm was raging. Reaching home, racked by misery and anger, she'd lost it when her mother started fussing, and spat out those fateful words – *I got rid of the baby* – unaware of what had happened to Tilly only half an hour before.

If only she had talked to Frances instead of refusing to discuss what had happened. Claudia thinks it was because, along with the devastation of being rejected by her first love, she was feeling utterly humiliated; an unbearable state when you're fifteen.

The years roll by, Anna marries, has a baby. And then one day Joe Hartman's wife walks into her yoga class. Anna can't resist. She has buckets of confidence these days, she knows she's good-looking and successful, she can hold her head up.

But not for long.

Joe confirmed that Anna became upset during their meeting at Overhill. It's only his word, for what that's worth, but Claudia believes him. After he told Anna he wasn't interested, she threatened to report him for rape. He denied it because he could. There was no evidence. Amongst Anna's effects are papers concerning an abortion carried out in the autumn of 2013, but as Michael Chancellor pointed out, they don't prove it was Joe's baby.

Claudia still watches the houses opposite from time to time, although it's not an obsession now, more a comfort. Not a day goes by when Owen Pemberton doesn't have a visitor. Claudia gives him six months before he starts seeing someone else, but suspects, with some malice, that that might be a generous estimate. He's put the house on the market, but even so, Lia Cockburn seems to be in and out of number 13 rather more often than is strictly necessary, even if she is managing the sale.

Claudia doesn't care if she never sees Joe again. He's tried to call her, leaving penitent messages, but she refuses to speak to him. She can't help resenting that he might get to start over. As with Owen, she somehow doubts he'll be alone for long.

When she closes the front door to 26 Culloden Road behind her, she feels lightness rather than the weight she's carried for so long. She sincerely wishes the best for the new owners and hopes they have more luck than her.

Acknowledgements

A huge thank you to: My agent Rebecca Ritchie for reading, critiquing and keeping my spirits up, and Harmony Leung, her amazing assistant. Oli Munson for looking after me this year. Finn Cotton at Transworld for his valuable comments and suggestions on the first draft. Sarah Hodgson for offering me a new home at Atlantic and helping me take *The Babysitter* to the next level. To Hanna Kenne and proofreader Liz Hatherell for their patience with my belatedly discovered bloomers. I promise the next book will be a breeze! Marketing and Publicity geniuses Felice McKeown and Kirsty Doole for getting this novel under the noses of readers. Lauren North for reading an early draft and giving me an honest opinion and extremely useful notes. All my author friends for the fun, the lunches and launches and the support. I honestly don't know how writers coped before the internet allowed us to introduce ourselves. I'd also like to thank the tireless book bloggers and reviewers who have read and reviewed this and my other books and of course those out there who read them purely for pleasure. It doesn't matter where you source your books: whether it's from an independent bookshop, a high street chain, a library, online, a charity shop or they've been passed to you by a friend, you are what makes an author's world go round.

411

DON'T MISS

THE
COMMUTER

COMING IN AUTUMN 2024